Jan Watson

SWEETWATER RUN

Tyndale House Publishers, Inc., Carol Stream, Illinois

Visit Tyndale's exciting Web site at www.tyndale.com

Visit Jan Watson's Web site at www.janwatson.net

TYNDALE and Tyndale's quill logo are registered trademarks of Tyndale House Publishers, Inc.

Sweetwater Run

Designed by Jessie McGrath

Back cover collage by Heather Aldrin

Edited by Lorie Popp

Published in association with the literary agency of Mark Sweeney & Associates, at 28540 Altessa Way, Suite 201, Bonita Springs, Florida 34135.

Scripture quotations are taken from *The Holy Bible,* King James Version.

This novel is a work of fiction. Names, characters, places, and incidents either are the product of the author's imagination or are used fictitiously. Any resemblance to actual events, locales, organizations, or persons living or dead is entirely coincidental and beyond the intent of either the author or the publisher.

Library of Congress Cataloging-in-Publication Data

Watson, Jan.
  Sweetwater run / Jan Watson.
    p. cm.
  ISBN 978-1-4143-2385-5
  1. Women—Kentucky—Fiction. 2. Kentucky—History—1865—Fiction. I. Title.
  PS3623.A8724S94 2009
  813'.6—dc22   2009006405

For Mary Martha Hall

ACKNOWLEDGMENTS

Some heart may be longing for only a word,
Whose love by the Spirit is quickened and stirred;
Now grant, blessed Savior, this service to me,
Of speaking a comforting message for Thee.
"MAKE ME A BLESSING TODAY" BY IDA TAYLOR, 1899

I am grateful to Jan Stob and Lorie Popp at Tyndale House and to my agent, Mark Sweeney, for helping me bring this sweet story to life.

As always my love goes to my children: Stephen, Andrew, Catherine, and Charles. This wouldn't be any fun without you.

An extra big thank-you to friends old and new who helped in so many ways as I wrote Sweetwater Run and promoted my Troublesome Creek series: Teresa Canter; Carol Conley; Connie and Bob Coppings; Angela and Jess Correll; Joy Frasher; Sharon, Bruce, and Dale Halstead; Elizabeth Hoagland; Sharon Kidd; Norma Linville; Ellen Nathe; Beth Neihof; Patti Price; Susan Tamme; Mandy Whalen; and the Grassroots Writers.

To my readers: I appreciate your cards, letters, and e-mails. Each one is a blessing to me.

To the staff of Bluegrass-Oakwood residential facility in Somerset, Kentucky: you entertain angels unaware. May God richly bless you.

CHAPTER 1

1893

MARCH HAD COME IN like a lion, and the lamb was nowhere to be found though the month was nearly over. Clouds the color of tarnished silver hung low over the eastern Kentucky mountains, spitting hard grains of snow. Cara Wilson Whitt stood on the porch wrapped in a knit mantle, disbelieving the scene in the yard. Six men gestured and talked in loud voices, the chief one being her husband. Dimm was not a talker. He never wasted words, but now he raised his voice, standing his ground.

There was the sheriff, a lawyer, the two accusers—Anvil and Walker Wheeler—her brother-in-law, Ace, and Dimm. And, oh yes, the cause of all the commotion: Pancake the mule.

Cara wondered for the thousandth time how it had come to this. How was it that Dimmert was in danger of losing his freedom for stealing his own mule? Ace had cautioned Dimmert about tangling with the Wheelers—perhaps his mule had wandered onto Wheeler property and they commandeered it, more or less. But Dimm knew his mule didn't stray. His animals were so well fed and pampered they had no reason to look for greener pastures. It ate at Dimm and he took to spying on the Wheelers. One day he saw Walker Wheeler take a club to Pancake when he balked at the traces, and he determined to get his animal back. It was either that or shoot Walker, and Dimm had never been given to violence.

When Dimmert relieved Anvil Wheeler of the mule, he didn't even have to get the winter-withered apple from his pocket to lure Pancake from his pen; the mule was that glad to see him. Of course the Wheelers tracked the mule's prints to Dimmert's barn and turned the case over to the sheriff.

Cara paced, her feet drumming on the wooden porch floor. She wanted to be out there. Dimmert would listen to her. But she kept her place like a good wife should. "Don't say nothing," she wanted to shout to Dimmert but didn't. "A mule ain't worth going to jail over," she would have cried out if a woman's words counted in a yard full of men. Dimmert didn't have much in the way of worldly possessions, but he had his pride. She knew better than to mess with that.

Ace sprinted to the porch. "We need that picture you had took, Cara, the one of you and Dimm with Pancake in the middle. Can you fetch it while I go down to the cellar for an apple?"

Sometime last year a traveling photographer had come by the place to make a picture of Dimmert and Cara. Dimm, of course, wanted Pancake in the picture. It was a nice portrait of Dimm in starched overalls and Cara in her Sunday dress with her hair swirled on top of her head—and Pancake's long bony head hanging between their shoulders. Dimm and Cara were staring straight ahead, sober as a preacher at a brush arbor meeting; not a smile creased either countenance. But Pancake was a different story. His smile was big and horsey, showing lots of strong, square teeth and so lopsided it made you grin to look at it.

Cara could hardly bring herself to leave the porch. She didn't want to tear her eyes off Dimm.

"I'll go get it," Dance, Ace's wife, who kept watch with her, offered. "Where do you keep it, Cara?"

"It's in the Bible in the corner cupboard," Cara said.

Dance opened the door, and a welcome drift of warmth sailed out along with the excited voices of Dance and Ace's children, who'd been sent in out of the cold. "You kids hush up," she heard Dance say before she came back out.

Lickety-split, Ace was back at the scene. The sheriff took the picture and the apple. He studied the likeness for a bit, then held it up beside the face of the mule.

"Can't they tell that's Dimm's mule?" she asked Dance. "Dimm don't lie."

"Lookee," Dance replied. "There's a brand on that critter's rump."

"Pancake doesn't have a brand."

"Exactly," Dance said. "That Walker Wheeler's gone and put his mark on Dimm's mule."

A cold wind railed around the side of the porch. Cara's skirts billowed. She anchored them between her knees.

The sheriff handed the apple to Dimm, who held it just in front of Pancake's long nose and did everything but stand on his head, but Pancake would not crack a grin or open his mouth for his favorite treat. The stubborn mule just stared balefully at Walker Wheeler, who was doing all the smiling today. Cara watched as Dimm laid his face alongside Pancake's in his sweet, forgiving way.

Finally the sheriff gave it up. "Anvil, are you sure this here's your mule?"

"Sure as I'm sure Walker is my son," Anvil answered.

Walker guffawed, picking up the apple Dimmert had pitched to the ground and taking a big, crunching bite.

"What if Mr. Whitt just gives back this mule?" the sheriff asked. "I hate to take a man to jail over a simple misunderstanding."

"I'd settle for that," Anvil said. "That and an apology to Walker. Dimmert saying this mule's his stock is the same as calling my son a liar." He turned to Walker. "You don't lie, do you, boy?"

Walker took another big, slurping bite. "No, Daddy, I surely don't. I bought this here animal off old Clary Lumpkin two days before she died."

"Then that's that," Anvil said.

"Dimmert?" the sheriff said.

Now it was Dimm's turn to clamp his mouth shut like Pancake had done. Only his eyes did not stare balefully but instead shot sparks at Walker Wheeler.

"Come on, Dimm," Ace pleaded. "It ain't worth going to jail over."

Dimm let loose a veritable torrent the one time he should have kept quiet. "This here's my mule, Walker Wheeler. I know it and you know it! And you know you're a bald-faced liar!"

A deaf owl could have heard the collective intake of breath at Dimm's misguided speech. "I ain't giving Pancake over." Dimm stood his ground. "It will be a cold day in Satan's shoes before I apologize to the sorry likes of you."

"Well," Anvil Wheeler said, "I gave you a chance. Walker, get the mule."

Walker stood glued to his spot.

Quicker than a rabbit's kick, Dimmert's fist shot out and sucker punched Walker Wheeler. Bits of apple flew out of Walker's surprised mouth as he toppled backward to the ground. Surely as caught off guard as Walker, the sheriff rushed at Dimm and wrestled his arms behind his back.

Dimmert gave no protest, however, but stood meekly with his wrists crossed behind his back.

Mumbling and fumbling, the sheriff trussed his hands. "That was plain ignorant, boy."

Walker wasn't hurt other than his pride, but he couldn't resist throwing a taunt. "You'll pay for that, you horse's behind."

"I'll pay for more than that if you ever take a club to one of my animals again, Walker Wheeler," Dimm said. "You see if I don't."

Next thing Cara knew, the Wheelers were leading Pancake away.

Ace ran back. "Come tell Dimmert good-bye," he said to Cara.

"Good-bye?" she said. "I can't tell my husband good-bye."

Ace made to lead her off the porch.

She pushed his hand away. "Walker Wheeler stole the mule first," she yelled and saw the sheriff look her way. "Dimmert did nothing wrong!"

"Cara," Ace soothed, "don't be making a scene. That lawyer, Henry Thomas, says he'll get Dimmert out of the pokey pronto. All we'll need to do is pay a fine. He says it's just a formality."

Tiny black spots shimmered in Cara's vision. Her knees buckled. "Mercy, I feel like I'm going to faint." She was glad now for her brother-in-law's supporting arm.

"You can do this," he said. "Come on. Dimmert needs to see you strong."

Dance gave her a nudge. "Go on with Ace. You'll be glad you done it later."

"I'm so sorry, Cara-mine," Dimmert said, his words so soft only Cara could hear. "I never aimed to leave you all alone."

Cara wanted to lean into him. She wanted to let his strength absorb her weakness, but instead she drew herself up. "You're not to worry for one minute. We'll get this all sorted out."

"Come on now, Whitt," the sheriff said. "It's time to get going." Pellets of snow gathered in the crease of the sheriff's black felt hat. His eyes met Cara's. They were not unkind. "Mrs. Whitt, you can come to visit."

Soon Dimmert was sitting on a pack horse behind the sheriff's big bay mare. He didn't look back as the horse was led away. Cara was grateful for that.

❦

Three weeks later Cara tossed and turned the whole night long. The bed was big and lonesome what with Dimmert gone. Midnight found her on the porch of their small but sturdy cabin, staring out into the darkness like she could conjure up her husband if she gave a concerted effort. It might not be so bad if she owned a rocking chair. Rocking soothed an unquiet mind. But she didn't have a rocker, so her thoughts roiled like sour milk in a churn, and there wasn't much comfort in the idea of visiting Dimm in jail.

She wouldn't be so lonesome now if she weren't so isolated. What had possessed her to let Dimm drag her from their spacious three-room house on Troublesome Creek up here halfway to nowhere? Ah, but Cara already knew the answer to that. Dimmert Whitt was the sweetest man she ever laid eyes on. Plus, he had an interesting face, not really handsome but arresting, like you could study it all day and never get the least bit tired. And that gingery hair—the color of spice cake fresh from the oven—Cara was a sucker for that hair.

Still unable to sleep, she decided she was thirsty and got up for a drink. The screen door squeaked as she opened it and went to the water bucket on the wash shelf.

Taking a dipper of well water from the granite bucket, she drank it before giving in to a yawn, and then her feet traced the familiar path to bed. After a quick prayer for Dimm's safety, she held his feather pillow close, like she would have held him if he were here.

The morning would be better. Morning's first light always filled her with promise; seemed anything was possible then, even Dimm's salvation. Thanks to her friend Miz Copper, she had radish and lettuce seed to set out in her spring garden. Nothing made a body feel better than a hoe in hand and fertile soil underfoot. Dimm was right about that part. This side of the mountain couldn't be beat for growing things. Pulling the cotton quilt over her shoulders, she turned, seeking comfort.

As Cara drifted off to sleep, she thought of Copper Pelfrey and how good she was to come all the way from Troublesome to bring plants and seeds from her garden. When Cara had first spied the Pelfreys yon side of the creek, she got so excited she dropped her favorite yellowware bowl and broke it all to flinders. Now what would she mix her gritty bread in? Quick like, she'd tucked up her hair and hung her apron on the peg behind the door. She reckoned it'd been three weeks since she'd spoken to another soul—except for Ace Shelton, who came by once in a while to see if she needed any little thing.

Miz Copper brought more than lettuce and radishes. She brought marigold and zinnia seed for planting in May and a little poke of money for Dimmert's lawyer. Copper's husband John made himself scarce. He said he needed to patch that hole he saw in the barn roof while she and Copper visited. But Cara knew he was sparing her embarrassment. He knew she'd be mortified to take money from anyone but his wife—and that was hard enough.

"How are you, Cara?" Miz Copper asked after she settled at Cara's table with a cup of fresh-brewed sassafras tea.

"Good," Cara said, but she couldn't meet Miz Copper's eyes.

Miz Copper laid her hand upon Cara's own and said again, "How are you?"

Tears pooled in Cara's eyes. Miz Copper had always been discerning and kind—ever so kind. "It's hard," she replied. "I've never been alone a minute in my life, and now alone is all I am."

"Oh, honey," Miz Copper said. "You could come stay with us."

"Dimm would want me here."

"Yes," Miz Copper agreed, "I expect he would."

Cara squeezed her eyes shut. The least little bit of sympathy and she was near tears again. "Do you remember the brave girl I used to be? Remember when my mama had the twins and I was the one helping?"

Miz Copper moved her chair close. She put her arms around Cara, and Cara leaned her head on her friend's shoulder. "I sure do. I never met a braver girl than you were that night."

Cara felt her tears wet Miz Copper's shoulder. "I don't know what happened to that girl. Now every little thing spooks me."

"Part of that is your being alone. I remember when I first came back to the farm after Lilly's father died. I felt so overwhelmed and weary at times, I cried just like you're doing now."

"What did you do? How did you stand it?" Cara asked, straightening up so she could see Miz Copper's face.

"I turned to the Lord," Miz Copper said. "You'll see; God won't put more on you than you can bear if you will turn to Him in your sorrow and your fear."

Cara nodded. She knew Miz Copper spoke the truth, but she didn't know for sure if God would listen to one such as herself, one being such a stranger at God's door.

Time passed easily as they chatted, even laughed a little, remembering good times. You couldn't be around Miz Copper without smiling.

Miz Copper's daughter, Lilly Gray, came in from the porch. "Mama," she said, "Daddy John says he's almost finished with the roof."

"Lilly Gray, you are as pretty as a picture," Cara said.

The girl leaned against her mother's knees and laid her head against her mother's shoulder. She looked up at Cara from underneath long black eyelashes. Her finely arched eyebrows, heart-shaped face, and porcelain skin reminded Cara of a china doll. Shyly she said, "Thank you, Miz Cara."

"Show Cara the locket Daddy John gave you for your eighth birthday."

"Oh, that's real pretty." Cara admired the intricate scrollwork on the small gold locket.

"It opens," Lilly said, coming to Cara. She fiddled with the jewelry and clicked the latch. "It's got pictures of my two daddies. See?" She held the open locket out. "My one daddy Simon and my now daddy John. Daddy Simon is in heaven with Jesus."

Cara met Miz Copper's eyes over the top of Lilly's head. Miz Copper gave a little shrug. Cara felt embarrassed to be complaining about being alone. The story of what happened to Miz Copper's first husband was widely known. He was thrown from a horse and mortally wounded, leaving her a widow with a baby. Miz Copper brought Lilly to the mountains and set up housekeeping on her own. Cara would do well to follow her example.

Cara felt like crying for herself as well as Miz Copper. She felt like crying for all the pain in the world. Instead she changed the subject. "Where's your little brother today?"

Lilly snapped her locket closed. "Oh, he's home with Miss Remy." She sidled closer to Cara. "Do you want to know a secret?"

"I purely love a good secret," Cara replied.

Lilly Gray cupped her hand around Cara's ear and whispered, "We're going to have another baby."

Mr. John appeared in the doorway. "Hey, girls, we'd best get started if you want to call on Fairy Mae."

Lilly skipped out to meet her daddy. "Can I hold the reins this time?"

"Sure as shootin'," Mr. John said. "We'll wait in the buggy, Copper."

Miz Copper drained her tea, then pushed her chair back and withdrew a leather sack from her skirt pocket. "Ace was good enough to come by and tell John how much Dimm's fine is, Cara."

"I'll pay you back every cent," Cara said, embarrassed but grateful.

"No need," Miz Copper said while tying her bonnet strings under her chin. "John said he owed that to Dimm for helping clear land last fall. Count it out before you pay the fine. I believe there's enough extra to tide you over." She hugged Cara hard. "I'm praying for Dimm and for you, dear heart."

"Thank you," Cara said, her voice husky with unshed tears. "I'm real happy about your new baby."

Miz Copper patted her still-flat stomach and laughed. "I expect little John William will be right peeved when this one comes. He's used to being the center of attention."

"Good thing you've got Remy Riddle to help out," Cara said.

"My goodness, yes. She has been an answer to prayer." She held Cara's face between her hands. "Now you take care of yourself."

"You too," Cara said, holding the screen door wide. "You take care of yourself too."

Now Cara pounded her pillow and laid her head in the indentation. She was trying to be strong since that visit. She was trying to follow Miz Copper's model; she really was. Daytime wasn't so bad, but nights were pure torture.

Her mind stirred up again, dragging out worn trunks of worry like a widow in an attic of memory. She threw the covers aside, her feet hitting the floor. Where had she hidden that money last? First she'd put it in the sugar bowl; it was empty anyway. But that seemed too obvious, so she'd moved it to the top of the corner cupboard. When that didn't satisfy, she pried up the end of a loose floorboard in front of the fireplace and stuck it down there. But what if a mouse took a liking to that little leather sack? Silvery moonlight spilled in through a high window and lit that place in the floor like a spotlight. If a robber came in, he'd make a beeline there.

"Ouch!" Cara sucked her palm. Why hadn't she noticed that nail in the floorboard before? Now she'd more than likely get lockjaw from the rust. She'd be all alone, jaw tight as the lid on a pickle jar, unable to take in a teaspoon of water to slack her raging fever. Just the thought made her thirsty. Might as well draw some fresh water. But what to do with the poke of cash money? For now she'd stick it in her pillow slip. It'd be safe there unless the robber was sleepy.

The mantel clock chimed twelve thirty. At this rate she'd still be awake when Ace came for her in the morning. He was carrying her to the county seat. Dimmert had finally been granted visitors. Cara was beginning to think she would never see him again. It would be the first time she'd visited a person in jail. She wondered how it would be to have bars between her and Dimm. Would she get to touch him? run her hand over his dear face? Probably not. There were surely lots of rules to follow at the lockup. She didn't want to break a one.

New green grass tickled her feet as she walked barefoot to the well. She relished the mild spring night. The lamb had finally banished the lion. Hand over hand, Cara pulled the wooden bucket up the pitch-dark shaft until she placed it teetering on the rock ledge. Holding the bucket steady, she dipped palmful after palmful of cold water to her lips until she'd had her fill.

Weariness seeped into her long bones with a dull ache and made the thin bones of her fingers and toes twang like fiddle strings. But still her bed did not call. She gathered her gown around her, sat on the single step to the well house, and leaned her head against the doorframe. Sleep found her there, deep and dreamless as the well. She didn't wake until the rooster crowed.

"Did ye bring me some shoes?" Cara asked later that morning when Ace rolled up in the buggy.

"Dance sent her extra pair," he said.

"Thank ye. These are sure nice." Cara was so thankful. The soles of her shoes had separated and flapped like an old man's gums when she walked about. Looking the many-buttoned boots over, she asked, "Do ye reckon I've got time to throw a little polish on these?"

"Don't take long at it. Dimmert's lawyer's supposed to meet us at the jailhouse."

Cara hurried inside and rummaged around for the tin of black polish and a rag. In seconds the shoes had sheen on the toes. It was a little more effort to get them on. Her hose kept bunching up at the heels and pulling at the toes. The boots were at least half an inch too short. Dance was about her size except for her feet. Frustrated, Cara tore off her stockings and flung them aside. She'd have to chance a blister. Try as she might with the button hook, Cara couldn't get the ones around her ankles to fasten. She shrugged and gave up. What did it matter as long as she was shod to go to town? Her skirts would hide her ankles anyway. After pulling her go-to-town gloves from the bottom drawer of the chiffonier, she was ready.

The buggy jounced along, tilting to the driver's side on the narrow roadbed. Cara kept sliding into Ace.

"Did Miz Pelfrey bring you the money?" he asked.

"I've got it right here," she replied, patting the bottom of her linen carryall. Carefully, she'd counted out the fine this morning, put the leftover folding money in a small drawstring purse, and pinned it inside the carryall. "Do you reckon they'll let Dimm out today?"

"I don't hardly see why not. That lawyer said all we need to do is pay the fine." Ace looked like a lawyer himself in his shiny black suit. "After all, it was his own mule he stole."

"Dimmert's a fool about his animals," Cara said.

"That fellow who accused Dimm would steal the dimes off a dead man's eyes," Ace said. "I would have done the same thing Dimmert did."

Cara clung to the side of the buggy. Her teeth rattled when they hit a deep hole. "He could have gone about it in a different way, though."

"That's water under the bridge now."

Tears under the bridge, Cara thought. *Enough tears to make a river.*

The jailhouse was situated on a side street, right beside the sheriff's office. Ace held the door as Cara entered a room furnished with a rolltop desk, a straight chair, and a coatrack. A man with a star on his chest that proclaimed *Deputy* sat slouched in the chair. One hand rested on his holstered gun. With a brown hat set low over his eyes, he seemed to be sleeping.

Ace caught Cara's elbow and ushered her back outside. He closed the door softly. "We don't want to catch him unawares," Ace said, then made a show of loud talk and letting the door bang shut before he got it open.

"Help you folks?" the deputy asked, sitting ramrod straight and taking off his hat.

Ace stepped forward. "We're here to see Dimmert Whitt. This here's his wife, and I'm his preacher."

"Visits on Saturday mornings only," the deputy said.

Cara couldn't hide her dismay—to be so close and not see Dimm. She covered her mouth with her gloved hand as tears pooled in her eyes.

The deputy jangled a large brass ring holding many keys. "I reckon it won't hurt to make an exception." He stood and looked kindly at Cara. "Now if we was full, I'd have to turn you away, you understand."

"Yes, sir," Ace replied, his hat in his hands.

"Thank ye, sir," Cara said.

"Turn your pockets inside out," the deputy instructed, "and, ma'am, you can hang your sack on the coatrack there."

A key turned in a large black lock and a door swung open. "There's only the two cells," the deputy said. "Whitt's in the last one."

Cara felt her heart break at the pitiful sight of Dimm clutching a set of steel bars as if he'd fall to the floor without their support. She stood back a ways, not sure how close she was allowed to be.

Ace pressed his hand to the middle of her back, urging her forward. With a nod he indicated the deputy standing with his back to them in the open doorway. "Take advantage of small favors," Ace whispered in her ear.

She leaned toward Dimmert and kissed his cheek through the open bars. "Dimmert, are they treating you well?"

"It's tolerable," he answered.

"Ace brought me to see your lawyer," Cara said. "We aim to get you out of here."

Dimm eyed his brother-in-law. "You plan on preaching a sermon whilst you've got a captive audience?"

"Figured looking as good as a lawyer wouldn't hurt your case none," Ace said.

The two men bantered while Cara looked around. The cell was small, probably twelve by twelve, with walls of mortared stone. It had four bunks hooked to the walls by chains and one open but barred window which Dimm could see out of if he stood on tiptoe. That window gave her great comfort.

There was one other man in the cell rolled up in a khaki-colored Army blanket on one of the lower bunks.

Dimmert saw her looking. "That there's Big Boy Randall," he said.

"You're joshing." Ace stepped in for a closer look.

"One and the same," Dimm said.

Cara was aggravated with them—acting like it was a source of pride to be locked up with such a notorious figure as Big Boy Randall.

As if he read her thoughts, Big Boy Randall opened one eye and touched the tips of two fingers to the side of his forehead, saluting her with the small gesture.

Her heart hammered with a trill of fear. Ace and Dimm were still jawing and didn't take notice. She swallowed and turned away from Big Boy's staring eye.

"Henry Thomas was supposed to meet us here," Ace said.

"I ain't seen him but once the whole time I been in this hoosegow," Dimmert replied.

"We'll go down to the office then," Ace said. "I'll be just outside, Cara."

Dimmert fixed her with a look of such longing she thought she couldn't stand it. "Cara-mine," he said, "do you miss me still?"

"Only every second of every hour of every day." She would have kissed his cheek again except for Big Boy Randall's presence on the bunk behind.

"It's time, missus," the jailer said.

"We'll be back for you, Dimmert," Cara promised.

CHAPTER 2

CARA FELT RIGHT SILLY as she took the extra place setting from the table. She'd been so sure of bringing her husband home today that she'd set the table for supper right after breakfast. Now she stood in the middle of the empty room cradling the white ironstone plate against her hollow chest. The white china had been a gift from Miz Copper when she and Dimm married. *So young,* she thought, *at eighteen we were sure we were all grown-up.*

Cara went to the black-and-white calendar that hung on the back of the kitchen door. Avery's Feed and Seed, it advertised. Turning the month from April to May, she studied the days. Dimmert had drawn a black circle around their special day—the mark signified their sixth anniversary. Cara traced it with her index finger. To think Dimmert had stood thus so circling the day with a pencil just weeks before as if they'd forget without a reminder. And now he was gone—penned up in the jailhouse like an animal.

Their wedding day had been full of regret. Cara supposed she and Dimm were marked for sorrow from the start. She remembered as if it were yesterday how beautiful she felt and how Dimmert stood so proudly beside her in his new overalls and his borrowed jacket. Her dress fit just so, and her short veil fell softly around her shoulders. Even her contrary hair, brown and fine as a baby's, obeyed for the day. It was supposed to be a double wedding—she and Dimm alongside Miz Copper and Mr. John. But there'd been that terrible accident with Miz Copper's friend Remy Riddle, casting a long shadow upon the sunny day.

Cara smiled to remember Miz Copper insisting that their wedding go on as planned, though Cara protested. Miz Copper and Mr. John had waited so long, and then to have their plans cast aside . . . Cara sighed. She still felt the injustice of it all. Not that she and Dimm weren't happy that day—oh, they were—but it was a sorrowful happy.

Things had worked out in the long run, though. Once Remy recovered from the accident that nearly took her life, Miz Copper and Mr. John had married and moved into a fine new house. Miz Copper said they were building an extra room off the back since another baby was on the way.

Cara missed Miz Copper and Lilly Gray, who was a big girl now. Cara would sure feel better if Miz Copper were at home, but she was away visiting her folks in Philadelphia. Mr. John and Miz Copper and their children had left soon after their visit to Cara. She supposed they wanted to travel before Miz Copper got too far along.

Letting the calendar page fall back to the proper month, Cara walked to the table. After wiping the plate with her apron, she put it back upon the shelf, on the stack with the other plates—twelve in all, with matching saucers, cups, and bowls. She reckoned Miz Copper thought Cara and Dimm's table would soon be full. That proved false hope.

The old nagging hurt welled up. Maybe she'd stay in the little pantry, closed up behind the curtain she'd made from printed cotton and hung on a length of heavy twine. On a better day, Dimm had pounded a nail at each side of the open doorway and watched while she strung the curtain panel on the twine, then wound and knotted it around the nails. He'd laughed to see how the curtain puddled on the floor. She'd been aggravated at how she'd misjudged the hem. "I'll have to do it all over again," she said.

But Dimm jerked the nails out of the wood with his claw hammer and pounded them in higher up. He never even unwound the twine or took the curtain panel off. And when he finished, it hung just so. She'd rewarded him with a fiery kiss. Now her lips were lonesome—missing him.

The next morning, after Cara washed up her cup and bowl, she looked aimlessly about the kitchen. What would she do with her day? Maybe she'd walk to Dance's, visit with her and the children. Cara's face brightened with purpose. Leaving her apron on, she headed out the door only to scoot back in to retrieve the borrowed shoes. She thanked those shoes for three blisters.

It was a pleasant two-mile hike to Dance's. Way different from when she and Dimm had first settled so close to the Sheltons. It had taken most of their spare time that summer for Dimm and Ace to clear a decent path between the two cabins. Now Dimm kept it passable by running the heavy drag over it on occasion. Who'd keep the weeds down for her now?

She couldn't help but dwell on seeing Dimm in that awful cell. Her mind went round and round. Why didn't that lawyer fellow get him out, and why wasn't he in his office like he'd told Ace he would be? She and Ace had found a cardboard sign in his office window that read, "Be back in the office Tuesday next. Sorry for the inconvenience."

A right smart inconvenience, Cara thought as she walked along, plucking leaves from low hanging branches and shredding them with her anxious fingers. They'd had to go back to the jail and beg the sheriff to let them tell Dimm. Cara could see by the deputy's warm brown eyes he would have let her go back again, but the sheriff said, "Saturdays for visitors." He had to uphold the rules, she reckoned. He sent them outside, around back of the jail, to stand under the window and wait for Dimm's head to appear.

Ace told Dimm the news while Cara swallowed tears.

"Don't worry none," Dimm called after them when they walked away. Then he hollered, "Cara," when they got to the corner of the building. She didn't want to look back, afraid she'd lose all composure, but of course she turned around. "Cara-mine," she heard but only saw his fingers wagging out the narrow bars.

Now her mind conjured up the things that could happen to Dimm left alone with Big Boy Randall. Big Boy'd probably eat up all his plate and Dimm's too. How long did it take for a body to starve to death? She counted Dimm's ribs in her mind.

Just ahead bluebirds flushed up from the low branch of a budding apple tree. She counted two bright blue males with rusty chests and one washed-out female. Her daddy always said bluebirds carried the hue of heaven on their backs. Her mama said bluebirds brought happiness. Cara listened to their soft warbles as they flitted off. Maybe God was sending her a sign—maybe Dimm would get to come home the next time she and Ace went to town.

At least try to think positive, she chided herself. But it was hard.

"Hello to the house!" Cara yelled as she approached the Sheltons' yard, giving notice of her intrusion.

Jay ran across the porch floor, shouting, "Aunt Cara! Aunt Cara!" before he nearly bowled her over.

Cara returned his fierce hug. "What have you been up to, Jaybird?"

"I'm too old for Jaybird now," the boy replied, all serious.

"Sorry. I forgot," she teased. "How old is too old?"

"I'm six. Don't you remember? Six going on seven." He grabbed her arm and tugged her toward the house. "Did you bring me a riddle?"

"I did. Do you want it now?"

The boy stopped and looked up at her. "Yup, I think I do."

"Can you fetch me a glass of water first? I'm parched from my walk."

Jay ran ahead up the porch steps and to the weathered wash bench that looked out over the yard. Snatching up the water bucket, he stood on tiptoe to empty what was left into a granite pan before scampering away. "I'll bring you fresh," he shouted over his shoulder.

"Come on in," Dance called from just inside the door.

"I'll sit here a minute," Cara responded, "until Jay hears his riddle."

The screen door squeaked open. Dance handed over baby Pauline. "Then take this'n for a while." The screen door squeaked again. "And this'n too. I've got beans that need a stir."

Cara settled in the porch rocker with three-month-old Pauline in her lap and thirteen-month-old Cleve on the floor. If she sat just so, she could steady Cleve between her feet and still rock Pauline. Wonder where Merky and Wilton were.

"Ace took the middle young'uns with him, else I never would have got these beans on the stove," Dance said from the kitchen as if she'd read Cara's mind.

"He'll have his hands full with those two." Cara pictured four-year-old Wilton, a little ball of fire, and two-and-a-half-year-old Merky, the prettiest baby girl she'd ever seen.

"He needs to have his hands full," Dance said, stepping out onto the porch with a wooden spoon dripping brown bean soup. "You know what that man had the nerve to say to me this very morning?"

"I couldn't venture a guess," Cara answered.

"I was nursing this'n—" she pointed the spoon at Pauline—"and chasing that'n—" the spoon leveled at Cleve—"when Ace says to me, 'Dance, ye need to turn off your baby maker.'"

Cara laughed so hard her feet lost purchase on little Cleve and he rolled over on his belly.

"It ain't one bit funny," Dance said. "Ye wouldn't be laughing if it was you."

Cara choked to a stop. "I'm sorry. What did you tell him?"

"Didn't tell him nothing—just bounced the skillet off his thick head."

"Dance!"

"Oh, it was just the little two-egg skillet." Dance held the spoon down for Cleve to mouth. "Didn't hurt him none."

"Forgive me. . . ." Cara guffawed, tears of laughter leaking from her eyes. "Forevermore. What if you'd had the chicken fryer in hand?"

"Reckon we'd be walking around his body," she said before the screen door slapped behind her.

Cara shook her head. There was no hope for those two. "I brought your shoes back, Dance," she said toward the open door. "Thank ye for the loan."

"You can keep them. I don't go nowhere that calls for shoes no way."

"They're too tight for me. I've got blisters on my blisters."

"I've got a pair that used to be Mommy's," Dance replied. "I'll find them for you before you go."

"Here you go," Jay said, handing Cara a cup of cold well water. "Now can I have my riddle?"

"All right, listen close: Way down yonder at the forks of Sweetwater I found a pile of timber. I couldn't rack it. I couldn't whack it, for it was awful limber. What is it?"

Jay concentrated so hard his freckles stood out like raisins in a dish of oatmeal. "Couldn't rack it. Couldn't whack it," he repeated. "That don't make no sense."

"Riddles don't make sense until you figure the answer," Cara said. "That's what makes them fun."

Jay ambled out into the yard, picked up a stick, and started knocking the tops off a stand of weeds. "Rack it! Whack it!" he yelled each time a horseweed fell.

Cara felt in her skirt pocket to make sure Jay's penny was still there. She had precious few left. Sitting with the two babies, drinking the cold water, and watching Jay, she was truly happy for the first time in days.

"Jay," Dance shouted, "stop that foolishness and go fetch some taters—if they's any left."

"What can I do to help?" Cara asked.

"Nothing better'n what you're already doing." Dance walked out and settled Cleve on her hip. "Jay! Go on now! These young'uns . . ." She shook her head. "I tell you the truth."

"This is the best water I ever tasted," Cara said.

"Ace found a spring up yonder. He rigged some sort of trough to run down to the well house, then fashioned a spigot that drips cold water into a wooden bucket." Dance rolled her eyes. "It *has* to be a wooden bucket. Took him two weeks—he could have been helping with these young'uns."

"Still, it is good water," Cara said as she rocked on, content as a mother robin on a nest. Seemed like children either settled you down or drove you to distraction, one or the other. Though, to give Dance credit, Cara didn't have to take them home with her. That thought made her heart pinch up. It didn't seem fair, Dance having more than she wanted and her having none.

After a noon meal of fried potatoes and pinto beans, Cara gathered kindling to start a fire under the washtub in the side yard. It wasn't hard to tell from the overfull basket in the corner of the kitchen that the washing hadn't been done on Monday. Soon water was boiling and she was stirring a pile of whites with the laundry paddle. Jay was a good help, lugging water for rinsing and cords of wood to keep the fire going. If she hurried she should get half a wash done in time to dry. It looked like it had been a while since Dance did anything but diapers. Diapers you had to do every day.

"Want me to rinse them out?" Jay asked. "I know how."

"No, honey," Cara replied, the pail of dirty diapers in hand. "You watch the fire—now don't get too close—and I'll take these to the outhouse."

"Law," she said when she opened the outhouse door, "this needs a scrubbing." After dipping the used diapers several times in a bucket of water laced with lye soap, she poured the slops down the outhouse hole.

It was with considerable pleasure she hung a dozen snowy white nappies on the line. A quick spring breeze sent them flapping in the sunlight. She knew from doing many a wash for her brothers and sisters that sunshine was a sure cure for diaper rash, and she had noticed a fine red spray on Pauline's tiny bottom.

Cara thought she'd take to coming over on Mondays. She could do her little bit of laundry along with the Sheltons'. It would take a load off Dance, plus give Cara something to do. Just the thought gave her new vigor as she scrubbed down the outhouse. There ought to be enough wash water for the porch too. Cara loved wash day for that very fact—all that leftover soapy water for scrubbing. She was never more content than when she had a broom in hand. It made a body proud to see how much work could be done in one day.

Once the porch was done, she slipped into the house, mindful of the babies' naps. Dance lay curled like a puppy around Pauline. Toddler Cleve lay across the same bed, his pudgy feet touching the small of his mother's back. Dance's eyelids fluttered open. *She looks so pale,* Cara thought. Her skin held no more color than skim milk.

Pauline fussed, waving her little hands about.

Dance opened her blouse to the baby. "I'm so tired, Cara. I can't hardly stand it."

Cara spoke quietly, telling Dance about her Monday plans and asked what else she could do. "You know I'm glad to help."

"Ace is like a banty rooster strutting round here like he's in charge of the world. He thinks we don't need help." Dance's sigh spoke volumes.

When Cara went back outside, she found Jay sitting forlornly by the burned-out fire. "I guess I won't get a penny today," he said. "I can't figure that riddle you gave me."

"I'll give you one clue. Go get your daddy's rasp."

Jay ran off and returned with the tool.

"Take this piece of wood and run the file over it. That's right—back and forth several times, Jay."

Tongue stuck out, Jay labored with the file until finally he stopped and looked at the little pile of dust he'd made. "Can't rack it. Can't whack it. Sawdust! Yippee! Do I get my penny now?"

It was dusky dark when Cara made her way back down the path to home. She had overstayed, purposefully lingering at the Sheltons' until Ace got home, then making an excuse to get him alone for a minute. "I'm worried about Dance," she told him. "How has she been, other than being run-down, I mean?"

Ace rubbed the pump-knot on his temple. He'd soon have a black eye to go along with the knot. "Well, ye can see she's got good aim. Hit me smack upside the head with a cast-iron skillet this morning. I'm glad I'd already eaten my eggs."

"She might have had good reason for that."

"I know. You'd think I'd learn." He shook his head. "She had a bad spell last week—took to crying and wringing her hands, said her head was splitting. She sat and stared at the wall awhile before she came out of it."

"I could take some of the children for a time."

"I won't never split my kids up. Thank ye anyway, Cara." Ace drummed his hat against his leg. "She always gets a time of grace after the bad spells. Besides, I leave Jay home when I have to be gone. He watches out real good."

"Whose funeral did you preach today?" Cara asked.

"Some feller I didn't even know by the name of Orban Hanson. He lived over to Meeting House Branch. There was a right smart crowd."

"How do you work that out—with the children and all?"

"There's always some lady or two just itching to get their hands on a little one again. They never fail to make my kids welcome." Ace rubbed his jaw. "I might start taking Cleve along too. Dance can handle Pauline, I reckon."

His words lingered in her mind as she walked home. She hoped Ace was right. Dance's mommy's shoes hung over one shoulder from the knotted strings. A briar plucked at her dress. She stopped to pull it off and saw dozens of sticker weeds on her skirt tail. They'd be hob to get off. In the distance a dog howled. She picked up her pace. It would soon be dark.

CHAPTER 3

TUESDAY CAME and with it Ace to carry her back to town. Cara met him on the porch. She fretted about him leaving Dance alone until he told her he'd dropped the whole bunch off at Dance's grandmother's. "Fairy Mae was that glad to see them," Ace said.

"That's wonderful," Cara remarked, "but how did you get Dance to go?"

"I was surprised myself when she took a notion to go over there. Usually takes a shoehorn to pry her off the place."

"How is Fairy Mae?" Cara asked.

"Frail, crippled up from rheumatism."

"I'm sorry to hear that," Cara said, stepping to the door. "I'll be just a minute, Ace. I've got to get my shoes and my bag."

Soon they were on their way to town once again. Cara prayed for better luck this time. "What if Mr. Thomas's office is still closed?"

"We'll sit on the stoop until he gets around to opening it," Ace said.

"Can't we just give the money for Dimm's fine to the sheriff?"

Ace flicked the reins and the horse picked up speed. "Don't work that way. You've got to get a receipt so nobody can pocket the money and say you didn't pay. Lawyers know all about that stuff. Mr. Thomas will protect your interests—so to speak."

"I just pray he's there," Cara said.

"You worry too much," Ace replied. "It will all work out. You'll see."

Cara wished she'd thought to slip her Bible into the linen sack along with the leather poke of money and the packet of cold ham biscuits for her and Ace to eat. She had taken to carrying the Bible around since her talk with Miz Copper. Just knowing it was there would give her comfort. She'd burned the midnight oil last night, darning socks and patching the knees on a pair of Dimm's work pants, her nerves jangled and her stomach in knots, anticipating the trip to the jail. Finally she'd fallen asleep at the table with her head resting on her arms, a dark whisper of smoke staining the lamp's glass chimney like a warning.

If it had not been such a daunting journey, Cara would have enjoyed being in town. Their first stop was Mr. Thomas's office, where the sign in the window read, "Closed: Back in one hour."

"One hour from what?" she asked Ace.

He pulled on a watch fob and withdrew a fancy round watch from his pocket. With a practiced move he snapped the case open. "Well, it's ten o'clock now, so we'll walk around for a while—give it half an hour or so."

"But what if he comes and leaves again? What if he puts another sign in the window?" Cara twisted a hankie with her gloved fingers.

"Cara, look around. This ain't New York City. You can see every building on this street from wherever you are."

"Sorry. I just feel like I'm jumping out of my skin."

Ace unsnapped his watch from the fob. "Here, you carry this and watch the time. That'll make you feel better."

Touched, Cara felt a spurt of tears as she fingered the heavy, filigreed case. "This is very nice, Ace."

"My folks gave it to me when I was ordained into the ministry. They came all the way from Maryland for the ceremony on Troublesome Creek."

"How'd you wind up in Kentucky if your folks are from Maryland?" They walked along companionably, window-shopping. Cara's nerves began to settle like birds on a wire, quiet for the moment.

"There was a big camp meeting over in Virginia that my folks went to. I met Dance there—she was with her family then, though generally she lived with her mammaw Fairy Mae. I was lost from the moment I first spied her. When she went home to Kentucky, I followed like a lovesick hound dog."

They paused in front of the pharmacy. Cara gawked to see so much merchandise displayed in the window. White granite basins, rolls of tape, thermometers, and metal bed warmers with long wire handles vied for attention. "That bed warmer sure would feel good on winter nights," she said.

"Dimmert will soon be home to warm up your cold feet," Ace replied.

"I sure hope you're right about that," she said.

"We'll want to cross here." Ace steered her into the dusty street. "You don't want to go past the pool hall. There's some rough customers haunts that place."

While Ace was busy watching for a safe time to cross, Cara clutched his arm and looked back. Men lounged on benches in front of the hall, spitting tobacco juice onto the wooden sidewalk and even out into the street as if trying to best each other's aim.

Unbidden, her eyes met those of a burly, red-bearded man slouched against the rail of the hitching post. The man gave a little two-fingered salute. "Missus," he said.

She dropped her gaze as Ace towed her across the busy street. Big Boy Randall had served his time it seemed. "That man scares me," she said.

Ace stopped smack-dab in the middle of the street. "Who's that?" he said, taking a gander at the pool hall. "Oh, you mean Big Boy Randall?"

She tugged on his arm to get them out of the street. She could feel her face flame with embarrassment. "Ace—"

"You don't need to fear Big Boy. He's like Robin Hood—steals from Peter to pay Paul."

"Still, he was in jail."

"So is Dimm, and we know how trumped up the charges against him are."

True enough, Cara thought.

Who should they run into on the other side of the street than Dimmert's sister Darcy? Darcy was a close friend and had been her confidante until Cara moved away from Troublesome Creek. "Darcy," she called in delight, reaching out to hug her friend.

Darcy's face crinkled with a smile. Dimples deepened on either side of her round and rosy face. "Oh, my goodness, Cara, I ain't seen you in a coon's age. Ace, Mammaw's right glad you brought Dance and the babies over this morning." She stared hard at Ace. "What in the world happened to you?"

Ace fingered his black eye. "It's a long story."

"What brings you to town, Darcy?" Cara asked.

"I'm going to Coomb's Dry Goods to pick up some dress material and a new bobbin he ordered for my machine. Want to go along?"

"Better not." Cara checked Ace's watch. "We've got to get to Mr. Thomas's."

Cara could swear she saw a blush sweep over Darcy's face at the lawyer's name. What was that about?

"Dimmert's being turned loose today," Darcy said, "right?"

"Supposed to be," Ace answered. "We're here to make it happen."

"Mind if I come?" Darcy slid her hand through the crook of Cara's folded arm. "I'd surely like to see when Dimm gets out so I can tell Mammaw he's okay. Having a grandson in jail has just about broken her heart."

The little party walked on down the street and saw Mr. Thomas's door was finally open. The lawyer leaned on the doorpost as if he'd been watching for them. Darcy's hand trembled on Cara's arm.

"Henry," Ace said, "this is Dimmert Whitt's wife and his sister Darcy."

"Ace," Mr. Thomas replied and then with the sweep of an imaginary hat, "Ladies. Please come in."

Mr. Thomas's office was spacious and very tidy. The dark wood floor was oiled to a gloss; papers were captured in brown manila folders and placed in a neat stack on a substantial oak desk that sat at the end of the room. A horsehair settee graced one wall, and two gentlemen's armchairs upholstered in burgundy leather faced the desk. Oil paintings of Indian chiefs wearing ornate headdresses and riding muscled horses adorned the walls over the settee and behind the desk. A large shadow box on legs sat in front of the settee like a table. Under the glass, Cara saw chert spear tips, arrowheads, bird points, and scrapers nicely arranged in a radiating pattern, like the spokes of a wheel. A tomahawk adorned by a large brown feather accented the display.

"Miss Whitt." Mr. Thomas indicated the settee, then pulled out one of the gentlemen's chairs for Cara. Ace took the other. Mr. Thomas settled into the rolling chair across from them.

Cara could hardly stop herself from stroking the supple leather of her chair. All along the bottom of the seat and at the edge of the arms were fancy brass tacks. She wished she could go outside and dust her skirts before she sat.

"Now what can I help you with?" Mr. Thomas asked.

Hopefully hidden by the desk, Cara felt in her bag and slipped the poke of money to Ace. He held it up as if it had been in his possession all along. "We're here to pay Dimmert's fine," he said with no little authority. "We aim to take him home today."

The lawyer rolled his chair backward and put his booted feet, crisscrossed at the ankles, on the edge of the desk. "Well, now, there's a problem."

Cara's heart sank. She clasped the arms of her chair so tightly she could feel the rounded tack heads pressing into her palms. She looked at Mr. Thomas. His eyes were black as chips of coal. There was no sympathy there.

"What do you mean?" Ace asked. "Give it to us straight."

Darcy moved to stand behind Cara. Her touch was warm on Cara's shoulders.

"The law's taking Mr. Whitt to the penitentiary at Frankfort today. He got two years."

Cara gasped. Tears streamed from her eyes. Darcy handed her a handkerchief. "But we brought the money," Cara said through sobs.

"It's too late," he said. "The fine was supposed to be paid last week."

"But you weren't here," she said, disbelieving the turn her life had taken. "We came and you weren't here."

Mr. Thomas had the grace to drop his feet as well as his eyes. "I'm sorry. I did all I could." He cleared his throat and stood, whisking his palms together as if he was ridding himself of nothing more significant than a little dust. "There's the matter of my fee. Do you want to settle up now?"

Cara shook her head. What had he just said? Surely he didn't expect payment for letting Dimm get sent to prison? "I don't understand how you let this happen. How did this happen?"

"Miz Whitt, we don't have the benefit of a sitting judge in this town but instead have trials and clear up other legal matters whenever the circuit judge comes around. He was here yesterday and heard Mr. Whitt's case. There wasn't a thing I could do."

"What do we owe ye?" Ace said.

Mr. Thomas named a fee and then added in the fine which was still owed. "It would be best if you settled this so there won't be interest charged," he explained. "That way when Dimmert's served his time, he'll not be beholden to the court."

Ace peeled off bills and laid them on the desk. "I can't rightly thank you for this half-baked job, but we'll pay what we owe."

Mr. Thomas strode to the door and held it open. "Call on me if I can be of other service," he said as if he hadn't just put a stamp of misery on Cara.

She stepped across the threshold, turning slightly to look back, trying to think of something to say—something to convey her loss to this heartless man. She saw he had a self-satisfied look on his face, like a cat at the cream pitcher.

"If you hurry, you might see Dimmert before they take him away," he said.

A few steps down the sidewalk, Ace stopped. "Wait just a cotton-pickin' minute," he said, marching back into the office.

Cara and Darcy hurried along behind him, but Ace shut the door in their faces.

They could hear words hot as baked potatoes being tossed back and forth, but soon enough Ace was outside again. He took one of Cara's arms and Darcy took the other.

"Come along, Cara," he said. "Let's go around to the jailhouse."

<hr/>

Surely I'm trapped in a dream, Cara thought when she saw the deputy leading Dimmert, shackled by a chain to two other prisoners, out of the jail. A man waited on the seat of an odd-looking buggy that reminded Cara of a hearse. It was like a long black box, all enclosed except for the driver's seat. The tailgate hung open, and she could see narrow benches along each side. Big metal rings protruded at intervals from the floor. She reckoned the prisoners' chains would be fastened to them.

Dimm shuffled along, tripping over his bindings, his head hung low. Cara wished she hadn't seen and thought Dimm would hope so too. No man would want his family to see him thus shamed. She thought to turn back, but it was too late.

"Dimm!" Darcy called out. "Dimmert Whitt!"

He shook the hair that had fallen over his face and looked their way. Confusion crossed his features until his eyes rested on Cara. He straightened his shoulders and stood tall; a smile lit his face. "Cara-mine," he mouthed, words meant only for her.

Ace walked up to where the deputy and sheriff marched the pris-oners toward the buggy.

"Back away," the sheriff said, and Ace did as he was told.

The first prisoner was a short, round man with stumpy legs. When he tried to step up, his foot missed purchase and he nearly fell on his face. The deputy bounded up into the bed and grabbed the fellow's hands while the sheriff hoisted him by the waistband of his britches.

The second man seemed just a boy. His face was all pimply, and his Adam's apple stuck out sharp as a knife blade. He tried a brave swagger, but his binding forced short, jerky steps. "I'm heading to the Rock Hotel," he yelled. "A sledgehammer will be my new sweet-heart." He looked at Cara and Darcy. "Can you tell my mommy where I'm gone?" All bravado gone, his voice cracked on a high note. "She'll be worried if she don't know where I am."

"Get on up in there, Lemuel," the deputy said. "Stop bothering the ladies."

Cara wanted to ask his mother's name, but fear stopped her tongue. She didn't even call out her own husband's name. Didn't say good-bye. Didn't say, "I love you." Her heart fluttered like a trapped bird's wings.

Before Dimmert could step up into the wagon's bed, Ace took a small black Bible from his pocket and held it aloft. "I'm a minister of the Lord," he said to the sheriff. "Can I have a word?"

Dimmert's chain pulled taut as Lemuel took his seat.

The sheriff leaned against the buggy. "Hurry it up."

"This here's for all you men," Ace said. "God don't forget you just because you're behind bars. Take this Scripture with you and it will give you comfort. 'The Lord is my shepherd; I shall not want. He maketh me to lie down in green pastures: he leadeth me beside the still waters. He restoreth my soul: he leadeth me in the paths of righteousness for his name's sake. Yea, though I walk through the valley of the shadow of death, I will fear no evil: for thou art with me; thy rod and thy staff they comfort me. Thou preparest a table before me in the presence of mine enemies: thou anointest my head with oil; my cup runneth over. Surely goodness and mercy shall follow me all the days of my life: and I will dwell in the house of the Lord for ever.'"

Before the sheriff could stop him, Ace reached out and pumped Dimmert's hand. "God be with you."

Cara heard a rattle of chains, a man's heavy sob—not Dimmert's, no, not Dimmert's—a horse's impatient whinny, a creak of a wagon's wheel, and then her life rolled away as quick as that.

CHAPTER 4

Henry Thomas crossed his lean but muscular arms and with narrowed eyes watched Dimmert Whitt's family walk toward Spring Street and the county jail. Ace Shelton's angry words rang in his ears. Who was Ace to rebuke anyone? Henry had wanted to smash Ace's face in. But he tamped down his temper, for an angry man was a man who had lost control, and Henry strove to be in control.

He walked to the jailhouse to watch the action. There they were, the whole lot of them, Ace strutting around importantly, Cara and Darcy with their heads together. Henry stood behind a tree and looked on as a string of prisoners was led out of the jail toward the waiting transport. He could tell Dimmert's wife was wiping tears.

He supposed he should feel a smidgen of pity for Cara. She seemed a nice enough sort and pretty, he'd admit, but not his type. Now Darcy—there was something about that girl. He'd made it his mission to watch for her to come into town. They'd had a few pleasant conversations thus far. She always blushed prettily when she was in his presence. Obviously she was ripe for the picking. A snap of his fingers and she'd fall right into his arms.

It didn't take long for the prisoners to be dispatched, although Ace had held things up by prissily bringing out his Bible and preaching the Word, as if that was going to help anything. Henry bided his time until Darcy said good-bye to her family and headed up the street alone.

"Darcy," he called.

She looked back and smiled. "Henry," she said.

Just the sound of her voice calling his name filled him with a joy he'd never felt before. "I'm real sorry about your brother," he said.

"Thank you. It's just about killed my mammaw and Cara." Darcy's eyes filled with sorrow. "Poor Dimm didn't steal that mule, you know."

Henry dared to cup her elbow in his hand and walk alongside her. "I tried every way in the world to help him. I want you to know that." If Henry had been a child, he would have crossed his fingers behind his back—canceling the lie, so to speak. But lies slid smooth as molded butter from Henry's mouth.

"I know. I'm sorry Ace was so mad at you. We're just all upset about Dimmert."

"Sure you are," he said. "Why, I'm upset myself. Dimmert Whitt's a good man. Say, could I interest you in a little lunch over at the inn?"

Darcy paused on the sidewalk. "Do they serve liquor? I couldn't go in there if they do."

"Strongest thing they serve at the inn is coffee." His grip tightened slightly on her arm. "What do you say? It would do the both of us good."

"I suppose it would be all right, seeing as we'd be in public."

Henry had to stop himself from putting his arm around her waist and drawing her close. "Darcy, there's not a thing wrong with a man taking his best girl for a bite to eat."

They were seated at a table near the window where a dusty fern hung suspended from a chain. Darcy perused the limited menu as if she had done this many times before. Henry was surprised. He figured she'd never been off the creek.

"Goodness," she said, "it's been a long time since I ate out."

Henry leaned on his elbows and stared at her. He felt a prick of jealousy. Had she been here with another man? "So, what did you have last time you were here?" he asked ever so casually.

"Oh, I've never eaten here," she said, slowly pulling her gloves off one finger at a time. "I don't get the chance to eat out except when I'm in Lexington, but Mammaw's been too sick for me to go there for a while."

He studied her face. She had a smattering of freckles across her pert nose and a generous mouth. Her cheeks dimpled when she smiled, which was often. Being in her presence was like walking in sunshine. She unrolled the napkin from her silverware and placed the knife, fork, and spoon correctly around her plate. The napkin she placed on her lap.

"Lexington?" he said.

She sipped her ice water. "I like to get there twice a year, look at fabric, buy patterns, and take measurements, but like I said, Mammaw's been sick."

Not long after they ordered, a girl placed Darcy's chicken salad and Henry's ham steak in front of them. Darcy took a dainty bite.

Henry waited for her to swallow before he commented. "You have a business? Up here in the hills?"

Darcy buttered a bite of bread. "I do. I'm a seamstress. I sew pretty gowns for society ladies."

Under the table Henry pressed his knee against Darcy's. She put her bread down and looked at him with wide eyes. Brazenly, he traced the blue vein up her wrist. It was all he could do not to bring it to his lips. "What's your middle name?"

"Mae, after Fairy Mae Whitt," she stammered.

He captured her eyes with his own. "Someday, little Darcy Mae, you'll be wearing pretty gowns of your own."

Spots of color stained her cheeks. "Did you mean what you said back there?"

He busied himself with his knife and fork, meticulously severing a bit of gristle from his ham, drawing out the moment, playing with her like she was a fish on the line. "What would that be?"

She dropped her eyes. "You said I was your best girl."

"Best and only," he said with his most disarming smile. "If you'll have me, that is."

After Henry saw Darcy to her horse and buggy, he returned to the office. He sat in his chair, turning it toward the many leather tomes lined in alphabetical order behind the glass doors of two walnut bookcases. The classics he had read filled one case while the other held leather-bound books on law. It seemed to him that those books held all the knowledge one could ever hope to find, and Henry had studied each one. Yet he couldn't reason out why he was falling for a simple mountain girl. It was like his heart called out to hers, like it had a mind of its own.

Henry swiveled the chair and faced the desk. He wanted Darcy. He did. But he wanted to want her on his terms, not because of some hold she had over his emotions. Propping his feet on the corner of his desk, he leaned back, then rested his head on his crossed fingers. She had a killer smile, though. And the way she looked at him—he'd give a pretty penny to see that look again.

Maybe he could have it all if he was careful. What was it Darcy had said over lunch, her grandmother was doing poorly? How long could she last anyway? Bait the trap, reel Darcy in, have the woman he wanted and that beautiful land she would inherit when the old lady died at the same time.

He smiled. Life was beautiful.

CHAPTER 5

CARA WOULD HAVE SWORN she was all cried out, but watching her dear sweetheart, trussed up like a Thanksgiving turkey, being hauled off to prison proved her wrong. She'd given Dimmert no comfort other than perhaps her presence.

Now riding home, she wished she'd run to him and thrown her arms around him even if the sheriff and his deputy had to drag her off. The picture in her mind of her husband bravely stepping up into what Ace called the jailbird cage caused a storm of fresh tears.

"I'm sorry," she cried and hiccuped. "I can't seem to stop."

"That's all right, girl," Ace replied. "I feel like bawling myself. Poor Dimmert."

Cara doubled over, burying her face in her lap. "What will happen to him?" Her muffled words gave voice to her greatest fear. How could her sweet, kind husband bear life in prison?

"I had occasion to visit a buddy once at Kentucky State Penitentiary," Ace responded. "This was back in my wild days before I gave my life to the Lord."

Ace settled against the buggy seat, letting the reins slack. Cara knew she was in for a story, for Ace loved to talk more than anyone she'd ever met. She mopped her tears and listened as the horse picked his way down the graded gravel road.

"You probably wouldn't think it of me, but I used to make moonshine—had the best still for a hundred miles, I warrant. Men lined up to buy my shine whenever I made a batch, all of them dry as a lizard on a hot rock." Ace took off his hat and set it on the seat between them, then shrugged out of his suit coat. The day was heating up.

In spite of herself, Cara was enthralled. Ace's stories meandered like a rocky creek bed, but he always entertained.

"The secret to my liquor was the water. I found a run of the coldest, sweetest water you ever tasted bubbling out of a spring up the mountain from my house—"

"That is good water," Cara interrupted. "Jay gave me a taste last week."

"Dance wasn't overly impressed with me taking the time to pipe that water downhill, I can tell you," Ace said, shaking his head. "She was cross as a goose in a chicken house for two weeks."

Absently, Ace rubbed the bruise on the side of his face. "Anyway, one of my friends back then was Lump Lumpkin. His grandma was Clary Lumpkin, God rest her soul. Clary was a saintly woman and her own children followed suit, but those grandkids . . . Man, something bent the twig there."

The warmth of the sun, the sway of the buggy, and the sound of Ace's melodious voice began to work on Cara. Her stomach unknotted, and she could feel the tension seep from her shoulders. Her eyes closed for just a minute. A dip in the road nearly sent her flying off her seat. Down and out the buggy's wheel went and she was fully awake.

". . . so then Lump and me started filling fruit jars with the stuff."

Evidently Ace hadn't missed a beat while she caught a nap. She guessed that was one reason he was such a sought-after preacher. Folks sleeping while he talked didn't deter his enthusiasm.

"This one time," Ace continued with a chuckle, "Granny Lumpkin chased me and Lump out of her cornfield. She was winding up like a baseball player, pitching green walnuts fast as spitballs. 'Ouch,' Lump yelled. 'Granny, you're killing me.' 'I'm a-trying to keep you out of hell, son,' I heard Granny yell back, while walnuts pinged off trees and off Lump's head. 'A man who'd steal corn from his own family is sliding down a slippery slope.' Lump earned his nickname that day, I reckon."

Ace stroked his chin. "I've been sorry for stealing from that sainted lady ever since. I started growing my own corn after that."

"So," Cara asked, "why did Lump wind up in the penitentiary?"

"He shot a man. Shot him straight through the heart one night when he caught the fellow stealing some of our homemade brew. I never even knew Lump had a gun." Ace's voice dropped to a hoarse whisper as if tears clogged his throat. "I'll never forget the smell of liquor mixed with blood and fear. Did you know you can smell fear, Cara?"

He covered his mouth with his hand. Cara could barely make out his next words. "Lump ran off, but I couldn't leave a man to die all alone, so I stayed—crying and praying for hours like a woman in labor. The next morning I went to find the sheriff. I was figuring me and Lump both was through. But I got off and Lump got life. I ain't never been able to forgive myself for that."

"Oh, Ace," Cara said. "It wasn't your fault."

"I didn't pull the trigger," Ace replied, "but I set up Lump's stumbling block when I built that still."

"I don't understand," Cara said. "Unless you gave Lump the gun, I don't see why you blame yourself."

Ace patted the empty seat between them, then reached down to retrieve the jacket that had fallen to the floor. He held it over the side of the buggy and gave a little shake. "Aggravation, now I'll have to press it again." Taking a small, well-worn Bible from the inside coat pocket, he handed it to Cara. "Look up Romans 14:13 and read it aloud."

Cara thumbed the pages. Her fingers felt thick as corncobs. Her family had never read the Bible much when she was growing up. Though she knew Ace didn't judge her, she felt ignorant as she let the books of the Old Testament slip through her fingers like falling leaves: Genesis, Exodus, Esther, Psalms, Amos, Micah, Malachi, and many others, but no Romans.

"Look in the New Testament," Ace said kindly. "You'll find Romans between Acts and Corinthians. It's one of Paul's epistles."

Cara wasn't about to tell him she didn't know what an epistle was, but she found Romans just where Ace said. She scanned the first chapter and lit on verse 7. "'Beloved of God,'" she read, "'called to be saints: Grace to you and peace from God our Father, and the Lord Jesus Christ.'"

Ace hung his carefully folded coat over the buggy seat. "Go to chapter 14, verse 13."

Cara took a breath and squinted at the small type. It was not to be taken lightly, she knew, speaking the words of the Lord. She wasn't sure if she was worthy, but she'd read it for Ace, who was laudable in her eyes. "'Let us not therefore judge one another any more: but judge this rather, that no man put a stumblingblock or an occasion to fall in his brother's way.' So you're saying your whiskey still was Lump's stumbling block?"

"Well," Ace replied, "it led him to the path of his destruction."

"You're awful hard on yourself."

"Preachers are held to a higher standard than other folks," he said, reining the horse in.

"But you weren't a preacher then," Cara responded. "Don't ye reckon God means for you to forgive yourself the same as you'd forgive someone else?"

The buggy rolled off the road and stopped under a canopy of beech and hickory nut trees. It was deep in green shadow and so quiet Cara could hear her own heart beating.

"Thank ye for that, Cara. I ain't been at peace with myself since Lump's funeral."

"What happened to Lump?" she asked, though she wasn't sure she wanted the answer. Probably beaten to death or starved at that prison. She couldn't help but picture the same for Dimmert.

"Caught the grippe the first year he was sent up, God rest his soul. I always figured it to be a blessing." Ace jumped down from the buggy seat and reached for her. "Are you up for a walk? I want to show you the spring where the sweetwater runs."

"I'd surely like to see that." She bent over to unbutton her high-tops. "Just let me slip off my good shoes first."

Ace walked ahead, stopping now and then to hold back a briar for her safe passage or to snap a low-hanging twig that threatened to poke him in the eye. The farther they went, the lighter her heart became. They walked for fifteen minutes in harmony, the only sound their own footfalls upon the forest floor.

Cara stopped when she spied a stand of white dogwood on a ridge high above. Hands on hips she took in their beauty. She might climb up there on the way back and get a spray to take home. And she wouldn't mind having a small limb if she could find one already on the ground. Cara liked to whittle, and the hard wood from a dogwood tree made sturdy round-headed clothespins and handy sharp skewers. She'd add it to her store of carving supplies.

Where had Ace got to? This particular area was not familiar to her. And what with hungry bears not long out of hibernation and rattlesnakes hiding under flat rocks just waiting for a tasty ankle to pass by, she didn't fancy getting lost. What would happen to a body if she got snakebit while all alone with no one to suck the poison out? She reckoned the venom would race straightaway to her heart and stop its beat sure as an unwound clock lost its tick. She listened until she heard Ace's heavy tread, then hurried to catch up.

His white shirt shone in the forest's gloom like a candle flame on a dark night. Cara liked how Ace dressed up whenever he preached or went to town on business. It gave him some authority. One evening while visiting with Dance, she'd watched him press his black suit. She could still hear the hiss and pop of the heavy sadiron as he heated it on the cookstove and sense the heavy smell of wet wool as the suit coat steamed under a pressing cloth. Dance had sat at the kitchen table looking at him wearily. Cara had never seen a man with a sadiron in his hand.

"There you are," Ace said when she caught up. "The spring is right around the bend."

She could hear the burble of water as Ace directed her path. The spring issued forth from a rocky ledge and formed a long, narrow run through the grassy meadow like a small creek. "Where does it end?" she asked.

Ace pointed. "This part goes underground right over there in that stand of sycamores. But it also feeds the creek that runs by your place. I came upon the spring because I knew if I saw sycamores there'd be water. I was hunting for a good place to set up a still."

Cara looked around. "You must have hid it good. I can't see a thing."

"I burned it to the ground when I got saved," he said, "and buried the ashes."

Cara nodded. She wondered if Ace had shared his sorrow with Dance and then figured he had not. Dance had burdens enough. While she watched, Ace tinkered with the plumbing he'd set up to carry some of the springwater down the mountain to his place. "That's amazing," she said. "How did you know to do that?"

"I like to fiddle with things. That's all." He indicated a fallen log. "Sit here and I'll fetch you a drink. I keep a tin cup around here somewhere."

Soon they were seated side by side sharing a cup of pure mountain water so cold it made her teeth ache. "Thank ye, Ace, for bringing me here. It took my mind off things for a little while."

"Time will pass. Dimm will be home before you know it."

She passed the tin cup to Ace. "You were going to tell me what it's like inside the prison. Tell me true."

"It's big," Ace said, "sits on several acres near the Kentucky River. It's built of limestone and has these funny turrets on the front—looks kind of like a castle. Armed guards are stationed along the walls in watch boxes to keep the prisoners from escaping. Inside, the walls are brick except for the cell house, which is the same limestone as the wall."

Cara shuddered. The prison sounded cold and desolate. She couldn't picture her husband there.

"Don't fret. It ain't so bad. Dimm will do fine if he stays out of trouble."

"What will he do all day?" She imagined Dimm shut up with nothing to occupy him. "Dimm ain't one to sit around."

"Oh, the prisoners work. They make chairs and cabinets, wagon beds and even shoes. Now that would be good, wouldn't it?" Ace polished the toe of one shoe on the back of his pant leg and held it out for Cara to see. "Dimm could make new shoes for us."

Cara tucked her bare feet under her skirt. "Dimm might like making wagons. Maybe he'll make one and roll on out of there."

"That wouldn't be such a good idea. They'll double his time if he tries to escape."

"I was just joshing. Dimm knows better."

"The good thing is he'll be busy and the time will go quicker that way." Ace reached up and broke a small limb, then hung the tin cup on the stub. "Even the women have jobs in prison."

"Women! I can't imagine why they'd pen a woman up like that."

"Most anything a man is capable of doing, a woman is also. Plus, seems to me women get taken advantage of more than men."

Cara followed Ace back the way they had come, being careful to keep up in the fading daylight. "What kind of work do the women do?" she wondered aloud.

"They mostly run the looms weaving hemp into bagging and rope. We'll pray Dimm isn't sent there. The dust coming off that hemp will choke your breath." Ace held a long, weaving branch of blackberry briar so Cara could pass by. "I always thought that's what happened to Lump. They told him to grow a mustache to filter the dust, but it didn't help any. I reckon his lungs filled up with that nasty stuff."

"Poor Lump." Cara touched Ace's arm and he turned to her. "I'm so sorry about your friend, Ace."

Though he was right before her, Ace seemed far away, as if his eyes saw distant worlds. "God works in mysterious ways to teach us life lessons. I wouldn't be a preacher today if Lump hadn't died."

Goose bumps covered Cara's arms, and a chill went up her spine. Somewhere a goose had walked over her grave. Following where Ace led, careful to mind her step, she pondered what had just been said. Was there something she needed to learn from losing Dimmert? She couldn't imagine any good coming from a thing so painful. God was up there somewhere, but she didn't reckon He had time to reach down with His powerful finger and stir things up on earth, like she'd stir her coffee when she couldn't find a spoon.

Nope, hard times were just hard times, something to be survived. Ace's sureness bothered her a little, though, and made her feel as if she was missing something important.

CHAPTER 6

THE REST OF THE RIDE HOME was quiet except for the sudden swarm of yellow-eyed, black-feathered grackles swooping en masse to light in the treetops lining the road. Cara covered her ears against their high-pitched rising screech. The birds sounded like hundreds of rusty hinges. Ace didn't take notice; he seemed lost in thought. Cara let him be. She had enough words in her head to last awhile.

Her house looked lonesome from the road, the windows like haunted eyes, the door a dark reproach. When Ace stopped the buggy, she couldn't seem to get out. Her legs were heavy as lead and her arms lay useless in her lap. Tears slipped from her eyes and tracked down her cheeks.

"Why don't you go with me to pick up Dance and the young'uns?" Ace asked. "You could visit with Fairy Mae and Darcy—even spend the night if you want. They'd be glad to have you."

"All right," she said before she had time to think differently. "If you don't care to take me."

Fairy Mae Whitt's sturdy little cabin was awash in light. Cara's belly grumbled at the smell of fried chicken.

"Come on in here," she heard Mammaw call out. "Come let me hug your neck."

Mammaw, withered with age and crippled with rheumatism, sat propped up with pillows in an invalid's chair. The big round wheels and the wide seat seemed to swallow her, but her eyes twinkled with merriment. She still had use of one arm, and Cara melted in the warmth of its embrace.

"Oh, Mammaw," she said, "I don't hardly think I can stand this."

"I know, honey." Mammaw gave an extra squeeze. "My heart's a-breaking too."

A little hand tugged at Cara's skirt. "Merky," she said, "my baby girl. Who's been playing with your hair?"

Merky popped one finger out of her mouth and pointed at Darcy before Cara swung her high in the air.

Soon Wilton demanded his share of attention and even little Cleve held up his arms for a swing.

Jay sidled over to his great-grandmother's chair. "Do ye have a riddle for me, Aunt Cara?"

Dance jiggled little Cleve on her hip and reproached the boy. "We don't have time for playing."

"It won't get no darker in the time it takes for him to answer one riddle," Ace said from the doorway.

Cara met Ace's eyes. He shrugged. "Listen, Jay," she said. "Here's your clue: A house that carries its master. A house with eyes and mouth. A house that travels. Now you unravel."

"That's too easy," Jay said. "It has to be a terrapin."

Cara ruffled his dark hair. "You're right as rain. I'll have to think harder next time."

"Do I still get my penny?"

"Me too," Wilton demanded. "Where's mine penny?"

"No penny for you, boy." Dance said. "You'd eat it or stick it up your nose."

Cara fished in her pocket for Jay's penny and handed Wilton the bright blue jay feather she had forgotten was there. "This is for you, Willy-boy."

Wilton took the feather and tasted the quill end.

"What do you say?" Ace asked.

"Thank you, Aunt Cara," Jay said.

"Fanks," Wilton echoed.

"Do we have to go home now?" Jay said. "I was just starting to have fun."

"You could let the big kids spend the night," Darcy said. "I could bring them home in the morning."

"I reckon not," Ace replied, retrieving the sleeping Pauline from a laundry basket and shooing his brood toward the door. "The house ain't right without everybody there. Thank ye anyway."

Soon the Shelton family was gone and Darcy had helped her mammaw to bed. Cara busied herself straightening the front room. It was strange to be in someone else's house after dark.

"Let's pop some corn," Darcy said when she came back. "Then we can have a hen fest—just us girls."

The corn popped when Darcy held the long-handled wire basket over the fire in the fireplace. The young women settled together on the hearth, a blue earthenware bowl between them.

"Wish we had some fudge," Darcy said. "I like sweet and salty together."

"This is enough for me," Cara responded. "I don't know when I ever ate popcorn last."

"Was today real hard for you—seeing Dimm carted off that way?" Darcy asked.

"That's why I'm here. I couldn't stand to go into our house tonight, but I reckon I'll do better tomorrow. It's not like I haven't been living there alone for a while. I just hoped . . ."

"I know. I know." Darcy patted Cara's knee. "I couldn't believe what happened."

"I blame that lawyer, that Henry Thomas. If he'd have done his job, Dimmert would be home tonight. Ace was hopping mad at him."

Darcy's face clouded.

She's as easy to read as the weather in June, Cara thought. *Clear as window glass.*

"I thought he was a right nice fellow," Darcy said.

"I could be wrong," Cara replied. "It's not like I know anything about the law, but it seems he could have tried harder."

Darcy slipped off the hearth and knelt before Cara. "Can I tell you something? I'm going to bust if I don't tell somebody!" Darcy's round face was as innocent as Merky's. Her brown hair was dressed for bed and hung in a single pigtail down her back.

A knot formed in Cara's chest. Darcy was sweet as an all-day sucker and as easily shattered, Cara feared. "What do you want to tell me?"

"Today after I left the jailhouse, I happened to run into Henry—"

"Henry? You're calling him by his first name?"

Darcy began to bank the fireplace ashes. The night was not so cold that they needed to keep it going. "He asked me to," she said, sighing like the fire.

Cara carried the rest of the popcorn to the kitchen table and sat it beside the kerosene lamp. Darcy took a chair across from her. "Tell me the rest, Darcy."

Darcy bounced in her seat; her eyes glowed. "Henry wants to court me! He called me his best girl."

Cara was caught off guard. She didn't like what she saw in that lawyer fellow. "What does Dance think about that? Shouldn't you discuss this with her?"

Darcy shrugged as if her sister was of no consequence to her. "Dance doesn't listen to anything but what's inside her own head. Ever since my brothers and sisters left to live with Pa and his new wife, I haven't really had a sister."

"You must miss them something awful," Cara said.

"Missing them is the hardest thing," Darcy said. "It hurts worse than when my ma died, and I never thought I'd say that."

"Why didn't you go with them and your daddy?"

"I couldn't leave Mammaw. I know you and Dimmert would have taken her in, but she needed me, and she was so good to us kids, giving us a home when we had nowhere else to go."

The embers in the fireplace dimmed, and the popcorn grew cold. Cara took a shawl from the back of the chair on which she sat, wrapped it around her shoulders, and settled in to listen to Darcy's story.

"I thought all us young'uns would starve to death after Ma took sick," Darcy said. "Pa was off somewhere. He was a circuit riding preacher, you know. He didn't even know when Ma died."

Darcy began to weave the end of her long pigtail through the loom of her fingers. "It wasn't that us big girls didn't know how to cook; it was that there was nothing in the house to cook. And then there were the little kids to look out for and no milk for them to drink. Dimmert kept us going with whatever he could kill—squirrels and possums mostly. Possum ain't bad if you bake it with onions."

Cara kept quiet. She'd always wondered about Dimmert's childhood, but when she asked, he dismissed her questions and rarely told her anything. He wasn't one to dwell on the past. When she'd press, he would always reply, "Don't let yesterday take up too much of today."

"Anyway, Pa finally came home. Soon as he buried Ma, he packed up all us kids and brought us here to Mammaw Fairy Mae's." Darcy chewed a piece of corn and washed it down with tea. "Did Dimmert ever tell you how him and me wound up living with Miz Copper?"

"He's told me some."

"Mr. Pelfrey came by Mammaw's one day—he was always doing this or that for her—and asked if maybe a couple of us bigger kids could go over there and help Miz Copper out. She was all alone with Lilly Gray, trying her best to make a go of that farm. Well, it was decided that Dimmert and I would be the ones. And am I glad. Miz Copper is the best, and the money she paid helped Mammaw take care of the others. And then of course, that's how Dimmert met you, Cara, because of Miz Copper."

"And am I glad," Cara teased, getting up to pour more hot tea. "Yes, Dimmert first came by my house when Miz Copper was taking care of my little brother."

"That was an awful thing when Kenny died."

Cara shook her head. "Boys . . . they sure can cause a lot of grief."

Darcy stirred honey into her tea. "That's why I'm only having girls," she said, holding up the honey pot. "Want some more long sweetening?"

"No, I've got plenty."

"When did you first take notice of Dimm?" Dimples played in and out of Darcy's round cheeks. "Was it love at first sight?"

Cara grinned. It was good to talk about happy times. "I'd have to say I liked his manners, and it didn't hurt a bit that he was riding a good-looking horse."

"That Star," Darcy said. "He was aggravating as sin."

"Now Star just hangs out in Miz Copper's pasture getting fat and sassy," Cara said.

"He was already plenty sassy if you ask me." Darcy stood and stretched. "I'd best go check on Mammaw. I put an extra quilt on your bed."

"Good night, Darcy."

Darcy hugged Cara tight. "Sweet dreams."

<hr />

Sunlight woke Cara the next morning. Chagrined, she leaped out of bed and hurried to the front room. Coffee perked on the stove, and a plate of biscuits and eggs sat waiting on the warmer.

"Good morning, sleepyhead," Darcy said, poking her head out of Mammaw's room. "Help yourself to breakfast."

"I'm sorry to have slept so late," Cara replied.

"I expect you needed it. I'm just finishing Mammaw's bath."

Cara started for the bedroom door. "Can I help?"

"You can pour me another cup of coffee and have one yourself." Darcy's voice held a smile that warmed the room.

Cara cut into her egg, then sopped up the bright yellow yolk with a piece of buttermilk biscuit. The first sip of coffee hit the spot. She felt her shoulders soften as tension drained from her body. Looking around, she took in the just-mopped floor, the light streaming in the windows, Darcy's sewing machine and dress forms laden with bright fabrics and wished she could take the feeling of this room with her when she left. Maybe she'd never go home—just stay here in this sunny kitchen forever.

She'd scraped her plate and put it with others in the dishpan when Darcy bounced into the room. "Mmmm." She sniffed the steam from her coffee. "Thanks, Cara. This is just right. Bring your cup and come on. Mammaw's ready for devotions."

Mammaw, propped up by pillows, her open Bible on her lap, gave Cara a smile to rival Darcy's. "Come give me some sugar," she said.

Leaning over, Cara bussed the old woman's soft cheek, spider-webbed with wrinkles. Mammaw smelled of starched linen and coffee. Every case on her pillows was embroidered with flowers and birds and butterflies. Even the collar of her gown was brightly stitched. It was as if she lay in a flower garden.

Darcy sat cross-legged at the end of the bed, so Cara did the same.

"I feel like reading from Psalms today," Mammaw said, flipping the Good Book's pages with her crippled fingers. "Listen to this, girls, from chapter 84. 'Behold, O God our shield, and look upon the face of thine anointed. For a day in thy courts is better than a thousand.

I had rather be a doorkeeper in the house of my God, than to dwell in the tents of wickedness. For the Lord God is a sun and shield: the Lord will give grace and glory: no good thing will he withhold from them that walk uprightly. O Lord of hosts, blessed is the man that trusteth in thee.'"

The verses from Psalms ran through Cara's mind as she walked the long way home later that morning. How was it that she'd wished for some warmth to take home with her and then Mammaw's devotion spoke of the Lord God as a sun and a shield? Could Mammaw read her mind? Did God even know she, Cara Whitt, existed? It seemed a mighty stretch of imagination to think so. Cara was sure God had bigger things to think on. Maybe she'd start thumbing through her Bible, though, like Mammaw and Ace did. She wouldn't mind having the strength it seemed to give them.

She walked along, switching the tall grasses in front of her with a long stick, hoping to give warning to any varmints lurking there. She stopped for a moment to watch a long green lizard slip off a flat rock. Being the same color as the new spring grass, he disappeared easily, hiding in plain sight no doubt. She wasn't afraid of lizards, but all the same she didn't want to step on one. Just the thought gave her the willies.

Soon she came to Troublesome Creek. She'd have to cross it. All sorts of creepy things hid in the dark water—tadpoles with their ugly bug eyes, snapping turtles, and slithery water moccasins, maybe death itself.

Dimmert had taught her to throw rocks in the water before she waded in. He said the snakes would go up under the riffles if they felt threatened, but what about the turtles? Wouldn't they be too slow? What if one mistook her big toe for a tasty treat? She reckoned if that happened, she'd have a turtle hanging off her foot until the next storm. Once a turtle clamped its jaws shut, it wouldn't let go until it thundered or until a cow bawled. There was no cloud nor cow in sight.

She stood wavering on the bank for the longest time. When had she become so afraid of things? She wasn't like this as a girl. In her growing-up years she'd helped her mother birth babies, tended her siblings' cuts and scrapes, and helped her daddy kill hogs without the blink of an eye. Now she was scared of itty-bitty tadpoles. It started when her brother died and got worse when she nearly lost her mother. Ever since then she saw danger lurking around every corner.

Something jumped from the bank and hit the water with a splash. She ventured a little closer, chucking a small, smooth stone into the water. Ripples circled ripples until the rings broke at the water's edge.

"'The Lord God is a sun and shield,'" she spoke loudly as she waded across the creek. The cold sent shock waves up her spine. "'The Lord God is a sun and shield,'" she said again and felt the comfort of the words circle her like the rings of water circled the impact of the stone. Soon she was on the other side, shaky but safe as she made her way home.

The house was no more welcoming than the day before, but she wasn't as dejected as she had been. Spending the night with Mammaw and Darcy had been a rare treat, and before she left, Darcy insisted on fitting her for a new dress, though she knew Cara couldn't pay her for it. The fabric Darcy chose was yellow- and brown-checked gingham. With a mouth full of straight pins, she darted and tucked while Cara turned this way and that dressed only in her in her muslin chemise. Cara would have picked from the stack of floral-print feed sacks, but Darcy would have none of it. "You're going to have a dress of nice fabric and that's that," she said.

Fetching her whittling knife and a small piece of hardwood, Cara settled down on the top step of her porch. The sun felt warm, so she took off her sweater and folded it for a cushion. She closed her eyes and studied the wood with her hands, allowing it to tell her the shape it would take. Soon slivers of aromatic walnut sang from her fingers like a long-remembered melody. She'd make a small basket to thank Darcy for the dress.

Maybe she would wear that dress to church. Ace took his children nearly every Sunday, though Dance rarely accompanied him.
Dance wasn't much for crowds. Ace had been after Cara to go along.
He said she needed to hear the Word. He said things would be easier
to deal with if she had that comfort.

CHAPTER 7

Darcy Whitt adjusted the window shade. The glare was giving her a headache. Frowning, she maneuvered another piece of pattern on the material laid out across the kitchen table. If she worked it right, there should be enough left over to make a new bonnet to go with the dress. Cara had been easy to fit; she was tall with broad shoulders but slender. She'd fallen off a lot since Dimmert's trouble, and her clothes hung on her like a scarecrow's. Next time she came over, Darcy would take her skirts in.

It had been fun to have her spend the night, Darcy mused while marking bust darts with a sliver of Fels-Naptha. Laying the soap aside, she picked up her dress shears and bent over the fabric. Darcy loved this part of dressmaking—the first snick of the scissors, fitting the dress form, pinning and basting—the anticipation of the finished garment. It was like painting a beautiful picture. Truthfully, she should be finishing the order for Mrs. Upchurch, an evening dress of velvet and lace trimmed with velvet roses. The roses lay completed on the sideboard waiting to be handstitched to the gown, one at the shoulder and several trailing down the side of the skirt. Personally, she didn't think pink complemented Mrs. Upchurch. Lavender or perhaps dusky green would have been a better choice.

Mrs. Upchurch was her best customer, though, and Darcy meant to please. Another thing to thank Miz Copper for. Five years ago Miz Copper had sent Darcy to Lexington to train under a dressmaker there. Now she could barely keep up with the orders from Mrs. Upchurch and her high-society friends. She'd make more money if she moved her business to Lexington, but that was no place for Mammaw.

She had enough money to keep herself and her grandmother fed and to have a few nice things—hand-finished underwear, rustproof corsets, and fine-milled soap—but someday she wanted a reason to wear corsets and fancy gowns like she made for others. She felt herself blush. Maybe that reason was Henry Thomas. It didn't hurt to dream. Dreams kept life from being so ordinary.

Fishing a straight pin from the corner of her puckered mouth, she secured a piece of pattern to the fabric. If Mammaw slept another hour, she could finish cutting Cara's dress and start on the roses. The evening dress needed to be in the post to Lexington no later than the end of the week if it was to arrive in time for the ball Mrs. Upchurch was attending.

Tap-tap-tap. Someone was at the door.

Spitting out the pins, she hurried to open it. "Dylan?"

"Hey, Darcy." Dylan smoothed a shock of yellow hair from his forehead. "Look what I found."

"Oh, pretty," Darcy replied, standing in the half-open door. "I'm surprised daffodils are already blooming."

"Over on Troublesome," he said. "Daffodils and flags, but the flags are still furled."

"Too bad. Irises are my favorite flowers."

Dylan smiled. "My mom's too. She says they smell like summer."

Darcy knew she should ask about his mom, perhaps invite him in for a cup of coffee, or at the very least pour him a glass of water, but Dylan didn't need encouraging. He was as hard to get rid of as a stray cat with a litter of kittens. "Well," she said instead, "thanks for showing me the daffodils."

"I meant for you to have them. I thought you and Miz Fairy Mae would enjoy them."

Darcy took the flowers. "Thanks," she said again.

"Would your mammaw like some company?"

"I'm sorry. She's sleeping, and I've got work to do."

"All righty then." Dylan stepped off the porch and walked backward across the yard, keeping his eyes on her. "See you soon."

"Soon," Darcy said and wagged her fingers before closing the door firmly behind her.

"Was that Jean Foster's boy?" Mammaw called from her room.

Darcy sighed, resting her bowed head against the closed door. Mammaw was awake; she'd have to put her sewing aside. She took a breath and went to Mammaw's room. "Yes, it was. And just look what he brought you."

Mammaw stuck her nose deep into the yellow bouquet. "Don't they smell pretty?"

"Let me get some water. You can keep them on your bedside table."

"I think Dylan meant these for you." Mammaw's eyes twinkled. "Looks like somebody's stuck on you, Darcy."

Darcy plopped down on the side of the bed. Butter yellow blossoms drooped from her hand. "Oh, Mammaw! Dylan's just a boy."

"He's a year older than you, Darcy Mae Whitt. Twenty-two's hardly a boy."

Uh-oh, when Mammaw called her by her full name, that meant she was aggravated. Mammaw liked Dylan and made no bones about it. Now Darcy was leery of telling her Henry Thomas was coming to call on Sunday after church. She could wait, just let him show up. When Mammaw saw how handsome he was—chiseled cheekbones, perfectly straight nose, and hair black as midnight—she was sure to warm up to him. Not to mention he was educated. *My, my, such a catch wanting to court her.*

Darcy fingered the buttons on her blouse, one after the other telling her fortune: Doctor. Lawyer. Merchant. Chief. Doctor. Lawyer. *Lawyer—the very last one!* That settled it; she was meant to marry a lawyer.

"Darcy," Mammaw said, "you're smashing the jonquils."

"Sorry. I'll just get that water."

Soon the flowers sat prettily in a tall blue vase and Mammaw was up in her invalid's chair. "Is it warm enough to take in some air? Those daffodils make me want to be outside."

"I think so," Darcy answered. "Let me fetch your shawl just in case."

It was pleasant outdoors. Darcy spread an old quilt on the porch floor and sat there with her needle and thread. Mammaw, parked in a patch of sunshine, held the fabric roses on her lap, handing one to Darcy when she was ready. The ball gown was lovely with its skirt spread out across the faded glory of the quilt.

"I made that quilt you're setting on when I was first married," Mammaw said.

"How old were you?" Darcy asked, snapping a thread with her teeth.

"Fifteen," Mammaw said with a chuckle. "I thought I was a grown-up."

"Were you happy? Did Papaw Whitt make your heart flutter?"

"Through the first four babies I reckon he did—early on. Here's a truth for you, little gal: when hard times come through the door, young love goes out the window."

"Oh, Mammaw, I hate to you think of you unhappy." Darcy placed her sewing aside for a moment, laying her head on her grandmother's knee.

Mammaw stroked her hair. "I don't reckon anybody gets through this life without some hard times. Faith ain't true unless it's tested."

Darcy took up her sewing. It was Mammaw's much-used thimble that rested on her finger. "Tell me a story. Tell me how your faith was tested."

"Law, I haven't talked about this for fifty years, though I've thought of it every day." Mammaw handed Darcy another rose and a small green felt leaf. "It was dead of winter. I had a new baby that year—Donald, your daddy. There was four other young'uns—Tad, Elwood, Perry, and Amanda. She was the nearest to your daddy. Your papaw was off somewheres. I can't rightly recollect where. He was always working. . . ."

Darcy's flying needle paused. She looked up to see a cloud cross Mammaw's eyes. The twinkle that was nearly always there was replaced by the shimmer of tears.

"I took it in my head to mop the floor while Herbert was gone working. Seemed like every day he tracked in something for me to clean up. The baby cried, and I set the mop bucket under the kitchen table so the boys wouldn't knock it over." Mammaw covered her eyes with her hand. Darcy knew something bad was coming.

"She was a pretty little thing, Amanda was, golden curls and round blue eyes . . . Merky favors her. The kids all settled at my feet in front of the fire. I was in the rocker, the baby nursing. I guess I nodded off but surely not for long. I always watched my young'uns close."

Darcy's hand closed over Mammaw's.

Mammaw shook her head as if she could change the outcome of her story. "Perry was there. And Tad and Elwood. But Amanda, my little toddling girl, was not. I remember stopping the rocker, laying the baby down by Elwood, rising up from the chair. I knew before I turned around what had happened. In my mind's eye, I saw her blue face and her curls wetly plastered to her head. I thought to sit back down, take up the baby, and turn back time, but the icy fear that walked my spine told me it was too late."

Darcy choked back sobs. Tears stored a long, long time, she figured, washed down Mammaw's weathered cheeks.

"I reckon I could have stood it if when I turned around, I hadn't seen her tiny feet, still pink, rising up out of the mop bucket. Those feet gave me false hope." Mammaw sighed, long and deep, and shook her head again. "Herbert said when he got home, the kids were still huddled at my feet, quiet as mice, Elwood holding the baby. There was no light to greet him except what issued from the fireplace. He sent Tad to fetch a neighbor lady whilst he pried Amanda from my arms."

Darcy hugged her grandmother tight. "Oh, Mammaw, I'm so sorry."

Mammaw leaned into Darcy's arms. "You're a good girl, Darcy Mae. God sent me the best granddaughter to replace Amanda, I reckon."

"I'm glad," Darcy replied. "I'm so glad to be yours."

While Mammaw took her afternoon's rest, Darcy finished Mrs. Upchurch's gown. She folded it into a sturdy pasteboard box tucked all around with white tissue paper. As a surprise she slipped a lady's fan made of clipped, white faux ostrich feathers into the folds of the skirt. The ostrich feathers had come from New York City. She'd ordered them herself. Cara had carved the fine wood handle. Next she thought she'd try peacock feathers trimmed to size. It was amazing what a body could order through the mail.

All the while Darcy worked, she thought of Mammaw's story. She wondered if this was the selfsame table little Amanda had drowned under. Poor wee thing—it was too sad to think on. When she had babies, she'd name her first daughter Fairy Amanda, for Mammaw and the little lost one. She tried it out, "Fairy Amanda Thomas," then blushed at her own conjecture.

But Henry was real and his attention to her was not false. She could tell by the look in his eyes. After finding a pencil, she settled at the table and began to sketch a wedding dress. Darcy had been designing her wedding ensemble ever since she attended Cara and Dimm's wedding. She always knew her prince would come, and she wanted to be ready. Now maybe he had. As the pencil glided over the paper, a beautiful gown appeared. Hat or veil? Bustle or modified train? Hat and bustle, she decided, nothing too fancy for the church on Troublesome Creek. But then again, if she and Henry were to marry, she needed something stylish. Mrs. Upchurch's husband was a banker, which Darcy fancied was the next best thing to being a lawyer, and Mrs. Upchurch always dressed as if she were receiving visitors any moment.

Before Darcy knew it, an hour had passed. Time always slipped by quickly when she designed. The high-necked, long-sleeved frock was only pencil on paper at the moment, but Darcy imagined it in pale lavender satin brocade overlaid with ecru lace. The full skirt would be edged with ecru fringe, but to keep the outfit from being too sophisticated, she'd wear a simple pouf of lavender netting instead of a hat.

Goodness, she'd better wake Mammaw and rustle up a little supper. Milk toast would do, easy for her to make and easy for her grandmother to swallow. She stood and stretched. One leg had fallen asleep and it stung like fire. Hobbling around, she gathered up her sewing. The dress design she secreted under a quilt in the corner cupboard with the others. Mammaw wasn't ready to see that.

Later, over supper, Mammaw was still in a pensive mood. "I don't have much of an appetite," she said, pushing half of her milk toast aside.

"Can't you eat just one more bite?"

Mammaw speared one piece of the toast Darcy had cut up for her; the bread hung from the tines of the fork like a fish on the line. "Someday soon this will all be yours, Darcy."

Darcy squirmed in her chair. "What do you mean?"

Mammaw swept the air with her one strong arm. "Why, this house, child, and the land that goes with it. All the hills and the hardwood trees and the coal seam buried underneath will belong to you and you alone. I wonder if it will be a blessing or a burden."

"I don't understand. What about the other grandkids?"

"Dance has got her share and Dimmert also. You know I deeded them property when they married. My other grandchildren have moved away. You and Dance and Dimmert are the only ones that stayed. The land was meant to have Whitts living on it." Mammaw shrugged. "That'd please Herbert, I suppose." •

Darcy dribbled honey on Mammaw's milk toast, then lifted the fork to her grandmother's mouth. "You're still trying to please Papaw," she teased.

Mammaw's face was hard to read. "That wasn't an easy job."

Darcy was taken aback. She'd never heard her grandmother say a word against Papaw. "How so?"

"Herbert Whitt was a rambling, gambling man. That doesn't make for the easiest life for a woman."

"Did you ever want to leave?"

"And go where with them young'uns?" Mammaw swallowed a bit of toast. "I made my bed. Besides, ain't no man is perfect. They've all got warts."

That made Darcy laugh. "You're a sight, Mammaw."

"A woman never gets over her first sweetheart, and Herbert Whitt was my first and last. There were as many good times as bad, I reckon."

Darcy poured more buttermilk into Mammaw's cup. "Tell me a story about the good times."

CHAPTER 8

MONDAY AGAIN, Cara trudged to Dance's under cold and sodden skies that threatened rain. Why must it always rain on wash day? She was sick of hanging clothes indoors to dry like she had done the last two Mondays, especially at Dance's, where the children made a game of hide-and-seek among the sheets and pillowcases. Her own package of wash—two dresses, one dish towel, and some drawers—was clutched under her arm like a fancy purse.

She was glad for the job, though, and the excuse it provided to leave her own desolate house for the hubbub of the Sheltons'.

"Hello," she hollered when she reached the yard. "You all to home?"

Jay sped out the door and across the porch. Wilton followed, missed a step, and rolled across the ground.

"Whoa, there, little fellow," Cara said, tickling his tummy with her bare foot. "Where are you going in such a hurry?"

"We been watching out the window," Wilton said.

"For me?" Cara asked, inordinately pleased.

"Sure, Aunt Cara," Jay replied, "but I ain't allowed to ask for pennies."

"You're not? Forevermore, why?"

"Ma says it's the same as begging." Jay tucked his chin, his face crestfallen. "Too bad. Solving riddles was the only way I had to make a living."

Cara had to hide her grin behind her hand. Jay talked so grown-up. "What if we do riddles for fun? And what if I hide a penny and you happen upon it?"

Jay stroked his chin. "That just might work."

Cara limped across the yard, Wilton clinging to her lower leg like a baby possum on its mother's back.

"Get off Aunt Cara's leg, Wilton," Jay demanded.

"He's all right, Jay," she said, swinging Wilton along. "Now listen up. Katydids can't cipher, june bugs can't write, but I know very well a bug that can spell. What is it?"

"Aunt Cara's gonna stop coming if you two boys don't quit pestering her." Dance leaned against the doorframe, her hands tucked under her armpits. "You ain't aiming to wash today, are ye? I cain't stand another day of dripping clotheslines in my kitchen."

"I'd thought to," Cara replied. "It is Monday."

"I know what day it is," Dance barked. "I ain't as stupid as you and Ace think I am."

Cara hesitated in the doorway and then held forth her little bundle. "I'm sorry. I never thought anything of the sort. It's just—well, it is wash day."

"It ain't like it's a law. Monday wash day! Tuesday ironing! Friday scrubbing! Saturday baking! The world wouldn't come to an end if we mixed those days up, now, would it?"

"I reckon not," Cara replied. "What if I scrub the floors instead of doing a wash?"

Dance motioned Cara to look at the dark clouds. "Cain't you see it's coming a frog strangler? Why do I need clean floors when these young'uns is going to be tracking in and out all day?"

Cara had had enough of Dance's peevish mood. "I think you're overtired. I'm going to gather your dirty clothes and take them to my house. I'll bring everything back when it dries."

Dance picked up Pauline and sank into a chair at the kitchen table, resting her head on her folded arms. Like little sentries, her children gathered round her. Jay patted her shoulder, and Merky and Wilton leaned upon her knees. Cleve crawled between her feet. Pauline lay across her lap. "It don't matter none to me. Do whatever you want."

"Jay," Cara said, "can you go to the barn and fetch the wheelbarrow?"

Jay looked into Dance's face. "Ma?"

"Go on," she said.

Cara went to the double bed in the corner of the room. She straightened the covers and fluffed up the feather pillows. "Come lie down, Dance. You need some rest."

Dance didn't need much prodding. Cara nestled Pauline by her side. "I'm taking the other kids with me," she said.

Dance sighed with not enough wind to blow out a candle. "Would ye bring me the starch from the table before ye go?"

Cara didn't argue. Finding the small blue box, she handed it to Dance. "Will you and Pauline be okay until Ace gets home?"

Dance nibbled the edge from a lump of starch. "You sound just like Ace, forever minding me," she retorted, then grabbed Cara's wrist. "I don't mean to be ugly to you. I'm just at the end of my tether."

Cara's heart turned over. "That's all right, Dance. You get some rest."

Soon the wheelbarrow was loaded with laundry tied up in a bedsheet. Merky and Cleve perched like monkeys on top. Jay and Wilton walked alongside.

"I can push that for you, Aunt Cara," Jay offered.

"That's okay, honey. I'll push while you figure the riddle."

"Fun," Merky squealed and clapped her hands. "We having fun."

"You hold on to your brother, Merky," Cara said, straining to push the ungainly conveyance over a tree root.

All of a sudden, the barrow tipped to the right. Children and soiled clothing spilled out onto the muddy path. Merky's happy smile turned upside down. She'd landed on her bottom, but where was Cleve?

"Uh-oh," Jay said, on his knees digging under the laundry.

"Uh-oh," Wilton repeated.

And there was little Cleve, muddy as a piglet in a hog wallow but none the worse for wear. Cara repacked the barrow and started up again.

There were no more mishaps during the rest of the journey, but the cold rain that had sprinkled on and off all morning broke loose just as they approached the barnyard.

"Hurry," Jay called as he ran across the yard with Wilton. "Hurry, Aunt Cara."

Cara unloaded Merky and Cleve at the end of the porch. The children were soaked; the laundry lay in a heap like a dirty reproach. Beyond her closed door there was no warmth. She knew the fireplace was stone cold. What a stupid thing to do—bringing these little ones out in this weather. They'd probably take pneumonia. No wonder God had never sent her children of her own. She'd make a terrible mother.

"Is it a spelling bee, Aunt Cara?" Jay asked, while Merky did a dance on the porch and Cleve laughed in delight at her antics.

Wilton pushed at the door and it popped open. "Why are you standing in the rain?"

Why indeed? Cara wondered, hurrying to shoo the kids inside and bundle them in quilts. Dry kindling filled the wood box, and she had plenty of coal in the coal bucket. First she'd start the fire and then make some cocoa and pop some of the corn Darcy had sent home with her last week. The children would dry. The laundry would get done—if not today, then tomorrow. As Dance would say, "The world wouldn't come to an end."

"Is it, Aunt Cara? Is the bug that can spell a spelling bee?"

Cara hoped her smile warmed her small niece and nephews. "That's exactly right," she answered, scooping Merky up in her arms. "Now who wants hot chocolate and popcorn?"

The children chorused, "Me!"

It was way past pitch-dark when Ace came for the children. Cara had pulled two straight-backed chairs to face the fire, and now Cleve and Merky shared them with her. Jay and Wilton lay on their full bellies, drowsily drawing with fat red pencils on a used brown paper sack.

"Hey, fellows," Ace said as he ruffled first one head and then the other.

"Daddy," Merky squealed, holding up her arms.

"Hi there, princess." He took Merky from Cara, settling down on the hearth. "Thank ye, Cara. I don't know what I was thinking leaving Dance alone so long. You've been a right smart help."

"I don't have so much time for thinking when I stay busy," she replied.

"Thinking can get you in trouble; that's for sure."

"Ace, Dance was eating starch today."

Ace's forehead knit. "I know. I've packed three boxes of the stuff home from the store in the last couple weeks."

Cara laid Cleve down beside his brothers. "I've heard of women eating dirt and even wallpaper paste."

"Why do ye reckon?"

"Mama always said it was low blood. Beef liver's the only cure I know of."

"That's hard to come by." Ace scratched his chin. "I can go into town tomorrow, ask around, see if anybody's butchered a calf."

"Then you might as well leave these young'uns with me for the night," Cara said. "Drop Dance off here in the morning. A change will do her good."

Ace stood and stretched. "I don't rightly think I'd like to leave the kids."

Cara bit her tongue. "Mercy sakes, they're all asleep." Indeed Cleve's and Wilton's cheeks puffed out with soft little boy snores. Even Merky drooped against her father's shoulder, and Jay was losing his fight, yawning mightily and rubbing his eyes with balled fists.

"You win," he said. "I'll be back in time for breakfast."

"Bring some eggs then. All my chickens ran off."

Ace smoothed his hair and positioned his hat just so. "Chickens don't run off. Weren't you feeding them?"

Cara could feel anger flare, staining her cheeks. "Well, of course," she snapped. "Why would you think otherwise?"

"Whoops." Ace smiled and danced some clogging steps. "Looks like I stepped on somebody's toes."

"Sorry," Cara said. "I don't know why those chickens up and left. I think they went looking for Dimmert."

"Did they pack little valises?" Ace asked, his eyes twinkling. "Did the rooster have train tickets? I wouldn't be surprised if the whole lot of them was setting off for the Kentucky State Penitentiary." He bent down so he could look in Cara's eyes. "It is a fowl place, you know."

Cara's fit of giggles lasted well past Ace's leave-taking. As she tucked Merky and Cleve in her bed and covered Jay and Wilton where they lay, notions of hens with tiny suitcases tucked under their wings entertained her. All in a flock, they tittered and cackled, following the proud red rooster as he hurried toward a westbound train.

Finally settled down with an ironstone mug of hot sweet tea, Cara took stock. Even though a week's worth of dirty clothes lay waiting in the corner, and even though she'd had to scramble through every cup and tin in the corner cupboard to find a penny for Jay, her heart was light. She tested a grin, then let a full smile spread across her face. Her problems no longer seemed insurmountable. After all, two years wasn't a life sentence, and she would find a way to make ends meet until Dimmert was home again.

She spread her arms and breathed deeply. She hadn't felt so free since she was a girl. Dreamy, half-formed memories of her growing-up years crowded her mind, begging for attention.

Her family had been poor but proud all those years ago on Little Creek. Folks said Cara favored her mama, with her high cheekbones and dove gray eyes. But really, it was her father she pined to be like. Unafraid of the slightest thing, he was a strong and determined man.

A remembrance of him slid into place like a picture card in a stereoscopic viewer. Tall and broad shouldered, he was captured mid-stride, arms outstretched, blacksnakes hanging by their tails from each hand. She remembered as if it were yesterday her nine-year-old self running to meet him, fascinated in spite of her natural fear.

"What you aim to do, Daddy?" she'd asked. "Why'd you bring them snakes home with you?"

"Run open the corncrib door, Daughter," he'd replied. "I caught us some good mousers."

From that day after, it was her job to rummage in that corncrib for feed for the chickens. At first she had to force herself to approach the round wired bin, but she'd gotten used to it—just like her father said she would.

Cara began to unwind her braided hair. She laid her combs and pins aside and brushed a hundred strokes as her memories continued. She liked high places when she was a girl, liked climbing to the tops of trees, liked scaling the beams in the barn. She liked the going up but not the coming down. More than once she'd gotten herself stuck and had to wait for her father to come in from the fields to get her down. He would stand under the tree she was in or under the trusses in the barn and encourage her descent until she could step out onto his dependable shoulders. He'd swing her down, and she'd be out of harm's way once more.

Wearing britches like her brothers, she was always up for adventure. There was that one time—egged on by the boys—she'd hopped on the back of the big red bull and rode him like a horse until he flipped her off in a pile of manure.

A sip of hot tea, and her mood turned contemplative. When had she lost that girlish bravery? The teaspoon clanked against the mug, round and round like her mental whirlpool of apprehension. She'd held these thoughts off for so long. Why did they have to come knocking at her door this particular night? It was the children, she supposed, those sleeping innocent bodies surrounding her with untested faith. Like she'd once had: faith in her daddy, faith in her husband, faith that countenanced courage because of someone else you could lean on when you faltered.

Cara stood so quickly her head got swimmy. Sliding her mug and spoon into the dishpan with the children's cocoa cups, she washed and rinsed them slowly, stretching out the task, keeping ruin at bay.

There now—all was tidy; all was secure. All she needed to do was turn out the coal-oil light and slip into bed between Merky and Cleve. The children would warm her body, calm her mind, and chase her worry—that old, sick trepidation—away.

Cara's hand trembled at the lamp. Her fingers stiffened, refusing her mind's order to blow out the light. It was time to look backward, time to figure out how she'd gone from being a stalwart, fun-loving girl to an insecure woman with a heart full of dread.

She turned the wick just a bit, then found her Bible. This very book was what had kept her mama together when Kenny died. Cara flipped through some pages, wondering where to find succor there. "'And they removed from mount Shapher, and encamped in Haradah,'" she read, her tongue stumbling over the unfamiliar names. "'And they removed from Haradah, and pitched in Makheloth.'" This was the book of Numbers, she made out. It seemed like a history of some sort. She'd have to ask Ace about it. He'd know the books of comfort. This couldn't be what Mama had read during that awful time.

Kenny, poor little buddy. Just a tad of a boy, looking for fun on a hot Sunday morning, swinging out over the swimming hole on a grapevine. Then falling . . . falling . . . to land so badly on a piece of debris caught in the creek. It was hard to lose a brother that way—his lifeblood flowing out like spilled milk from a glass.

Cara had been brave then. She was the one who'd thought to go get Miz Copper, who was the closest thing to a doctor they had. And she was the one to help Miz Copper bind Kenny's wounds. Cara remembered standing at the edge of Kenny's grave the next day, shoring up her mother, shedding not one tear.

Absently, Cara stroked the Bible's worn leather cover as her memories continued. Miz Copper had come again on Christmas of that very same year, when Mama nearly died birthing the twins. "Pray out loud," Miz Copper had shouted as she struggled with the birthing, finally guiding two tiny slippery bodies into the world. "Pray hard."

Miz Copper had bragged on Cara's strength and fortitude that night, and Cara had been proud. So proud she'd tucked her fear way back in the farthest corner of her mind. There wasn't time to sort things out right then. Too many brothers and sisters to help care for, too much worry about her mama to think about herself.

Rain started up again, pounding furiously on the tin roof overhead. *Just like tears,* she thought, *pouring out in a veritable torrent's fall of grief.*

Then, of course, she'd fallen in love with Dimmert and everything changed. He did all the taking care of. It seemed his delight was in hers. Most times she didn't even have to voice what she wanted—Dimm discerned it. Whether it was a cup of sassafras tea on a cool evening or a warm shawl to drape across her shoulders on a cold winter's morn, her husband supplied it before her thought of need was even fully formed.

It seemed she and Dimm had grown up together in the years they'd been married, molding each other in the best of ways. His listening to her rattle on about whatever was on her mind was something she'd never had before—an audience. His unconditional love let her give voice to her odd quirks and fears.

She taught him to laugh and to play, something Dimmert had

never been allowed as a boy. He had barely talked when first they met, and then only in response to her queries. "What are you thinking, honey?" she'd ply. Or "What is your favorite color? food? day of the week?"

The tiniest of smiles tugged the corners of her mouth to recollect Dimmert's replies. "I reckon if I had to have a best color it would be that gray shade of your eyes, Cara-mine." And his favorite food: "You can't never get enough taters." But the answer she loved best was his favorite day of the week: "Any day I wake up next to you."

Cara turned off the lamp and went to kneel by the bed of her sleeping niece and nephew. Was it any wonder fear had overtaken her when she lost Dimm? She prayed for God to send back to her the resolve she'd felt earlier in the evening. *This time make it stick. I don't want to live the next two years afraid of tadpoles and typhoid—well, maybe it makes sense to be afraid of typhoid. Okay, Lord? Can You start with tadpoles and maybe snakes? I used to not be scared of them, so that shouldn't be too hard.*

Giving Cleve a little nudge over, she crawled into bed. But something nagged her. What had she forgotten? "Oh!" Crawling back out, she knelt with eyes closed and hands folded. *Amen,* she finished.

If Cara was going to talk to God, she needed to get herself to church and learn His ways. She knew most Sundays Ace went to the church on Troublesome. She would ask if she could go along. Though Dance rarely went, Cara knew she would not mind if Cara did. Plus, they could take the children, except the baby, of course. Cara could cook a big meal and carry it over to Dance's on Sunday mornings. They could eat together as a family after service. It seemed a really good plan.

Merky popped her thumb in her mouth and curled up against Cara. Little Cleve's foot poked her ribs. Sleep overtook her. It was the best rest she'd had in months.

CHAPTER 9

DARCY WAS ALL ATWITTER. Three dresses spread their skirts across her bed. It was a good thing her corset tied up the front or else she'd have had to leave it off because Mammaw's crippled fingers could not have helped her with the fastening. Then she would be in a pickle, for without the corset none of her dresses would fit. Standing tall as her five-foot frame would allow, Darcy sucked in her stomach and pulled on the corset ribbons until she saw stars. *Hmm, which dress . . . which dress?* The blue brought out her eyes, but the green flattered her brown hair. "Wonder what Henry's favorite color is."

"Did you say something, Darcy?" Mammaw called from the other room.

"Just thinking out loud. Trying to decide what dress to wear."

"You're going to be late for church if you don't get a wiggle on," Mammaw fussed.

The blue, Darcy decided, definitely the blue. "Now don't fret. Remember the trip's much quicker now that we have roads." She tugged the dress down over her full bosom and peered in the chiffonier mirror. "I look like a powder pigeon. Why can't I be tall like Cara?"

"Let me see you, girl," Mammaw said.

Darcy swished her skirts as she stepped into the kitchen.

"You're the spitting image of me at your age, Darcy Mae. If you think you're big now, wait 'til you start nursing babies."

Darcy leaned over to peck her grandmother's finely wrinkled cheek. "Oh, Mammaw."

Mammaw tweaked Darcy's collar, then patted her waist. "What have you got on under that dress?"

"It's a corset—and a nice one too. Didn't you ever wear a corset?"

Mammaw smiled and shook her head as if she'd never heard of the like. "No, and you won't find anybody on Troublesome who does."

Darcy poured her grandmother another cup of coffee. "I like to look nice. There's nothing wrong with that."

Mammaw cocked her head. Darcy saw her studying look. She could never put anything over on her sharp-witted grandmother.

"I might as well tell you. I'll be bringing Henry Thomas home after church. I thought I could ask him to stay for dinner."

Mammaw patted her chest. "Henry Thomas? What about Dylan Foster?"

"Dylan is just a friend." Darcy sighed. "You've always read too much into that."

"Is anybody to home?" a rough voice called from the porch.

"There's Remy," Darcy said with relief. *Just in time. Thank the good Lord for Remy Riddle.*

The screen door screeched as Darcy swung it open. "Come on in. I've saved you some coffee."

"Let me hug your neck," Mammaw said, and Remy did. Darcy bet Mammaw was one of the few humans Remy Riddle would allow that close.

Fastening her hat with a long, jet-beaded hat pin, Darcy said, "I'll be off then. Thanks ever so much, Remy."

It was a fine spring day. Birds chirruped overhead, a soft breeze blew, and all along the road, trees fairly burst with new growth. Despite the harsh winter recently past, the road was in good shape. *Better than the one that led into town,* Darcy thought as her little bay mare trotted along. Dimmert had searched high and low to find a horse for her. Chessie was just right, not too big for Darcy to handle. He'd taught her how to curry Chessie's coat for the ultimate sheen and how to braid Chessie's pretty black mane.

Darcy missed her brother. They were the closest of all the kids in her family. She wondered how he was today and if he got to go to church. Would he go if he could? Darcy hoped so. She didn't know how he could make it if he didn't have the Lord to help him through the next two years. Poor Dimmert, poor Cara. They didn't deserve what had happened to them. She'd ask the preacher to pray for them during the service.

"Giddyup, Chessie." She flicked the reins lightly. "We've got people to see and things to do."

Church had already started with all four verses of "Onward, Christian Soldiers." Darcy wanted to save the aisle seat for Henry, but she scooted over on the wooden pew when Ace nudged her arm. Wilton and Jay scurried in ahead of their father, who carried Cleve. Oh, well, she'd save the other side. But, no—here came Cara up the outside aisle to sit beside her there. Cara carried Merky. Then Wilton pitched a little fit to sit beside his aunt Cara. With a stern look, Ace shook his head at his misbehaving son.

The preacher stopped midverse on "Bringing in the Sheaves" to let the family settle. "Page 104, Brother Shelton," he said kindly.

Wilton screwed up his face, and Darcy knew it was not to sing. She was glad Henry was late. She wouldn't want him to see this scene. As Wilton took another breath, Ace reached around the perfectly behaving Jay to thump Wilton on the back of the head with the knuckle of his index finger. Darcy swallowed a smile. She remembered her father reprimanding her in the same way during the long church services of her youth. She would have taken Wilton onto her lap, but she didn't want to muss her dress. Instead, she patted his knee. Giving in, Wilton leaned against her arm.

"'We shall come rejoicing,'" Darcy sang, "'bringing in the sheaves.'" Looking Cara's way, she raised her eyebrows in question. She couldn't remember the last time she saw Cara at church. It was odder than seeing her sister Dance here, and Dance rarely darkened the doors. Cara shrugged and took her side of the songbook. Darcy wondered if she knew the words.

When the song service was over, the minister asked for prayer requests. Mrs. Sharp asked for prayer for her son who had enlisted in the Army. Mrs. Hackley brought up the needs of a neighbor as she always did. She looked out for others. Several folks stood and asked for this or that to be remembered. Cara didn't stand and neither did Ace, so Darcy kept quiet. She couldn't rightly ask for prayer for Dimmert and Cara with Cara sitting right there.

She couldn't stand anyway, for Wilton had slumped across her lap in sleep. A large patch of drool stained her skirt. She wanted in the worst way to turn and glance at the benches behind her. Maybe Henry had slipped in and was sitting in the back. She didn't dare a glance, though. If he was there, she wouldn't want him to see her need. Better to have him looking for her. It was good to have Wilton tethering her to the spot. She'd let him sleep until the service was over.

The sting of disappointment dampened Darcy's sunny mood as she gathered her fussy nephew, her Bible, and her knitted purse and stood for the doxology. Henry Thomas was nowhere to be seen. What could that mean?

The congregation filed out the open door, stopping on their way to shake the preacher's hand and exchange a few words about the service. Darcy had the misfortune to follow Mrs. Sharp, who always took more of the reverend's time than was proper. Wilton hung like a deadweight on her hip. He was much too big a boy to be carried, but it was that or listen to him scream.

Straining to peek around Mrs. Sharp, Darcy noticed folks gathering in small groups to chat. Usually Darcy loved to participate. Invariably she'd get a compliment or two on her apparel, and everyone always asked after Mammaw's health. But today she just wanted to get away to nurse her heartache in private.

Wilton swung his legs, kicking in frustration. She was glad Ace was already outside or else the boy would have been in for a spanking. One of his feet landed a soft blow on Mrs. Sharp's posterior, and the woman shot him a mind-your-manners look. Darcy acted like she didn't notice. Truthfully, she wanted to kick Mrs. Sharp along herself. Long-winded old biddy.

Goodness gracious—where'd that come from? Mammaw would take *her* to the woodshed if she heard Darcy say such a thing.

To make up for her hateful thoughts, Darcy took extra time to converse with Mrs. Sharp once they stepped outdoors. She heard about her family and her chickens and her ducks. Darcy feigned interest. Mrs. Sharp never paused for a reply anyway.

Then she saw him and her heart skipped a beat. Henry Thomas stood in all his glory just on the other side of the knee-high wall that delineated the churchyard. Darcy's grandfather had helped build that dry-stacked rock wall. *Oh, my goodness.* Henry held the reins to Chessie as well as to his own powerful-looking horse. *My, my, tongues will wag if people notice.* She sort of hoped they did.

Looked like someone already had, for on his way across the yard, Dylan stopped on a dime and gawked at Henry. Ever since Darcy could remember, Dylan had fetched her horse for her after services on Sunday. Often they rode their horses together until she peeled away in the direction of her house and he continued on to his. *Child's play,* she thought. He'd have to get used to the fact that she was a grown woman now and she would choose whom she wanted to spend her time with. Still, she didn't aim to hurt him, and the crestfallen look on his face let her know that she had.

She didn't speak as she crossed his path on her way to Henry, for really what could she say? Even worse than Dylan's reaction was the look Darcy saw pass between his parents. Mrs. Foster was Mammaw's good friend, and she'd always been nice to Darcy. Mammaw would not be happy.

She kept her back to the folks in the churchyard as she exchanged a few words with Henry. She was afraid if she looked back, it would spoil the mood of excitement Henry stirred in her.

Forevermore, Darcy thought as Chessie trotted along behind Henry's horse, *who put me in charge of everybody's sentiments anyway?*

Soon she forgot all about anyone's feelings but her own, captivated as she was by the way Henry sat in the saddle. It took a man to handle a horse like his, and Henry, with his stature and sure ways, was quite the man for her.

With one motion, Henry indicated for Darcy to follow him off the road up an unfamiliar logging trail. It wasn't far, maybe a quarter of a mile, before he reined in his horse and came to help her down.

"I was wondering," Henry said as his gaze swept the forested land. "Is this part of Fairy Mae's place?"

"Um, no, Mammaw would never allow any trees to be cut. Her three hundred acres starts the other side of the road and goes down the mountain. It ends at Gristle Creek. I know that for sure. Dimmert staked it all out when Mammaw gave property to him."

"Just wondering." Henry tapped the trunk of an oak tree with the knuckles of one hand. "This timber must have sold for a bundle."

What Darcy saw was devastation. Where once huge oak, cherry, and walnut trees spread their branches heavenward, now the ground was littered with stumps and dead limbs. "It's an abomination if you ask me," she said, "just an abomination to strip the land this way."

"There's plenty more where they came from." Kneeling, Henry fingered a tiny sapling growing beside a rotting log. "See here? The forest will take care of itself."

"A bird couldn't land on that. A squirrel couldn't build a nest there."

Henry looked up, his black eyes deep as a bottomless pool. Darcy could willingly drown there. "I hope you're not one of them, Darcy Whitt."

Darcy swallowed hard. Whatever "them" was, she wasn't, if Henry didn't want her to be. All she needed in the whole wide world was to have those dark eyes looking at her.

Henry rose to stand beside her. The little sapling torn from the earth hung from his fist. If she moved half an inch, her leg would be touching his. She didn't dare breathe. "What do you mean, Henry?"

"Tree lovers." Flinging the sapling down, he ground it under the heel of his boot. "Folks who want to hold on to the past with no thought to the future."

Darcy thought she'd never heard a person speak with such conviction, such passion. His hand brushed hers as he gestured. Sparks hot as cinders shot up her spine. Devil take all, she was lost.

"Sorry," Henry said, turning those eyes on her again. "I get carried away sometimes."

"That's okay," she replied, hypnotized. "I could listen to you all day."

"Really?" His hand found hers. "I could *look* at you all day."

The kiss was as natural as sunshine on a spring day. Darcy didn't give a thought as to whether it was right or wrong. It seemed inevitable. She hoped it would never stop. Surely this was what she was born for—loving and being loved.

After long seconds, Henry broke away. "Did you like that, little Darcy?" he asked, cupping her chin.

"Can I have a second helping?"

Henry saw Darcy to the edge of Fairy Mae Whitt's property line. Though she'd asked him to stay for noon dinner, he'd begged off. He wanted to scout the land down along Gristle Creek—see if Dimmert had put any stakes there when he surveyed the property. He could feel the title already changing hands: from Fairy Mae to Darcy and then by rights to him. A smart man controlled his wife's inheritance; no court of law would deny him.

Henry didn't notice the fine spring day. He took no pleasure in the ride toward Gristle Creek, though his horse moved like a well-oiled machine. Dollar bills blinded his sight as row upon row of hardwood trees fell like wounded soldiers in his mind's eye. If the plan hatching behind his fevered brow came to fruition, he would be rich beyond measure. Money wasn't his ultimate goal, but with wealth came power and with power he could acquire each inch of Whitt property. This land should have been his already.

At the creek, he tethered his horse and hiked for an hour or more until he could look down on Fairy Mae Whitt's humble cabin. Unbidden his finger brushed his lips and turned his thoughts to Darcy. He had just kissed lips that had never been kissed before; he was sure of that. Henry had tasted adventure. He'd clawed his way out of these mountains when barely past childhood—gone to law school in Illinois, served in a prestigious firm, and squired his share of young women—so why had that one kiss taken him so by surprise?

Crouched down behind a tree, seeing but not seen, he watched the comings and goings in the house below. Looked like a family reunion, but he supposed it was just a regular Sunday dinner in the hills. In the yard a hound dog squeezed through a hole in the lattice surround underneath the porch. Pointing its long snout up, it sniffed the air, then turned Henry's way. He'd better get going before the dog sounded an alarm.

A boy he took to be Ace Shelton's eldest came out the cabin door and flung a bone—probably chicken; what else did women cook on Sunday?—over the side of the porch to the grateful mutt.

Then Darcy stepped out, still wearing the blue dress she'd worn to church. With a wave to the boy, she walked back up the road Henry had brought her down just a short time before.

He wondered where she was going and had to stop himself from following her. "Don't be a fool," he admonished himself. "It was just a kiss, no different from a hundred others."

But Henry's heart didn't listen.

The sapling was just where it had fallen. Tenderly, Darcy straightened the stem and peeled off some raggedy leaves. After wrapping it in a square of dampened newsprint, she carried it back toward home. She wished she could stay in the peace and quiet of the forest, reveling in Henry's kiss, but Mammaw would need her soon.

What a day. She'd barely made it home, trembling and flushed, when Ace pulled his wagon up. All the kids plus Dance and Cara carried in loads of food for dinner. Cara had prepared everything the night before, then persuaded Dance to come and visit Fairy Mae. Ace had gone home after the service to pick up her and baby Pauline. It was a true blessing, for Mammaw was so distracted she never got around to wondering why Darcy was home late from church and what had happened to Henry's proposed visit.

Now Darcy hurried back, glad to have in her possession something Henry Thomas had touched—unmindful of the portent of a once-thriving plant now broken and bruised. She thought only of her lover and the promise in that kiss.

CHAPTER 10

CARA WALKED SLOWLY HOME, carrying her pots and pans in a gunnysack slung over her shoulder. She put herself in mind of that old riddle: "Yonder it goes, here it comes, uphill, downhill, rain or sun, served many a hoof and leg, yet has never moved a peg."

Pots shifted, clunking against each other. She paused to readjust her poke and brush a wayward lock of hair from her eyes. She'd been so excited to go to church this morning that she'd tried a new hairstyle, a twist she'd once seen Miz Copper wear. It looked pretty with Miz Copper's thick red tresses but not so good with her own. Her light brown hair was so fine and silky the combs kept slipping out. Cara's back slumped. Yes, she was as plain as the path she trod, a brown wren compared to a bright cardinal. Useful, though. She'd really enjoyed preparing the meal that everyone ate at Fairy Mae's.

Darcy looked pretty today but distracted. She kept catching Cara's eye like there was something she wanted to tell her, but they never got the opportunity what with the kids running in and out and dishes needing doing. And then, just when they were ready to say their good-byes, Darcy disappeared. Good thing Remy Riddle was still there with Fairy Mae or they would have had to linger on. Cara could tell Fairy Mae was tuckered out by that time. Darcy took good care of her mammaw though. Nobody could fault her. But it was good she had Remy to help out now and then.

The closer Cara got to home, the quicker she walked. She was anxious to get to her knife and her whittling wood. Darcy had given her an order for half a dozen fan handles and paid her cash money for the one she'd already made. Cara had taken pains to curve the handle to fit a woman's hand. All along the flared top she'd drilled tiny holes for Darcy to stick fancy feathers in. Now Cara had some change in her pocket and the promise of more. That was a good feeling. Maybe she'd look for some shoes that fit next time she went to town.

Cara was as distracted as Darcy had been. When she reached her house, she walked right in the front door, although her mind clearly told her there was something out of sorts. She paused. What was that on her porch? Maybe her eyes were playing tricks. She cracked the door and chanced a peek.

Just to the right side of the steps sat the finest rocking chair Cara had ever seen. Seat and back of woven rush, arms wide enough to hold a cup of coffee, rockers carved with as much thought as her lady's fan—it was a work of art. But where in the world had it come from?

Hesitantly, she searched the periphery of the porch for clues. A well-worked wad of tobacco lay in an ugly lump beside the stepping stones. She didn't know a single man who chewed, not a one who would bring her such a gift as a rocking chair. Taken aback, she rushed to the open door. Her mouth formed his name before her mind remembered his absence. "Dimmert!" she cried. But there was no solace there.

Dusk, that most melancholy of times, was settling in, ushering in the night. It was too late for her to go back to the Sheltons'. She'd have to chance the dark alone. Again. Taking a seat on the top step, she tucked her skirt under her jittery knees. It seemed a thousand eyes watched her from the woods beyond her yard—waiting, waiting. For what?

"Take a hold of yourself," she said with a mental shake. "What kind of threat is a rocking chair?" Probably her daddy had brought it, though it was many a mile to his house. And Daddy didn't chew. And where would he get a rocking chair anyway? And if he came, so would her mama, and she would never leave without seeing Cara. Mama would stay all night if necessary.

Cara's mind teased the riddle like a cat with a mouse while her knife carved a length of rosewood. The heft of the woody tissue soothed her. She had found its heart and it bowed to her command, taking the shape she desired it to. Lines from this morning's sermon came to her. "The wind and the wave obeyed His will," Brother Jasper preached. "Would you do less than the wind? less than the wave? Would you dare not bend to the Savior's will?"

Was God trying to shape her? Was He trying to bend her to His will? How did a body know what He wanted? Standing, she stretched out the kink in her back, then took her work inside. The Bible was where she'd left it. She held it close and wished she could read it through her fingers like her touch read whittling wood.

Making ready for bed, she braided her hair and turned down the covers. The floor was hard under her knees as she prayed an extra long time, but she finally felt unafraid. So unafraid that she chanced to open the door onto the darkness of the night and drag the pretty rocking chair inside.

The next morning ushered in a fine spring day. May had been nice thus far. A breeze blew soft and sweet as Cara grabbed her hoe and started for the garden. She needed to check on the salad yield. She'd taken a chance planting so early. A cold snap would kill it all.

But so far so good. The cut-and-come-again lettuce looked good enough to eat, though still quite small. The radish she yanked from a burgeoning row was not much bigger than a marble, and the early bunch onions' green tops were still pencil slim. Her mommy always made a fuss over the first mess of lettuce, radish, and onion—"kilt salad," she would call it. Cara supposed it was because she killed the lettuce by smothering it with hot bacon grease. Sometimes Mama made the dish with dandelion greens for a different taste.

Kneeling, she tested the soil—still too early for most vegetables or her flower seed. But she should go ahead and get the potatoes ready. A light frost wouldn't hurt. They'd do fine as long as a freeze didn't come. Ace had laid off two rows three feet apart with his mule and a one-horse plow. She'd put the hills every foot and a half down the furrow. That was more potatoes than she could eat, but it was good to have more than you thought you needed. Plus, she could barter some at the store.

The root cellar was in back of the cabin. Cara opened the door, went underground, and hauled a bushel basket of seed potatoes up the wooden steps and out into the light. The morning was so pretty, so warm and fresh, she sat in the yard to cut the potatoes, making sure there were two eyes to each piece. When she was done, she spread the pieces out on the porch, leaving them to callus over. That would take a few days, but it was necessary to prevent rotting in cold or wet weather.

She'd also brought out the last of the winter apples, and now she sliced a piece and popped it into her mouth. Suddenly the unmistakable bray of a mule blared from the direction of the open barn door. Startled, Cara nearly stabbed herself with her own knife. Ace must have come round with his mule while she was cutting up potatoes. Curious, she walked that way, enjoying her apple as she went.

Hee-haw . . . Hee-haw . . . The sound became louder with each step.

Oh, my stars. Cara was losing her mind. The apple and the knife slipped from her grasp, and she covered her mouth with both hands. There stood Pancake in his stall, his teeth bared like a possum's. Cara shook her head to clear her vision, but it was Pancake all right. She'd know that smile anywhere.

"Oh, Pancake." Cara threw her arms around the mule's scruffy neck. It was almost as good as hugging Dimmert. "I'm so glad to see you."

Pancake rubbed his long nose along the crook of Cara's neck as if to say, "Not as glad as I am to see you."

If mules could cry, Cara thought while he snuffled into her shoulder, *then Pancake surely was bawling.*

She felt like crying tears of joy herself as she fetched the fallen apple and watched a grin return to Pancake's face. After finding the halter where Dimmert had left it, she led the mule from the barn. Soon both were on the way to the Sheltons'. Cara couldn't wait to get Dance's and Ace's opinions on the strange goings-on at her place.

❦

The Sheltons were in the garden when Cara rode in. The children scattered up and down the rows like chickens searching for bugs, except for Jay who wielded his own pint-size hoe. Cara could see Dance nudge Ace, then point at her before all sizes of Sheltons swarmed her way.

Cara slid off as Jay said, "Is that there Pancake?"

"The very same." Cara nodded.

"How in the world . . . ?" Ace started.

"He just showed up this morning," Cara replied.

"He must have wandered away from the Wheelers'. We'd best take him back."

"No, Ace. Pancake didn't wander. He was shut up in his stall when I found him."

The children wanted turns on the mule's back, so Ace lifted them one at a time to sit on Pancake as the grown-ups pondered the situation.

"What if the Wheelers accuse you like they done to Dimmert?" Dance asked.

Cara hadn't stopped to think of that. She turned to Ace. "Could they?"

Ace traced the brand on the mule's rump. "I wouldn't put it past them."

Cara tugged the leather lead until she could rest her face against Pancake's. "What am I to do?"

"Now I know you don't much like him," Ace said, "but I figure we'd best call on Henry Thomas. He can tell us if we need to get the law involved."

"I can't afford to pay that flimflam man again!"

"I figure his advice will be free now that he's calling on Darcy," Ace said.

"How did you find out?" Cara said, then wished she could take it back. It was Darcy's news to share or not.

Ace hefted Jay up for his turn before settling the baby in Jay's arms. "Ain't they a pretty picture?" he asked, changing the subject.

"Ace, stop your teasing," Dance warned.

"Didn't you see Henry waiting for her after church on Sunday, Cara?" he asked.

"Sunday . . . are you for sure?"

"He was waiting for her outside the rock wall. They rode off together."

"I reckon I was too busy gathering the children, but Darcy never said a word during Sunday dinner." Cara felt foolishly betrayed. It seemed like Darcy would have told her something so important.

Dance took baby Pauline from Jay's arms, allowing the boy to nudge Pancake into a ride around the barnyard. "Mark my words about that Henry. I seen his eyes the day Dimmert was taken from your place, Cara, and they was cold as a snake's belly in January. He's no good, I warrant."

Ace removed his slouch hat and ran his fingers through his hair. "I know you're disappointed in him, Cara, and I was right mad myself, but Henry ain't so bad. He come up rough and now he's made something of himself. You got to give him credit."

"I don't have to give him nothing," Dance said.

"So what should I do?" Cara asked, anxious to deflect the argument brewing between Dance and Ace. You'd think Ace would know by now not to stir Dance up.

"It's either talk to Henry," Ace said, "or make a call on the sheriff."

Just the thought of going to the law gave Cara palpitations. "I can't go in that jail again. My heart couldn't stand it."

"Pshaw," Dance said. "You got to stop being so lily-livered."

Stung, Cara felt dreaded tears forming. Who was Dance to be calling names? She wished she hadn't come here. Maybe she should ride Pancake to her mama and daddy's and stay there until Dimmert came home. She picked up Merky, who was pulling at her skirt, begging for attention. Nestling the little girl in her arms, she bent her head to hide her face from Dance.

"It's up to you," Ace said. "You know I'll help you whatever way I can."

Cara's head spun with a decision she was unable to make. Why was every little thing up to her these days? Why was her husband sitting in jail when she needed him so bad? Why wasn't it her own baby in her arms? She cleared her throat of unshed tears. "I'll have to think on it." Then falsely bright, as if she had not a care in the world, she said, "I'd best get back to my garden."

"Jay!" Dance hollered in Pancake's direction. "Come go with your aunt Cara!"

"That's a good idea," Ace replied, giving his wife's shoulder an affectionate squeeze. "Jay can run home for help if you need anything, Cara."

"That's what I was aiming for, Ace," came Dance's sharp retort. "You don't have to be explaining what I say!"

Cara hated to hear the two still sparring as she guided Pancake out of the yard, but she was touched by Dance's unexpected kindness.

"Mommy and Daddy sound like blue jays fussing over a piece of corn," Jay said from his roost atop the mule.

A body couldn't help but laugh.

* * *

Cara and Jay spent the rest of the day chopping weeds. Come late afternoon, Cara baked a round of corn bread, though she'd had to stir the ingredients in a cooking pot, seeing as how she'd carelessly broken her mixing bowl. Jay greased the cast-iron skillet, and she stuck it in the oven to heat. The cornmeal mix sizzled when she poured it into the hot pan.

As a treat, she'd picked a bit of the early lettuce, some small radishes, and a few slender onions. They'd have a salad and hot bread for supper.

"Jay," she said, "run down to the cellar and grab a pint of blackberry jam. We'll have it for dessert."

It was warm enough to leave the door open, and she watched as her nephew disappeared around the corner of the house. Pancake was wandering around the barnyard, munching on new green grass. Later she'd have to put him up for the night and pray he would still be there in the morning. It was sure comforting having Pancake home.

After laying a few pieces of thick-sliced bacon in a cold skillet, she checked on the corn bread. It was nearly finished. As she tore the lettuce, cut up the radish and the onion, and turned the meat with a fork, Cara felt content. The oven door squeaked when she lowered it. The bottom of the bread was just the right shade of brown when she flipped it onto a plate. The bacon was crisp as she pinched off a bite, the leftover grease still hot enough to wilt the lettuce after she added a measure of vinegar and a sprinkle of sugar.

"Can I sit in the new chair for supper?" Jay said.

"What word's most likely to get you what you want?"

"Please?"

"You certainly can," she replied, putting two pieces of bacon on the boy's plate.

"Thank you," he said.

Cara slathered a slice of hot corn bread with butter, then reached for her fork.

"Wait," Jay said. "We need to talk to the plate."

She folded her hands in her lap, bowed her head, and listened to the boy who was more in touch with the Lord than she would ever be.

"Bless this food and the hands that made it," he prayed in a perfect imitation of Ace, "and bless us that eat it. In Jesus' blessed name we pray. Amen."

"Thank you," she said. "That was very good of you."

"I think I should come live here," Jay said between bites. "Looks like you need a man around the house."

"You've got that right," she said, filling his glass again from the jug of milk she'd brought home from the Sheltons'. "But I don't think your ma and pa would give you up."

Jay wiped his milk mustache with the back of his hand. "Probably not. I'm the onliest one who can keep Wilton out of trouble."

Cara laughed. "That's a big job."

Jay nodded. "Don't I know it."

CHAPTER 11

DARCY HURRIED to finish her morning's routine. Breakfast over, dishes done, floor swept, front window washed . . . only because Mammaw said she couldn't see out. Darcy bit her tongue as she searched for the vinegar and some newsprint. There wasn't a thing wrong with that window. Just because Mammaw used to wash her windows once a week didn't mean Darcy had time for the same. Sometimes her grandmother could try the patience of a saint.

Darcy's face flamed. A saint wouldn't be sneaking around, and a saint definitely wouldn't have entertained the thoughts she'd had all week. *But I'm not really sneaking,* Darcy consoled herself. *I have to go to town anyway to get Mrs. Upchurch's order to the post office. It's not by my design that Henry's office is just down the street.*

She wrapped a bit of newspaper around her index finger and wiped a streak from a pane. Standing back, she admired her handiwork. "Clean as a whistle," she said, untying the apron strings from behind her neck.

"Ain't you going to do the outside?" Mammaw asked from her wheeled chair. "Seems to me a window ain't really clean if ye only do the one side."

"Remy will be here any second, and I need to get to the post office early this morning."

Mammaw sighed. "All right then, honey. I don't want to hold you back."

Darcy hung her apron on the peg behind the door, picked up the jar of vinegar water, and started toward the pantry to put it back on the shelf.

"That window glass puts me in mind of a half-baked pie," she heard Mammaw's quiet lament.

Darcy jerked her apron from the peg and opened the door. "Maybe I'll just finish this window before I go," she said through clenched teeth.

"Well, if it ain't too much trouble," Mammaw answered.

Just as she was twisting the zinc lid back onto the glass jar of window wash, she heard Remy's crutch hit the porch floor.

"Morning," Remy said in her strange, rusty voice.

"Am I glad to see you," Darcy replied, then dropped her voice. "Mammaw's in a mood."

Remy was not one to waste words. "Warranted, I reckon."

Thank Remy to cut to the crux of the matter. After hobbling all the way here with the aid of a crutch, she put Darcy in her place.

Darcy held the door and Remy hitched inside. Mammaw had nodded off. Her double chin rested on her chest, which rose and fell with faint snores. Remy took a seat in a nearby chair.

Darcy tied a fancy bonnet under her chin and fetched the box that held Mrs. Upchurch's order. "Good-bye," she mouthed. "Thank you."

Remy dismissed her with a nod.

The moment she stepped away from the cabin, Darcy's spirit lightened. As much as she loved her grandmother, and though she thanked God every day for her, sometimes Darcy was nearly smothered with her constant need. How would she care for Mammaw if she and Henry chanced to marry? Darcy's mind took fanciful flight as she hitched Chessie to the light buggy. He would live here, of course. She saw him tenderly feeding Mammaw her Cream of Wheat while Darcy stitched another of her creations. When he was finished, Darcy would hand him his just-whisked suit coat as he left for the office.

Darcy's lips tingled at the thought of his good-bye kiss. She could see herself waving Henry off before she turned back to Mammaw, who hid a tender smile behind her hand, a smile that recognized Darcy's good fortune.

Startled out of her reverie, Darcy pulled hard on the reins when a wagon loaded with pigs approached from around a hairpin curve in the road. The buggy wheel slipped dangerously close to the narrow shoulder, the only thing between Darcy and a deadly plunge into a deep ravine. At a sharp flick of the reins, Chessie picked up speed. Gravel flew. Pigs squealed. A flock of doves lifted from the branches of a pine tree. The other driver shook his fist.

"Sorry," Darcy called above the clamor of the doves.

"I need to stop daydreaming and pay attention to the road," she said to Chessie. "A body could get killed out here."

But it wasn't just wishful thinking, Darcy knew as she righted her bonnet. It was a dream about to be fulfilled.

Henry had daydreams of his own, and they all had to do with reclaiming his heritage. His office door was propped open to the warm spring day while he did some bookkeeping. His fine script in navy blue ink filled page after page in leather-bound ledgers. At the present he was entering accounts received, his favorite task. Henry trusted numbers, especially numbers that stood for dollars. Each column on each page took up the same amount of space, nothing overlapped, and not a letter or a number was less than perfectly printed.

Henry paused to refill his pen from the bottle of ink in the ink-well. He'd have a larger income if he'd stayed in Chicago. He'd clerked in a law office to pay his way through school. They'd offered him a good position with a good salary when he graduated, but Henry had old scores to settle and they couldn't be settled in Chicago.

Henry grew up poor as dirt and just as disrespected. His father—long gone now—had been a layabout, his mother so broken down by childbearing she hardly knew Henry existed. He remembered as a boy tagging behind her as she begged for credit at Coomb's Dry Goods. He remembered his family being turned out of one tenant house after another when Henry's father wouldn't keep the place up, wouldn't work on a bet if the odds were in his favor. The last place they'd lived in had cracks in the walls big enough to pitch a cat through.

But things were different now. When he walked down the street, folks practically bowed and scraped. "Morning, Mr. Thomas," he'd hear. Or "Fine morning, Henry. I need to see you about a little something." Henry was privy to the business of nearly everybody in the county, and scores of them owed him money. Sometimes he called in his obligations; sometimes he didn't. There was power in having folks in his debt—power and control.

Taking a clean sheet of paper from a stack, Henry angled it in the middle of his desk and began to draw. From long-entertained memory he sketched the footprint of what had once been his grandfather Thomas's farm. Carefully he blotted the ink, then further outlined a rough draft of the external border of the various Whitts' property: Fairy Mae's, Dimmert's, and through Dance, Ace Shelton's. He knew what he searched for, of course, knew the answer before pen and ink revealed it in truth: his grandfather's lost legacy. What should have been Henry's birthright, acre upon acre of buried coal and richly timbered land nearly touched the black-inked borders of what now belonged to the Whitts.

Over a period of time, ten acres here and twenty there, Herbert Whitt had by hook or by crook obtained most every smidgen of property once owned by Henry's grandfather. By all accounts, Fairy Mae's husband had been a shrewd businessman and a first-rate card shark. Obviously Henry's grandfather had been neither. But Henry remembered his grandpa's kindness and the stick candy he kept in his pocket especially for his namesake. He always had cinnamon, Henry's favorite. "You're the smartest of the bunch," he'd tell Henry.

Henry's pen rested too long in one place, and now an ink stain besmirched his drawing, spreading across the paper like the acid of anger stained Henry's heart.

Opening the middle drawer of the desk, Henry withdrew a key and went to the standing display case in front of the horsehair settee. He slipped the key in the lock and opened the case with one quick turn of his wrist. Next to money, the objects there were Henry's treasures and a reminder of his great-grandmother's Cherokee heritage. He fingered a sharp-tipped arrowhead. The workmanship always gave him pause. He'd seen his great-grandmother only one time, but he remembered with the clarity of youth her beauty and her dignity. He laid the arrowhead in place.

Unconsciously he ran his fingers through his thick, coal black hair, then traced the outline of his fine, long nose. Though not vain, Henry was aware of his good looks. While in Chicago, at every dance and debutante ball Henry could swing an invitation to, the young ladies had flocked to his side—even the daughter of the president of the law firm he clerked for. But Henry didn't attend parties to meet women; he went to learn manners and social decorum.

"All wasted here," he said aloud. Taking a ceremonial tomahawk from the display, he gripped the handle, slung it over his shoulder, and brought it forward, slicing the air but with no release. The silky eagle feathers attached to the handle with a leather thong fluttered with the motion. It had been a while since he'd practiced with the hatchet. Maybe he'd take it with him whenever he had the opportunity to stake Ace Shelton's land. He could hardly wait to see that place. It was sure to be as rich as the other Whitt properties. One pleasant thought led to another and then to the fair Darcy.

As if he'd orchestrated her appearance, Darcy peered through the door. "Henry, are you to home?"

Henry's pulse quickened. Quickly he replaced the tomahawk, turning the key once more. Darcy stood in the doorway backlit by sunshine. In a few strides Henry was across the room, extending his hand to her. "Come in. Please come in."

"Well," she said, "I don't know if that would be proper. Maybe you'd best step out here."

"There wouldn't be a thing wrong with you coming in. Folks will think you're here on business."

"Are you sure? I wouldn't want any gossip to get back to Mammaw."

With one hand he captured her elbow and pulled her across the threshold. Her scent reminded him of Ivory soap, so clean, so pure— just being in her presence made him feel special. Could that be love? Henry didn't know what love was supposed to feel like. The only person who ever cared for him was his grandfather, and that was years ago. Henry's desire to kiss her innocent lips was so strong he nearly grabbed her right there. Instead he moved back to let her in, sliding the doorstop away with his foot. "What brings you to town, Darcy Mae?"

With a little dip of her knees, Darcy placed a large box wrapped in brown paper and tied up with string on the display case. "I had to mail this package. Your office is on the way—um, just across from the post office." She stumbled over her words. "I guess you already know that."

Her cheeks looked like bright red apples. Henry had to hold himself back from taking a bite. "I'm glad you thought to stop by. I really enjoyed having lunch with you."

With small movements she twisted her shoulders from side to side and ducked her head like a girl in a schoolyard. "Really?"

"Really. Come here." He guided her to the back room, where he kept an Army cot, clothes, office supplies, and a big black safe.

"Henry? I don't think . . . I shouldn't . . ."

He silenced her with darting kisses, first her ripe apple cheeks, then her sweet, sweet lips.

"Oh my," she said. "Henry."

He pulled her as close as close could be. "What is it about you, little Darcy?"

She stood on tiptoe and returned his quick kisses with the softness of a butterfly's wings. It seemed as if Henry had been hungering for this all his life.

He reined himself in. "There," he said with a light but lingering kiss upon her willing lips. "We'd best stop."

"Yes," she replied, not moving from the circle of his arms, "we'd best."

The bell over the office door dinged. He pulled away and straightened his tie. Cracking the supply room door, he edged around it. He'd get rid of the visitors while Darcy waited unseen.

Of all people, Ace and Cara stood waiting. He nearly swallowed his Adam's apple.

"Your sign said to come on in. Sorry to interrupt." Ace cocked his head and strained his neck, looking around Henry.

Dimmert's wife turned her head. "Ace," she murmured, "we can come back later."

"No need for that. I was just counting supplies." Henry cleared his throat. What in thunder was Ace looking at? Chancing a glance behind, he could feel the color drain from his face. A froth of skirt and petticoat was caught in the door. Inch by slow inch the skirt tail was being tugged from its trap. *Stop!* he thought to say, though he didn't open his mouth, for with one more jerk the door popped open. There stood Darcy with her bonnet askew, her eyes round as wagon wheels.

"What?" Ace exploded.

"Ace," Darcy choked.

"Oh, dear," Cara chimed in.

"I can explain." Henry's calm, detached lawyer's persona took over. "Miss Whitt was taking my measurements for a new suit coat."

"Behind closed doors?" Ace said, his eyes narrowed, one fist thumping the other palm.

"That door swung too when you opened this one." Henry pointed at the office door. "It always does that." He squared his shoulders and stared back at Ace. "Sorry to put you in a bad light, Miss Whitt."

"Goodness," Darcy said, righting her bonnet and picking up her package. "I'd best get this mailed."

"Perhaps another time for the measurement, then," Henry said without breaking his eye lock with Ace.

Ace backed toward the open door, keeping Henry in sight as if he were a rabid dog. "I'll measure you, Henry Thomas. I'll measure you good if this happens again. Darcy! Cara. Let's get out of here."

As the door slammed closed behind Ace, Henry had to admit he was shaken. Shaken and embarrassed—feelings of weakness he was not used to entertaining. Those emotions took him right back to his wretched childhood. He'd allowed the fetching Darcy Whitt to penetrate his carefully constructed armor. That made him as big a fool as any other man.

He paced the room, rounding his shoulders and letting them drop until embarrassment turned to anger, an emotion Henry could deal with.

CHAPTER 12

DARCY CRIED all the way home. Chessie trotted along the familiar road, needing no direction to take Darcy's mind off her desolation. She hoped they'd meet the wagonload of pigs again. It would be easier to be pitched over the side of the road than to face Mammaw once Ace got finished. And Dance was there with the kids and Remy, who was sure to tell Miz Copper. Oh, the shame of it all. Darcy just couldn't stand it!

At a wide place in the road, she pulled the buggy over and waited. Soon Ace stopped his vehicle behind hers. He approached from the side. Cara trailed along.

"Ace," Darcy pleaded, "please don't tell Mammaw and Dance."

Cara joined in. "Ace, does Fairy Mae need to know? It would only cause her worry, and I'm sure it won't happen again. Right, Darcy?"

With all her heart Darcy surely hoped it would, but she couldn't lie right to their faces. "We were only kissing," she said between sobs. "I don't see the harm. . . ."

Ace looked like he might bust a gut. "Darcy Mae Whitt! You know better. You're an unmarried woman, and you were behind closed doors with a man who is no kin to you. You were raised better than that!"

"You and Cara go all over together, and nobody says a word against it."

Darcy heard Cara's sharp intake of breath. "Darcy," she said like she couldn't believe her friend would say such a thing.

Ace turned his head, took off his hat, and settled it again before he answered. His words were soft and kind. Darcy could have handled it better if he spoke in anger. "Folks don't say anything because there is nothing to say. Cara is my sister, the same as you are. Don't try to justify your actions."

Darcy took a shuddering sigh. She was sorry she'd sunk so low as to hurt Cara, but they didn't understand. "Does it help that I love Henry and Henry loves me?" She straightened her small frame and tossed her head. "We're the same as promised to each other."

Ace put one foot on the buggy and leaned in close. "Has he asked you to marry or made any sort of promise to you?"

Cara sat down beside Darcy and put one arm around her.

Darcy fished a hankie from up the cuff of her sleeve and blew her nose. "I know his intent. Truly I do."

"Darcy, Darcy, Darcy." Ace shook his head. "You're treading deep water."

"Is it wrong to want to be happy?" Darcy dabbed at freely flowing tears. "All I do is take care of Mammaw and go to the post office once a week. Henry is the answer to prayer."

"You've got blinders on, girl. God don't condone sneaking around, hiding your sin."

Darcy flinched.

Ace's voice softened. "I can see how Henry charmed you, sister. He sure had me fooled. Henry's as smooth as a snake-oil salesman, but he ain't the type to tie to."

Under cover of the handkerchief, Darcy crossed her middle and pointer fingers in childish rebellion. "I'll do better, Ace. Just promise you won't tell on me."

Ace's palm rasped over his beard stubble as he gave in. "All right, this one time, though it's against my better judgment."

"I'll ride the rest of the way to Fairy Mae's with Darcy," Cara said. "You want me to drive?"

Darcy turned over the reins and slumped back against the soft leather of the buggy seat. She and Henry would have to be more careful.

＊＊＊

Henry cursed his own stupidity. He needed to get outdoors and work off his anger before acid ate a hole in his stomach. As he flipped through his engagement diary, he saw a one o'clock appointment with the Hanson family. Ever since the patriarch of the Hanson clan died—Orban must have been a hundred if he was a day—the family had been feuding over his thirty acres of rock, one rickety lean-to, and six coonhounds.

Henry had seen the dogs—sleek, reddish brown coats and long, pointed noses. Orban had a reputation for training the best hunting dogs. For sure they were the only thing Orban owned that was worth fighting over. Henry might like one of them himself. Maybe he'd take one or two in payment of settling the estate. If things continued according to design, he'd soon have plenty of land to run them on.

Henry had hatched his plans on a day late last fall after seeing Fairy Mae and Dimmert leaving the courthouse. With her grandson's help, Mrs. Whitt hobbled down the steep steps. Henry had made it his business to peruse the will Fairy Mae had just filed. His mind ticked with possibility when he found what Darcy stood to inherit after the old lady passed.

Then when Ace came to Henry for legal advice after Dimmert was accused of stealing the mule, Henry saw the way to make his wishes reality. Dimmert's land lay sandwiched between what Darcy would come into when her grandmother died and that previously deeded to Ace's wife. It wasn't a great leap to figure what might happen if Dimmert didn't pay his fine. And if Dimmert didn't pay his fine and went to prison for thieving, would his wife be able to pay the taxes on Dimmert's land? Fat chance.

Henry would save the day by snapping the property up at a fair price before it was auctioned off on the courthouse steps. Even Ace couldn't question his intent if he was one of the family, if he was husband to the fair Darcy Mae. He'd work on plans for Ace's property once the others were his. It shouldn't be too hard. Everyone knew Dance Shelton was loco, and she was Ace's weakness. Something was bound to happen there, and when it did, Henry would be quick to offer his assistance.

Back to the day at hand, Henry stepped to the door and looked down the street. If he moved swiftly, he could put his Out of the Office sign in the window.

No such luck, for there came the Hansons ten minutes early. Henry meant to make quick work of their complaints. It shouldn't take long to divide up thirty acres and six hounds—minus two.

⬥⬥⬥

Cara stuck close to Darcy's side as they made their way into Mammaw's house. Darcy smiled brightly as she lifted Merky onto her hip. Merky was a great distraction, fiddling with the bow of Darcy's bonnet, begging to try it on. Dance sat at the table with a cup of coffee while the other children ran through the kitchen screaming like banshees.

"Where's Remy?" Darcy asked.

"She lit out as soon as I brought these young'uns in," Dance said, giving Darcy a measured look. "Can't say as I blame her none."

"Is Mammaw . . . ?"

"Sleeping—or trying to. You kids hush." Dance blew on the steaming coffee. "What's got you all worked up, Darcy?" she asked before chancing a sip.

Of all the times for her sister to act like a sister. Darcy was dumbfounded. She couldn't remember a time when Dance inquired about her feelings. She was always much too busy taking her own temperature to fret about anyone else's fever. Now, the one time Darcy wanted to be overlooked, Dance paid attention.

Darcy's mind raced with possible ways to answer that wouldn't be a lie. "Why do you care anyway?" was what came out.

Dance gave her a dismissive look. "Where's Ace?"

"Right here," he said, filling the doorway. "You young'uns ready to go home?"

The children flocked to their father.

Dance set her coffee cup back on the saucer and stood with the baby. "You going our way, Cara?"

Cara trailed the Sheltons. "Will you be all right, Darcy?" she whispered at the door.

"Yes, I've just got to pull myself together before Mammaw wakes up." Darcy gave her sister-in-law a quick hug. "Thank you, Cara. Thanks for being so understanding."

"Well," Cara said with a quick smile, "I know all about pining after a man."

When the house was quiet again, Darcy set about washing Dance's coffee cup and righting the things the children had left scattered across the room. One of the little ones had been in Darcy's sewing kit, and now her soap marker was broken, tape measure unfurled, and the apple-shaped pincushion was missing. Darcy wondered, not for the first time, what was wrong with Dance. What kind of mother let her children meddle in another's belongings? What kind of woman didn't wash her own coffee cup?

Darcy fretted while she curled the tape measure around her finger. Why couldn't her sister be a sister? That was all she'd ever wanted from Dance. She worked herself up into a righteous wrath until she remembered a sermon sometime back where Brother Jasper spoke of Peter asking Jesus if he should forgive his brother seven times. She supposed she hadn't come close to forgiving her sister seven times, much less seventy times seven.

Darcy put the measure back in the lidded basket where it belonged. She reckoned she'd best not be pointing fingers today. Why did she go behind closed doors with Henry? Why did kissing him today seem so wrong when kissing him last Sunday out among the trees felt so right? Was it because she'd been caught today? Regardless, just thinking of Henry's kisses made her head swim.

On hands and knees, Darcy spied the pincushion behind the corner cupboard. Stretching, she dragged it out and dusted it off. She might as well clean under there while she was of a mind to. After Darcy fetched the broom from the porch, she covered its business end with an old pillowcase. Back on the floor, she jabbed the broom back and forth until there was not a speck of dust remaining under the cupboard. What a senseless plight women had, cleaning dirt from dawn to dusk and then being buried under six feet of it.

Darcy sat back on her heels and looked around. What else might she clean under now that she had the broom in hand? Crawling across the floor like her nephew Cleve might do, she set about poking the broom under the cookstove. One thrust, then two, and she was sorry she had started. The pillowcase was brown with grime, and a streak of grease besmirched the front of her pretty blue dress. If she didn't get the grease out quickly, it would be ruined.

Standing at the ironing board in her corset, muslin petticoat, and knee-length drawers, Darcy rubbed renovation soap into the dress skirt and brushed it off with a boar's hair brush. Darcy learned to make the special soap while apprenticed to Mme Pacquin at her House of Couture in Lexington. Mme Pacquin insisted the care of clothing was as important as its construction. Darcy could still see her teacher at the blackboard, ticking off the list of ingredients for the soap with a long, pointed stick: alcohol, beef's gall, borax, turpentine . . .

"Darcy Mae?" Mammaw called from the bedroom. "Honey, can you come here?"

One more brush and the greasy stain faded away. With a flip of the dress, Darcy laid it across the board. She wished she had some renovation soap for the stain of sin that soiled her conscience before she had to face her grandmother.

***

Finally the Hansons were done wrangling over Orban's modest estate. Now Henry was out behind the office, repairing a fence for his latest acquisitions, Lester and Daisy. Henry was pleased with the dogs Orban's nephew brought back in payment, though the male was obviously past his prime. Daisy leaped around the yard while Lester circled a spot of sunshine, winding down for a little nap.

"Daisy! Down!" he commanded when she knocked against his knees in her exuberance.

The dog slunk off, disappearing through the open gate into the shade of the stable at the back of the lot.

Henry heard his horse nicker a welcoming sound. *That's good,* he thought.

The day heated up as he pounded nails and dug new post holes. He pulled off his jacket and his stiffly starched boiled shirt and hung them neatly over a rail. He shattered a rock with a pickax, then flung the pieces out of the way. He could feel the muscles of his arms bunch against the short sleeves of his knit undershirt. It felt good to be outdoors working off the frustrations of the day. He'd lost his head this morning with Darcy. Falling in love was not an option. She was just another girl, only a cog in the wheel of his plans; he needed to remember that.

As he stood back to admire his progress, he wiped stinging sweat from his eyes with the tail of his undershirt. Daisy tried again to make his acquaintance. This time she stuck her long snout into the curve of his palm. He laughed as he rubbed her silky ears and ran his hand along the ridge of her bony back. Daisy was one fine animal, and Lester would do to teach her to hunt.

Henry had never owned a dog before. But when he was around seven years old, a beagle pup started hanging around the yard. Henry took to saving half his own meager supper to sneak out to the dog. That worked for about a week. Every night the little creature lapped beans and corn bread soaked in bacon grease from Henry's hand. Then Henry's mother caught on and cut Henry's portions. "We cain't be feeding no mangy mutts," she said when Henry cried.

He'd tried. He really had. For three nights he fed the beagle instead of himself, and then his own belly let him down. He never knew what happened to that pup.

It was almost dark when he finished the fence. It was past time for supper. He slipped on his shirt and his jacket and started off for the boardinghouse where he took his meals. He could see the top of Daisy's head as she jumped behind the fence. Turning back, he opened the gate and soothed the dog. "I'll bring you something tasty," he told her and Lester. "You'll eat well. I promise you that."

CHAPTER 13

CARA SHRUGGED OUT of Dimm's old work shirt, then laid it aside. The sun was heating things up nicely this early Tuesday morning, and she was bent on cleaning the place, starting with the corncrib. She picked through ears of corn in the wood-sided structure and tossed any molded pieces out the door. Soon there was a small pile out there. She hadn't been a very good steward of last fall's hard work or else she wouldn't have let the corn spoil. Dimmert kept it turned and aired out. She should have done the same.

A smile tugged at her lips when she remembered picking the heavy yellow ears of corn with Dimm. "Good as gold," he'd remarked, running his thumbnail between rows of perfect kernels. As she remembered it, everything about that fall day had been perfect—the air crisp with the promise of winter to come, leaves swirling in jeweled colors, corn shucks rustling when they brushed by.

Once the corn was harvested, Dimm cut the stalks and left them on the ground to cure. After the forage had wilted and partially dried, it was Cara's job to bundle and bind the tops with supple osier twigs. The loosely packed shocks looked like rows of tepees when they were set upright. She'd really liked working beside her husband in the fields, sharing the harvest. Seemed like all her resolve had wilted like fodder shocks when he went away.

There. Most of the corn was still good. She chose a couple of ears for Pancake and latched the door. Perhaps she'd hunt for a black-snake to keep in there as her father had done. "Yeah, sure," she said. Chuckling at her own foolishness, she turned to find a chicken peck-ing at the moldy corn. She popped some golden kernels from a good ear with her thumb. The hen scurried over, scratching around Cara's feet and clucking at her lucky find. Cara watched as a dozen more chickens emerged from a wooded hillside. A strutting red rooster followed, claiming the barnyard as if he'd never left.

"I guess you've got no news of Dimmert then?" she asked while shelling more corn with the heel of her hand. They sure looked like her lost hens. As she gathered the moldy ears, she thought of the day's work ahead. She'd burn the bad corn, clean out the chicken house, plant some seed corn now that she had animals to feed. Why she might go to the Sheltons' and retrieve the cow Ace was milking for her. With a cow and chickens she'd have cream and eggs to sell in town, and that meant money in her pockets. She wouldn't have to borrow from Miz Copper when the taxes came due.

She was full of purpose and resolve. One thing she wasn't going to do was worry. Somehow the good Lord had sent her a rocking chair, a mule, and now chickens. Starting today she was going to count her blessings.

Inside the henhouse she opened a small window to let some sun and air in. My, the stench nearly took her breath. Miz Copper would never have let her coop get in this condition. "Elbow grease doesn't cost a cent," Cara could almost hear her say.

"Come on in," she said to the rooster, who stuck one yellow clawed foot through the open door. "I reckon you're ready to bring your chick-ens home to roost—so to speak. Just give me a minute here."

"*Plawk,*" the rooster agreed in his rooster language while he circumvented the room in an exaggerated strut. "*Plawk, plawk, plawk.*"

Cara collected the feeding trays and the watering jars, then set off toward the spring-fed creek that divided their property from the Sheltons'. Sweetwater, Ace had dubbed the creek. She agreed with the name, for it was an easy, meandering little stream not given to fits of flood and destruction like Troublesome Creek. Dimmert had formed a dam of rock and clay a little ways upstream, so she had a nice deep pool in which to rinse the metal trays and the glass jars. With a handful of sand from the creek bottom, she scoured the feeders. Fluffs of downy pinfeathers whirled like tiny shipwrecks in the current.

Enjoying the sun on her back and the cool water at her fingertips, Cara sat down on the creek bank. She plucked three broad leaves from the branch of an overhanging sycamore and christened them the *Niña*, the *Pinta*, and the *Santa María*, then launched her leaf ships and watched as they sailed away. What must it have been like to leave the old world for the new? Where did they find the courage? Whoops! The *Santa María* nearly capsized, and the *Niña* was threatened by a muddy-brown newt. Without a thought to fear, Cara plucked the salamander from the water and let him swing from her fingers by his long tail. The newt hung motionless, his tiny limbs folded, his bright eyes dulled.

The little creature's reaction to the disturbance Cara caused to his world made her feel mean. "I didn't aim to bother you." She released it to scurry under a pile of decaying leaves. Nothing really harmed newts. Their bad-tasting skin protected them good as a knight's armor. Too bad the newt didn't have knowledge of that.

Cara wrapped her arms around her knees and rested her head there, trying to recollect the Scripture Ace had told her to commit to memory. It was just yesterday on their ride to Fairy Mae's from the lawyer's office. They were traveling at a slow pace behind Darcy, who seemed in no hurry to get home. There was plenty of time for talk. Cara had been glad for the opportunity to ask Ace about the books of comfort. He said for her to study Matthew, Mark, Luke, and John. "That will take a while," she replied. "I'm a slow reader. Can you give me something quick to hold fast to?"

Last evening she sat on the front porch in her new rocker with her Bible and searched until she found Psalms. The Bible was divided in books, Ace said, and the books had chapters like any other book. Psalms was in the Old Testament. Matthew, Mark, Luke, and John were in the New Testament, which had all of the words of Jesus. That was why they were so comforting.

Now sitting on the creek bank, she spoke a verse from the chapter in Psalms Ace told her to commit to memory: "'Yea, though I walk through the valley of the shadow of death, I will fear no evil: for thou art with me; thy rod and thy staff they comfort me.'" That sure was pretty. It was one of the verses Ace read to the prisoners that day Dimmert was carted off.

A tear slipped down her cheek and settled in the corner of her mouth as a sure knowing of God's love settled in her heart. Was she not as important as a mindless lizard? Wouldn't God cover her with protection as surely as He'd provided the scurrying woodland creature a protective skin? It didn't mean she'd never be plucked up, never have her world turned upside down by unknown forces, but it did mean she was not alone, whatever befell. And being alone was what she really feared, not tadpoles and spiders and not even lockjaw . . . well, maybe lockjaw still, a little bit.

A warm spring breeze ruffled the surface of the creek. One of Cara's little ships whirled around in an eddy, broke loose, and sailed downstream. It was so peaceful on the bank of Sweetwater Creek. Cara felt her shoulders release the knot that had formed there when Dimm was led away by the sheriff.

Just as she released her fears, a slithery snake raised his head from the water. Screaming, Cara scrambled to her feet. Ha, she wasn't as brave yet as she meant to be. She tossed a piece of shale in the water moccasin's direction. *Plop!* Rings formed in the water, then broke upon the bank. Taking its sweet time, the snake swam away. Cara tossed one more rock for good measure. *"I will fear no evil: for thou art with me."*

Leaving the water jars and the trays to dry in the sun, she went to the yard and started a fire under a medium-size cook pot that she filled with water from the rain barrel. Once the fire was under way, she got a rake, a shovel, and an old broom worn down to a nub from the barn. Back in the chicken house, she tied a scarf around her nose and mouth before she removed stale straw from the nests. She stood on an overturned box and scraped manure from the overhead perches with the stubby broom, glad she had on her oldest bonnet, a worn cotton shift over her dress, and Dimmert's work shirt.

Dimmert had built the perches from 2½-by-1-inch slats so the hens and rooster could rest upon them rather than clinging with their toes wrapped around the more usual narrow poles. He said this resting position allowed the birds' feathers to cover their feet so they wouldn't freeze in the coldest weather. He was a marvel, her Dimm. A frozen-toed chicken was a sad sight, she would admit. She hoped the chickens appreciated him as much as she did. The rake made it easy to move the refuse to the door, where she could shovel it into the wheelbarrow to burn later with the moldy corn.

The water was at full boil when she returned. After pouring half the water into a common bucket, she took a kitchen knife and shaved half a pound of hard soap into the pot. With a long-handled spoon she mixed until the soap dissolved. Swinging the iron crane to the side, she removed the cauldron from the fire. Slowly, carefully, she added a measure of kerosene and mixed until all was absorbed. This she poured into the pail of hot water and stirred some more.

Now she was ready to paint the nest boxes, the perches, and every crevice in the hennery. The chickens would be happy to be spared the torment of lice. She would have to leave her shift and bonnet on the porch until wash day or else she might carry some of the mites to her own bed.

Cara's muscles were sore and she had a crick in her neck after the day's chores. As usual, she'd planned more work than she could do, but that was good. For supper she crumbled stale corn bread into a glass of buttermilk and carried it out to the porch. Pancake wandered over, and she went back in the kitchen to fetch a piece of bread for him.

Across the barnyard, chickens straggled toward the henhouse. It made Cara happy to think of their clean perches, sweet-smelling straw in their nest boxes, quart jars tilted in chicken saucers dripping clean water, and trays full of feed from the barn. Soon the hens would start setting, then hatching their eggs. The yard would be full of doodles, little bits of fluff and promise.

Cara was content until a little itch of worry demanded scratching. She still didn't know what to do about Pancake. Walker Wheeler could come in the night and take him from the barn easily enough. Her rocker picked up speed, and her spoon clanked against the rim of her glass. There was an old cot in a stall that Dimmert kept for bums, those poor souls without a bed to call their own. Dimm always gave them a job for a day or a week, fattened them up some before they drifted off again. She reckoned she could sleep on the cot out there.

But what if some mites lived in there? The very thought made her skin crawl. She scraped the last bit of tasty corn bread from the bottom of the glass and sat back in her chair. Ace was going to talk to the sheriff, clear everything up, but until then Pancake would have to leave his comfy shakes in the barn. The Walkers weren't getting easy access to him.

Dressed for bed, she sat on the porch and let down her hair. Bending over her knees, she brushed and brushed until she was satisfied there were no critters hiding there. Dimmert loved her hair, though it was nothing special. Dimmert said her plain brown hair shimmered in the sunlight. He said he could see strands light as corn silks there. Her heart ached like her shoulders did when she thought of her husband. Dimm saw beauty in everything—even a dumb mule, even a hobo down on his luck, even her.

He didn't even mind that her womb couldn't hold a baby. With every loss he'd kissed her tears away as if he needed only her and no other. As she wove her hair into the familiar braid, she wondered how he was tonight, her Dimm. She envied every person in that awful prison who might sit at his supper table, who might work alongside him, who might be granted a piece of his generous heart. My, she hoped he had a window. Maybe he was looking up at the same moon that shone down on her.

Laboriously, once a week she wrote and mailed a letter, though she wondered if it was worth the trouble and expense. Would anybody read it to him? She supposed a note from home might give comfort even if he couldn't make out the words. Surely he would know it was written with love from her.

Cara rubbed the back of her hand across her lips, missing him. It was getting dark out. She hadn't even got out her whittling gear though she needed to finish a cherrywood handle for one of Darcy's fans.

Darcy. Cara was afraid she was in for a world of hurt. For one thing, Henry Thomas seemed much older than Darcy. If she had to venture a guess, she'd say ten years. Maybe more. And he was a man of the world—polished, you could say. What was it he saw in Darcy Mae? Cara stopped the rocker and carried it into the house. Not that Darcy wasn't fetching—she was—and smart in her own way. But Cara would bet a pretty penny he'd kissed many lips before.

Cara felt her cheeks get hot. *My gracious, what a thing to think about.* She'd let her mind go idle. She opened the window by her bed. "Pancake," she called into the night. "Bread?"

Pancake stuck his long head over the windowsill and nibbled delicately from her hand.

Cara laughed and scrubbed the sweet spot between his eyes. Drawing his lead through the window, she looped it over the bedpost before she blew out the coal-oil lamp. "Sleep tight. Don't let the bedbugs bite."

Cara slept hard that night, rousing only once to pull a quilt up against the chill night air. She didn't wake fully until the rooster crowed.

Now she knew the answer to her sleeping woes: a rooster for an alarm clock and a mule's head stuck in her window.

CHAPTER 14

DARCY HAD NEARLY FINISHED eight of the sixteen button-holes down the front of the Eaton Basque she was sewing for Mrs. Charlotte Inglebrook. "Wouldn't it make you tired, Mammaw, to pack a name like that around?"

"What name's that, sugar?" Mammaw asked.

Darcy snipped a thread and tied a new knot. "Mrs. Charlotte Inglebrook—you know, the lady I'm making this jacket for, the one who's a friend of Mrs. Upchurch. We were just talking about it."

"I was thinking of making a stack cake," Mammaw said. "Jean Foster's coming to call tomorrow, you recollect. We've got some of them dried apples left, don't we?"

Darcy's stomach sank. She'd pushed any thought of company to the far reaches of her mind. Truthfully her hope was that Mammaw would be napping when Miz Foster called. If Dylan had spoken to her instead of her grandmother, Darcy would have told them not to come. But no, Dylan had to come round the other day while Remy was over. Now the posy of apple blossoms he'd left dropped brown petals on the kitchen table. She should pitch it.

"I was thinking of making a stack cake," Mammaw repeated.

Darcy bit her tongue. Mammaw had one good arm. She was thinking of Darcy baking a stack cake. "Mammaw, I really need to finish these buttonholes. I was meaning to get the braid trim on and do the buttons before dark."

There, the eighth buttonhole was perfect. Mrs. Inglebrook was even more particular than Mrs. Upchurch, if that was possible. Darcy thought she would be pleased. Bending over the sturdy shirting, she started number nine. Her needle punched through from back to front. "Ouch!" A fine spray of blood stained the fabric. "Those brats!"

Mammaw looked up from her Bible and raised one eyebrow.

"I still haven't found my thimble after Dance let her children scatter my things."

"I'll thank ye to remember them brats are your nieces and nephews," Mammaw said.

"Does that mean Dance doesn't have to bother herself to make them mind?"

"Darcy Mae Whitt, what's got into you? You're as sour as curdled milk these days." Mammaw slipped off her reading spectacles and set them on the side table. "Well, lookee here. Your thimble is lying on this table, hidden in plain sight."

Darcy sponged blood from the jacket with a clean white rag and cold water. "I'm sorry. I shouldn't have said that about the kids. You know I love them."

"Poor Dance," Mammaw said. "She struggles so to raise them young'uns right."

Darcy couldn't see whatever it was that made Mammaw favor Dance over all the other grandkids. As she blotted the wet spot with dry toweling, she wondered aloud, "Why did Dance leave Mommy and Daddy and come to live with you when she was little?"

Mammaw pulled at her shawl, straightening out a wrinkle. "You was just a set-along baby when she came here. Dance was the oldest before Ezra, then Dimmert, then you. Dory was the least one, barely out of the oven and your ma was with child again." Her head moved slightly, more tremor than shake. "The Whitt men was always good at making babies." Mammaw fell into silence. Her softly wrinkled face took on a pensive look.

Darcy put her sewing aside and went to sit at her grandmother's feet. "Go on, Mammaw."

"Your daddy came to fetch me all the way over to Virginia. I stayed right at three months that time, and I couldn't help but notice there was something fey about your sister. She was nearly eight years old, but she'd rather sit in a corner chewing the end of her pigtail or flapping her hands in front of the face than wag the baby around. I never knowed a girl who didn't like to get her hands on a new baby, kind of turn it into her own. Like you was with Dean and Dilly, remember?"

Darcy leaned her head against Mammaw's knees. "Indeed I do. I bathed them and mashed up their meat and taters, changed their diapers . . . I reckon I was more mommy than my ma."

"She was so wore out, your mommy. You older kids was such a blessing."

"Tell the part about Dance."

"Well, like I said, she was an oddling, nearly drove your mommy to distraction. She didn't have the time to keep up with Dance and everybody else at the same time, even with my help. That summer she was carrying Dawn. Then one night Dance just disappears. We put all the young'uns to sleep in the loft that evening, but the next morning Dance was nowhere to be found. Gone out into the night and left the door ajar for anything to walk right in."

Darcy pulled off Mammaw's felt slippers and began to massage her feet, being careful not to touch the tender bunions.

Mammaw sighed and leaned her head against the pillowed headrest of her chair. "That feels good, child." Her knobby hand stroked Darcy's head. "It was a sight that morning, your ma wringing her hands, baby crying, Dimmert and Ezra running in and out asking where to look next. We never even got the biscuits baked that morning. Then around about noon, here Dance comes walking over the ridge behind the house, hair full of cockleburs and sticker weeds."

Mammaw wiggled her toes as Darcy kneaded the balls of her feet. "Get some of that good-smelling salve from the bedside table."

Darcy returned with two colorful tins. "Do you want this Malvina cream, 'The one reliable beautifier,' or the Seven Sutherland Sisters' petroleum rub, 'Guaranteed to make your skin smooth as a baby's bottom'?"

"I reckon it's too late to beautify my tired dogs. Let me smell that Seven Sisters." Mammaw took a sniff after Darcy unscrewed the top. "Who was it sent this stuff?"

Darcy wondered what was happening to Mammaw's memory. It was wearing her patience thin, telling her grandmother everything over and over again. "Miz Upchurch sent you the petroleum rub, and Miz Copper brought the Malvina last time she visited. Wasn't that thoughtful?" She propped Mammaw's feet on a stool and untwisted the top from the Seven Sutherland Sisters. This would be good for her dry hands as well as Mammaw's feet. Henry was sure to notice, Darcy dreamed.

". . . never did figure out where she'd been." Mammaw had continued the story without her.

"Was she hurt?"

"Not so's we could tell. Then one night she did it again. Only this time Dimmert followed. He was just six years old, but he was already old beyond his years. They was always close, Dimmert and Dance. He let her have her fill of walking, and that is all she did: walk with her arms stuck out straight in front. Dimmert said she was in a trance."

When one foot was happy. Mammaw rested it and stuck the other one out. "Well, that liked to have pushed your ma to the end of her rope. Soon as your pa came home from his circuit—did you ever hear him preach? He's a fine hand at preaching, your pa is."

"I only heard him once. He took us older kids to a revival he was doing. He had people confessing and speaking in tongues, handling snakes . . . everything. Me and Dimmert, Ezra and Dory was all baptized there where he was preaching."

"They's no telling how many souls your pa has saved. Makes a tired old mommy right proud."

Darcy took a file to Mammaw's toenails. "Finish about Dance. What happened when daddy got home?"

"We had a powwow. Me and your papaw and your ma and pa. Herbert had come to carry me back home, said he was tired of beans. We knew we had to do something before Dance walked off a cliff or got eaten by a panther. So then it was decided Dance would come to live with your papaw and me. We would have liked to bring Dimmert also, but your ma needed him."

What about me? Darcy couldn't help but think. Why was it always Dance? Why was Darcy treated like the redheaded stepsister?

"Of course we couldn't break up the family any worse than we were already doing. I wouldn't've minded to have the whole passel of you young'uns. But you know, your mommy loved you in her way, and you all was good at looking out for each other."

"So then Dance always lived with you and Papaw Herbert until she married Ace."

"I tell you what. She was good company when your papaw died. I don't think I could have stood it without Dance."

Darcy smeared a little cream on her own elbows. "Do your feet feel better, Mammaw?"

"I was thinking of making a stack cake," Mammaw said. "Do we have any dried apples left?"

Darcy might as well give in. Mammaw would worry it into the ground until she saw a dried-apple stack cake dripping frosting. "How many layers do you want?"

"Six or eight will do. Time was I built the tallest stack cake of any woman hereabouts. Do we have any apples, Darcy?"

Darcy straightened the pillow on the back of Mammaw's

invalid chair. She'd just as well put her sewing away. By the time she reconstituted the apples, baked the layers, and boiled the icing, it would be noon tomorrow. "I'll go check the pantry. What else do I need?"

Mammaw turned the pages in her Bible until she found a thin piece of folded paper. "You must always remember where this is. Your papaw's mother wrote this down from her mother's recipe." She unfolded the paper. "Look what a fine hand she had. Her name was Mary Golden." Once her spectacles were back in place, Mammaw commenced to read. "'Soak apples in cider with sugar and spice.' Then for your stacks you need flour, sugar, baking powder—not soda, Darcy Mae—then some ginger and some cinnamon, salt, lard, eggs, vanilla, and sorghum."

"What about the icing?"

"It's mostly just sugar, butter, and a little sweet milk, and oh, some of that vanilla. Ye just kindly pour it over the stacks like a glaze."

"Do you want to take a rest while I heat up the oven? I'll wake you when I get ready to bake the layers. We can let the apples sit overnight and build the cake in the morning."

"I am tired. Will you get the measurement right without me?"

"Sure, you taught me about teaspoons and tablespoons. Remember I used to do all of Miz Copper's cooking and baking." Darcy pushed the chair to the bedroom and helped her grandmother transfer to her bed.

"Herbert likes a piece of stack cake in the evenings with his coffee," Mammaw said. "It's about time for him to come in from the fields. I'll just close my eyes for a minute."

Darcy bussed her Mammaw's cheek. "I'll be sure to save him a piece."

A tap at the door brought Darcy out of the pantry, a bag of dried apples in one hand and a pail of lard in the other. Nudging the partially closed kitchen door open with her elbow, she saw Dylan standing there.

"Do you need some milk, Darcy Mae?" He lifted the lidded bucket to chest level. "It's all strained and everything."

"Thanks, Dylan." She turned to set the cake makings on the table, then went back into the pantry for a gallon jug. Stepping outside, she shut the door. "Mammaw's asleep." She set the jar on the wash bench.

Dylan upended the bucket and poured milk streaked with ribbons of rich yellow cream into the mouth of the jar. "Do you need this right off or do you want me to put it down the well?"

Darcy dipped water from the rain barrel into the dirty bucket. "Put it down the well whilst I scrub this bucket."

He secured a zinc lid onto the jar, then walked down the stepping stones. She stood in the deep shadow of the porch and watched as he turned the corner. My, it was a beautiful morning. The sun said ten o'clock as it cast a welcoming warmth over the yard. Leaving the bucket to soak, she followed Dylan to the well. Bright green blades of grass tickled the soles of her bare feet, and the air around her was soft as an oft-washed quilt and smelled of pear trees in bloom.

Dylan had propped open the door to the well house, and she stood just outside as he attached the jar ring to a rope on a pulley. The mechanism hung far enough over the lip of the well to lower the milk without getting in the way of the water bucket, keeping it fresh and cool until it was needed.

"Your ma is coming by tomorrow," Darcy said.

Dylan startled. The rope jerked in his hands, and the top of the jar bobbed into view. "Whew. You caught me off guard. I almost smacked the jug against the rocks."

"Sorry."

Dylan looked over his shoulder at her. "Ma won't say anything to upset Fairy Mae, if that's what you're worried about."

"Who said I was worried? Who says I have anything to worry about?"

"It was all the talk on Sunday," Dylan replied. "You going off with that Thomas fellow."

"I didn't go off with Henry—Mr. Thomas. I wanted him to meet Mammaw. That's all it was." A pang of guilt reverberated through Darcy. She tossed her head but found she couldn't meet his gaze.

"Did he, then? Meet your grandmother, that is?" Dylan stepped out of the well house to stand with her in the sunlight.

"No, not really. He was in a hurry. He's a busy man, being a lawyer and all."

"Business? On Sunday?" Dylan had no trouble with his gaze. It didn't dart here and there as Darcy felt hers doing.

"Probably something that couldn't be helped," she said, staring at the ground.

"Well, it ain't any of my concern no ways." He stooped to grab a small stone and sent it sailing through the air. With a thunk the stone hit the base of the maple tree in the side yard. A blue jay answered with an angry, raucous call. "I just come to bring Miz Fairy Mae some milk. I'll be back with more in a couple of days." Head up, he walked away.

Darcy wondered why she felt such a sense of loss. "Dylan," she called, "I'm sorry."

He didn't stop, didn't turn his face to her, only acknowledged her regret with a backhanded wave.

CHAPTER 15

CARA SMILED to herself. She couldn't believe how rested she felt after her night with Pancake. But the mule, poor thing, leaned against the porch railing. His snores sounded like an old man's. "Extra feed for you today," she said.

The morning was busy with her work readying the soil for the beans she wanted to plant. Now that the warm weather had settled for good she could get serious about her garden. With her hoe she mounded hills of dirt. Taking the sturdy six-foot poles saved from last year's crop, she shoved them in each hill at a thirty-five-degree angle pointed toward the north. Set in this way the vines would climb better, bear earlier, and the pods would be straighter and be more easily picked.

On her knees she planted six beans to a mound. Once they had a good start, she would thin to the four strongest plants and allow those to climb to the top of the pole before she pinched the tops off. Her chickens scattered around her, pecking hapless bugs. Cara sat back on her heels, watching as a buxom hen tugged at one end of a fishing worm. The chicken pulled with all her might. With a final tug the worm snapped in two, the head end plowing back into the earth, the tail end hanging from her beak, a fancy feast. Cara was ever so glad to have her chickens back. They would keep her garden clean, and she would soon have fresh eggs to eat.

When the sun was straight up, she walked down to the creek to wash her hands. Once she'd eaten a little noon meal, she'd ride Pancake over to the Sheltons'. Dance might like to have the bean seed she had left over. Cara could stay and help her for a while. Ace had promised her some Crosby's Egyptian table beet seed; she could plant them tomorrow if she picked them up today. Dimmert always sowed beet seed real thick so they could pull the surplus for a mess of greens, allowing the remainder to grow large bottoms. She could feel beet juice dripping from her chin already. What she didn't eat this summer, she would pickle in quart jars for the winter.

Cara said a prayer of thanksgiving over her onion on corn bread sandwich. For the first time in a long time she felt hopeful and grateful. After taking her bonnet from a peg behind the door, she pulled it shut, then went looking for Pancake. He must be in the barn.

The barn seemed dark and brooding when she approached. She didn't much like being in here. A barn without a man seemed as lonesome as a kitchen without a woman. The interior was deep in shadow, though some light streamed in through the door and through small windows. Against the far wall, dark brown tails of cured tobacco stuck out around a press, the last hands Dimmert had tied, she figured. He liked a pipe now and then. Walking over, she released the lever to the press and removed the tobacco stick, expertly sliding the hands off onto a stripping table. A pungent yet not unpleasant herbal scent made her sneeze.

"Pancake," she yelled and clapped to wake the animal. Funny how he put himself in the stall whenever he wanted. He raised his big head and gave her a goofy smile. "Let's take a ride." She held out his lead and he came willingly.

Where was it Dimm kept the woven rug he threw over Pancake's back before he rode? She peeked in each empty stall until she came to the one farthest from the barn door. At first she was not afraid by what she found there. Instead, she tried to reason out the folding bed set against the wall with a dark green woolen blanket tossed across the foot. Beside the bed an overturned wooden box served someone as a table. There was a twist of chewing tobacco there and the stub of a candle on a cracked saucer. A half-eaten apple lay browning on its side.

Her first thought was to flee, but she determined to not let her fear take command over her as it had in the past. With great trepidation she knelt and looked under the bunk. Her mouth went dry at what lay there—a shotgun and an empty tooled-leather knife sheath. Ice water ran through her veins, flushing away any trace of bravery she had previously acquired. She tried to rise, but her legs turned to jelly.

While still cowering on her knees, she sensed a dark presence at the door to the stall. "Pancake?" she squeaked, praying it was so. Her heart knocked hard against her rib cage as her brain trilled with alarm. Slowly, one hand on the cot for support, she stood and turned to face whatever blocked the doorway.

Her eyes widened as Big Boy Randall tipped his hat. He was a massive man, way bigger than she remembered. As he stepped forward, she retreated, catching the back of her knees on the cot, which sent her sprawling on the narrow bed.

Lord, help me, she prayed. Clinching her eyes tight, she lay there helpless and more frightened than she had ever been.

"Missus," Big Boy said, "I don't aim to do you no harm."

She sat up screaming, "Get out." She threw the apple and the cracked saucer at Big Boy's head.

He ducked and darted away.

Breathing fast, she sat on the side of the bed until her heart settled. She tried to swallow, but her mouth was dry as a moth's wing. How long had Big Boy been living in her barn? Had he watched her every move from the shadows—watched as she drank her tea, brushed her hair, set on the porch in her nightgown? Feeling violated, she crossed her arms over her chest. The best thing for her to do would be to sneak out a window and make a run for the Sheltons'.

She pushed the wooden box across the hard-packed dirt floor and positioned it under the high-shuttered window. There was no glass in the barn windows, so all she had to do was open the single shutter and slither through. *Better be quick,* her brain warned, *before he comes back and catches me.* But her fingers felt big as sausages and fumbled at the latch over her head.

There, the latch lifted. She pushed and pushed, but the wooden shutter was warped and stubbornly held its place. Standing on tip-toe, she pounded on the window with both fists. "Give way," she grunted under her breath. "Please give way."

With alarm she felt the box beneath her tip. Her fingers grappled for the window ledge but did not find safe purchase; instead she fell heavily, cracking her head on the corner of the wooden box.

Stars danced in her vision as she lay stunned for a long moment. When her head cleared, she saw she was within reach of the weapons under the bed.

Anger nudged away her fear and fueled a firm resolve. Fuming, she withdrew the shotgun from under the cot. She'd shoot him if she had to.

The stalls were empty; the barn was empty. Pancake was gone. That crook had stolen her mule! She forced herself to take deep breaths and think. Big Boy would hardly set up housekeeping in her barn if his aim was to take Pancake. Perhaps what he really wanted was her. Maybe he planned to kill her and throw her lifeless body into Sweetwater Creek. Her heart caught in her throat. Could she do it? Could she shoot a man? even one who might harm her? She tightened her hold on the weapon. Perhaps she'd shoot over his head first, fire a warning shot.

She crept into the space behind the open barn door and peered out through the crack. Forevermore, there stood Big Boy Randall beside the mounting block, holding Pancake's lead like he was wait-ing for her to come out and ride away.

Straightening her spine, she walked out with the barrel of the gun pointed over the peak of his hat. "I'll thank ye to unhand my mule," she said with as much command as her wavering voice would allow.

"Do you want me to load that there weapon?" he asked, his voice as sincere as a deacon at a foot washing. He took the gun right out of her sweaty hands, cracked it open, and slid a shell in its chamber. "I reckon I deserve to be shot—scaring you that way." While stroking Pancake's long nose, he shook his head as if disappointed. "I was just hoping we could talk."

Despite herself, Cara was intrigued. Her legs still wobbled like a toddler's, but she felt God's arms surround her, holding her up, giving her courage. Out here in the light Big Boy didn't seem threatening at all. "If you come to the porch, I could fix you a bacon and onion sandwich," she surprised herself by saying. It was so like something Dimmert would do. "Then you'll have to leave my property or I'll get the sheriff."

Big Boy held his arms up in surrender. "No need for that. Just hear me out and I'll be on my way."

A few minutes later Cara returned to the porch with Big Boy's sandwich. She sat in the rocker while Big Boy took the top stepping stone. He washed his sandwich down with sweet milk before he patted his stomach and belched. "Man, that hit the spot. I was so hungry I could have et my shadow."

"I think I just figured out who brought me this chair," Cara said, "and Pancake. But why?"

Big Boy rolled the milk glass between his meaty palms. "I brung Pancake home because I couldn't stand the way that Walker Wheeler done Dimmert."

"But can't you see that what you've done may get me in serious trouble? The Wheelers could accuse me of stealing Pancake just like they accused my husband."

Big Boy cast a knowing look her way. "I wouldn't worry none about that coward Walker," he said, then aimed a stream of tobacco juice out into the yard. "He won't be claiming Dimmert's mule again."

Cara's stomach sank. She wasn't sure she wanted to know how he had come upon the chair that gave her such comfort. "I guess you'd better tell me the whole story."

"Me and Dimm was bunkmates in jail, you know," Big Boy began. "I don't reckon I ever met a man kinder than Dimmert Whitt." With a sweep of his arms, all of a sudden he was talking like a poet. "'Ointment and perfume rejoice the heart: so doth the sweetness of a man's friend by hearty counsel.'" He closed his arms and dropped his head. "Proverbs 27:9."

Cara made a mental note to check that out. Proverbs sounded like the Old Testament to her.

Big Boy slid down to the bottom step, propped his elbows on the top one, and leaned back. Stretching out his long legs, he crossed his feet at the ankle. When he took off his hat, his hair, red and wild as a burning bush, sprang out in all directions. His legs looked thick as tree trunks, and Cara had never seen bigger boots. He seemed right at home. That thought gave her pause.

"They weren't much to do there but talk," Big Boy continued. "At first Dimm was stiff as a corpse, wouldn't talk to save Satan, but I didn't mind to carry the burden. I've always liked me an audience."

His back was to Cara, but she didn't need to move her chair closer to hear. His voice was as big as the rest of him. He reminded her a little of Ace in the way he could draw you into a story— make you listen and care despite yourself. She watched him pat his pockets.

"I must have left my twist in the barn," he said.

Pancake ambled across the yard like he was coming over to listen. Big Boy released the bit from the mule's mouth and took off his lead before he settled on the porch steps again. Cara began to wonder if this would go on 'til suppertime.

"Funny thing happened whilst me and Dimm was shut up," he said. "Dimm took to leaving crumbs on the outside windowsill for this blackbird every morning. Soon that thing was pecking biscuit from his hand. Next thing you know, Dimm could bring that bird inside and ride it on his shoulder. Strangest thing I ever seen."

Somehow Cara doubted that. She would bet that Big Boy had seen many strange things, most of which she wouldn't want to hear. "Dimm has a way with animals." She thought she might tell him about the chickens, about how they had left when Dimm did and how she thought they were grieving for him as much as she did. But she didn't want to start a conversation. She didn't want Big Boy to see her as a friend. "You'd best tell me about how you got Pancake and why you thought to bring me this chair."

"It was like this, you see. Dimmert told me about Pancake. There weren't no justice there that I could see, so I figured to right what wrong I could. Dimmert wouldn't allow me to bust him out of jail, though I told him he could hide out with me for as long as was necessary."

Cara nearly laughed. Big Boy was hiding out in Dimmert's barn. Did he think Dimm would have hidden there too? Big Boy was kind of silly. His words tickled her funny bone.

"I had the perfect solution to pay Walker Wheeler back for his thieving ways. I found me a dead polecat and nailed his hide to Walker's stable door; then I put me half a dozen live ones in with Walker's prized horses after I led Pancake out of there." Big Boy gave a contented-sounding snort, like he'd put a big one over on the Wheelers.

"But, Big Boy," Cara couldn't help but ask, "how in the world do you catch a skunk without getting sprayed?"

Big Boy looked around his shoulder at her and raised one eyebrow as if he couldn't believe anybody wouldn't know the answer to that. "Why, you snatch them up while they're sleeping and pack them tight in a gunnysack. They can't shoot you if they can't raise their tails."

"Hmm. I didn't know that." Valuable information, she supposed, if you could figure out when the striped varmints slept. "I don't see how skunks are going to keep the Wheelers from coming after Pancake."

"Thing is," Big Boy said, "Walker Wheeler knows his kin. Him and striped kitty are same as kissing cousins. It was a goodly reminder of the coward that he is. Besides, it's kind of my trademark. Believe you me, that old boy don't want to mess with me or mine." He leaned back on the step, resting on his forearms. "'Whoso diggeth a pit shall fall therein: and he that rolleth a stone, it will return upon him.' Proverbs 26:27."

"That's true enough of Walker," Cara said, "but what about Anvil? He might not feel the same."

"Walker Wheeler wouldn't have nothing but a rabbit farm if not for his old man. From what Dimmert told me, I suspect Anvil knew the truth all along. He just didn't want to call his son out in front of the sheriff and everybody."

Pancake nudged Big Boy with his long nose. Big Boy pulled a clump of grass from beside the step and held it up. "What's the matter, you lazy bum? Cain't pull your own grass?"

Cara had a sinking feeling. She had grown used to having a rocking chair. "So, what about this chair? Please tell me it doesn't belong to the Wheelers."

"Nope. It sort of used to be on the porch of the funeral parlor."

"'Sort of used to be'?"

"Thing is, they had half a dozen and you had none." He turned to look at her again. His face wore not a hint of shame. "Dimmert told me how you'd always wanted a rocking chair."

"But . . . but . . . you can't go stealing chairs from off the undertaker's porch!"

"I beg to differ," Big Boy said. "Way I see it, I wasn't stealing. I was just evening things up, so to speak. They had plenty and you had none. Now you have one and they still have plenty."

Cara hid a smile. "I beg to differ" sounded like a prim old maid. He was funny and entertaining, she'd give him that; but funny or not she needed to get him and his ill-gotten gain from off her porch before the undertaker and the law came calling.

Cara pulled the fancy rocking chair to the edge of the steps. "You have to take it back. Dimmert would never approve of you taking someone else's property and bringing it to me."

"Well, if you're tore up about it . . ." Gathering his bushy hair up under his hat, he fixed her with an innocent look. "I was only doing a favor for a friend. Dimmert asked me to look out for you, missus."

"And I appreciate the gesture. But you have to know this isn't right."

Hands the size of small hams rested on Big Boy's hips as he turned her words over. "Cara Whitt, you are a woman to be prized. Proverbs 31:10. 'Who can find a virtuous woman? for her price is far above rubies.'" Standing, he gave her a courtly bow. "Can I borrow your mule for a spell?"

"Of course, and there's one other thing. You can't be sleeping in the barn."

"I reckon there won't be no need once I take this here chair back to the funeral parlor. Of all the men setting out front of the pool hall after the chair went missing, I'm the onliest one the law questioned. Figure that," he said with a wink, like he got his own joke. He put the bit and the lead back on Pancake. Hoisting the chair with one hand, he started out across the yard.

Soon she watched him come out of the barn. Pancake was fitted with a saddle blanket and an upturned rocking chair. Big Boy stopped and gave a salute. "I'll bring your mule back directly."

Despite herself, Cara waved, like she was sending a sweetheart off to war. She gathered her skirts around her and took the step Big Boy had just vacated. She missed the rocking chair already, but somehow she thought she hadn't seen the last of Big Boy Randall. What a puzzling man he was, stealing chairs and retrieving mules and quoting Scripture. What was it Ace said about him playing Robin

Hood—robbing the rich to give to the poor. Misguided, if you asked her, but she sure was glad to get Pancake back.

She thought to get her leather strop and sharpen her whittling tools, but a bigger project came to mind. While in the barn she'd noticed a pile of lumber stuck up under the worktable where Dimmert stripped tobacco. Now was the time to investigate. She hurried to the barn.

With a satisfied smile she pulled several oak boards out from under the stripping table. As she ran her hands down the grain, she fancied she could still smell the live tree.

With a carver's practiced eye she chose just the right boards for making long rockers for wide, smooth rides. After they were cut, planed, and sanded, she'd pick out wood for the arms. Before summer, she would have a rocking chair for herself. Why hadn't she thought of this before? If she wanted, her porch could resemble the undertaker's. Cara laughed aloud. Wouldn't that be a sight?

Two would be enough for her porch, one for her and one for Dimm. When he came home, they'd sit together enjoying the dimming of the day as lightning bugs flashed and whip-poor-wills sang. When the days got short, they'd take the chairs inside and toast their toes in front of the fireplace.

It warmed her heart to think Dimm had reached out to comfort her from behind bars. She guessed if Dimm trusted Big Boy, she should do the same. How else would she loan him the mule? She was beginning to understand his mercurial nature. But she'd keep an eye on her things, just in case he knew a widow down the road somewheres who needed her bread bowl or her hominy pot worse than she did. Cara laughed at herself. It felt good, laughter.

The barn seemed homey now as she bent to her task. The shadows were just shadows, and the dust motes that danced in the streams of sunlight spoke of work being done and dreams coming true.

CHAPTER 16

A FIVE-LAYER DESSERT SAT proudly but precariously on a cut-glass cake stand in the middle of the kitchen table. There would have been six layers, but one stuck to the pan. From her station at the cookstove, Darcy cocked her head. The cake seemed to be leaning to one side. Before she could react, the top tier slid off the stack, continued over the side of the table, and plopped to the floor. Good thing she hadn't iced it yet. Without a moment's hesitation, she dusted the layer and stuck it back in place. She always kept her floors clean enough to eat on, after all. As if mocking her, the top started its slow slide again. She had a mind to fling the whole mess right out the door.

Taking the errant layer off, she laid it on a plate, then went to the pantry for the inside broom. With a quick snap she had a single thick straw. Carefully, she positioned the misbehaving piece in place and drove the straw right through the middle of all five layers. Some of the sulfured apple filling oozed out and dripped down the side. She figured she could cover all that with icing. What an aggravation this had been. Why had she listened to Mammaw anyway?

Back at the stove, a niggling worry begged attention. Like a mouse with a hard crust of bread, it kept gnawing at her. There was something wrong with Mammaw. While Darcy stirred cream into brown sugar and melted butter, she tried to figure out exactly what was different. Mammaw seemed like her old self when Darcy got her up this morning, but soon she was back to the pattern that had started about two weeks ago. Like one of Dance's little kids, she asked the same thing over and over. It was as if her mind was a sieve. She even forgot how to feed herself sometimes.

Darcy didn't mind the added physical work. Her grandmother deserved the best, and Darcy took pains to keep her spotless and comfortable with frequent linen changes and as many sponge baths each day as necessary. But the endless questions made her short-tempered. Just this morning Mammaw asked for biscuits and gravy three times even though she'd already eaten her breakfast.

The brown-sugar mixture bubbled in the pan. Darcy added a shot of vanilla and let it cook for several minutes, stirring until her arm got tired. When the icing had cooled and was starting to thicken, she poured it over the stack cake, letting it dribble down the sides. The cake took on a whole new look as Darcy swirled the caramel icing. "Pretty as a picture," she said.

The clock on the mantel chimed twelve times. Where had the morning gone? Dylan's mother was coming for her visit early after-noon and Darcy still had the kitchen to clean up and Mammaw hadn't had her dinner. Darcy looked around. What should she do first? Feeling guilty but rushed, she decided to take advantage of her grandmother's extra-long nap to wash the pans and mixing bowls. Mammaw wouldn't be happy if Jean Foster saw the kitchen in such a state and neither would Darcy.

Everything seemed a mess and a worry. Darcy had a secret weapon against melancholy, however. Thoughts of Henry put a smile on her face. She danced around the kitchen with a dishrag and a mop.

In no time at all order prevailed. The five-layer stack cake stood proud as the queen of England on the table, where Mammaw, in a freshly ironed day dress, could admire it from her rolling chair. Darcy hoped she didn't count the layers—hoped she wasn't disappointed if she did.

If Darcy had been worried Jean Foster would spill the beans about her boldness Sunday last when she'd gone off with Henry, it was unwarranted. Miz Foster was as gracious and kind as ever. She even complimented Darcy on the stack cake, which could have used less salt and more sugar. Mammaw paid no notice, however; she kept asking for more until Darcy was embarrassed for her.

"Mammaw," she finally said, "don't you want to save a slice for Papaw?"

Miz Foster seemed startled for a moment, but then she patted Mammaw's withered hand and gave Darcy a look of recognition.

When Miz Foster left, she motioned Darcy to follow to the porch. "Dear, my own mother became much like Fairy Mae in her declining years. It is a heavy burden but one the good Lord will surely guide you through." She gave Darcy's arm a gentle squeeze. "You are a good granddaughter, one I know Fairy Mae is proud to call her own. I will be praying for both of you."

Darcy could have cried, but she held back. "Thank you. Mammaw needs your prayers."

"I'm right over the hill if you need me," Miz Foster replied. "Just holler and I'll come running, night or day. You hear?"

Dylan was waiting for his mother. He gave Darcy a wave but he didn't speak. Both the Fosters made Darcy feel uncomfortable in a way she couldn't put her finger on. They were just so . . . good. But Darcy was not a bad person. She went to church and read her Bible. She took care of her grandmother and supported her. That counted for something, didn't it?

So why was she standing on her own porch feeling . . . guilty? That was it—like she'd opened a jar of tomatoes and found them spoiled, still pretty on the outside but festering on the inside. She

searched her conscience, but she didn't have to search far to find
Henry Thomas.

She went into the house and took the tablecloth from the table.
Mammaw was asleep again. Her chin rested on her chest, and her
soft snores filled the kitchen. Back outside, Darcy gave the tablecloth
such a shake it flew from her hands and landed on the lilac bush. A
red-winged blackbird took advantage of the cake crumbs that scattered beneath the lilac, his heavy beak thwacking the ground. Darcy
watched his maneuvering as he hopped under the sweet-smelling
bush to eat his treat in safety. Each time he darted into the light to
fetch another crumb, his glossy feathers shone like wet coal. A small
house wren boldly thought to join the feast but quickly flew away
when the blackbird flashed his wings' red stripe in warning—*don't
come too close*.

Just like Henry, she thought. He was her beautiful blackbird with
a flash of danger, but she was not a wren. She was not about to fly
away from him.

After retrieving the tablecloth, she shook it again, more gently
this time. Maybe Mammaw would like to sit outside awhile and
watch the birds. She could scatter some stale corn bread. Maybe the
blackbird would come back. Maybe Darcy could take a minute to
dream of Henry.

Night was closing in when Henry came by. Darcy had just gotten
Mammaw settled, thank goodness. He didn't seem to mind if they
got caught, but Darcy did. She wanted to talk to Mammaw first,
smooth the waters, but the time never seemed right. Mammaw was
so upset the first time Darcy mentioned Henry. Darcy wasn't quite
ready to deal with that again.

Darcy was at the porch rail, dribbling water from the rain barrel
onto the tiny tree she'd brought home and planted in an old coffee
tin. It was on the porch railing, where it could catch some sun, and
she was careful to keep the soil moist. Still, it struggled.

"Darcy," she heard a voice from the shadows. "Little Darcy Mae."

She didn't have to look to know who called her name, for his voice was as dear to her as one could ever be. Awash in pleasure, she slid the spindly plant out of sight behind Mammaw's red geranium. She pinched a leaf from the geranium and crushed it in her palms. It smelled as good as the finest perfume from Paris, France, Mammaw always said. Darcy never questioned how she knew.

Darcy turned and eased the kitchen door closed, then flew down the steps, across the yard, and into Henry's waiting arms. His kisses were darting, teasing, leaving Darcy weak in the knees.

"Come up to the logging trail with me," he said. "I want to ask you something."

"I can't," she whispered. "I can't leave Mammaw."

He tipped her chin and kissed her again, slow and easy this time. "Come on, little Darcy. Do it just for me."

A longing overtook Darcy—a need to fulfill his need. It seemed to come from the very marrow of her bones, which turned to water; from her heart, which forgot to beat; from her breath, which caught in her throat. Darcy had never wanted anything more than she wanted to do Henry's bidding. But what if Mammaw called out and no one was there?

"Please," she said, "don't tempt me so."

"Listen," he said. "I love you."

On her tiptoes she put her arms around his neck. "I never thought to hear such pretty words."

He hugged her tight. "Run away with me and I will marry you tonight."

"What about my family? And I'd thought to make a dress." Darcy leaned back to study him. He was so handsome with his high cheekbones and long, straight nose it took her breath, but his eyes were dark and brooding.

Henry dropped his arms from around her and turned, staring off into the gloom.

Darcy's heart sank. Was he mad at her? She dared to go in front of him, tried to kiss his cheek, but he shrugged her off. "What did I do?" she asked.

With a quick movement he was on horseback looking down on her. "Go on back in the house. Go on back to your mammaw."

Shamelessly she grabbed his coattail. "But you said you love me."

His horse took a side step away. The saddle creaked as he reached to unclasp her fingers. "Yes, I did, but you never said the same. I need a woman who puts me first."

Darcy twisted her hands together, not daring to touch him again. "I do love you, Henry. I love you so much it pains me."

With one strong grasp under her arms, he lifted her off the ground. She could feel his muscles bunching up, straining against the sleeve of his jacket as she felt the press of the saddle against her chest. For a moment she thought he meant to carry her off and she wished he would. But instead he kissed her hard enough to leave his memory on her mouth for a good long time.

"If I come for you again, you'd better be ready. I've asked you once. I might ask you twice, but there'll be no third." Easing her down, he removed his arm and flicked the horse's reins. The horse trotted off smooth as Henry himself.

Darcy stood there in the yard for the longest time, stood with the manly scent of saddle leather surrounding her, stood with the kiss stamped on her mouth and Henry's desire stamped on her heart. She wished she could stand there in that selfsame spot until he returned.

Darcy was tugged in two directions. Mammaw was like her child now. Her need pressed like butter in a mold on Darcy's heart. While Henry . . . Henry made that same heart sing with longing.

The night was bringing a damp cool with it. Lightning threatened in the distance. Darcy pulled her apron up over her arms against the chill. How her life had changed since she met Henry. She'd never thought to know such passion, had not known of its existence. Her own father and mother lived like strangers in the same house. She'd never seen them kiss. Ace and Dance had a certain passion, she supposed. Ace did toward Dance, anyway—you could see it in his eyes—but Dance didn't look the same way at him.

Thunder rolled across the sky ever closer with each wave. Darcy kept her place, lost in rumination. Dimmert and Cara loved each other truly; Darcy bore witness to that. But theirs was a sweet and simple love, like flowers blooming or summer sunshine across your shoulders. Henry's love was thunder and lightning and wild whipping wind stirring her emotions like the sudden spring storm fast approaching.

Lightning splintered the night sky with many fingers of fire. Darcy hurried inside. The little house lit up with each flash of lightning, trembled with each cracking boom. She stood just inside the screen door, mesmerized by the storm's display. She could smell the rain before it started, hear each fat drop spatter against the wooden porch floor before the drops joined forces, hurling buckets of water across the porch. Her dress front was soaked before she thought to close the door. She leaned against it and slid slowly to the floor, resting her head on her knees.

Teardrops mimicked the rain as she sat there. It didn't seem fair that love would hurt so much. If she turned her back on Mammaw, she would never forgive herself, but if she turned Henry away, she would never be happy again. Outside, the storm raged on as inside, Darcy wept and prayed for guidance.

⋘⋙

Henry almost made it home before the storm overtook him. He couldn't believe what he had just done—begging Darcy to run off with him, telling her he loved her. He'd meant to *ask* her to marry, not demand. But then she wouldn't even go a step away from her grandmother to please him. That got him mad—who did she think she was?

All the plans he'd put in place, all the property to be acquired, all the money yet to be made . . . He'd come that close to throwing it all away over a woman! How dumb could he get? Henry sank in a quagmire of self-pity. Once—just once—he'd like somebody to love him best.

His horse didn't like the lightning and the thunder, so he took extra time with his care when they got to the stable. He talked gently as he rubbed the animal down and put some timothy hay in his feed box. Lester lay curled up on a gunnysack under a bench, safe and dry. Henry let the old dog be. Through a flash of light he saw Daisy dancing with excitement at the yard gate, and he lifted the latch to let her out. With wagging tail she waited at the stable entrance. She knew not to approach until he was finished with the horse. Darcy Mae should be so obedient.

Finished with the rubdown, he put the horse in a stall. Daisy stuck her nose in his cupped hand, looking for the small piece of beef jerky he always brought her. He patted her bony head and shared his conundrum. "I made a fool of myself tonight, Daisy. Of all things, a woman's managed to get my heart in a vise."

Daisy leaped up and planted a slobbery kiss on Henry's cheek. He slid her long silky ears through his hands. "Come on, girl. Let's go in the house. I know just the thing to get me thinking right again."

Henry sat in his rolling chair with the land survey sheets spread out before him and waited for the rush of excitement to come. The coal-oil lamp sputtered, and he turned up the wick. Rain beat a lonesome sound on the tin roof. Daisy sighed from her bed on a thick rag rug under the desk. Henry shifted position and reached for his pen. With a precise X he marked the spot where he would build a house once the land was his. First he'd fell some timber, then knock down that shanty Darcy called home.

He tapped the pen against the blotter on the desk and drew a circle around Fairy Mae's piece of property. How long could the old woman last? Not much longer surely. Being married to Darcy beforehand would be to his benefit as far as said property went. He'd almost blown the whole deal tonight. Darcy was not quite as malleable as he had supposed. That would change once they were wed.

Hours passed as he studied the drawings and made his plans. Finally he got up and twisted the combination lock on the safe he kept in the back room. He didn't even have to think to turn the knob clockwise, then counter, now clockwise again, for his fingers held the code and his ears were attuned to the familiar clicks. By lamplight he studied the bills and sacks of coins inside the safe. Just for the joy of hearing the sound, he jingled a few gold pieces.

That joy was fleeting tonight, however. Darcy's face wavered between him and his money. He saw the hurt he had caused. Over and over he ran his thumb across his lower lip. He could still taste her sweet mouth.

"I have to rethink this," he said. "I'll ask her right and give her time to make a fancy dress. The land will be mine whether we marry now or later and so will she."

Reacting to her master's voice, Daisy stuck her nose around the doorpost. Yawning, she stretched and bowed her back. He had interrupted her sleep.

"Daisy, I'm perplexed. Darcy Mae keeps getting in the way of me counting my money. Did you ever think that day would come? I think she's put a hex on me."

He smiled at that notion as he turned the dial until he heard the lock click into place. Without undressing, he lay down on his bed and closed his eyes. Daisy flopped across his feet.

Instead of counting sheep, he ticked off each item of his plan. Arrange to marry Darcy—that was the first and most important step. Put the squeeze on the county tax assessor to raise the taxes on Dimmert's place—favors were owed, so that would be easy. See what he could do about Ace's part of the original parcel of land. Ace would be the fly in his dumplings. He was already suspicious after catching Henry and Darcy together. Yes, Ace could cause real trouble.

Henry's mind swirled with plans. Since he was a young boy, he'd plotted how to avenge his grandfather's degradation by Fairy Mae's husband, Herbert Whitt. If he remembered correctly, Ace Shelton was once in trouble with the law over a whiskey still.

Easing his feet out from under Daisy, Henry left his bed and began pacing in the dark. He always thought better on his feet. What was the story? Henry had been away in school when it happened, but he remembered hearing rumors when he came home for a visit. A man was shot and killed, and Ace was involved somehow. That was it. Henry rubbed his chin. He needed to find out which judge let Ace Shelton walk.

Henry felt better. He lay down again and stared into the darkness. First thing in the morning he'd hightail it to the courthouse and look up some records. It was good to have a plan.

CHAPTER 17

A FEW DAYS after Big Boy Randall took the funeral parlor's chair away, Cara was sitting on the front porch, sharpening her small-bladed whittling knife on a leather strop. She had begun to think Big Boy was not going to return the mule. And what could she do if he didn't? Go to the sheriff and say, "Someone stole the mule my husband stole that someone stole from him"?

As if in answer to her quandary, she heard, "Morning, missus," from across the barnyard. "I brung your mule back."

Cara laid the tool aside and stepped out into the yard. She didn't want to encourage Big Boy to come up on the porch. She aimed to keep his visit short. She needn't have worried, however, for Big Boy dismounted and with a jaunty wave strode away, leaving Pancake by the barn. Cara guessed he was going to cross the creek and head back to the road.

"Well," she said, retrieving the leather strop. *Slap, slap, slap*—the blade stroked the strop at an angle. Cara ran the mirrored edge of the blade across the surface of her thumbnail to check for nicks.

The midafternoon air was soft and balmy. Who didn't love the first sweet days in June? The porch was quiet, and Cara fell into a meditative state as she carved a chunk of butternut. Strangely, she was let down by Big Boy's quick departure. She'd thought they'd share a few words. After Big Boy's visit the other day, she searched the Bible until she found the book of Proverbs, and she read every word aloud. The rhythmical flow of the short verses put her in mind of the cadence of whittling—each line a beat as each score with her knife was also a beat.

She had memorized her favorite verses, and now she recited them. "'There be three things which are too wonderful for me, yea, four which I know not: The way of an eagle in the air; the way of a serpent upon a rock; the way of a ship in the midst of the sea; and the way of a man with a maid.'" That was pretty to say. The whole book reminded her of the riddles her daddy had taught her when she was a girl and which she now taught to Jay. Each one had a lesson at its core.

Wood chips flew through her fingers as the rough face of a doll emerged from the butternut. Tiny ears appeared on the oval shape; a slight dimple creased the chin. Given a chance, she might have asked Big Boy about the spider verse. It puzzled her: "The spider taketh hold with her hands, and is in kings' palaces." Was that some kind of warning? Cara didn't like spiders. She kept knobby green hedge apples under the bed and in each corner of the house to keep the creepy things away. She thought of one time she'd seen a hairy wolf spider big as a half-dollar crawling up the bedpost. She smacked it so hard with a cord of wood that she busted the post. Dimmert laughed until he cried. The thought made her laugh too. My, she missed her husband.

She turned the doll's head in her hands, searching for rough spots. Merky was sure to like having her own baby to play with. Darcy said she would make a dress and bonnet for the doll. She had stopped by yesterday on her way to mail some packages. Cara gave her a letter to post to Dimm. Darcy was too dressed up for a quick trip to the post office. Cara wondered if she meant to make a call on that lawyer again. But she bit her tongue. Darcy didn't need her playing mother hen.

Time to put her project away; she could get it out again this evening. The sadiron was already on the stove and her ironing waited. Such as it was—one dress, some bedclothes, and a few shirtwaists. But if she was going to do Dance's laundry tomorrow, she needed to get her ironing done today. Maybe Dance didn't care if her wash wasn't done until Wednesday, which put her ironing off until Thursday, but Cara did. No wonder Dance was always out of sorts. She had no pattern to her days.

She positioned the wooden ironing board in front of the window, which was propped open to catch the breeze. Wrapping the handle of the sadiron with a dish towel, she tipped it and spat. The spit sizzled on the flat surface, and the starched pillowcase hissed when she pushed the hot iron across it. It made Cara feel wealthy to sleep on ironed linen. Her mama had never enjoyed such luxury. They were lucky to have blankets. It didn't seem to matter back then, though. Daddy told them a story every night before Mama tucked them in with a kiss. That was luxury enough.

In little more than an hour her ironing was done. A pot of butter beans simmered on the back of the cookstove, and a round of corn bread baked in the oven. Her mama always cooked butter beans and fried potato pancakes on Tuesday. Cara kept the tradition. Dimmert loved her potato pancakes.

She was just folding up the ironing board when she heard Big Boy's booming voice again. "Missus, I caught you some dinner."

She looked out the window and saw he had a string of fish. Her mouth watered—fried fish with the beans, potatoes, and corn bread? That would be a feast. She covered her mouth with her hand. How could she take the fish without asking Big Boy to eat? Yet how could she turn the gift down without hurting his feelings? Her toe tapping, she peeked out the window again. All right, she'd have him to supper and then gently explain that he could not be hanging around the place. Surely he would understand.

She walked out to the chopping block by the barn. Before she could say, "Stay for supper," Big Boy was cleaning the fish. Shiny scales flew in all directions before he slit one down the middle of the belly. He expertly removed the insides and the bony spine. The lungs lay still inflated on the block. "We used to play with those." Cara pointed. "My brothers would float them down the creek."

"It takes a good hand to get the lights out without busting them," he replied, sliding the cleaned fish into a pan of water.

"I could fry these up for supper if you have time to eat before you get on your way," Cara said, congratulating herself on her way with words.

Big Boy scaled another fish. "I figured to leave these with you. But if you want me to stay . . ."

Cara could have kicked herself. She'd been thinking too much as usual. Now what could she do but invite him to stay for a meal? "I'll have it ready in no time, and you can take the extra with you."

Soon she and Big Boy Randall were sitting at the kitchen table, which she had pulled out on the porch. She prayed no one would come along and see them sitting here. But she couldn't very well have him in the house. The worry was giving her indigestion. She'd have to get out the baking soda once he left.

Big Boy ate half a pot of beans with his potato pancakes and his fish, then sopped up the bean soup from his plate with a piece of corn bread. He pushed his chair back and rested his arms on his belly. Cara thought it was big as the rain barrel. He must be eating somewhere regularly.

"Thank you, missus," he said. Pulling a short piece of straw from his shirt pocket, he worked it around his teeth. "Them was mighty good beans."

With her elbows on the table, Cara folded her hands under her chin. "So, where do you go from here?"

"Now don't be fretting about me," he said with a wink. "I got friends all over yon hills."

"Might I ask you something?" Cara said.

"Shoot," he replied.

"There's this verse in Proverbs that has me puzzled. It's the one about the spider in the palace. What do you take that to mean?"

"To understand a part, you got to look at the whole—"

"I'll just fetch my Bible," Cara interrupted, starting to stand.

Big Boy motioned her to sit. "No need," he said, tapping his head. "I got the whole of Proverbs right here—Ecclesiastes too. That particular verse speaks to the wisdom of little things, like spiders and ants, conies and locusts. It's saying a spider can spin her web in a king's palace as easy as she can spin anywhere else."

"What do you reckon a coney is?"

"Do you know I had that selfsame question? Mr. Webster says it's a kind of rabbit. It's kindly hard to picture a rabbit making a home in the rocks though, ain't it?"

"You sure know your Bible," she said.

"They don't call me Preacher for nothing," Big Boy responded.

"Preacher? I thought your nickname was Big Boy." Cara dished up two bowls of peach cobbler and handed one across the table.

"Big Boy's my given name," he said around a spoonful of cobbler. "My family calls me Preacher."

Cara shook her head. Despite herself, she had to hear how a person got such a moniker as Big Boy.

Big Boy polished off his dessert and licked the spoon. "I feel like I died and went to heaven after that peach pie. Reckon I could have just a tad more?"

Cara made the second helping extra large. "How did you come by such a name as Big Boy?"

"My daddy was a little banty rooster–size man. First thing Daddy said after I was born was 'That there's one big boy.' It stuck."

Cara chuckled. "I'm sorry, but that is funny. It makes me wonder what your brothers and sisters are named."

"Everybody else has got regular names." Big Boy counted off on his fingers. "There's Shacklett, Halona, Aloda, Lulie, and Yeary. I'm the least one. I guess Mammy plumb run out of names by the time I came along."

"Hmm," Cara said. "Those are all real pretty."

Big Boy stroked his beard. "I've been pondering on paying a visit to Dimmert. What do you think?"

Cara's heart beat painfully. She ducked her head to hide quick tears. "If you do, would you tell him that I miss him something awful?" He kept his eyes straight ahead. Cara figured he could hear the anguish in her voice. "Could I maybe send him some things?"

"I'm fixing to head toward Frankfort in the morning. You bundle up whatever you want me to take and set it here on the porch. I'll come by for it early."

Cara threw caution to the wind. "You could stay in the barn tonight, Big Boy."

He looked sideways at her. "Tell you the truth, if things were different, I'd take you up on the offer. I love Dimmert like a brother, which kindly makes you my sister, but I'd better get on the road. I'll go up Crook-Neck to my brother Shacklett's. I don't want to set folks a-jawing and speculating."

"Didn't you think they might talk when you hid out here before?"

Big Boy shrugged. "Nobody was the wiser then. I made teetotally sure of that."

"You're a good man, Big Boy Randall."

"Tell that to the law," Big Boy replied, then laughed.

"Seems like you go out of your way to get arrested, taking chairs from the funeral parlor and stirring up the Wheelers," she said. "Why would you do that?"

Big Boy stretched his big arms over his head. "I could never stand one person having plenty and another doing without. I was always trying to even things out."

Cara bided her words. She didn't want to seem judgmental, but clearly Big Boy was in the wrong. "Don't you reckon there might be a better way of doing that than staying just this side of the hoosegow all the time?"

"You might be right. I felt silly sneaking that rocking chair back to the funeral parlor." One at a time he cracked his knuckles. Their popping sounded overloud in the stillness of the evening. "You might not understand, but being with Dimmert Whitt for the short time stirred my soul."

"How do you mean?" she asked.

Big Boy leaned forward, resting his elbows on the tabletop. "Dimm's so quiet, it's like he's always thinking. He listens to your words and then turns them back on you. Makes you come up with your own answers. You know what I mean?"

"Yes," she agreed.

"And a body can tell, Dimmert's a man of strong conviction. He would rather go to jail than lie. Me, I always had me a little fun twisting facts to suit myself."

It was getting late. Cara stood and started scraping the plates. Big Boy's was clean as a whistle. "You should take Pancake. He'll make your journey to the penitentiary easier."

"Thank you, missus." Big Boy stood and retrieved his hat from where it perched on the back of his chair. "I'll take you up on that. I expect Dimmert would druther see Pancake than me anyway."

"Would the prison guards let Dimm see Pancake?" Cara thrilled at the thought.

Big Boy gave her his slow wink again. "Don't you worry none about that. I'll see to it."

Later that evening Cara took a worn tablecloth from the press and laid it out flat on the floor. She folded a flannel shirt and a pair of overalls and put them square in the middle. From the top chest drawer she took a cotton union suit with knit cuffs and two pairs of wool socks and added them to the stack. That didn't seem enough somehow. What else could she add to remind Dimm how much she loved him?

The screen door slapped shut behind her. She searched through her stack of whittling wood. There was a small chunk left over from the doll's head. Butternut was a soft wood, which made for quick and easy carving. She didn't even sit on the porch steps but stood in place as a heart the size of a silver dollar emerged from the scrap of wood. *DW + CW,* she scribed on the heart. Back inside, she stuck it in the pocket of the flannel shirt.

That task finished, she fired up the cookstove. When the oven was hot, she slid in a pan of biscuits.

At 3 a.m. Cara was still cooking. She couldn't seem to stop. There was fried chicken, boiled eggs, biscuits, baked sweet potatoes, another round of corn bread, and Dimm's favorite—fried apple pies. When the food cooled, she wrapped it in oilcloth and packed it in a clean lard bucket. As she poured leftover grease from the skillet into a grease keeper, she smiled at the thought of Dimm receiving her gifts—if the food even made it to Frankfort, given Big Boy's big appetite.

She wouldn't question though, wouldn't give orders. It was enough that Big Boy was going to see her husband. She caught her breath. She could go with him! Who was to stop her? For a moment her resolve flamed bright as a new penny. Then she found her senses. It wasn't fitting for a woman to up and take off as if it didn't matter what others thought. Her daddy always said the only thing a man packs all his life is his name, good or bad.

Besides she had a feeling that Dimmert would not want her there. The prison sounded like a hard and lonesome place. It would be easier for him to bear the time if time was all he had to bear. While the cookstove still held heat, she put on a pot of coffee. There was no reason to go to bed this late. She might as well wait for morning.

When the rooster crowed, she woke with a crick in her neck. Her coffee had long since gone cold, but there were live coals under the stove burner, so it wouldn't take long to get a fire going. Twice-heated coffee would be strong enough to stand a spoon in, but she welcomed that. She opened the kitchen door expecting to see the bundle of clothes and the lard bucket full of food waiting to be picked up. Instead there was another Big Boy–type gift.

Leaving the door open, she sat at the table and rested her weary head in the crook of her elbow. The early morning sunlight filtered though the screen door, bathing her face in warmth. The rooster sang another earsplitting wake-up serenade. The aroma of nearly burned coffee called her to get going.

After adding a healthy dash of cream to her mug, she went out to the porch and settled in the newly delivered rocking chair. She was pleased to see the rockers she had made fitted perfectly well on a wide-bottomed chair. Big Boy must have worked all night long. There was no way he went all the way to Crook-Neck and back. She wondered how he knew she had made rockers.

The coffee didn't taste half-bad. Soon as she finished she'd let the chickens out of the coop for the day. Then she thought to hoe some weeds from around the potato hills before she headed over to the Sheltons' to do the wash.

It would be nice to have a cat, she reckoned. A cat was good to curl up in your lap when you rocked. Her mind started to scratch around, searching for a worry or two to keep her company. Seemed like she couldn't hardly work up to a good head of worry though, seemed like rocking and fretting didn't go together. Her daddy used to say, "Let every day provide for itself and God send Sunday."

Absently, she tucked a strand of hair behind her ear. Draining the last of her cup, she stood. Her eyes took in the wealth around her—the burgeoning garden; the wild rose climbing a trellis on the whitewashed henhouse; the fragrant patch of orange marigold beside the porch; the white ironstone mug that fitted her hand perfectly; the sturdy rocking chair. Big Boy was taking her heart to Dimm. Cara was thankful.

CHAPTER 18

Darcy spread three yards of linen across the table. She'd washed it for shrinkage yesterday and hung it to dry in the shade so the pale pink color wouldn't fade.

"Ain't ye going to press it before you cut?" Mammaw asked.

"I did that already," Darcy said.

"Let me feel of it."

Darcy suppressed a sigh. She had the flimsy pattern pieces all ready to pin to the fabric. The pattern had cost fifteen cents—kind of pricey, probably because it called for double ruffled sleeves and a ruffled collar. Last night she went through her trunk of fabric and selected the handkerchief linen for a blouse and a piece of lightweight wool worsted for a skirt. The dark rose color of the wool contrasted nicely with the light pink linen. Because she had a short waist, she'd use whalebone in the skirt to keep it from rolling over. Darcy hoped for the hourglass figure that was all the rage in the latest fashion magazines Mrs. Upchurch sent her through the mail.

"Are your hands clean?" Darcy asked as she draped the fabric across her grandmother's lap.

Mammaw's mouth quivered as she held up her good hand for Darcy to inspect. The gesture made Darcy feel small. She hugged her granny, letting the touch last longer than usual. "Of course they are. I'm sorry."

Mammaw fingered the linen. "Is this for you, Darcy Mae? Is it for something special?"

Darcy turned away and busied herself with the piece of wool. "I'm going to take this out to the clothesline. It still smells of mothballs."

The wire clothesline was strung between the well house and a skimpy locust tree. Darcy chose the shaded end, then pegged the folded wool cloth to the line. With any luck the birds would be busy elsewhere this morning.

How did Mammaw know she was up to something? Darcy had been so careful to keep her feelings to herself, so careful her stomach was in knots most of the time. All she'd been able to eat since Henry's insistent visit was toast and weak tea. That was probably what had Mammaw suspicious, for usually Darcy was a hearty eater. Surely Mammaw hadn't seen the two of them out her bedroom window that night. She would have said something if she had.

Why did everything have to be so hard? If Henry came with his proposal again, what would she do? How could she turn her back on her grandmother? Hadn't she made her choice, though, when she picked out the fabric for her wedding dress—going with practical linen and wool instead of the silk she had once dreamed of? Darcy undid one clothespin and pulled the fabric tighter on the line before she fastened it again. Scooping up the free end of the wool, she buried her face and inhaled the sharp mothball fragrance until her head floated. The least bit of a Scripture came to mind—*"moth and rust doth corrupt."* As she let the fabric fall, Darcy wished she had some mothballs to put around her heart.

A warm wind kicked up, wafting the scent of lilac her way. The woolen fabric snapped on the line. Darcy scanned the sky. Smallish gray clouds skittered like playful kittens across the sun. She stepped into the well house for a minute's peace and rested her weight on her palms; then she leaned over the rim of the well. "Hello," she shouted.

Hello . . . Hello . . . Hello . . . The echo floated up from the shaft.

"It's me, Darcy!"

Darcy . . . Darcy . . . Darcy . . .

She leaned farther in, careful to keep her footing. "I don't know what to do!"

To do . . . To do . . . To do . . .

"Are you tetched in the head?" a familiar voice queried from behind her, "or did somebody fall down the well?"

Startled, Darcy's palms slipped against the rock ledge. She nearly took a tumble. "Forevermore, Remy. You could have made me fall in."

"Humph. Weren't me playing games in the well house."

Darcy pulled the door shut behind her and turned the wooden peg that held it closed. "What are you doing here?" Her voice sounded sharp even to her own ears. "I'm not going to town today."

Remy stared at the ground. "I hoped to visit Fairy Mae."

Darcy realized she didn't know Remy the least bit, though the woman had been helping her with Mammaw for months now. She studied the woman who was always . . . what? Available? Darcy couldn't even put a name to who Remy was to her. Her conscience plagued her. This wasn't the first time today Darcy Mae Whitt had felt mean.

"Mammaw would love a visit," she said. "I'll make us some tea."

Darcy followed Remy's slow progress, taking in the other woman's thin frame, her halting gait, the trail left by the pull of her wooden crutch through the grass. Truly, Darcy thought, what with her white hair, pale complexion, and washed-out blue eyes, Remy was the oddest person she ever chanced to meet. And her voice, like a rusty screen door, sometimes caught Darcy off guard even though she'd heard it a thousand times.

Darcy recalled the first time she laid eyes on Remy. It was in May of 1887, the day before Miz Copper was to marry Mr. John in a double wedding with Cara and Dimmert. The women of the household gathered in Miz Copper's bedroom that warm afternoon, trying on their dresses. Darcy loved her pink mull frock. It was the fanciest dress she'd ever owned. And Miz Copper—oh, she looked like an angel in her pretty gown with her hair caught up with pearl combs. It was such a happy day until Mr. John stumbled across the threshold with Remy's crumpled body in his arms. Darcy could still see dark red blood spilling down the front of Miz Copper's moss green wedding dress.

She'd been shot of all things, Remy had, by old Hezzy Krill when she mistook Remy for a four-legged varmint stealing eggs from Hezzy's henhouse. Remy had nearly bled to death, and she still walked with a limp. She must be lonely now, living by herself in the house Miz Krill left to her in her last will and testament.

Remy's bad luck was Darcy's good fortune. Because Remy was always on hand to sit with her grandmother, Darcy could get to town on occasion and Remy came every Sunday morning so Darcy could go to church service. Remy went to service on Sunday nights. It worked out perfectly. Why, if it hadn't been for Remy, Darcy might never have met Henry.

Darcy stopped in her tracks. Of course, why hadn't she thought of this before? She tapped Remy's shoulder. "Might I have a word with you before we go in?"

"Suit yourself," Remy said, leaning back against the raised porch floor and resting her crutch by the step rocks.

Darcy dived right in. "What if I was to go away for a short time— you know like when I go to the city to visit with Mrs. Upchurch and her friends. Could you come and stay with Mammaw for a spell? I know she usually goes to stay with Dance when I'm gone that far, but . . ."

"What does Fairy Mae want to do?" Remy asked. "I wouldn't want to go against her wishes."

Now it was Darcy who stared at the ground. "I was thinking something might come up all of a sudden. Like so quick I wouldn't have time to make other arrangements," Darcy stammered. "I would need your word you would take care of Mammaw until I got back or until Ace could come and carry her to his house."

Remy studied her. Her odd, pink-rimmed eyes never blinked. Darcy felt sneaky as a sheep-killing dog. "I don't aim to stir your pot."

"Believe me, Remy. I'd tell you if I could."

Remy stuck her crutch under her arm and deftly climbed the steps before she paused. "I'd never forsake Fairy Mae. All ye need do is send for me."

Darcy was almost giddy with relief as she reached around Remy to hold the screen door for her. Seemed her prayers had been answered. Henry was going to be surprised the next time he proposed.

Remy mumbled something peculiar as she ducked under Darcy's outstretched arm. "The devil is in his broth a-brewing," Darcy thought she heard.

How fey. Whatever did Remy mean by that?

<hr />

Cara was disappointed to see that the children, except for Jay and baby Pauline, were off somewhere with their father. At least Dance was in a fair mood—or seemed to be. It was often hard to tell at first glance. It was a warmish day with only a smattering of gray clouds that didn't amount to much. Still, she'd have to hurry to get the wash on the line in time for it to dry.

But Dance had already started the fire under the wash pot. A line of infant gowns, bibs, and diapers flapped in the breeze. Pauline napped atop a pile of laundry, and Jay dug fishing worms at the edge of the garden.

"Whee, that's a good one," he'd yell every so often before he tucked it in an old tin can.

"I had fresh fish for dinner yesterday," Cara said before she thought.

"Been fishing, have you?" Dance asked. "I don't know when's the last time I had time to fish." She kept one fist knotted at the small of her back as she stirred the laundry with a long wooden paddle.

"No, I didn't catch them. Someone brought them by. I should have thought to save you some."

"That boy yonder will catch a mess. He's a natural with a pole and a wiggle tail."

"Want me to take over the stirring?" Cara asked.

"I wouldn't mind. My back's a-killing me." Dance fished a pile of linen from the bubbling water and dropped it into the rinse tub. "You stir and I'll wring."

Cara eased the baby from one pile of laundry to another, sorted out the children's clothes, and added them to the wash water. "Do you think it needs more soap?"

"Be spare," Dance remarked. "I didn't get as much made as I should have last fall."

"You make the best soft soap, Dance. What do you do different?"

"I copy Mammaw. She only ever used rainwater and only pure lard, no refuse grease."

Cara scrubbed the knees of a small pair of pants up and down the washboard. "Looks like Wilton was trying to wear these out."

"They were already thin when he got them. One of Ace's lady friends thought she needed to give my young'uns her kids' castoffs."

"Lady friends?" Cara nearly choked. "I can't picture Ace being that way."

"I don't reckon I'm worried none. It's just the church women are always feeling sorry for poor old Ace." Dance wrung a piece of clothing, then gave it a quick shake. "I call them his lady friends when I want to rile him some."

"You know, Ace is plumb crazy about you."

"Yeah, I know," Dance replied, stooping to pick up the full laundry basket. "I know that for a fact."

"So how about you?" Cara dared to ask. "Are you still crazy about Ace?"

"Well, Cara—" Dance sashayed toward the clothesline—"why do ye think I've got five kids?"

Cara laughed and stirred, laughed and stirred. It did her good to get a little fun out of Dance Shelton. She noticed a nearly full box of starch sitting on a ledge rock, which served as a fine shelf, along with a box of bluing. The beef liver Ace bought in town must have done her good.

"Ma! Ma!" Jay shouted. "Can I go drown these worms?"

"I'm standing right here. You don't need to holler," Dance said as she worked. "All my kids think I'm deaf."

Jay came closer, his pole on his shoulder, his tin can full of dirt and worms.

Cara ruffled his hair. "Be careful of that lid. You don't want to cut yourself."

Jay stuck out one dirty paw, showing off a long red scratch. "I did already."

Cara took the tin. She moved the jagged top back and forth several times until it snapped off in her fingers. Obediently, Jay washed up while she poured soapy water dipped from the washtub over his hands. "Here's a riddle for you, Jaybird: Way down in the deep, a fish struggled to keep. Coughed up on the shore, he couldn't stand it no more. Who is it?"

Jay giggled. "Oh, that's too easy. It's Jonah, ain't it? I learned all about him in Sunday school."

"You're getting too smart for me."

Jay glanced at his mother, who was back at the clothesline. "Reckon you'll hide me a penny?"

"Reckon I will."

"Ma! Ma! Can I go now?"

"Yes, go on." Dance waved dismissively as she pegged clothes. "Don't be falling in. I ain't washing no more clothes today."

Cara stood and watched the boy skip off in the direction of the creek. The pole bounced on his shoulder. He whistled a nameless tune. An old, sad yearning came over her. If she had managed to carry her first pregnancy to term, she might be teaching her own son to fish.

Pauline wiggled and gurgled in the laundry at Cara's feet. She scooped the baby up and nuzzled her neck. "Roly-poly Pauline," she sang as she swung the baby high. "Who's the prettiest baby on Sweetwater? Who's the sweetest baby on the creek?"

Settling Pauline in the crook of her arm, she joined Dance at the line. "If you don't have the prettiest young'uns, Dance."

"Pretty hungry," Dance said, eyeing Pauline, who was chewing on one fist. "If you'll finish hanging these clothes, I'll go feed this one."

There was only one load of darks left, and Cara made short work of that. Scrubbed, stirred, rinsed, wrung, hung, and done. She saved a pair of Jay's britches for last and pegged them waist side up with a penny in one pocket. Hands on hips, she looked at the wash. Sunlight sparkled off the whites so brightly she had to turn her eyes away. Was there anything more satisfying than a sunny day with no threat of rain and fresh-washed clothes on the line?

She walked between the two lines just to enjoy the cool dampness and the clean scent given off from clothes drying in the sun. Some folks laced their soap with oil of sassafras or oil of caraway, but Cara much preferred the honest bouquet of lye.

Before she married and left home, Cara had spent many a pleasant hour making hard soap with her mother. Mama would save grease drippings all winter. Then come spring, they'd start the process by boiling the grease in water until it was nice and white: the whiter the grease, the finer the soap. This was a dangerous process; Cara had a nasty burn mark on her right arm to prove it.

When the clean grease was accumulated, she'd help Mama with the measuring and the dissolving of lye and rosin in water. Once this was done, they would ever so carefully add the grease and borax to the pot one small piece at a time. This they would boil for about two hours, stirring all the time until the grease was taken up. As soon as the mixture became soapy, Cara or Mama would add a tumbler of salt dissolved in warm water and continue cooking for half an hour or so. When the soap was just right, they poured it into a tub that had been soaked in cold water. The fun part was cutting the cold soap into bars, which they stored under one or another's bed, usually Cara's and her younger sisters', because that was coolest and driest place in the house. Maybe that was why she still favored the scent of lye over most any perfume. The smell reminded her of home.

By the time Cara was finished daydreaming of making soap with her mother, she had cleaned the porch floor and the outhouse to boot. Dance sat under a twisted apple tree with the baby, watching Cara work.

Finished with the scrubbing, Cara poured two cups of coffee and joined her under the branches laden with tiny green pieces of fruit. "You're going to have a bumper crop of apples this fall."

Dance's mouth worked back and forth like she had something to say.

Cara stayed quiet, wondering what it was. Pauline was lying on her belly across Dance's outstretched legs. A fat and sassy bumblebee worried over the few apple blossoms that had not turned brown. Cara sipped her coffee.

"Cara," Dance said, "I don't know why you are so good to me. It ain't like I ever do anything for you."

Cara wished she dared to reach across the wide divide Dance used to set herself apart and just hug Dance Shelton close, sister to sister. "I reckon you don't know how much it means to me to come here to your lively house. Sometimes I get so lonely-hearted I don't think I can take one more minute in my quiet place, much less one more day."

Dance set her cup aside and reached up the cuff of her sleeve. "I wouldn't tell nary a soul this but you . . ." With her pointer finger wrapped in the handkerchief, Dance dabbed the inner corner of one eye.

Cara didn't breathe; she was so afraid she'd break the spell Dance seemed to be under.

Dance took a long, shuddering sigh. "You know I love these young'uns—all of them—and most days I care for Ace. But sometimes I get a longing to flee out the door and run right over a cliff."

Cara couldn't think of one comforting thing to answer back. "Is there any little thing I can do for you?"

"You're already my washerwoman," Dance replied with a shrug. "Reckon them whites are dry?"

Cara started to rise, thankful for something to do.

But Dance's fingers gripped her arm and held her in place. "You stay," she said, handing the baby over. "I ain't used to sitting this long."

CHAPTER 19

DARCY WAS RIGHT PLEASED with herself. Her new pink blouse would be finished as soon as she set in the sleeves, and she'd only cut it out the day before. The ruffled collar was so pretty. Maybe she should try the bodice on.

The ruffles pinched under her chin, making her neck disappear. "Look at this, Mammaw," she said, turning from the mirror. "Does it look as bad as I think it does?"

"Kindly puts me in mind of a chipmunk," Mammaw replied from her rolling chair. "Makes your cheeks look nice and full."

With a sigh, Darcy began to rip out the top ruffle. It was one setback after another. She'd aimed to go by Cara's today and see if she had finished some more handles. An order for half a dozen feathered fans had come in yesterday's post. Evidently they had become ladies' necessities in Lexington. Darcy popped a stitch and worried. Would she have time to finish her outfit before Henry came again?

Once she had one offending ruffle off, she slipped into the blouse again. "Much better, don't you think?"

Mammaw cocked her head to one side, then the other. "You're pretty as a speckled pup in a red wagon. Now, why did you say you're sewing this?"

Darcy gathered her courage. It was time to tell her grandmother the full story. Turning back to the looking glass, she watched herself begin to speak. It was easier than watching her grandmother's face. "I know it's not right, but I've been hiding something from you."

Mammaw made a funny snorting sound.

"Just listen. Please." Darcy peered closely at her reflected image. One bust dart seemed a hair lower than the other, so she adjusted the blouse before she plunged ahead. "I'm in love with Henry Thomas, and we aim to wed."

There, she'd said it. She held her breath and waited for her grandmother's reply. The silence made her nervous. "We'll probably go away for a short time, Henry and me," she chattered on, unable to turn around and face the music. "He ain't of a mind to tarry. That's why I'm working so hard on this outfit. I don't want to be wed in an ordinary dress."

Slipping out of the half-finished blouse, Darcy fitted it on the dress form that sat beside the mirror. "I don't want you to worry none. Remy has promised to care for you while I'm away—or if that don't suit, I'm sure Ace will come and take you to his house." She felt desperate as a fish floundering on a line. Why didn't Mammaw say something? "And Cara—you know Cara will help out. Gracious, Mammaw, say something. It ain't like I'm leaving you for good, just a few days—a week at the most. Then you'll have me and Henry both."

An uneasy aura, like seeing buzzards circling in the distance, stopped Darcy's chatter. Slowly she turned around. Mammaw was slumped in the chair. Her face was like wax. Her good hand was fisted and drawn up under her chin.

"Help us, Lord," Darcy moaned an all-inclusive prayer as she dropped to her knees in front of the invalid chair. "Mammaw! Mammaw!" She stroked Mammaw's cheek. Was she drawing air? Was she dead?

Darcy ran to her room and fetched her tortoiseshell hand mirror, a gift from Miz Copper. Back in front of the invalid's chair, she held it under her grandmother's nose. "Please, Mammaw, don't die on me."

Darcy's hand trembled so violently she nearly dropped the mirror, but there was the sign she hoped for—Mammaw's breath visible on the surface.

She sat back on her heels and, careful as careful could be, laid the mirror aside. The mantel clock ticked loud as buckshot. The air grew dense and still. For a moment she thought she'd killed her grandmother. Laying her head on Mammaw's knee, she sobbed and sobbed. "I'm sorry. I'm so sorry."

Behind her the screen door squeaked. "What's happened here?" Remy asked. "What's wrong with Fairy Mae?"

Darcy stood on wobbling legs and mopped up streaming tears with the hem of her apron. "I don't know. I was telling her about going away—just trying to prepare her, you know, so it wouldn't come as a shock." She tripped over words so heavy with guilt she might need a wheelbarrow to carry them.

Remy dropped her crutch and shook Mammaw's shoulder. "Fairy Mae, you wake up."

Darcy watched hopefully as Mammaw's good hand relaxed and fell limply to her lap. Her eyelids fluttered open, and she smiled the sweetest smile.

"Mammaw," Darcy cried as more tears spilled down her cheeks, "you like to have scared me to death."

"Reckon she needs some honey?" Remy asked. "I used to give Hezzy honey whenever she had spells."

"She seems back to herself," Darcy replied. "You're all right now, ain't you, Mammaw?" she yelled.

"I expect she can still hear. Ain't no need to deafen her."

Darcy's short laugh was shaky with relief. "You're right, Remy. I don't know what I'm hollering about. I'll make us all some tea and put extra honey in Mammaw's."

Remy patted Fairy Mae's hand. "You're going to be fine as frog's hair now. We'll have some tea; then we'll get you down for a nap. Does that sound good?"

Mammaw didn't speak, but she nodded. The childlike smile still lit up her face.

At the stove, Darcy spooned leaves into a tea ball and hung it over the edge of a porcelain teapot. It struck her that as many times as Remy had visited this house, this was only the second time they had taken tea together. Of course most times she was leaving when Remy came. And Remy wasn't exactly easy to get to know.

Mammaw looked like a baby bird, stretching her mouth in a big O each time Remy lifted a spoon of tea from the cup.

Darcy took the opportunity to freshen Mammaw's bed. She pulled clean linens from a cupboard and tucked one sheet tightly over the mattress. Then she folded the top sheet to the bottom of the bed and slid the pillows into crisply ironed cases. As she plumped the feather pillows, she wondered if Mammaw realized how hard Darcy worked to provide such nice things for her. If it wasn't for her sewing, no telling what would happen to both of them. Since Mammaw was a widow and Darcy wasn't married, they'd be at the mercy of her brother Dimmert or Dance's husband, Ace.

At least they had relatives who would be glad to help if needed. Some women were not so lucky. When she lived with Miz Copper, they used to see the old widow Case being hauled back and forth over the road to one son's house or another. Her journey was as regular as the change of seasons. Story was Mrs. Case had four sons, which meant four daughters-in-law, none of whom were particularly fond of their husband's ancient mother. There she'd be, eighty-seven years old, sitting in a straight-backed chair in the bed of a hay wagon, clutching a tattered carpetbag in her lap. Darcy used to wonder what she kept in that bag.

Once Mammaw's bed was ready, Darcy wheeled her in for her afternoon rest. Mammaw seemed glad to be in bed. Her eyes closed as soon as her head hit the pillow. Darcy said a quick prayer of thankfulness before she joined Remy at the kitchen table.

"That old lady you lived with, were her spells like Mammaw's?" Darcy asked, scared to hear the answer.

Remy perched on the edge of her chair. She poured hot tea in her saucer before taking a loud slurp. She seemed to be studying the question. Darcy wondered if she ever talked without mulling her words over first.

"Not perzactly," Remy allowed. "Hezzy'd be gathering eggs one minute or sweeping the front porch and the next she'd be flat out on the ground. Usually she'd know beforehand. She'd say, 'I'm having a sinking spell.' I learned to fetch the honey pot then."

Darcy stirred her tea. She'd yet to take a taste. "I sure wish Miz Copper was home. She'd know what to do."

"She's good at doctoring," Remy said.

"Have you heard from her? Seems like they'd be back from visiting her father and stepmother by now."

"She got grounded by the doctor up yonder. Says she can't travel until the young'uns are borned."

"Young'uns? She's having twins?"

"Yup."

"Forevermore. I'll have to tell the folks at church. I know Miz Copper will want our prayers." Darcy brought a spoon of tea to her lips, but she couldn't swallow. Guilt backed up from her heart, nearly strangling her. "Do you reckon I shocked Mammaw so bad she had a stroke?"

Remy fixed her with a steady look. "Sticks and stones. If words could kill, we'd all be wearing oak-board overcoats."

Darcy slapped a hand over her mouth, but she was so tickled she couldn't help but laugh. Her teacup rattled in the saucer, and the spoon clattered to the floor. "Remy," she sputtered, "that's the funniest thing I ever heard."

"It's the truth though, ain't it?" Remy said before taking another long sup.

"Remy," Darcy started, then hesitated. It was hard to spit out words that should have been said many times before. "I thank you for being so kind to me and Mammaw."

"I ain't much use for anything except being good to old folks and animals," Remy replied with her usual frank stare. "I reckon it's my talent. The one the Lord gave special to me."

Darcy relaxed. It felt right to be chatting with Remy. Maybe she wasn't so different after all. "Whatever happened to that fox that used to follow you around?"

"Foxy got old and passed on like everything is prone to do. I figure I'll see her again when I pass through the pearly gates."

"That's sure a happy thought," Darcy said and drained her cup. "More tea?"

"Nope. I'll just go check on Fairy Mae; then I'm heading home."

Darcy tapped her two fingers against her lips. "I was thinking I'd like to measure you for a dress before you go. I've got some printed calico you might like."

For a moment Remy's eyes looked wary, like a barn cat's when offered a treat. "I wouldn't want nothing fancy," Remy finally said. "And it would have to hang straight down. I don't like me no bindings."

Darcy smiled. She felt as if Remy had given her a great gift. The gift of trust.

"I wouldn't even need a pattern," Darcy responded, fetching her measuring tape. "How about a pretty bonnet to match?"

<hr />

A week to the day later, Darcy stepped outside the cabin into the most melancholy of times. Twilight in lavender hues of loneliness tiptoed down the mountains and crept across the yard. When she was a girl, she and her brothers and sisters would play Mother, may I? or hide-and-seek on summer evenings. She remembered her mother sitting on the porch with her face turned away. Was she missing

Darcy's father when she sat like that, lost in sadness? Did she yearn for him like Darcy now yearned for Henry?

The gloaming of the day was different for children, she supposed. Dusk was just a signal to squeeze in a little more fun before they had to go indoors and wash their feet before bed. Somewhere from beyond the yard, a mourning dove cooed its plaintive song. Lightning bugs flew low to the ground, flashing their strange cold light, like lanterns signaling a sweetheart.

Darcy sank down on a bench placed against the wall of the porch, hugging her arms close against the chill night air, glad to have a minute to herself. Mammaw had eaten cinnamon toast and applesauce for supper. Darcy carefully cut the toast in small squares and watched as Mammaw pinched each piece between her fingers and aimed for her mouth. Same with the applesauce spoon—sometimes it landed closer to her ear. It was like watching Dance's set-along baby, Cleve, eat. Mammaw seemed to enjoy supper, though, banging her spoon against the table with a smile instead of frustration like she sometimes used to do.

The upshot of Mammaw's spell last week was that childlike manner. Nothing seemed to bother her except Remy's leave-taking. Remy came each day now, helping with one thing or another. Darcy enjoyed her company, and she thought Remy stood three inches taller when she wore her new dress and hat to church last Sunday evening. Funny what a pretty frock would do for a gal's outlook.

A salty tear ran the length of Darcy's face and settled in the corner of her mouth. She shook out a fancy handkerchief with crocheted edges and dabbed delicately at her nose. It hurt to think of Sunday—for Henry hadn't come calling as she had hoped. And yesterday, when she took a package to the post office, the cardboard sign in the office window said, Closed.

Another tear slipped down her face, and her heart ached just remembering how it felt to stand there on the sidewalk—missing him. How could you love a person as much as she loved Henry and not even know where they were on any given day?

She still couldn't believe what she'd done next, sneaking down the alley between Henry's law office and the barbershop next door. Thankfully, the street was quiet and nobody seemed to take notice. Maybe he was out back saddling his horse or some such manly thing. She was surprised to find the lot behind the office was enclosed by a high wooden fence. The fencerow was neat as a pin. Neither a weed nor an unruly blade of grass could be seen. Beyond the yard she could see a stable painted black.

Gathering her courage, she had marched right up to the stable and knocked—like she had every right to be there. She pressed her eye to a crack between the double doors and peered into its shadowy depths. "Henry?" Her voice quivered. Her burst of bravado was quickly fading.

But something stirred beyond the door. Her heartbeat quickened in anticipation. But, no, she realized, it was not Henry, just an old dog unfurling from sleep on a bed of gunnysacks. The dog yawned and stretched before he ambled over and stuck his graying muzzle through the narrow gap in the door. She slid her hand in sideways and scratched the top of his long nose. She didn't even know Henry had a dog.

"Barooo!" she heard from behind. A second dog barked and threw itself with mighty thumps against the yard gate. "Barooo!" It sounded like a hound and maybe a mean one. Soon barks and brays from all up and down the street answered the call. Half a dozen or more dogs of various breeds shot through the alleys and headed her way. With a mighty heave, she slid one of the heavy, double-hung doors open just far enough to slip through. She'd take her chances with the old dog.

Everything inside the barn was as orderly as Henry himself. His tools from saw to claw hammer were tidily arranged in order of size on a shelf. A rake, shovel, and pitchfork hung from nails against the wall. The absence of his horse told her he was gone.

She stayed in the stable for the longest time, watching dust motes dance in a beam of sunlight. Stayed until the pack of dogs wandered away—stayed even though she wasn't sure Henry would be glad to have her there. After a while, the old dog went back to sleep and the other one stopped throwing itself against the fence. Darcy crept out then, like a thief in the night, but the only thing stolen was her dignity.

Now she sat on her own porch in the twilight still unsure of Henry's intent. Was he finished with her? Why had he said he loved her anyway? And what would a man like Henry, so handsome and so sure, want in a woman like herself?

Thinking of Henry stayed her restless heart for a little while—until the dove cooed again. There was something so forlorn about the bird's call, like all the hurt in the world settled right there in that one sound. Darcy's thoughts turned inward. Would Henry ever come for her again? Would she go with him if he did?

From the road she heard the sound of a horse's hooves fast approaching. Could it be Henry? She tossed her apron toward the bench and raced barefoot across the darkening yard. The horse didn't slow, and the stranger upon its back didn't even tip his hat when he saw her standing there.

Disappointed, Darcy turned back. Once safely off the road, she scooped lightning bugs from the air. Though they were captured in her cupped hand, their flashing signals did not cease but sped up as if they sensed their time to find true love was threatened. Taking pity, Darcy uncurled her fist and watched as the tiny beetles climbed to the ends of her fingers before launching heavenward.

Darcy smiled for the first time that evening. Life for the fireflies was fleeting, lasting only a season—and love was hard to find. She would take her chance with Henry. The light of love was worth it.

CHAPTER 20

CARA'S GARDEN WAS BURSTING with life. She had been neglectful of it, busy helping Dance and also visiting with Fairy Mae since her health took a setback last week. Cara scooted a basket along the ground with her foot, dropping fistfuls of green beans into it as she went. Soon she'd have enough beans to can a dozen quarts. And there would be more tomorrow.

When she was a schoolgirl, Cara had learned about a beautiful garden, one of the Seven Wonders of the Ancient World. Her teacher, Miss Chandler, had each student in her fourth-grade class write a paper on a different wonder. Cara's piece was the Hanging Gardens of Babylon.

Cara could recall nearly every word she'd written: "There was a king in Babylon, Nebuchadnezzar, who married a mountain princess. The king had a brick terrace built four hundred feet square and seventy-five feet above the ground. He filled the garden with flowers and all manner of fruit trees. The beautiful Hanging Gardens of Babylon were watered from the Euphrates River. King Nebuchadnezzar built this wonder because he wanted his mountain princess to feel at home."

What a romantic story. She remembered her little girl self puzzling over the name Nebuchadnezzar, practicing the spelling of it over and over with chalk on slate before daring to set it down. Miss Chandler had doled out one sheet of lined paper for each student, and Cara was determined not to mess hers up.

Cara had loved her teacher. Miss Chandler was from someplace up north as foreign to Cara as Babylon. She always wore a snow-white blouse with a navy blue skirt, and her laced-up shoes never lacked for polish. She was by far Cara's favorite, though she taught only one year in the one-room schoolhouse on Troublesome Creek. Teachers didn't last long there.

Cara stopped among the pole beans. Gazing out over her little patch of ground, she wondered how things would have turned out if she had stayed in school. Miss Chandler taught so much more than reading and writing and arithmetic, simple things, really, about manners and hygiene and how to present oneself. She could still hear her teacher's voice: "*Ain't* fell in a bucket of paint," she would say whenever one of her students used that word, and, "Monkeys' words and monkeys' faces always appear in public places," when she caught one of the boys carving his initials on his desk.

Cara bent to pick up a couple of beans that had missed the basket. Fourth grade was her last year of formal schooling, but Miss Chandler's lessons stayed forever with Cara.

On her last day as their teacher, Miss Chandler had called Cara aside. "Stay in school. When you graduate, write to me. I will help you get into teacher's training."

All of Miss Chandler's words were pearls. But Mama needed Cara at home. There were babies to help raise and times were hard. Daddy saw that each of his children made it through fourth grade, though. It was a gift he gave.

"I wonder," Cara quizzed the june bug that buzzed around her ears, "would Miss Chandler be proud of me? Or would she be disappointed in how I've turned out? Just one more woman with a hoe in a garden patch. Just one more woman up a holler trying to keep her feet steady on the ground where she was planted." The bug lit on a dark green tomato leaf, the perfect camouflage. "Good choice," Cara said, deciding to let him be. "Land on the ground and the chickens will have you for dinner."

Now Cara took in her surroundings. Though it was midmorning, a cool curtain of fog still outlined the banks of Sweetwater Creek. In random places sunbeams penetrated the heavy mist, casting golden beams on a radiant cucumber blossom here, a tiny cushaw baby there.

High overhead, a mockingbird trilled a festive song, flitting from one melody to another quick as a honeybee on clover. Creek water burbled over moss-covered rock, its tune sweetly underlying the mockingbird's call. Just as sweetly, the sharp scent of wild honeysuckle tickled her nose, and she sneezed lightly into the handkerchief she kept tucked up the cuff of her sleeve.

Surely there wasn't a prettier place on God's green earth than her garden on this day. It was as if she had her own piece of Babylon right here—for a garden was a garden. And Cara's was beautiful and full of grace.

When Cara was finished with her chores, she walked the familiar path to the Sheltons'. Dance was chopping cabbage at a makeshift table under the shade of a maple tree. She wiped sweat from her forehead with the crook of her arm. Pauline napped on a pallet under the table, and beside her Cleve gnawed on the core from a cabbage. Merky sat on one end of the table with a pan of soapy water, playing at washing canning-jar lids.

"It all came on at once," Dance said, indicating a bushel basket of cabbage heads.

"Worms got most of mine. But my beans need putting up." Cara looked around the yard. "Where're the boys?"

Dance gave a small jerk of her head toward the mountain beyond the well house. "Off with their pa. He's in a twist because his springwater has dried up. Some critter tore into the plumbing most likely."

Cara sliced a head of cabbage neatly in half, then quarters. Dance worked her knife over the pieces until all was slivered, ready for making kraut. Little Cleve banged his piece of cabbage against Cara's bare ankle. Merky laughed as water splashed the front of her shift.

Dance shook her finger. "Merky Mae, stop wasting that water."

"At least she's staying cool," Cara said. "Man, it's hot today."

"It's summer," Dance replied. "Supposed to be hot."

"Well," Cara said, "that's true enough. She popped a piece of cabbage into her mouth, liking the good, solid crunch of it. "Have you heard from Fairy Mae since we all went over Sunday?"

"We went by last evening. Darcy says she ain't talking anymore." Dance's chopping was even faster. She slid her blade under a mound of cabbage and added it to a nearly full pan.

Cara sighed. "I'm sorry, Dance."

Dance let down her guard. "Mammaw was always good to me. I cain't hardly stand to see her slipping away."

"Me neither. If there is a better person than Fairy Mae Whitt, I've never met them." Cara whacked another globe of cabbage. "Do you reckon Darcy needs me to come help out for a spell? I could stay as long as needed if Ace could watch out for my garden and my chickens."

"Darcy's got that friend of Miz Copper's staying over right now. Mammaw seems to like her."

"Oh, Remy Riddle, sure. She's a good hand with old folks. She took care of Hezzy Krill, you recollect." Cara set to washing and rinsing jars before carrying them to the kettle of steaming water set over the fire. "So you think Darcy's doing okay?"

Dance shrugged dismissively. "Darcy Whitt will do fine as long as that oily Henry Thomas keeps his distance."

"She seems to be taken with him."

Dance snorted. "She's got no business. Man like him has only one thing on his mind."

A welcome breeze stirred the leaves over their heads. Cara lifted her skirts above her ankles for a moment. "I expect she's pretty lone-some sometimes."

Dance whacked her knife through a cabbage so hard the blade stuck in the tabletop. "Play with fire, set on the blister," she said, rocking the blade out.

Even though the breeze continued, it seemed like the tempera-ture shot up ten degrees there under the sugar maple. Cara could see that Darcy was a sore subject with Dance. "Can I have some lids, Miss Merky?"

"Here you go," Merky sang, fishing them one by one from the soapy water. "Here you go again."

"Just dump the water off, Cara," Dance said. "Merky, get down."

Chastised, Merky crawled under the table to play with Cleve.

Cara handed her a piece of cabbage. "You'll be nice and cool under there, little girl." She wished she'd thought to bring the doll she'd finished last evening. Finally happy with the head, she'd attached it to the body Darcy had sewed and stuffed with cotton batting, then fitted with the dearest dress and bonnet. This would have been a good time to give the gift to Merky, while the boys were off with Ace. She didn't want them to feel left out. Perhaps she should whittle a couple of whistles for them and a rattle for Cleve first.

"Cara!" Dance said. "Why are ye just standing there with your hair on your head and your teeth in your mouth? Them jars are boil-ing dry."

"Oops, sorry. I'll just slip these lids in." Cara hurried over to the kettle with the clean lids. She didn't mind Dance's sharp words. It was just her way. Also, Cara thought it a good sign that Ace had taken Jay along with him to fix the springwater contraption. Things were looking up for the Shelton household.

Cara stayed for supper, much of which she cooked. Jay caught a pullet for her and held its feet while she neatly chopped the head off and set it down. The headless hen took off, trailing blood, until it collapsed a few feet away.

"I don't hardly like seeing them run that way," Jay said.

She studied the boy while she rinsed the hatchet. Her brothers had always laughed when watching a freshly slaughtered chicken's last movements. And the yellow, clawed feet were toys for them. You could pull on a tendon and make them open and close. Jay was different—compassionate, probably because he'd had so much responsibility at a very young age.

"Now, Jay, that chicken's not suffering. Once you cut off the head, it can't feel pain. That's just a reflex."

"You know that story in the Bible where the pigs run over a cliff? That's what it puts me in mind of. Maybe that chicken's demon possessed."

Cara had no reply. Sometimes Jay was too quick for her. "Why don't you ask your daddy about that?"

She retrieved the pullet, dunked it in scalding water to loosen the feathers, plucked it, and singed the pinfeathers off before gutting it and cutting it up for the skillet. When she was finished, she had twelve pieces plus the liver. "Do you want to do the gizzard, Jay?"

"I reckon," he said, taking it and washing out the grit. "I don't mind any part of killing chickens once I know the thing's really dead."

Cara smiled at the brave little boy. "How about the eating part? I cut the pulley bone out just for you."

"Thanks, Aunt Cara." Jay added the clean gizzard to the pan. "How'd you know that's my favorite?"

Ace had just finished saying grace over fried chicken, cream gravy, biscuits hot from the oven, cabbage slaw, new potatoes with pearl onions, and cold sweet tea when they heard a "Hello, anybody to home?" from the yard.

Cara stood so quickly her chair nearly tipped over. "That sounds like Big Boy Randall. He must be back from his visit with Dimm."

Ace, Jay, and Wilton headed for the door. Ace pushed it open. "Come on in here, Big Boy. Dance will fix you a plate."

Dance had one baby on her lap and another hanging off her leg.

"Don't get up," Cara told her. "Big Boy can have my place." She left her chair and took a seat on the bench with the children.

Soon Big Boy was polishing off his second helping. He'd talked a little but not much, for he was too busy eating. Cara steered her heart toward patience. She'd waited this long; she could wait a little longer.

"I'm finished," Jay said. "Can I go see Pancake?"

"Me too," Wilton chimed.

"Go on," Ace allowed. "But stay away from his backside. Mules got a powerful kick."

Cara picked little Cleve up off the floor. She mashed a potato with gravy and fed him small bites.

Big Boy patted his stomach. "My, my, my. I was so hungry my belly was eating my backbone."

Ace and Cara exchanged glances.

"Is there something you're holding back from us about Dimm?" Ace asked.

Fear made Cara's whole body tingle. She was thinking the same thing but couldn't voice it. "Something has happened. I know it." Clutching Cleve, she stood and began to pace the kitchen. Cleve waved his spoon, and gravy slopped down the front of Cara's dress.

"Now, missus, it ain't as bad as you'd first think," Big Boy said. A toothpick bobbed in the side of his mouth. "Dimmert's been through a rough patch, but things are looking up."

Cara felt suddenly weak.

Dance handed the baby to Ace and took Cleve. "Cara, you sit down." She poured Cara another glass of tea. "Tell it like it is," she said to Big Boy. "It cain't be worse than what she's conjuring in her mind."

CHAPTER 21

HENRY GREW MORE SUSPICIOUS each day. Someone was minding his business, and he couldn't figure out who. He'd spent Wednesday in the Perry County Courthouse looking through record books to see if Ace had been charged with a crime over there. He got in late, tired and frustrated, only to find evidence that somebody had been snooping around in the stable. From the size of the muddled shoe prints he studied, it looked like a big kid or a woman.

It made no sense, but he'd started leaving Daisy in the stable whenever he went out. Obviously Lester wasn't much of a watchdog—not to mention he'd not been much help in training Daisy to hunt. Not that she needed it. That dog was sharp. Daisy had outshone herself the last time he took her coon hunting with some local men and their hounds.

Henry laid his tools neatly on the workbench. He'd spent the early morning changing the lock on both his office door and the one to the back room. When you had a lot to lose—and he did—it paid to be extra careful. Lester circled his bed and plopped down. He didn't want to do anything but sleep.

Henry pulled his watch fob from his pocket and flipped the watchcase open. Time to get back to business. Sam Follett needed help settling a property line dispute, and Henry was meeting him shortly.

Sam's neighbor had stirred up a ruckus, saying Sam had not surveyed the property correctly. The neighbor claimed a stand of black walnut trees belonged to him. While scouting the land in question, Henry discovered the crumbling rock foundation of an old cabin. Sam said his great-grandparents set up housekeeping there many years ago.

Leaving the door open a crack, he entered the office and took his seat behind the desk. He rarely met clients at the door. It was best that they saw him as a person with authority early on. As he rubbed his chin with his palm, he realized he hadn't shaved this morning. What was happening to him? His mind was so stirred up over everything he couldn't keep life straight anymore.

Dipping a pen in the inkwell that sat ever ready on his desk, he started a list.

1. *Why were charges dropped against Ace Shelton after killing of man at still?*
2. *Check newspaper accounts from the time.*
3. *If need arises, call in a favor from the sheriff in Perry. . . .*

His mind wandered. The bell over the door dinged. Henry loved that ding; it sounded like money. Sam Follett walked in. As Henry slid the list into the desk drawer, he noticed number four read: *Darcy Mae Whitt.* Foolish as a schoolboy, he'd put exclamations after her name. He was losing it.

Sam Follett's case was much easier than Henry had expected. The man held no grudges and was more than willing to let his neighbor encroach a bit on his property line if it helped settle the affair.

Henry was astounded. Property was property, and as far as he was concerned, every inch was important. "You don't have to give up any of your holdings to this fellow. We can prove what's yours. We'll take it to court if necessary."

"I'd thought to take a sled over there and haul Grandpa's rocks over to my place. The rest I don't care so much about."

"I believe you should fight for what's yours. I'm more than will-ing to help you."

Sam was elderly, and when he stood to leave, Henry could hear the creak of his bones. "Love your neighbor as yourself," Sam said. "I reckon I'll be leaving this old earth shortly, and I don't want a jot nor a tittle against me in the Lamb's Book of Life."

Henry reached across the desk to shake Sam's weathered hand. The man might be old, but he held on with a death grip. His watery blue eyes pierced Henry's own. "What about you, son? What's writ on your page?"

Henry was taken aback. Nobody had ever questioned the state of his soul before. "It's probably not pretty—my page."

Sam leaned in a little farther. "It ain't too late. Do ye read your Bible?"

"I can't say as I do." Henry couldn't believe what he was revealing to this old gentleman. He had always been careful to keep himself in check—at least until Darcy came along, he'd never shown his feel-ings to anyone. Not since he was a young child.

With a final squeeze hard enough to bruise, Mr. Follett released his hold. "Prodigal Son," he said, like it was some special phrase just for Henry. "The Lord loves the Prodigal Son as much as any other. All ye need do is repent and God will welcome you back into the kingdom. The other steps will surely follow." He reached in his pocket and took out a jingle of silver dollars, which he stacked on Henry's desk. "I thank ye for your time," he said, his eyes never leav-ing Henry's.

Henry gathered the silver and handed it back. "No charge."

The bell rang again as Mr. Follett left, but this time it sounded like a warning in Henry's ears. Turning to the bookcase behind his desk, Henry crouched to see the bottom shelf. Somewhere, he vaguely remembered, was the Bible he had received when he graduated from law school. There, at the very end wedged against volume XYZ of a leather-covered law tome, was the Bible, Testaments Old and New.

Henry eased it out and laid it on his desk. Then he retrieved his list. With pen in hand Henry added:

5. *Prodigal Son.*

Henry arched his back. He'd been hunched over his desk most of the afternoon, meticulously drawing up a new deed for Mr. Follett. Ridiculous, if you asked him, giving way to someone else just to avoid an argument. Why, people had shot each other for less. Henry tapped the cap of the ink pen against his lower lip. Every time he tried to work up a good head of steam, Mr. Follett's eyes pierced his consciousness. His insides had been uneasy ever since the old fellow left his office.

Picking up the Bible, he turned it over and over but didn't crack it open. What could be between its covers that held any import for him? Prodigal Son—yeah, right. Henry Thomas had been son to no one since his grandfather died. And he'd done right well by himself.

Henry walked to the back room door and tried the new lock and key. Perfect, much sturdier. Going to the safe, he let the heavy door swing open. Gold and silver and paper money in stacks didn't give him the usual delight. Handing back Mr. Follett's silver had given him more pleasure. Henry rubbed his forehead hard. He was losing his edge.

Daisy came to stand beside him. Her long nose sniffed the strange contents of the safe. Henry closed and locked the door. "You don't need be nosing around in there. Let's go check on Lester; then I'll get you both some supper."

Daisy loped around back and through the open stable door. Henry followed, checking the fence for loose planks. Lester usually took his afternoon nap in the front yard, right under the office window. But Henry hadn't noticed him there today. He'd been busy, though.

In the shadow of the stable door, Daisy shook and whimpered.

"What now?" Henry said, taking in the dog's drooped ears and tucked tail. "Daisy, come." But she didn't answer his command, a first.

It was Lester, of course. Henry should have known something was wrong when the old dog didn't follow his usual course. On days when Henry worked at home, he let the dogs roam as much as they liked. Daisy always chose to be at Henry's side, but Lester's big adventure was to move from the backyard under the lilac bush to the front yard, snug up under the window. He never did anything but sleep and eat—but he was a master at both.

It hadn't been long, Henry figured, for the body was still warm. "I'm sorry, old buddy," he said, stroking the dog's bony back. He should have spent more time with Lester while there was time to be had. Most of his attention went to Daisy because she was the demanding one, the one who seemed to need him. While Lester . . . well, Lester kept his spot warm and his bowl licked clean.

Half an hour later Henry reined in his horse. He dismounted and lifted Lester down. The body was surprisingly heavy. The shovel struck rock as soon as he started digging, but Henry was determined to bury Lester right there a few feet from the worst roots of a giant water maple. Thankfully, he'd thought to bring an ax and a sledge-hammer along with the shovel.

It took longer to dig the grave, what with chopping roots and breaking rock, than it did to ride to the site. But Henry recollected one glorious night when the moon was full and Lester was still the best dog in the county for tracking and treeing. He belonged to Orban Hanson at the time. Orban was rightfully proud of Lester. That one night, Henry remembered, they all followed Lester's rich, deep bray to this same tree. When Orban flashed his lantern light upward, a dozen pairs of masked eyes looked down at Lester.

Yes, this was the spot all right. Henry figured Lester would have picked it if he could. With Lester's body in his arms, Henry stood looking down into the open grave. He couldn't bring himself to dump the body in. The grave looked so raw, so unwelcoming. "I'll fix this," he said as if Lester cared.

Back on the horse, he rode to a meadow full of ryegrass and wildflowers he had passed on the way. Once he had a good armload, he went back and lined the grave and eased the old bones down. Lester looked content lying there among nature's bounty.

Dirt fell soft as a blanket from Henry's shovel. He took his time. When satisfied, he packed and smoothed the mound. Finally finished, he covered the grave with the heaviest stone he could fine. Taking out his pocketknife, he scratched *RIP Lester, King of the Coon Dogs* on the surface of the rock.

Henry hunched down and chewed on the end of a piece of ryegrass, pondering how a body could be full of life one moment and dead the next. What was the point if all your life became worth no more than a mound of dirt and a heavy rock? A black cloud of hopelessness settled over him.

Suddenly, like the flash of Orban Hanson's lantern, Mr. Sam Follett's blue eyes pierced the darkness. "Repent!" Henry fancied he heard. "Repent."

Startled, Henry fell backward. Flat on the ground, he grappled for the shovel and flailed blindly at the old man's image. The shovel slashed the air impotently until Henry let it fall. He didn't try to rise but lay unmoving with his arms outstretched and his feet resting on the newly dug grave. Tears trickled from the corners of his eyes and pooled in the hollow of his ears.

A trio of heavy sobs escaped his lips before he got hold of himself and turned to crouch on hands and knees. It took all his strength to stand, gather his tools, and heave himself into the saddle.

Well before he reached the edge of town, he managed to discount the strange happening by the side of Lester's grave. This was no time to turn maudlin. The certitude of avenging his grandfather's memory was close at hand. Henry determined to let nothing get in his way.

Daisy was waiting when he got home. He had picked up supper from the boardinghouse: two steaks, Daisy's rare and his well-done. Her enthusiasm restored him somewhat as he cleared his desktop and spread his meal. He left the Bible on the far corner of the desk, afraid if he touched it the strange piercing light would come back. Henry had had as much of that as he could deal with in one day.

CHAPTER 22

CARA HIT THE FLOOR with a thunk. She felt her head bounce like a ball thrown against the side of a barn. The room spun like a merry-go-round. She thought she might lose her supper.

"Cara!" she heard Dance say just before something cold and wet hit her.

Little Merky patted her face while Dance wiped it with a rag. "Here, sit up," Dance said.

Cara closed her eyes, willing herself to ride the spinning room to unconsciousness. *Lord,* she prayed, *don't let Big Boy's words be true. You know I can't take it if Dimm doesn't come back.*

"Now, little lady," Big Boy said as he lifted her off the floor and set her in a chair, "Dimmert is going to be fine. Fine, you hear?"

"My word, Mr. Big Boy," Dance fussed, flapping the skirt of her apron like a fan in Cara's direction, "ye scared her near to death."

Cara held the cold tea glass to one cheek, then the other. "Goodness," she said, straightening the skirt of her dress, embarrassed to tears, "I'm sorry to be such a bother."

"For pity's sake," Dance said, "you men give her some air."

Ace and Big Boy stepped back from the table.

Cara took a deep, steadying breath. "Tell me true. I have to know."

"Well, to make a long story short: There was a ruckus in the prison stable and Dimm—"

Cara could feel the blood drain from her face again. "Just tell me he's all right, please."

"Now," Big Boy said, "would I tell you different if it wasn't gospel true?"

"No, you wouldn't."

Chairs rattled as the men sat down. Tea splashed as Dance refilled glasses. Merky climbed onto Cara's lap, like she was settling in for a story. Ace jiggled Cleve on his knee, and Dance rocked Pauline in her arms. Wilton followed Jay back in and sat at his mother's feet. Jay leaned against Cara's arm.

"Like I said," Big Boy started after a long draught of tea, "Dimmert had a spell of trouble. There was a—"

"Start at the beginning," Cara interrupted.

"I got there to the prison early in the morning," Big Boy said. "Fog off the river was so thick I had to take out my pocketknife and cut me and Pancake a door to go through."

Jay gasped. His little arm thrummed with excitement against Cara's own. She was glad for Big Boy's slow yarn-telling ways. She needed time to get ready for the end of the story.

"First thing I seen was several big fellers with big guns standing in little open huts high up on the walls of the prison. All the guns were pointed our way and us with no handy protection save that pocket-knife. Pancake didn't like it the least bit. He slicked his ears and took to walking backward. He wanted to be shut of that place. Clear as day, I could hear every one of them guns being cocked. 'State your business,' one of the men hollered.

"I hollered back, 'Don't shoot. Me and Pancake here has come to visit Dimmert Whitt.' I held the lard bucket high so they could see it. 'I've brought victuals from his wife.'

"'Approach the gate,' we was told, but you know Pancake—once he started backing up, he wasn't about to change his mind.

"I gave him a little poke in the side. 'You're going to get us shot.' I want to tell you I nearly swallowed my chaw when Pancake refused to put on the brakes. I was pulling one way—him the tuther. But before you could whistle Dixie, there was a dozen armed guards heading our way, and none of them looking for a social visit.

"'Set down that bucket,' one of them fellers said.

"And I says, under my breath to Pancake, 'This here's the time for a smiling mule, if there ever was one.'

"Well, the fog had thinned a right smart—"

"Did you cut it all to tatters with that knife of yours?" Jay interrupted.

"Hush up, Jay," Dance said.

"That's all right, boy." Big Boy reached in his overall's pocket. "Do you want to hold the knife while I finish?"

Jay knelt on the floor, unfolding and folding the knife's many blades. Wilton sidled up beside him.

Ace handed Jay a boiled potato to practice on. "Keep your fingers free of the sharp edge," he instructed.

"Now where was I?" Big Boy asked.

"Pancake was a-smiling," Wilton said.

"That's right; he was. And do you fellers want to know why?"

"Yes, yes," Jay and Wilton sang as Cara's voice caught in her throat because she knew the only reason Pancake ever smiled.

"As the sun popped up over the high prison wall," Big Boy continued, "the gates flew open and a short round man dressed like a preacher on Sunday came high-stepping out. 'Here, you men,' he hollered. 'Wait now.' Well, I aim to tell you the barrels of those guns dropped like dead ducks."

Big Boy's hands relayed the story as colorfully as did he. First they pictured a belly round as a keg, then gun barrels falling and finally flailing wings. Cara didn't hurry him along.

"Now, here's the best part. Pancake's grin split ear to ear and I just let him go. The prison guards parted like Pancake was Moses at the

Red Sea, for behind the man I took to be the warden came Dimmert Whitt himself. I could see he was limping bad, but he was on his own two feet."

"Oh," Cara said, "I wish I could have been there."

"Me too," Jay said.

"Me three," Wilton said.

"If you boys don't stop cutting in, you're going to the porch," Dance said.

"It was a welcome sight," Big Boy said. "It was certain to my eyes that Dimmert Whitt was well thought of by all. Soon as I was sure nobody was going to fill my hide full of buckshot, I handed Dimm your lard bucket, Cara."

"Was he hungry? Did they let him eat?" Cara asked.

"Well, now, you know Dimm. Soon as he pried the lid off, he started passing out chicken and biscuits. Next thing you know we're the same as having a picnic right outside the prison gates." Big Boy laughed and slapped his thigh. "Don't that beat all?"

Cara laughed along with everyone else. It was so Dimm. "Thank you, Big Boy. It's almost like I was there. Now tell us the hard part. How did Dimm get hurt? Why was he limping?"

Suddenly Big Boy got serious. "It is a strange and miraculous story. Dimm has been making wagon wheels and also caring for the horses and mules in the prison stables. The guards learned right quick that Dimm is a natural with animals. It seems that selfsame warden I done told you about has a little daughter about your age, Jay. The warden, Mr. Matthew, keeps a gentle pony stabled there at the prison for her. The warden's family lives on the prison grounds in a fine brick house. Women prisoners keep the house, do the laundry, and mind the Matthews' children. Prisoners too old to be a threat tend the yards and garden."

Jay pulled Big Boy's sleeve. "What's her name?"

"The warden's daughter?" Big Boy asked.

Jay nodded.

"Delphinia."

"That's real pretty," Jay said.

"I never saw the girl," Big Boy said, "but can't you picture big blue eyes and long yellow hair to go with a name like Delphinia? Anyway, the girl was watched over real close, being as she the same as lived with thieves and scoundrels. That's why it was such a shock when one day a prisoner assigned to the stable comes flying out the door into the prison yard yelling for help. Soon the stable was full of guards and prisoners all witnessing a frightful scene. There was little Delphinia backed into the corner of a stall by a powerful stallion. Each time a man tried to get in there with them, the horse reared and struck out with hooves sharp as ax blades.

"'Get back. You men get back,' a guard shouted as Mr. Matthew made his way to the scene only to find his sweet Delphinia about to be trampled to death. Of course, Mr. Matthew plunged right in and was flung backward by the horse's well-positioned kick.

"They say he collapsed like a sack of flour. 'Go get Whitt,' Mr. Matthew wheezed from his position on the ground.

"In no time, there was Dimm still carrying the wagon wheel he'd been working on. Dimm sized up the situation and turned to where Mr. Matthew slumped, supported by two guards. 'Get everybody out,' Dimm said.

"With an effort Mr. Matthew stood alone. 'Do as Whitt says. Leave us alone.'

"'With respect, sir,' Dimm said, 'I mean everybody.'

"The guard who told me this story—you didn't think Dimm would be a-bragging over it, did you?—said the warden's face got red as fire, but he followed the rest out. Of course they hung right outside the doors watching Dimm's every move and listening to his every word.

"The guard said it was the strangest thing he ever seen. Dimm didn't even hesitate when he opened the stall door, but he went in with his hands in his pockets like it was just an ordinary day and he was kind of singing." Big Boy paused and shook his head. "Even I can't picture that—old closemouthed Dimmert Whitt a-singing.

"The guard told me it was so quiet there on the grounds that it didn't seem natural. Nobody even dared to breathe. Next thing you know, there came Dimm out of the stall with Delphinia in his arms and a barn cat in hers. And there was that mighty stallion meek as a kitten following along behind."

"What a story," Ace said. "What a witness."

"Ain't it just?" Big Boy said, finishing off his tea.

Cara took a deep breath. Finally she could breathe again. "But, Big Boy, how did Dimm get hurt?"

Big Boy busted out laughing. He laughed until he wheezed. "I'm sorry. This ain't one bit funny, but it's so like Dimm." He mopped his face with his napkin rag. "After it was over and Dimm was going back in the stable, he stepped on a pitchfork. The handle caught him right between the eyes, and a tine pierced the bottom of his work shoe."

Big Boy is right, Cara thought. *This is not one bit funny.*

"I'm sorry, missus. Really I am," Big Boy said, catching her eye. "But it's another miracle that Dimm didn't either get lockjaw from the nasty pitchfork or brain himself one. He was still limping when I left, but he's just as smart as he ever was."

Well, that set everyone except Cara laughing right along with Big Boy. But soon she was smiling too. The story could have been so much worse, and to think her Dimm had saved the life of a child.

"I thank you, Big Boy. I reckon Dimmert did us all proud." Standing, Cara began scraping plates. As soon as the dishes were done, she aimed to head for home. She couldn't wait to get alone with her thoughts of Dimm.

"You go on now," Dance said as if she read Cara's mind. "I'll get these dishes."

Big Boy pushed back from the table. "I'll walk you home, missus. I expect Pancake will be right glad to get there."

"Can I go with you, Aunt Cara?" Jay begged. "Can I ride Pancake to your house?"

Cara couldn't resist his freckled face and pleading eyes. "You'll have to ask your daddy."

"Oh, Daddy," Jay said, "leave me go too."

"What do you think, Mother?" Ace asked.

"I ain't your mother, Ace," Dance replied, "but sure Jay can go. Wilton, don't even start!"

"Hey, Willy-boy," Ace interjected, "what say you and me go check out the plumbing for the springwater? I never did finish that job."

Cara was glad for Jay's presence when they got to the house. It kept her from tearing open the envelope as soon as Big Boy handed it to her. "I thought you'd want to read this privatelike," he said. Having Jay there on the porch with them also kept her from throwing both arms around Big Boy's neck and kissing his cheek. The man had brought her such happiness.

"Listen," he said, "I don't want to get your hopes up, but there's talk of a pardon for Dimm."

"Pardon? What's that mean?"

"It's like forgiving a sin—like being washed white as snow. Cara, a pardon would set Dimm free. He wouldn't even have a record."

"You mean he could come home? Just like that?"

"Just like that," Big Boy said. "It was no small thing Dimmert did. The warden is thankful his daughter was not trampled by that horse. There's to be an inquiry."

"Like a meeting? About Dimm?"

"Exactly," he said.

Cara had to catch her breath. Could it be? Were her longing

prayers for Dimm's return about to be answered? *Lord,* she prayed a simple prayer, *I thank You for the possibility.*

After Big Boy left, Jay found the dolly Cara had made for Merky along with the whistles and spinning tops she'd carved for him and Wilton. "She looks like Pauline," he said of the doll. "You're sure a good woodcutter."

"You were pretty good yourself with Mr. Big Boy's knife and that potato."

Jay's chest swelled with little boy pride. "Could you tell it was a horse I whittled from that tater?"

"I could tell. I got a quick look before Wilton ate it." Cara fiddled with the letter in her apron pocket. She couldn't wait much longer to read it.

"Where'd Mr. Big Boy go?"

"His brother Shacklett Randall lives up Crook-Neck Holler, and Big Boy has gone to visit. It was sure good of him to bring us news of your uncle Dimmert, wasn't it?"

Jay twirled a wooden play-pretty and sent it spinning across the porch floor. "Yeah, and he brought old Pancake home too. That was real good." With an agile hop he caught the top just before it went over the side. "Man, I can't wait for Wilton to see these tops." Taking a whistle from his pocket, he gave a mighty blow. "Ma ain't gonna like these whistles much, though."

Cara laughed. "Maybe you'd better play with them here."

"Good idea. I'm gonna go check on Pancake," he said, the man of the house. "You need anything before I go?"

"No. Thank you for asking, though." Cara settled into the rocking chair. "Why don't you get a biscuit from the kitchen to take to Pancake?"

The screen door squeaked open. Jay was in and out before it closed. He was almost to the barn before she had Dimmert's letter out. She wondered not for the first time if boys ever walked.

Her eyes blurred for a moment to see Dimm's words on paper—another thing to thank Big Boy for.

Cara-mine,

I hope this don't embarrass you, me giving my feelings to Big Boy for him to put down and carry to you, sweetheart.

It was sure good to see Pancake. Except for the missing you part, it ain't so bad here. I make wagon wheels and long-sided wooden slats for wagon beds. I am fat and healthy. We eat twice a day and have meat once, usually fatback in beans. But it ain't like your cooking. I hope you are well and taking good care.

I thank you for the little heart. Mine beats ever for you.

Your loyal husband,
Dimmert Whitt

(Hereby set down by Big Boy Randall, July 1, 1893)

Cara blotted a teary streak from the single page of stationery. She was overwhelmed to find her husband captured there on the written page. Dimm could just as well be sitting here beside her the words rang so true. Holding the page to her nose, she breathed in the hope of the scent of her husband.

What will Dimm think of me now? He left a girl afraid of so many things, really just afraid to live for fear of death. I'm so much stronger now. What if he misses that scaredy girl? A southwest wind ruffled the leaves in the ash trees that shadowed the yard. They flipped on their spindly stems, showing their silvery undersides. She welcomed the breeze. It would be raining by morning.

Neatly she folded the letter, being careful to keep the same creases, and slipped it back in the envelope. She would put it in her Bible before she went to bed. It was amazing to think she could get it out anytime and reread Dimmert's thoughts. Maybe she'd go ahead in the house and get the Bible. She could read a little bit before the light failed. Jay would enjoy hearing about the spider spinning in palaces and about the rock rabbits.

And when Dimm came home—her heart leaped and raced at the thought—she would read the Bible to him every night. It would be her gift.

CHAPTER 23

SUNDAY MORNING DAWNED with the promise of a scorcher. It rained during the night, leaving an overcast but muggy footprint on the day. Henry opened the back door into the fenced yard and let Daisy out. Like a puppy full of play, she fetched a length of knotted rope and begged a game of tug. A mug of strong black coffee sloshed in his hand as he sat on the wooden stoop and halfheartedly yanked on the free end of the dog's toy.

Daisy would have none of it. With a teasing growl, she flung the rope into Henry's lap, then stood back hopefully. Giving in, Henry sat the mug aside and threw the rope across the yard. Daisy ran half-speed, pounced, and shook the knotted rope between her teeth. If it had been a rabbit, Henry thought, she would have snapped its neck.

"Good girl," he said when she dropped the toy at his feet. The game repeated until Daisy couldn't hold his interest anymore. He had been in a black funk ever since he buried Lester.

Scrubbing his eyes with his knuckles, Henry let out a weary sigh. Last night he'd tossed and turned through a tormented series of nightmares all featuring his own rapid slide into ruin. Toward morning, he'd dreamed a herd of snorting hogs tore into his safe, gorging on gold and silver coins, trampling stacks of paper money under their cloven hooves. From the corner of the room, where the wall met the ceiling, Mr. Sam Follett's singularly brilliant eyes cast a searchlight over the rampaging swine. Suspended under those soul-bearing eyes was a ledger book made from gold with *The Lamb's Book of Life* scribed in emeralds and sapphires and rubies. The gilt-edged pages turned slowly by an unseen hand.

"Where were you last night when I needed you?" he asked Daisy.

With one paw on his knee and one on the step, the dog stared him down with her liquid brown eyes.

"What do you know about the Lamb's Book of Life?" he asked. Then it dawned on him. It was that parable about the Prodigal Son. That was where the nightmare came from. Of course, it made perfect sense. It had taken him half an hour last evening to find the passage in Luke about the rich man's lost son. Personally, Henry identified with the other son, the one who was never appreciated.

Daisy went for the coffee cup he'd set aside. Henry let her have it. Her long tongue lapped the rich brew hopefully. With a puzzled look, she stopped and snorted. Backing away, she barked at the cup like it had offended her in some way.

Henry laughed. With understanding, his bad dream began to fade. It was no more than a ghost story told to a child who then discovers goblins under his bed. He stood and stretched, kneading the small of his back with his fists. He was master of his own fate. That was all he needed to know. True, he had not been able to find anyone he could bribe to turn against Ace Shelton, but there were more ways than one to choke a cat.

Actually Henry was surprised to find out how well thought of Ace Shelton was. Seemed everyone knew him personally. He'd presided at this one's granddaddy's funeral and baptized that one's errant son, never charging a red cent. People acted like Ace's head was strung with gold. What a load of manure.

Henry wondered what Ace got out of it—traipsing up and down the hollers in his two-dollar suit, spreading cheer among the home folk. While Henry, who had actually done something with his life, was treated little warmer than a tax collector.

The sun beat down on his bare head. He poured the cold coffee over the side of the stoop. It must be nine o'clock, for the church bell was clanging—calling the sheep to Sunday service, calling the prodigals home. The secret, Henry surmised, was to make your own home, stock your own shelves, bank your own money. You'd never be a lost son if you drew your own map.

"Daisy," he said, "what say we take a trip up to the Sheltons' while Ace and his brood are busy at church? I want to look over that piece of property."

That's the ticket. Stay busy; make plans. He'd get the tomahawk from the glass-topped case and take it along. He'd been meaning to have a practice session for the longest time. Whistling, Henry went to saddle up. He felt better already.

⚘

The sun had begun its slow descent from straight up before Henry got to Ace's place. His horse had thrown a shoe. The farrier, along with everyone else it seemed, was at church, so Henry had to fix it himself. But he was not concerned. Odds were against Ace coming here today. He was probably at old lady Whitt's, filling his plate with fried chicken. Henry took a piece of beef jerky from his saddlebag. After slicing a piece for Daisy, he found a seat and had a bite himself. It should be easy enough to find a spring and refill his canteen.

The place Henry chose for his repast was about halfway between the boundaries of the Sheltons' land. Mixed hardwood stands of maple, beech, black walnut, and oak marched tall and proud as royalty up the mountain. The ground was spongy with moss, and great masses of maidenhair fern trembled in the breeze. Their waving fronds whispered against each other like girls telling secrets. Henry was thrilled with the place. He'd stepped off a goodly portion of the acreage and each step was golden. The forest alone was worth a fortune.

Following the sound of water, he was dumbfounded to find a strange setup of wooden barrels and pipes. It appeared Ace had rigged a plumbing system to run springwater down the mountain. The very sight of it irked Henry. "Stupid do-gooder. Ignorant hillbilly."

Retrieving the ceremonial tomahawk from his saddlebag, Henry smacked the hilt of it against his palm several times before winding up and letting fly. The weapon sailed through the air, its eagle feather adornment fluttering, seeking and finding the target with a hearty, wood-splitting thunk. Henry worked the tomahawk free of the elevated keg, watching with satisfaction as water sprayed out. He didn't stop his assault until the cask leaked like a sieve.

With the last throw, the ax sank into the wood so tightly Henry had to prop his foot on the keg and work the blade out.

"What are you doing there, Henry?"

With his hand still on the weapon's handle, Henry looked over his shoulder. Ace Shelton stood there big as day, a look of surprise on his face.

"Hey, Ace. I was just doing a little target practice. This isn't your place, is it?" Henry's words backed up like a crawdad trying to cover his tracks.

"Who else's might it be?" Ace's voice cracked with anger.

"Well, I don't know." Henry turned on the charm. "I was just out for a ride, exercising my dog here." Daisy stood in front of Henry, a low and menacing growl rumbling from her throat.

Ace stood with his hands on his hips. "So you take Sunday rides going around destroying other people's property for fun?"

With a crack of thunder, the day darkened. Clouds that had been merely streaks of gunpowder gray joined forces, obscuring the sun. What light there was turned a threatening greenish black. The air was charged with danger so thick you could almost taste it.

Henry jerked the hatchet free, letting it hang without threat at his side. He tried a smile. "Truly, I thought this thing was dry."

Ace didn't say a word, just looked at the springwater jetting out against the backs of Henry's knees.

Tree limbs whipped over their heads, and the first drops of rain dampened the ground. Henry turned toward his horse, dismissing Ace. "There's nothing that can't be replaced. I'm more than happy to pay for any damage I might have caused."

"I don't want your money, mister. I want you to fix what you busted."

"Sure thing. Another day, though." Henry wheedled like he was dealing with a recalcitrant child. "You'd better go on home. It's fixing to come a gully washer."

Ace strode toward Henry, not stopping until he was in Henry's face.

Despite himself, Henry took a step backward.

"Oh, I'm going," Ace said. "I'm going straight to the sheriff's office." He raised his hand and jabbed Henry in the chest with his index finger, each poke delineating each word. "You. Henry. Thomas. Stay. Off. My. Land." Ace was breathing heavy as he continued to threaten Henry. "Don't think for a minute I don't know what you're up to." With that, Ace turned his back and began to walk off. "And stay away from my sister-in-law," he threw over his shoulder. "She's too good for the likes of you."

Henry's emotions swirled like the gathering storm clouds overhead. Ace's angry wounding words took him right back to the little boy he'd been, clutching his mother's skirts while she begged credit at the local store. *Not good enough*—words sharp and jagged as broken glass slashed Henry's fragile ego. *Not good enough.*

The tomahawk in Henry's hand seemed to take on a life of its own. Just as the weapon had zeroed in on the wooden keg, it now sought the back of Ace's head. As soon as the hatchet left his hand, Henry wished to call it back. "Ace," he yelled in a warning already much too late and "Please, God, no," the first prayer he'd ever uttered.

Ace fell hard, facedown.

Henry stood staring, disbelieving what he had done. A gorge hot as acid rose in his throat, and he trembled violently. He shook so bad he could barely walk as he followed Daisy's lead to Ace.

The dog whimpered, tucked her tail, and turned pleading eyes on Henry.

Henry sank to his knees. As if observing from far away, he saw his hand go out and pluck the tomahawk from Ace's head. Before the blood flowed, Henry could see the stark white edges of Ace's skull plate and the bulge of Ace's brain. With the tips of two fingers, he felt for a pulse at Ace's neck. Nothing! Without a doubt, Ace was dead. No one could survive such an assault. He had killed a man!

"I can't leave him out in the open like this," Henry said, his chest heaving in panic. Maybe he could find something to cover him with. He grabbed Ace by the feet and began to pull him toward the spring. Once he had to stop, he was so sick. "Why'd you have to come up here, Ace?" he pleaded as he dragged. "Why'd you make me do this?" Stinging rain lashed his face, then turned to hail, pinging off the ground and off his back, hard as glass marbles. He cast about for a sanctuary for Ace.

The spring originated from under a cliff, which Ace, Henry surmised, had lined with rock. Now, grunting with effort, Henry positioned Ace's body there out of easy sight. Next, filled with impotent rage and wild with desire to cover up his crime, he flung the barrels and reeds of Ace's gravity flow system over the side of the mountain.

Cursing his bad fortune, Henry followed the plumbing down the mountain as far as he dared, jerking pegs out of the ground and shoving pipe down sinkholes. Back up the mountain, his fury replaced by anguish and fear, he retrieved the tomahawk and wiped the blade on the wet grass. The rain would take care of the blood.

"Come, Daisy," he called, mounting the horse. He had to get to town and decide his next move. There wasn't a chance in ten anybody would trace him back to Ace, but still he'd need to set up an alibi—maybe get out of town for a while.

His mind churned with plans that he discarded one after another. His mind and body were superalert as if he were a warrior in battle. And in a way he was. He was in a war to save himself.

The rain stopped as he neared town. Mud puddles steamed in the heat. Tree branches and sheared leaves littered the trail. He pulled off the road and dismounted near a creek to remove his shirt and examine his pants, looking for traces of blood. The driving rain had rinsed him clean. Still, he stooped at the creek's edge and splashed handfuls of water over his face and hair. Catching hold of Daisy's collar, he pulled her into the creek and scrubbed her hard. She shivered and whined but licked his face. Daisy was always on his side.

By the time he returned to the office, his strategy was set. He'd go to the boardinghouse as usual for supper and casually drop a few hints about a meeting in Cincinnati. Near dark he'd transfer the money from his safe into his saddlebags. The tomahawk he would clean and put back in the display case. His wet and muddied clothes he'd ditch somewhere between here and Chicago—his real destination.

Yes, that would work. Though ill and driven nearly mad by the day's events, he rubbed down his horse and filled Daisy's bowls. Bathed and freshly shaved, he stretched out on his cot for a moment. But every time he closed his eyes, he saw Ace fall again. His mind replayed the strange green light of the day, the splat of the ax seating itself in the back of Ace's head, the pull of the body as he dragged it uphill, the way it collapsed, as if boneless, when he shoved it in the rock-walled aperture of the spring.

He felt boneless himself as he walked toward the boardinghouse for supper—like he might just float away. The world had shifted on its axis in the course of a few mindless minutes on the side of a lushly timbered mountain. It seemed like arrows pointed from all directions, naming him a murderer.

Henry's lawyer's mind tried to make sense of the senseless. It wasn't murder exactly. He didn't set out to kill Ace Shelton. If Ace hadn't flung out his taunts, nothing would have come of it. So you could say Ace brought it on himself. Was that how a jury would see it? Henry wondered. Was that how he'd plead his own case? He hoped never to find out.

Greasy meat loaf and lumpy squash sat heavily in Henry's stomach as he trekked home. He barely made it to the house before he lost the meal. No matter the facts of the case, he couldn't make it right, and he couldn't bear his own company. He packed his saddlebags and prepared for the trip he'd mentioned casually to his tablemates over supper.

He packed little clothing. He could buy whatever he needed in Chicago. But he wanted his shaving kit, one of his ledgers, the money of course, and the packet of soiled clothing wrapped in oilcloth. At the last moment, for reasons he couldn't have identified, he added the barely used Bible.

The Out of Office sign bobbed in the window when he shut the door. With a twist of the key, it was locked. He forced himself to walk at a normal pace as he went around to the stable. Soon as the horse was saddled and the saddlebags were secure, he whistled for Daisy.

Down the middle of the road they went—man, horse, and dog, to the world's eyes innocent as innocent could be. Henry wondered if he'd ever be back.

CHAPTER 24

MONDAY MORNING AND Cara couldn't get started. Even her whittling basket couldn't keep her attention. She set it on the windowsill
and grabbed the broom. Ever since Big Boy planted the thought of
a pardon in her mind, she'd been good for nothing. She fought to
keep her emotions tamped, like a fire banked for the night, for Big
Boy had warned her not to set her hopes too high. These things had
to follow the letter of the law—it could be weeks or months or not
at all. Cara sort of wanted to call on that lawyer fellow, that Henry
Thomas, but Big Boy said wait up on that. He said sometimes it's
better not to get in your own way, and Cara knew that was true.

While she stayed out of her own way, she prayed. Praying went
along good with sweeping. The steady whisk, whisk of broom straw
against the wooden floor helped put her mind on her heavenly peti-
tions. Goodness, though, the porch was already clean as a hound's
tooth. She remembered her grandmother, her daddy's mama, used
to sweep her yard. Granny had the prettiest blue eyes and the sweetest smile. Her yard was mostly hard-packed earth with patches of
struggling grass much like Cara's own. So with broom in hand, Cara
stepped out in the yard. Yesterday's hard rain had settled the dust,
but she gathered pebbles and feathers and leaves into her dustpan.
Granny would be disappointed to know this was the first time Cara
had tidied her front yard this way.

Reluctantly, she hung the broom and dustpan back in place behind the door. She might as well build a fire and get to the laundry. August was fast approaching, and that meant she'd soon be elbow-deep in tomatoes and bushels of green beans. She really didn't have time to dillydally like she'd been doing the last few days.

But first she'd take a second to practice looking up the road. Shading her eyes with one hand, she stared hard. That was the way Dimmert would come, just over the ridge there. She meant for him to find her like this—standing and watching. As soon as she spied him, she'd take off running. He'd throw his arms around her and draw her close, and then they would kiss. Kiss and kiss like they'd never stop.

Oh, just the thought . . . how sweet—how very sweet.

Cara stared so hard where she expected to see Dimm she nearly missed the little boy heading her way. "Jay?" Even though he was still at a distance, she could see he was white as snow and clutching his side like he'd run the two miles from home.

Just like in her daydreams, she ran up the road, except to Jay instead of Dimm. The boy nearly collapsed in her arms. "Jay, whatever is the matter? Honey, what's wrong?"

Jay bent at the waist and sucked air. "Daddy—daddy didn't . . . Mommy's sick . . . Pauline's hungry . . ."

Heavy as he was, Cara lifted Jay and carried him to the porch. She handed him a glass of water.

The poor little thing gulped it down, then lay on the floor. "Daddy has been gone all night," he stammered, "and Mommy's sick with worry."

"You wait here while I get Pancake." Cara sprinted toward the stable. Thankfully, Pancake was in a traveling mood.

With Jay holding on from behind, they were soon on their way to the Sheltons'. Evidently Ace had gone off sometime yesterday afternoon and hadn't come home. That was not like Ace at all. There had been the threat of storm, so he didn't take any of the kids along, Jay related. And truthfully, Cara knew, Dance was so much better she could handle them alone. But still, Ace would never stay out all night. Cara's heart was in her throat the whole trip. *Please let him be home when we get there,* she prayed over and over.

The front door stood open, the screen door ajar. Merky and Wilton sat at the kitchen table.

"I fixed them breakfast before I left," Jay said. That would explain the oatmeal stuck to their faces and congealing in their bowls.

Cara grabbed a rag and washed their little faces and their little hands all the while keeping watch on Dance, who sat staring into the distance.

Cleve needed a diaper change and something to eat. He didn't cry but sat under the table like he was too tired to move. With a clean nappy and some soothing powder, he started fretting.

"Hey, Wilton," Cara said while stirring milk into the last of the oatmeal, "how about you feed your brother? Did anybody go to bed last night?"

"We all just watched for Daddy," Jay replied.

Cara approached Dance cautiously, murmuring words of comfort. Dance didn't resist when Cara took Pauline and did for her what she'd just finished doing for Cleve. "Here now, Dance," she said while helping Pauline to nurse. "Feed the baby."

Dance took the strong sweet tea Cara offered and drank it down. Cara buttered bread and broke a corner. "Take just a bite."

Dance's eyes cleared, though they kept a haunted look.

Cara gave the children bread and jam and poured yesterday's milk into their cups. From the pasture near the barn she could hear the cow bawling. That scared her more than anything. Ace would never let the cow suffer from lack of milking.

Dance clutched Pauline to her chest with one arm and with the other opened the screen door Cara had just closed. "Ace," she yelled. "Ace Shelton, where are you?"

Cara walked up behind her. "How long has he been gone?"

Dance stood with her hand on the door's handle. "It was late

afternoon yesterday. He was going to check that stupid spring again."
She closed the door. "He said he'd be home in time for supper."

The bawling cow tore at Cara. "If I bring the cow down to the
porch, do you reckon you could milk her, Dance? I thought Jay and
I would walk up the mountain and look for Ace. Maybe he's broken
a leg or fallen in a sinkhole or something."

Dance's face took on a hopeful color. "Maybe he has. It would be
just like Ace to break a bone and leave me with all the work to do."

Cara found the milk bucket and a rope lead for the cow. The animal didn't resist when she led her across the barnyard. On a sawed-
off stump nearby the watering trough, Cara noticed a dirty hatchet
lying on the chopping block. Ace must have killed a chicken for
yesterday's supper, but he would have washed the hatchet.

The swish and ping of milk against the side of the bucket accompanied Cara and Jay as they left the yard. The path was narrow and
steep, so Pancake was left behind. Just this side of the woods, where
the trail commenced, Cara stopped to look back. Dance sat on the
bottom porch step milking. The children gathered on the top step,
Wilton holding Pauline, Cleve bunched between him and Merky. A
flock of crows shot over the corner of the roof, cawing and dipping
their black wings toward Dance and her children. An ominous fore-
boding chilled Cara; she had to tear her eyes away from the picture
at the porch. *I'll never see them like that again,* she thought.

Jay plunged ahead, beating weeds aside with a stick. "Come on,
Aunt Cara. Time's a-wasting."

They climbed steadily for a time on a trail obviously familiar to
Jay. Cara never would have found it without him. Now and then they
stopped for Jay to exclaim over the destruction of his father's sweetwater run. "You think a wild hog did this?" he asked, his brows knit
together.

Cara had heard of feral pigs wreaking havoc on everything in
their paths, but she'd never actually seen one. "I don't know. Did
your daddy ever say anything about finding hogs here?"

Jay looked about the trampled grass. "He's told me stories about them. He's going to be really mad."

Cara didn't say anything. Pigs might uproot the system but in some places the pipes were missing. Hogs couldn't carry them away. Her bringing Jay was a mistake. She should have gotten one of the men from church or the preacher to help look. It took every ounce of her strength not to run away. But if Ace was hurt, the sooner they found him the better. She stepped ahead of Jay, following a path barely wide enough for one, and picked up her pace.

At least it was cool in the shadow of the trees. She marveled at Ace's ingenuity—running the springwater down the mountain in such a clever way. And she couldn't help but remember the day she'd sat with him, drinking the sweet, cold water from a tin cup.

She guessed it was forty-five minutes or so before they came into the clearing where Ace had discovered the spring. Jay headed for the busted keg, but Cara caught his arm. There was something very wrong beyond that smashed wood.

Cara knelt down to face Jay. "I need you to ride Pancake to Aunt Darcy's and—"

"But I've got to find my dad."

Cara made her voice stern, and she gave him a slight shake. "Jay, I think your daddy is hurt bad. Now listen and do as I say. Take Pancake and ride to Aunt Darcy's. Tell her to get Brother Jasper and have him bring some men up here."

Jay's face clouded over. His lips trembled. "I got a bad feeling in my belly."

She wanted to hold him and soothe his troubles, but instead she stayed firm. "The best way to help your daddy is to go for help. Can you do that?"

Cara watched the boy find his resolve. He'd never looked more like Ace. "What should I tell Mommy?"

"Tell her you're going for help. Tell her I'm staying here."

As soon as Jay disappeared from sight, Cara fought to find her own resolve. She kept her back turned from the opening of the spring, where she had caught a glimpse of a man's booted foot. It seemed a million locusts shrilled from the surrounding trees, but she could still hear the dreadful buzz of the green flies she'd seen lifting and settling there like a swarm of bees.

Queasy and shaking, Cara walked a few dozen paces away and eased herself down. The carpet of leaves was still damp from yesterday's storm. Wrapping her arms around her bent knees, she tried to figure what might have happened. It must be that Ace had fallen. He probably went on the cliff that overlooked the spring. The storm yesterday was sudden and caught him off guard. The ground gave way and caused his fall. But wait. It could be anyone at the bottom of the cliff. Just because Ace was missing didn't mean he was dead. It could be someone else's sorrow lying there.

She wasn't certain she could stand, but she needed to see if it was Ace. *Lord, give me strength,* she prayed.

Upright, she planted her feet firmly against the sudden tilting of the ground and saw a curious thing. With a dip of her knees, she plucked a long, thin strip of leather from among the sodden leaves. *Wonder what Ace was doing with this?* A sudden spurt of tears overtook her as she wound the leather thong neatly around her finger before secreting it in her pocket. And there—was that his hat rolled up against the trunk of a hickory tree?

Slowly, she turned to face the spring. The terrain she crossed might as well have been a raging river. Each step was hard as plowing in clay uphill without a mule. "Lord, help me," she whimpered over and over. "Help me. Help me."

He lay like a man in his bath in the aperture of the spring. Water burbled through the crook of his knees, seeking a path of escape. His clothes were soaked, and his face looked oddly swollen and scuffed. "Ace?" With a trembling hand she touched the familiar face, now still as death.

She knelt beside him in the pool of springwater and laid her tear-streaked cheek against his, which was cold and unresponsive. She noticed bits of grass and tiny twigs caught in his hair. With her fingers she began to comb them out. Ace was always proud of his hair. Her fingers found a terrible misshapen lump on the back of Ace's head. Screaming, she jerked her hand away.

Cara jumped up, nearly falling on the slick rock, and went to fetch his hat. "It will be all right, Ace," she said. "I'll just go get your hat."

As she went back to the spring, she brushed dirt from the crown of dark felt. She wanted so much to fix his hat back where it belonged, but her hands wouldn't obey. They didn't seem to be hers anymore. What did people do in times such as this?

Desperate to provide some dignity to her dear friend, she took off her apron, wafted it gently in the air, and let it fall to hide his face. That didn't seem covering enough, so she set his hat loosely on top of the apron. It was then she noticed the gash in the back of the hat's wide brim. He'd dashed his head on the rock when he fell, she figured. The wind from yesterday's storm blew the hat against the tree. It all made a perfect, dreadful sense.

As soon as she stopped her motions, the flies swarmed again—hateful, nasty things. Leaving her post for a moment, she broke a leafy branch from an ash tree and wielded it like a fan. "'Shall we gather at the river,'" she sang as she fanned his precious body. "'Where bright angel feet have trod . . .'" and "'Jesus, Lover of my soul, let me to Thy bosom fly . . .'" The fanning kept the flies away, and the songs kept her sane. It was like God's strong arms reached down from heaven and held her up, for her own strength could not sustain her.

It was hours before she heard the commotion of men climbing the mountain.

Brother Jasper was first to her side. He took the ash tree branch from her cramped hands. "Sister Cara, come away."

"I can't leave him here," she said. All afternoon she'd stood with her feet in the icy springwater keeping Ace as safe as he would ever be again.

Men gathered round. She could see them staring, pulling on their beards, blinking, trying to figure what had happened.

"Come, sister," Brother Jasper said again. "Jean Foster waits over yonder to take you down to the Sheltons'. You are needed."

All the horror of the day came crashing back at the mention of poor Dance and the children. Oh, what would they do? "Pray first, Brother Jasper. Ace would want us to pray for Dance and the young'uns."

The swish of hats preceded the bowing of heads before Brother Jasper's clear, firm voice was lifted to heaven. "Father God, we ask not why, for we lean not unto our own understanding but lean instead on Your everlasting arms. Lord, we know that Brother Ace is dancing on streets of gold. We just ask for mercy on his widow and his children. Be with Sister Cara as she goes to minister unto them. Fortify her for the long road ahead."

As soon as the prayer was finished, another man made his way into the circle. Cara recognized the sheriff. He held his hat in his hands. "Miz Whitt, I need a word."

"Can't this wait?" Brother Jasper interjected. "She's weak as water and near collapse."

"This won't take long," the sheriff replied. "You can stay with her, Reverend."

"Well, let's get her away from here at least," Brother Jasper said. "Here now, Sister Cara, lean on me."

Cara couldn't get her legs to work. She was rigid as a fence post. Brother Jasper on one side and the sheriff on the other seized her by the elbows and carried her to the fallen log where once she'd sat with Ace. Jean came up over the hillside. She sat beside Cara and put both arms around her. The sheriff didn't object.

He squatted down until he was eye-to-eye with Cara. "Tell me what you saw."

Cara choked on the words, but she managed to answer the sheriff's question. She told of seeing the booted foot and how she sent

Jay for help. She relayed how first she'd turned her back on Ace, disbelieving it was him, and then she'd spied his hat.

"Where exactly did you find the hat?" The sheriff's sharp question penetrated the fog surrounding Cara's brain.

"Um, let's see. I was sitting on the ground there." She pointed to the spot of flattened grass where she had rested. "The hat was kindly propped up against that hickory tree, but I didn't touch it at first. First I went to see if it was really Ace. I was hoping it was someone else, but then. . ." She shook her head. "Soon as I saw that hair, I knew. Lord help us, it was Ace."

"What happened next?" the sheriff asked.

Cara held out her hands stiffened into claws. "I combed my fingers through his hair and went to get his hat." She began to shake. Her feet danced a jig upon the ground. Jean's arms held tight.

Cara looked at the sheriff. "I wanted to comfort him someway, maybe set his hat back on, but I couldn't bring myself to touch him again." She doubled over; her head dropped to her lap. Her voice was muffled when she added, "I covered him with my apron and his hat."

The sheriff stood. "You can take her now," he said to Jean.

"Sheriff," she heard a man's voice call out, "you'd better get over here. I think he's moving."

The sheriff's head whipped toward the voice before he rushed away. "Get that hat and that rag off his face," he barked. "He's going to suffocate."

Jean held Cara's hand tightly as she hobbled toward the spring, holding her breath, afraid to hope. Some men stepped aside to give them access.

"Watch his fingers," the sheriff said.

Cara forced herself to look. At first she saw nothing, then just the slightest twitch from his right index finger, like he was trying to tap a message. With help she knelt there again. "Ace," she said while her tears fell on his face like fat raindrops. She reached out and stroked his cheeks, which were still cold as marble. "Ace, are you in there?"

His eyelids fluttered ever so slightly, and a muted groan escaped his lips. Cara was so light-headed with relief she thought she might pitch forward across his battered body. The sheriff caught her under the arms and lifted her, swinging her away from Ace as if she weighed no more than a child.

Leaning against Jean, she watched as the sheriff and a couple of men gingerly turned Ace on his side. The angry wound was now exposed for all to see.

The sheriff squatted and looked without touching. "Looks like the cold springwater saved his life. See here?" He pointed to a glistening bloodred clot. "This is the only thing standing between Ace and sure death. I reckon the chilled water has kept it from busting." The sheriff stood staring down. "Now the trick will be getting him down the mountain without causing more damage."

Brother Jasper removed the flannel shirt he wore. "What if we soak this in the water and wrap Brother Shelton's head in it?"

Cara heard the men murmuring among themselves. "It's worth a try," one said.

The sheriff pulled on his chin. "All right. We'll form a stretcher of arms and carry him." He turned to Cara and Jean. "You go on down and prepare his wife. It's likely he'll be dead before we get him there." He rested his hand for a fleeting moment on Cara's shoulder. His face looked stern, but she caught a flicker of sympathy in his eyes. "You did good, Miz Whitt. If Ace had laid out another night, he wouldn't have stood a chance."

CHAPTER 25

CARA REMEMBERED NOTHING of her walk down the mountain
to the Sheltons' cabin. One moment it seemed she was standing in
the spring beside Ace and the next she traipsed across his yard. She
expected to find chaos but instead found an improbable calm, like
the appeasing moment before a storm sets in, when even the birds go
silent and the leaves hang unmoving on the trees.

A woman she recognized from church sat in a chair on the porch
with the babies, Cleve and Pauline. Wilton and Merky sat on the top
step. As she got closer, Cara could hear the muted sounds of pots
and pans.

"The ladies are cooking supper," Jean whispered in her ear, like
a loud word would shatter Cara's thin veneer of control. "There was
more than plenty in the garden, and Dance had recently finished
milking."

"Where is she?" Cara asked.

"I was able to get her to lie down while we were waiting for the
men to assemble and start up the mountain," Jean said. "I hope she
is resting."

"Does she know?"

Jean patted her arm. "Honey, none of us knew what we'd find up
there, but Dance said she feared he was dead."

"Thank the good Lord I don't have to tell her that," Cara replied. "Not yet anyway."

Merky held her arms up as Cara approached. She swung the child on her hip. Merky buried her face in Cara's shoulder.

"Aunt Cara," Wilton said, "Jay didn't come back."

Cara looked at Jean, who shrugged. "I guess he must still be at Fairy Mae's."

"He'll be so worried," Cara said.

Jean stepped ahead and held the screen door open. "Right now you need something to eat to keep your strength up."

"Me too, Aunt Cara?" Wilton asked. "Do I need something to eat too?"

Cara ruffled the boy's hair, biting her lip to hold back a sob. "Why, I believe you do. That belly under your shirt looks near empty."

Willy pulled up his shirt and looked down. "It's a-talking to me."

A tear slid down Cara's face and caught in her smile. "What's that belly saying?"

"Taters and beans," Wilton replied, rubbing his stomach.

That was so like something Ace would say, it caught Cara off guard. Ace had to get well for his children. She cupped the back of Wilton's head. "Come along. Let's get that belly of yours some supper."

Someone had rigged a screen with a couple of blankets to hide Dance's bed from the bustle of the kitchen. Cara pulled the corner back and stepped behind. Easy as she could, she sat on the side of the bed and touched Dance's shoulder. "I'm here," she said.

Dance hid her head under the bolster pillow. "He's dead, ain't he?"

Cara puzzled over how to answer. She didn't want to get Dance's hopes up too high. "Ace has met with a terrible accident, but he lives. Right now he's drawing breath. The men are bringing him down. You need to get ready to help him."

Dance bolted upright and commenced screaming. It took all

of what little strength Cara had left to keep her from flinging herself off the bed. The screen was thrust away as several women rushed in.

Jean threw her arms around both of them. "Shh. Shh," she murmured. "Get ahold of yourself, Dance. You're no help to your husband this way."

Cara broke. Racked with sobs, she stumbled out of the house and leaned against the porch rail. She had nothing left to give to Dance. She reached for her apron skirt to blot her face and then remembered where she'd left it.

Jean came up beside her. "It's going to be rough here tonight. Mrs. Hackley and I will be staying over. Our men too, I'm sure. You don't have to do this alone. We'll do all we can for Ace and for Dance."

"I don't know what to do for Dance if Ace dies," Cara managed to say through her tears. "If only Dimmert were here or if Fairy Mae weren't so sick. She was always such a comfort to Dance."

"Do you want Dylan to go to Fairy Mae's and fetch Jay?"

Cara tapped two fingers against her lips, fighting for control. "I should go. Somebody has to tell him and Darcy what has happened." Fresh tears spurted like fountains. "Poor Darcy, she must be worried out of her mind."

"Why, Darcy isn't home. She left last night with that lawyer Henry Thomas."

"What?" Cara shook her head hard. Nothing was as it was supposed to be. "You mean she just left? ran away? How can that be?"

"When Jay got to Fairy Mae's with the news that something was wrong over here, Remy left him with Fairy Mae and came to fetch us. Poor thing, she'd hobbled all the way on her crutch—so out of breath I feared for her. When I asked why Darcy didn't come, she told me Darcy was gone."

"I can't take this in. I knew Darcy fancied she was in love—but to up and leave Fairy Mae? I can't believe it."

Jean Foster was the last person who would speak ill of anyone. "I'm sure Darcy plans a quick wedding trip. And she knew Remy would take perfect care of Fairy Mae."

"Wedding?" A tiny flicker of anger mingled with Cara's grief. It was enough to make a body sick.

"Darcy wouldn't go off with a man without the promise of marriage," Jean said in her kind way. "Darcy is a God-fearing girl."

"I know, but you can't just go running off willy-nilly to please yourself." Cara sagged against a post. "She didn't even tell me. And I thought we were close as sisters."

Jean nodded. "You're right, of course. She shouldn't have. It was the wrong thing to do on many counts, but I expect Mr. Thomas was pretty persuasive."

"So what do I do now? Who's to help with all of this?"

Through the trees they could hear the sound of the men coming down the mountain.

"The Lord sends what you need in times such as these. Right now you have many friends willing and able to help. I believe Ace has family in Maryland. We'll get the news to them." Jean rested a hand on Cara's shoulder. "One step at a time as God leads. One step at a time."

<hr />

When Cara got to Fairy Mae's, she found Jay feeding an apple to Pancake. *Lord, be with me,* she prayed. *This is the hardest thing I've ever had to do.*

"Hey, Jaybird," she said. "Looks like you're taking good care of old Pancake."

Pancake lifted the apple core from Jay's fingers. The boy began to tremble. He kept his eyes on the ground. "Why didn't my daddy come with you, Aunt Cara?"

"Will you come to the porch with me so we can talk?"

Jay hid his face against Pancake's neck. "Oh. Oh," he whimpered. "You're gonna tell me something bad."

Cara knelt on the ground and pulled Jay to her, taking in the sunshiny little boy scent of him. He stood still in the circle of her arms. "Jay, your daddy was up there at the spring." She swallowed hard and took a deep breath. "I think he fell off the cliff onto some rocks. Honey, your daddy's hurt, but we're going to take good care of him."

"I don't believe you," Jay said and gave Cara's shoulder a shove like he was pushing the truth away. "You're riddling me."

Cara tightened her grip. "Jaybird—"

"Don't call me that! I ain't a baby!" Jay struggled to break free. "Let me go. I need to see my daddy!"

"Jay. Jay," she soothed. "It's all right. Everything's going to be all right. Listen, I brought Wilton and Merky with me. See there in the wagon with Dylan Foster? They need to see their big brother."

"I better not cry. It'll scare them." Jay tucked his shirt into his trousers and dashed at his eyes with the back of his hand. "I'm sorry I pushed you."

Dylan jumped down from the wagon when they approached. He held out his hand to Jay. "You did a good job today, finding your way and taking care of your granny Whitt. A grown man couldn't have done better."

Cara looked at Dylan gratefully. Jay needed a man's words right then.

Jay pumped Dylan's hand. "Could you hand my brother and sister down? I reckon they need me."

As soon as Wilton's feet hit the ground, he was heading for Pancake. "It's my turn to ride."

"I'll help him," Dylan said. "You want to come along, Jay?"

Thankfully Cara had only Merky to deal with as she headed for the house. She needed to talk to Remy.

Remy darted out the door quick as a house wren. "It's bad, ain't it?"

Cara nodded. "Let me get Merky settled; then we can talk."

"Put her in with Fairy Mae," Remy said. "It will do them both good."

"Is Mammaw Whitt like this all the time now?" Cara asked as she and Remy left the bedroom where Merky lay snuggled up beside her great-grandmother. The little thing was tuckered out.

"Pretty much," Remy said. "She ain't eating, neither."

Cara collapsed on a kitchen chair. "Ace is near death. I think he fell off a cliff."

"I reckon Dance is tore all to pieces," Remy replied as she poured a mug of coffee and sat it in front of Cara.

Cara tipped a small pitcher and watched thick cream swirl into the coffee. "Tell me about Darcy. I can't believe she left you alone with Mammaw like this."

"Well, 'course Darcy didn't figure on nobody falling off a cliff when she set out with Henry Thomas," Remy said in her matter-of-fact way. "She asked me to look after Fairy Mae and I said yes."

"Goodness, Remy. I'm not faulting you or Darcy. I just need to figure it out. That's all."

"Funniest thing," Remy said, "After that storm blowed through yesterday afternoon, Darcy took to watching out the window, like she was expecting somebody to come calling. I teased her some: 'Ye expecting your gentleman caller?'

"She said, 'I wish.' Then right after dark up rides the devil all in a lather, and next thing I knowed, Darcy's packing a valise and she's out the door. But they'll be back directly."

Cara sighed. Her head ached something fierce. "How do you know they'll be back? Maybe we'll never see Darcy again."

"Oh, they'll be back," Remy said. "That lawyer feller left something important behind."

Cara wished she had some headache powders. "What did Mr. Thomas leave? His precious money?"

"His dog there," Remy said. "He left his dog in my care. Her name is Daisy."

Indeed there was a dog lying on a rug in front of the cold fireplace. At the mention of her name, the hound padded over and dropped her head in Remy's lap. Remy stroked her ears. "There's a good girl," she said.

"How can you be so calm? I feel like I'm about to fly apart."

Remy sat with her hand resting on the dog's head. "Ain't no use fretting about this old world. Ain't like we're in charge of nothing."

Boyish laughter sailed in through the open door. Cara looked out across the yard. Dylan had put his straw hat on Pancake. He guided the mule round and round the barnyard. Wilton laughed so hard Cara thought he might fall off. Jay stood off to the side, his mouth turned upside down.

Fresh tears cascaded down Cara's cheeks. How could a body make so many tears? "What's going to happen to these children if Ace doesn't make it?" Her whole body began to shake. "Dance can't hardly take care of Pauline, much less the rest of them."

"Then we'll have to do it, won't we? The good Lord provides, I reckon."

Cara was taken aback. Here she was crying and moaning over what might be and Remy, with scarcely anything to call her own, jumped right in with the answer.

Cara took her hankie from her sleeve, mopped her face, and blew her nose. "You're right. The good Lord does provide." She stirred her coffee, then took a sip. "Let's make a plan."

As that dreadful day closed, Cara lay awake in her own bed. Tears wet the pillow slip, but she reckoned it was all right to cry for Dance and the young'uns—and oh, for the sorrow of Ace. At least she'd stopped crying for herself.

Merky cried out once, then stuck her thumb back in her mouth. Cara was ever so glad for the little girl's presence. She wondered how

Remy was doing with Wilton. That brought a smile. Of all the kids, Wilton was the one who wanted to stay with Fairy Mae and Remy. Who would have figured that? But Remy enticed Wilton with the dog. She told him Daisy needed a buddy just like Wilton, for she missed her daddy too. Cara never would have thought to put it so—in words that a four-year-old could understand—giving truth and comfort at the same time.

Remy was a puzzle. Cara had never even contemplated Remy's life. She was always just there helping out—staying in the background, kind of like Martha in the Bible. Cara sat up and blew her nose. She reckoned she and Remy were much alike, both Marthas, neither wanting to be noticed. But Darcy was a Mary if there ever was one. Darcy was bright and shiny as sunlight on water, lighting up a room with her sparkle, always ready for a new adventure.

Lord, Cara added a new request to the day's constant prayer, *please be with Darcy. Keep her safe and bring her home fast.*

Cara's head pounded and her nose was so stopped up she could barely breathe. Giving up on sleep, she eased out of bed and drew a light quilt over Merky. One burner of the cookstove still held heat. She stirred the embers to flame, added a chunk of wood, and put the teakettle on.

When the water was near to boiling, she poured some in a small crock and added two heaping tablespoons of salt. Covering her head with a tented towel, she breathed the cleansing, salty air.

She was thankful to have this time to herself and thankful to Jean and to Mrs. Hackley, who insisted on staying with Dance and the babies tonight. Jay stayed there also. He would not leave his mother. Brother Jasper and two of the church elders were keeping watch over Ace.

Dylan was riding to Hazard to find a doctor and to dispatch a telegraph to Maryland. How sad, Cara mused, for Ace's parents to hear the news in such an impersonal way. Elder Foster said they should pray that they could get here in time to see their son before he passed on, but Cara would not. Ace would live. She knew it. God would grant a miracle.

Certain scenes from the day played over and over across her mind's eye: Ace's body lying crumpled in the spring; his brown felt hat rolled up against the hickory tree; her apron billowing out over his stony face; Dance standing on the bed, screaming . . . Cara wished the salt water would wash those dreadful images away.

And there was one more picture she couldn't get out of her mind. Just before she left Dance's and started home with Merky, she'd noticed the sheriff standing at the chopping block, holding Ace's hatchet up to the waning light.

His eyes narrowed when he saw Cara watching. "As far as you know, Miz Whitt, did anybody use this recently?"

"Not as far as I know. I thought maybe Ace killed a chicken yesterday."

"So you took notice of this blood here?" he asked, flashing the blade. "Any sign of that when you got here? When was it? Early this morning?"

"Um, well," Cara stammered, feeling like a moth in a spider's web. "No, not so early, maybe ten or so."

"Any sign of last night's supper? skillet? dishes?"

"I don't recollect—I was only thinking of finding Ace. I think the ladies from church washed some dishes."

"Let me ask you something else, Miz Whitt . . ."

Cara wished he'd quit calling her Miz Whitt. She looked around, hoping to see Brother Jasper or maybe Dylan. Why was the sheriff asking her these questions? She started to back away.

The sheriff kept his steely blue eyes locked on hers. "Did you ever witness any violence acted upon Mr. Shelton by his wife?"

Cara swallowed hard. "Violence? No—well, they had the normal tiffs, Ace and Dance, like any other couple."

"Did you ever see Ace Shelton lay a hand in anger on his wife?"

She shook her head.

"How about the reverse?"

"Why are you asking me these questions?"

"Just trying to figure things out," the sheriff replied. "There was talk around town about Miz Shelton's hair-trigger temper. A few weeks back Ace had a knot over his eye big as a hen's egg. He said his wife hit him with a skillet."

Now as Cara folded the linen towel and emptied the cold salt water, she pondered the sheriff's questions. What in the world could he be after? What was he thinking? From experience she thought it couldn't be good. She figured the lawman had more than questions on his mind, but surely he didn't think Dance had anything to do with Ace getting hurt. It was an accident, pure and simple.

Her headache had eased and she could breathe again. Best not borrow trouble—best not make too much of the sheriff's probing. He was only doing his job.

She scooted Merky's limp body over to make some room for herself. What was it her daddy would say when her mama would fret over some small thing? Oh yes. "Let every day provide for itself and God send Sunday."

Cara wondered if that was from the Bible. Probably not, for it seemed to her God provided every day. Now He would provide for Ace and for his family. She just needed to stop trying to take everything on all by her lonesome.

CHAPTER 26

THE NEXT TIME Henry came with a proposal, Darcy was ready. Somehow she sensed he would come to her this day. Maybe it was in the tension of the afternoon's summer storm, but it seemed like she could feel his presence, exciting and dangerous.

"Be quick," he said when she went out to meet him.

So she rushed to gather her things, all the while keeping an eye out the window to where Henry talked with Remy in the fading twilight. Darcy feared he would change his mind any minute and ride off, leaving her behind. She tucked tissue paper into the folds of her wedding costume before she packed it on top of her other things. Try as she might though, her new hat wouldn't fit in the valise. With a jet-beaded hat pin she secured it atop her head, then ran to tell Mammaw good-bye.

Mammaw barely opened her eyes when Darcy bussed both of her soft cheeks. "I'll be back in a day or two. Remy will take good care of you."

Seizing the moment, she paused to look at her reflection in Mammaw's dresser mirror. The lamplight cast a golden glow around her face as she pinched her cheeks and rubbed a little petroleum salve on her lips. The hat didn't go with the housedress she wore, but she wasn't about to leave it behind. Guilt stopped her in her tracks as she rushed through the bedroom door. With a sigh she went back to Mammaw's side. Kneeling by the bed, she took her grandmother's hand in her own. "I love him. Be happy for me."

The screen door screeched. Remy must have come back in. Darcy jumped up, gave herself one more look-see in the mirror, reset her hat, and grabbed her valise. With a "Thank you, Remy," she was out the door and into the arms of her soon-to-be husband.

Although Henry was in a dark mood she could not tease him out of, Darcy was in a state of giddy bliss all the way to the train station. It was happening. She was about to marry her beautiful Henry.

Through the night they traveled until they came to a town with a livery station where Henry could board the horses. She wasn't sure where they were exactly, but she wasn't about to vex Henry with questions. Once they got to the depot, he bought tickets and found them a bench on which to rest. Unable to keep her eyes open another minute, Darcy drifted off with her head on Henry's shoulder until a train thundered into the station and shook her awake. With a great belch of smoke and a terrible screech of wheels, the train stopped on the tracks.

"Henry," Darcy said, "are you sure that thing's safe?"

Henry had turned distant. He'd barely said three words during the whole night's journey. Now he guided her to the train with his hand at the small of her back. "Get on," he said.

A kindly fellow cupped Darcy's elbow. "Watch your step, little lady," he directed as he helped her up the steps. Henry was close behind, loaded down with Darcy's valise and a set of saddlebags. "I'll take those," the man said.

Henry replied, "No thanks."

They sat together in two seats that faced two other seats. Henry slumped against the window, pulled his hat down over his eyes, and fell asleep.

A well-dressed woman with a wicker basket and a portly man filled the facing seats. The woman looked Darcy over. Her questioning gaze rested on Darcy's left hand. The man leaned toward the woman and spoke in a low voice. She shook her head like he made her angry, then opened the wicker basket and handed him a meat sandwich.

Darcy kept her hands rolled up in her apron for hours until all of a sudden the train lurched to a stop and the other couple got off.

"Henry," Darcy said, poking his shoulder, "the train has stopped. We must be in Chicago."

Henry's eyes flew open. He looked under the seat, checking their luggage. "This one-horse town is not Chicago. Stay here and don't let anyone touch our things. I'm going to stretch my legs."

When Henry left, Darcy scooted over to his seat. She watched him stride across the wooden platform and disappear into the station. He was so handsome and so smart. She was proud to be his almost wife.

Soon he was back with two boxed lunches. "There's a ladies' necessary inside the station, Darcy. We'll eat when you get back."

The kindly man helped her down the steps.

"Thank you," she said, figuring it was the hat that got her special treatment. He probably mistook her for someone important.

The lavatory was cramped and not very clean. Darcy splashed water on her face and washed her hands. The roller towel was black with grime, so she used the skirt of her apron. Catching a glance of herself in a cracked mirror, she righted her hat and untied the apron strings. She'd stick it in her valise. The station platform was thick with folks coming and going—so exhilarating. Darcy could have watched all day.

An earsplitting whistle shook the air, and a blast of smoke sent sparks and cinders flying from the train's chimney stack. "All aboard!" she heard.

Back on the train, she noticed an upside-down water jug and a long tube holding a stack of paper cones. She pulled on a cone and three fell out. Embarrassed, she tried to stick them back up the tube. She was glad Henry didn't see.

The kindly man tossed the cones into a waste can. "Like this here," he instructed, gently pulling on the tip of one cone. He held it under the water jug and turned a handle. Water trickled into the cup. When it was full, he handed it to Darcy.

Darcy was delighted. The water was fresh and cold. "You must love your job," she said to the man.

"I expect I do."

The next time the train shuddered to a stop, Henry grabbed her valise and his bags and motioned her to follow him off the train.

"Is this Chicago then?" she asked as she scurried to keep up with him.

"No," he snapped, "this is Nowhere, USA."

"You don't need to be hateful," she replied.

With a sigh, he stopped on the platform and set down his load. "I'm sorry, Darcy Mae. I'm just weary." He caught her chin with his thumb and tipped it. "What if I kissed you right here in front of all these people? What would you say?"

"I'd say I love you, Henry Thomas." She melted when his eyes got warm like they were now, like she was the only person who mattered in his world.

"Afterward we're coming right back to this spot, and I'm going to claim that kiss."

Darcy's heart skipped a beat. Could it be? "After what?"

Henry pointed down the road. "Just the other side of the hotel there is the courthouse. I figured we'd take advantage of the opportunity. How about it, little Darcy? Will you marry me?"

Her heartbeat changed from a skip to a flutter. She was so happy she might die there on the spot. "Do I have time to change my clothes?"

At the hotel Darcy stood back as Henry procured a room. "Mr. and Mrs. Jones," she heard Henry say, and "two nights."

The desk clerk dipped a pen in a pot of ink and added their names to a list. Henry handed the man two packets from the saddlebag and watched as they were placed in the hotel safe.

"I'll wait downstairs," Henry said after he unlocked the door to their room and set her valise and his bags inside. "Take your time."

The room was pretty with flowered wallpaper and polished cherry furniture. Darcy emptied her suitcase and spread her dress across the bed.

A light knock at the door startled her. She cracked the door and peered out into the hallway.

"Hot water?" a maid asked.

"Please," Darcy replied.

The maid smiled and poured steaming water from a bucket into a blue and white pitcher that sat in a matching bowl on the washstand. From a cart in the hall the maid brought fluffy white towels and rose-scented bath soap.

"How did you know to bring me this?" Darcy asked.

"Your husband paid extra," she said. "You are a lucky woman to have a man so attentive to your needs."

"Yes," Darcy said. "Yes, I am."

Darcy's gloved hand trembled in the crook of Henry's elbow as they walked the short way to the courthouse and climbed the wide marble stairs. Again she stood back as Henry made arrangements. She saw money change hands before a clerk led them to a wood-paneled room where a man in black robes seemed to be studying a stack of papers.

"Everything's in order," the clerk said in answer to words she couldn't hear.

She and Henry waited on heavy wooden benches like church pews while the clerk went to find some witnesses. Tall windows let light stream into the room, but still it was an intimidating place. Darcy was losing her courage. In spite of her pretty outfit, this didn't feel like getting married. Where was her church? Where was her family? This was not the day her dreams had spun.

"Wait here," Henry said, rising.

Darcy clutched his arm. "Don't leave me in this place alone."

"I'll only be a moment," he replied, peeling her hand off his sleeve. "There's something I forgot."

Darcy's teeth chattered as she watched Henry disappear through an open door. She needed a water closet in the worst way.

The unmistakable sound of long skirts swishing against hardwood floors drifted in from the hall. Darcy took heart. Rushing out, she found a woman dusting the wide window ledges. "Is there a facility I can use?" Darcy asked.

With kindness the cleaning lady showed Darcy to a small room off one of the many corridors. When she was finished, Darcy washed her hands, pinched her cheeks, and stepped back into the hall. Now, which way had she come? All the corridors looked alike. Choosing one, she hurried along, looking into each room she passed, but there was no judge, no Henry. When she came to the end of the hallway, she turned and scurried back the way she had come and tried another. Frantic, she felt like screaming. She was going to miss her own wedding.

She nearly fainted with relief when she saw the charwoman with her bucket of rags wiping baseboards. Just beyond her was the judge's chamber; Darcy was sure of it.

Her heart settled when she saw Henry waiting. He handed her a posy of tiny white flowers and pink rosebuds nearly the same shade as her dress. "You have to have flowers on your wedding day," he said.

Suddenly everything was just right. She didn't need a church. She didn't need her family. All she had ever wanted was right here by her side.

***

Much later, after dark, Henry kept his pledge. Like children they swung hands as they walked back to the train station. There on the wooden platform, Henry took her in his arms and kissed her. "I love you, Mrs. Thomas. You are precious to me."

Darcy scarce could take it in. She was a wife in every way. Had any woman ever felt more loved than she did at this moment? On tiptoes she kissed him back. "I will love you forever, Henry. All I ever want is your happiness."

Making their way to a bent-willow bench, they sat together looking out over the train tracks. Gaslight illuminated their little corner of the world.

"I love this," Darcy said, "being here with you."

"What else do you love?"

"You mean besides you? Well, let's see, I love me a strong cup of coffee in the morning. And I like rain but not storms." Henry put his arm across the back of the bench, and she nestled under it. "I love the heft of an uncut bolt of fabric and a card of buttons." She thought for a moment, looking up at him from under his arm. "You know those pretty early summer flowers, irises? Mammaw calls them flags. I love the scent of iris. That's about it, I guess."

Henry tightened his arm around her. My, but it felt good to be with him. She wished they could stay here forever—grow old on this bench.

"Darcy . . ." Henry jumped up and paced a minute before stopping and staring at her. "I need to tell you something."

Darcy stood to face him. "Oh, it's okay. I already know. I'm not bothered in the least."

Henry appeared startled. "How could you know?"

The platform was empty, so she brazenly slipped her arms around her husband's waist and buried her face in his chest. "I don't mind being Mrs. Jones in our hotel room. It's the name on our license that counts."

He groaned as he lifted her off her feet. "You make me wish I were a better man."

The only thing that marred Darcy's happiness in the two days they spent in the town outside of Chicago was Henry's nervousness. He was always glancing over his shoulder or pulling aside a curtain to gaze out the window, like a man being watched. Otherwise, their time there was the happiest of Darcy's life.

"Can't we stay here?" she asked Henry on their last morning, interrupting his reverie at the window.

Henry let the curtain fall and took her in his arms. "I have business in Chicago. Important business."

She leaned back in his arms and studied his face, so dear and familiar to her now.

"Can I trust you?" he asked.

Hurt, she replied, "I'm surprised you need to ask me that. I'm your wife; that should stand for something."

In that way of his, he tipped her chin and looked into her eyes. "You may not like what I'm going to ask of you. You may be sorry you ever married me."

"Never," she responded, though fear coursed through her body. "Just tell me quick."

Henry started pacing again, then went to the window and peered around the curtain. It made her want to scream in frustration. His back was to her when he began to talk. "When we get to the city, I will have to leave you for a while—a week, maybe two at the most. I know a safe place you can stay. You'll like it there."

"But, Henry . . ."

Turning around, he raised his hand palm out, like he was speaking to a child. "Darcy, don't. Please don't question me."

Darcy wasn't sorry she married Henry, but she was ever so sorry they had to leave the town where she had become his bride. Her husband was a serious man. That would take some getting used to. That he needed them to be separate for a while was alarming and conjured up all sorts of disasters in Darcy's creative mind: Henry was ill and didn't want her to face a deathbed scene. Or—and this made her pulse beat fast—he kept a mistress tucked away in an apartment in Chicago. Darcy could feel heat rise in her face as she walked to the train with her husband of two days. If he had another lover and Darcy found out, there *would* be a deathbed scene. Darcy would see to that.

"What's your rush?" Henry said. "We have plenty of time before our train leaves."

Henry carried her stuffed valise and two pretty hatboxes. The saddlebags were slung across his shoulder. On one of their walks about town they had discovered a dress shop. Darcy drooled over the fashion displayed on a mannequin in the window. Henry insisted on buying the exact outfit in her size plus two new hats. No wonder he couldn't keep up.

Darcy adored the round boxes. One was pink with a green grosgrain ribbon that tied across the top, and the other was a sophisticated navy blue with a beige lid.

"Let me help," she said, reaching for her traveling bag.

"No," he insisted, though he sat her belongings down while he moved the saddlebags from one shoulder to the other. "Your things are not heavy—just a little awkward is all."

Darcy cocked her head and looked him over. Something wasn't right. The saddlebags were not as full as they had been. "Henry! Did you remember to get your packets from the hotel safe?"

His face blanched white as a sheet. He unloaded again beside a gas lamp. "See what you do to me," he called as he sprinted away. "You make me forget my head."

Darcy relaxed a little as she waited. Henry's mind seemed to be only on her. She didn't think she needed to worry. She just needed to trust.

CHAPTER 27

A WEEK LATER it was Darcy Mae Thomas who pulled back a velvet drape and peered out the window like she had seen Henry do. Beyond the smudged glass was a crowded sidewalk where people scurried about, busy as ants.

She sneezed before she could get her hankie out. Thankfully, she was the only person in the parlor at the moment. The other women who took rooms here in Mrs. Oldham's Respectable House for Young Ladies were always sizing her up. She'd heard them mimic her accent, knew they talked behind her back. Fingering the thick fabric, she noted the dust caught in the folds and sneezed again.

At least Mrs. Oldham was kind, and Darcy had found a position as a seamstress at a tailor's shop around the corner. It wasn't like she had to work, not like the other girls. Henry had already paid for her room and board, but she couldn't stand to sit around the house all day wondering when he would be back.

She tucked the handkerchief deep in her pocket and withdrew the gold ring Henry had put on her finger the day they wed. There were their initials *HT* and *DW* twined together by a prettily scribed vine. Darcy chanced to put it on. It broke her heart when Henry told her to take it off—that their marriage was a secret for now. He said she would understand in time. She didn't like it one bit, but she would do anything for Henry.

A tear tracked down her cheek, and she dashed it away before secreting her wedding band in her pocket again. She missed Henry so bad it hurt, and she was full of longing to see her mammaw. Before he went away, on whatever business was keeping him from her, Henry made her promise to keep their affairs to herself. That part wasn't so hard, for she hadn't a clue what they were doing in Chicago. He would be back soon, though. He had promised. For Henry she could wait.

Bored, Darcy wandered about the parlor, careful not to stir up any more dust. It was Saturday. She got Saturday and Sunday off, but she would rather be working. It was different, sewing men's trousers and jackets, not nearly as much fun as making fancy gowns for Mrs. Upchurch and her friends. Darcy was learning. Even though she'd worked for the owner of the shop for only three days, Mr. Mark frequently commented on her fine stitching. That was probably why the other girls in the house didn't like her. They worked there too and surely didn't like Darcy being singled out for praise, especially since they'd been employed much longer than she had.

Fortunately, Bridgett, who shared Darcy's room, wasn't like the others. She was sweet and shy with a freckled face and a tumble of dark hair. But Darcy couldn't understand a word Bridgett said. And it didn't seem Bridgett could understand Darcy either. They were foreigners to each other. At night after lights-out, Darcy could hear Bridgett's muffled sobs, and she was sure Bridgett could hear hers. Being homesick was a language they could both understand.

She found Bridgett in their room in front of a lady's desk. The writing surface was pulled down, and Bridgett was bent over her work. She waved a piece of stationery back and forth to dry the ink. "Jibberey jabberer jab," she said, or so it sounded to Darcy.

"You're writing a letter?"

"Momma," Bridgett said with the prettiest smile.

Darcy got that for sure. She watched as Bridgett folded the letter around some dollar bills. After addressing an envelope, she sealed the flap with mucilage from a small brown bottle. Standing, Bridgett reached for her hat, then pulled on white gloves. "Postage officer." She smiled at Darcy. "We go?"

"Post office," Darcy said. "Sure, I'd love to go with you."

It was a pretty late summer day. It wasn't as easy to discern the coming of fall here in the city. Tall buildings, bustling streets, vendors hawking their wares—from the boy with his newspapers to the man selling pretzels from a cart—all combined to shut out the subtle blend of one season with another. With a pang Darcy thought of how the mountains would announce the coming change. The trees would whisper, "Here it comes; here it comes," as the leaves turned jeweled colors of red, gold, and orange. The mornings would beckon coolly for sweaters and long-sleeved shirts. The air would smell of apples and ripening persimmons, stirring your taste buds, making you long for hot biscuits dripping with fruit butter.

"Scuse peas," Bridgett said when she bumped against a man whose arms were laden with brown paper packages.

"Watch where you're going," the man groused and hurried on.

Darcy drew Bridgett away from the foot traffic to a table at a sidewalk café. She snapped her change purse open and paid for two fizzy cola drinks over Bridgett's protest. "My treat," she said.

As soon as they were seated with the delicious icy treats, a fit of giggling overtook Darcy. "Bridgett," she said, when she got hold of herself, "say 'Excuse me, please.'"

"Scuse me peas."

"*Ex,*" Darcy said with an exaggerated mouth. "*Excuse.* Excuse me."

With a look of concentration Bridgett replied, "Es scuse?"

"Very good." Ice rattled in the glass as Darcy finished her cola. "We'd better get to the post office. I think it closes at noon on Saturdays."

Bridgett's forehead crinkled. She checked the clock on the bank building across the street. "Time going."

"Exactly." Darcy nodded as she linked her arm with Bridgett's. "We can practice your English while we walk."

As they headed down the street, Darcy bumped Bridgett with her hip. "Oh," she said, "excuse me, please."

"You peas *ex*cused," Bridgett said.

Darcy laughed all the way to the post office.

While Bridgett posted her letter, Darcy entertained herself by perusing an assortment of scenic postal cards. She chose four and laid them side by side for a better look. My, they were pretty. Maybe she would send one to Mammaw. Surely Henry wouldn't mind if she sent her a little note.

She selected two cards, one to keep and one to mail, then dug in her small purse for pennies. She wouldn't write anything specific, just that they were wed and that she'd be home soon. And she wouldn't put Mrs. Oldham's return address on the card; that way she could write to Mammaw and please Henry at the same time.

Using the fountain pen and blotting paper set out for such a purpose, Darcy carefully printed a note to Mammaw. Someone would have to read it to her since she was so poorly, probably Ace or Cara. Darcy wasn't sure if Remy could read. But it was okay; everyone could enjoy it that way.

Darcy grinned as she walked back to their lodgings with Bridgett. She could just see Mammaw's smile when she heard Darcy's words from so far away. She took Bridgett's hand and swung it with her own, carefree for the moment. "Let's go to the park and feed the ducks. Want to?"

Bridgett nodded. "We go ducks?"

"Yes," Darcy said, happy for the first time since Henry left, "we go ducks."

Across town, Henry's mood was dark. He hadn't had a good night's rest since the night on the train with Darcy. Every time he closed his eyes, he saw the fated tomahawk turning end over end as it catapulted through the air. Twice he'd wakened from nightmares in which he'd seen old man Follett's eyes judging him over Ace's fallen body. Relieved, he'd think, *It's a dream—just a dream,* until finding himself in a strange bed brought back every single grain of truth in the thing he had done.

After leaving Darcy at Mrs. Oldham's, he had traveled across town to find lodging of his own. He'd spent the first few days secreting his money in various banks—not too much in one place. He was careful not to raise suspicion. Although it was hard, he stayed away from Darcy. Women were a man's downfall; he'd witnessed that more than once. He questioned his own motives for bringing her with him.

It was the guilt and the fear, he supposed. After the accident with Ace, he'd gone back to his office for his money and for Daisy, meaning to hightail it out of town unencumbered by any other thing. But he couldn't keep his mind off Darcy. Unlike his usual, well-planned motives, he'd let his need rule his heart. Darcy had come tearing out of the house and thrown herself into his arms. He had stood for the longest time breathing in the scent of her. She was so sweet, so innocent, and it felt so right to have her in his embrace. Somehow just being with her made things seem bearable.

"Get your things," he'd said against his better judgment.

Of course all she wanted was the license and a ring. And to his surprise he wanted to marry as much as she did. There was something irresistible about her need of him. No, that was not it. It was her love that he couldn't easily walk away from. If he had ever had a doubt that she loved him fully, it was erased when she agreed to stay in the boardinghouse alone. "Don't cling," he'd had to tell her when he left her on the porch. "Act like I'm your brother."

But it had to be. Henry still might have to leave her to save himself. He felt like a fool and a coward, but he was not about to give up everything he had worked so hard for. Yes, he might lose the opportunity to reclaim his grandfather's land—that waited to be seen. He might need to head out west and start over. If so, he would go alone.

There was just one thing to do. Henry had to go back home and scout around, find out what was what. If no one had tied him to the death of Ace Shelton, then he and Darcy could return. If things were bad, Henry would have to leave Darcy. He would have no choice. He would be much too easy to track with a woman in tow. It would hurt her, he knew, and his heart sank at the thought, but he wasn't going to prison for love. He'd tucked a packet with plenty of money in her valise. She was a smart girl. She'd find her way home.

His mind made up, he journeyed back to Kentucky. Traveling by train and coach, he got as close as the foothills. Once there, he secured a horse from a livery station and bought some necessities along with coffee, jerky, canned beans, and a blanket roll. Traveling by night, he made it home in record time. If home was a camp with no more comfort than a thin blanket on hard ground, that was.

As soon as he'd arrived in Chicago, he'd shaved his mustache and let his beard grow. He wore a flop-brimmed hat pulled down low over his eyes, scuffed boots, overalls, and a shirt two sizes too big. Purposely, he dug his hands in soil, leaving his nails broken and dirty. He certainly didn't look like a well-paid lawyer anymore. For two days, in this disguise, he haunted neighboring towns, ferreting out any news he could get. Men talked—especially if it was about something out of the ordinary—and they seemed to find the assault on Ace Shelton way out of the ordinary.

Late the second night, in a dark and smoky tavern, Henry nursed a shot of whiskey and listened to the prattle.

"Well, I heard a bear was chasing him and he fell off a cliff," one guy offered. "You know the woods up there are plumb full of bears and panthers too."

"Wasn't Ace Shelton the fellow who had that still?" another said. "The one where that man got shot years ago?"

The first man swirled his whiskey before downing it with one gulp. "Yeah, I think you're right. Lump Lumpkin went to the hoosegow over that. Shame. Ace and Lump made the finest corn liquor I ever drank. Smooth as springwater."

"Maybe Ace set up another still," the second fellow said while motioning the bartender over. "Maybe he was kilt over it."

The other man studied the possibility as the bartender splashed amber-colored liquor in his glass. "Could be, I reckon, though I heard Ace had found the Lord."

A third man, who was listening as intently as Henry himself, chimed in. "You both got it wrong. I hear tell the sheriff is fixing to arrest that wife of his. Wasn't she a Whitt?"

The first two men turned the third man's way. Henry pulled his hat a notch lower but kept looking their way.

"Yeah, she's Herbert and Fairy Mae's granddaughter as I recollect," the second man said. "But that's a stretch, ain't it?"

The third man crossed his arms and leaned on the bar. "I knew Dance Shelton years ago. She's a fey one. Always was stranger than a two-headed cat." The man's eyes narrowed. "You know the sheriff's deputy is my wife's sister's mother-in-law's third cousin twice removed. It was the sister's mother-in-law that gave my wife the rundown on what the sheriff told his deputy. Who is my wife's sister's—"

"Yeah, yeah," the second man said. "So what about Ace's wife getting arrested?"

"Word is she split his head open with an ax. They found the ax on the kitchen table, dripping Ace's blood."

The men shook their heads and sipped their drinks.

"You never can tell," one said.

"That's for sure," another replied. "Think I'll get on home to the old lady."

"Good idea," the first man said. "Say, was that your wife I saw sharpening her hatchet today?"

The other man laughed as he slapped some money on the bar. "Probably was. She's been threatening to do me in."

The three men made their way to the door. "Reckon that Shelton woman will swing?" one asked.

"More than likely. That's pretty cold-blooded," another replied, shoving the door open and heading out.

"I'd say it depends on whether he dies or not," the man holding the door said. "They ain't going to hang her if he lives. She might get some time, but swing, no, that won't happen."

"Yeah," one of the men said, "and if he ever comes out of that stupor they say he's in, he might say she didn't do it."

"Could be," one agreed. "Could be."

Henry steeled himself to stay at the bar. Every fiber of his being wanted to follow the men out the door to hear the last snippet of conversation. He waited several minutes before he chanced to leave. After surreptitiously dumping his untouched drink in the spittoon at his feet, Henry put the right amount of coinage on the bar and stood to leave. Not one head turned to follow him out. Nobody even glanced his way.

He was out of town, well on his way to his latest hidey-hole, when the impact of what he'd heard hit him. Ace Shelton was alive! He would swear on his mother's grave that the man was dead when he left him on that mountain. This changed everything.

His mind churned with torment as his horse carried him up mountain. Back at camp he built a fire and put on a pot of coffee. He wouldn't sleep tonight. There were plans to be made.

CHAPTER 28

THE WATERLOGGED WOVEN BASKET that held Cara's whittling tools collapsed at her touch. Knives, a whetstone, the strop, and several small pieces of wood spilled out on the porch floor. Picking up her favorite tool, she examined its dull, rusted blade. She vaguely remembered laying the basket aside the morning she saw little Jay running up the lane. With the broom, she swept the mess out of the way; she'd see to it later. Now she needed to face her overgrown garden while she had the chance.

Chickens flocked round her feet, begging for attention as she walked across the barnyard. Taking pity, she opened the corncrib door and shelled two ears of corn upon the ground. The red rooster strutted around the perimeter, cawing in delight when a kernel popped his way. Since she had already detoured from the garden, she stepped inside the henhouse, took the egg basket from a peg, and started gathering the hen's fruit. Each nest held a clutch of eggs. The hens had been faithful even though neglected.

One fat dominick fluffed up her feathers as Cara approached her box. The hen clucked several times, stood, flapped her wings, and sat back down, determined to set her eggs. *She's out of season,* Cara thought, *but then so is everything.* With the basket dangling from her arm, Cara emptied the other nests. She'd have to candle the eggs this evening. Some might be rotten.

Startled by a creaking sound, she whirled around. The trellis Dimmert had made for the climbing roses now dangled across the doorway, blocking her exit.

Everything was falling apart and she no longer cared. Just going through the motions was more than she could manage. Minding the thorny branches that snaked through the lattice, she shoved it out of the way and went out.

Pancake ambled out of the stable and stood behind her. He hung his long, horsey face over her shoulder.

She stroked his nose. "I know. It's all such a mess."

She could swear the mule nodded; she could feel his agreement against her chest. Laughter bubbled up from a place she thought was gone forever. "Pancake, what would I do without you?"

Quick to take advantage, Pancake walked away and planted himself by the corncrib.

"I guess I can take a hint," she said, pulling out another ear of corn. "Do you need me to shell it for you?"

Showing his gums in appreciation, Pancake nibbled from her palm.

"I'm changing your name to King or Prince or some such high-and-mighty moniker," she said.

Down by the creek, she left the egg basket in the shade of a tree and faced the garden. It no longer vied in beauty with the Hanging Gardens of Babylon. Tomatoes lay rotting on the ground. Weeds strangled the green beans, and she could barely discern where the potato hills began. Her garden was a mishmash, a veritable vegetable stew.

A rustling sound caught her attention. Kneeling among the itchy cucumbers, she lifted a heavy vine and looked down the row. A possum flashed a toothy grin and gave what he thought was a fearsome hiss. Cara waved the vine back and forth. Overgrown cucumbers smacked against the possum's sides. With one more hiss and one more smile, the varmint turned and scurried away. Cara watched his long, hairless tail disappear down the bank of the creek.

"At least it wasn't a puff adder," she said as if someone were listening, "or a rattler."

Despair, thick as rock dust, choked her throat and clouded her eyes. It seemed each bit of strength and independence she'd worked so hard for all summer had dried up like the marigolds and zinnias at the edge of her garden.

Cara grubbed and hoed for a couple of hours, cleaning horseweed and pokeberry from the rows. Rotted vegetables went in a bucket to be thrown away. She wished she had a pig to feed.

The sun climbed toward noon, baking the garden and her with its unforgiving rays. She gathered up her skirts, then stepped into the creek and let the coursing water bathe her feet. A shaded ledge rock not ten feet away invited her to sit a spell. It was cool and quiet there on the ledge with her feet dangling in the stream. For a minute she could pretend that the last two weeks had never happened, pretend that she was just a girl with a mule waiting for her husband to come home. That seemed ever so doable now.

Finding Ace had been hard but not as hard as what came in following days, Ace unable to talk or sit up, just existing on sips of chicken broth, and then the sheriff turning his cold, searching eyes on Dance. Cara still couldn't believe anyone could see guilt stamped on Dance. Poor thing, she'd been sitting by Ace's bed day and night, barely taking time to eat and hardly sleeping. It was a wonder she still had milk for the baby. Thank goodness Jean was helping. And Jean's husband was a great source of comfort. Dance would be sitting in a stone cold jail cell today if not for Elder Foster's interference.

It was barely a week after Ace was found that the sheriff had come to arrest Dance on suspicion of assaulting him.

"The law's here," Jay had yelled, bursting into the house and letting the screen door slam.

"Jay," Cara reprimanded, "not so loud."

"But it's the sheriff," he replied, his eyes round with apprehension. "What's he want?"

"I don't know. Listen, I want you to slip over to the Fosters' and ask them to come here." She patted his backside, and he scooted out the door. "Be quick."

She watched the sheriff through the filter of the screen door. He was standing at the chopping block like on the day he questioned Cara about the hatchet. Wilton pushed against the door. Cara held it tight. "Wilton, don't. Go play with your top."

"It's broke. The twirler fell off." He pushed against the door again. The screen bowed out from the force of his hands. "Where's Jay goin'?"

Where she'd patted Jay, she swatted Wilton. His face crumpled, and he let out a howl fit to wake the dead. She swooped him up into her arms. He wrapped his legs around her waist. Fat angry tears wetted her shoulder. "I'm sorry, Willy-boy, but you must mind me."

"I want to go too," Wilton said.

So do I, Cara thought. "I know. I know." After wiping his tear-streaked face, she settled him at the kitchen table with a piece of gingerbread and a glass of milk. Food always worked with Wilton.

The rocking chair by Ace's bedside squeaked. Dance was taking the baby from her cradle. She paid no attention to Wilton. It was as if she couldn't see or hear past Ace's needs. Cara couldn't fault her for that.

"When's Merky coming home?" Wilton said, gingerbread crumbs spilling from his mouth.

"Soon," Cara said while cutting him another slice. "She's with Cleve at Mammaw's, you know."

He pounded the table with his fork. "I want to go to Mammaw's. I want to see Daisy."

Cara was itching to get back to the door. "Wilton, that's enough. If you don't stop whining, I'm going to take your cake and eat it myself."

She eased back to the door, not wanting to draw attention. The sheriff was not in sight, but she saw a play of shadows in the depth of the barn. What could he be looking for? What right did he have to poke around in other folks' property?

"Dance," she said, "I'm going to the barn. I'll be back directly."

Cara was halfway down the path that dissected the yard before she remembered her stained apron, her undressed hair, and her bare feet. Goodness, they'd all been so busy these past few days—who had time for primping? She took off her apron and hung it on a bush, then removed some hairpins from her flyaway hair and reshaped the bun at the nape of her neck. It wasn't that she cared two figs how she looked; she wanted to be perceived by the law as a person who had authority in this place.

Standing tall, she stepped inside the barn. "Are you looking for something in particular, Sheriff?" she said, hoping to catch him off guard.

He didn't even flinch. "Could be." He touched this and that, crouching to look under the workbench, then springing back up in a motion so fluid it seemed he made no effort at all.

The sheriff put her in mind of a copperhead gracefully slithering along the ground, waiting for the proper moment to strike.

"You don't have any right to be going through Ace's things." Her voice came out whiny, like Wilton's, instead of forceful like she'd aimed it to be.

The sheriff walked her way. In spite of her resolve she took a step backward. From the house, she could hear Dance start up again like she did several times a day now, crying and pleading for Ace to wake up. It was sad enough to make a stone weep. They watched as Wilton came out the door and scooted like a fat puppy under the rocking chair, hiding.

Cara raised her shoulders and let them drop. "Can't you see we're barely holding on here? Can't you leave well enough alone?"

The sheriff took off his hat. "I like Ace Shelton. He's a good man. I can't just ignore the fact that somebody bashed his head in."

Cara covered her mouth with her hands. It came back in a flash,

the sheriff that dreadful day at the chopping block and those questions he asked about Ace and Dance. "You can't seriously think
Dance could do something so dreadful!"

The sheriff's unflinching gaze fell on her hot as a brand. "Truth be
told, everybody's got a little of Brother Cain deep down."

Feeling weak, she found a sawed-off stump and sat down.

He came and crouched beside her, like they were friends or something. Snagging a long piece of grass, he stuck it in his mouth and
chewed. She watched his eyes narrow. He plucked the grass from his
mouth and used it to point toward the house.

"Way I see it, she got carried away that day. Ace done something
to rile her; then he left, went to his quiet place." The sheriff chewed
the stem of the grass. "She stewed over it—him leaving her with all
them young'uns again. Yep, she stewed 'til she was ready to blow like
the lid off a pot. She grabbed the hatchet and followed him, busting
his fancy sweetwater run as she went."

The sheriff looked her way. She knew he was judging her reaction. "Listen," she started, "for one thing Dance would never leave
the kids alone—"

He commenced with his theory as if she had not spoken. "There
was Ace, probably bending over where the spring bubbles out of the
ground, maybe getting himself a cool drink of water, maybe splash-
ing it on his face. She finds him there. Years of resentment come
to a head." The sheriff slapped his palm against his leg. The sound
cracked like lightning. Cara jumped.

"Quick as that," he said. "Ace reared up, then fell backward into
the water. Never knew what hit him."

Cara felt the strength draining from her body. She knew abso-
lutely that what he said was not true, but he was the law. "What do
you aim to do?"

"I'm going to take Miz Whitt to jail," he said, jangling a pair of
handcuffs clipped to his waist. "I've got no choice."

If Cara had had the strength, she would have lifted her hand and shoved him over—sent him sprawling in the dirt. Instead she sat there like a lump, not knowing what to do. "Lord, help us," she said.

They saw Elder Foster first—he came almost running into the yard. Then other folks appeared: Dylan, Jean, Brother Jasper, and Jay.

Cara's eyes met Jean's, which radiated distress. The men gathered round while Jean stood back, holding on to Jay.

The lawman stood and faced them. "I've come to arrest Dance Shelton for the attempted murder of Ace Shelton."

Jay jerked away from Jean. As if shot from a cannon, he rammed his head into the sheriff's belly. Any other man would have doubled over and gasped for breath but not the sheriff. He stood his ground like Jay was no more bother than a flea.

Dylan grabbed Jay around the waist. Jay's arms and legs spun like a whirligig as Dylan carried him off.

Now, days and miles away from that scene, Cara walked to her garden and stood over the bucket of mushy tomatoes and half-rotted cucumbers and felt a surge of anger so hot she nearly outshone the sun. In a burst of energy she carried the bucket to the back of the barn and hefted a large red globe.

Splat! The tomato burst, trailing juice and seeds down the rough barn wall.

Cara wound up and let an overgrown cucumber fly. "Yahoo," she yelled when shards of green sailed her way. Backing away, she let go again. Tomato followed cucumber, which followed tomato until Cara was panting and the bucket was empty. She could feel a wicked relief as she headed for the egg basket.

The first brown egg she aimed at the imagined image of the sheriff, who, she fancied, was now covered with vegetable guts. But the next was meant for Darcy, and when it popped she lobbed another. Soon she was cackling like an old, fat hen, her hairpins falling out, her dress no protection from the slimy, reeking mess she was creating.

"Good grief, missus," a voice she recognized broke through her tantrum. "What's got into you?"

She was midmotion with the last egg from the basket. Big Boy's eyes widened as he backed away. "Ha," she said. "I've got you on the run."

"Whoo-wee!" he said. "That stuff stinks."

Cara tossed the last egg. "Life stinks."

"I know. I heard about Ace. I'm sorry I wasn't around to help out. Me and Shacklett have just got back from a visit with our sister Aloda in Lexington."

"It's been terrible, just terrible."

"Tell you what," Big Boy replied, "why don't I do some work in the garden while you clean up a bit. Then we'll talk."

"That sounds good," she said, "but I don't have much time. I only came home to see about a few things. I need to get back to Dance's."

"I'll walk over with you," he said. "Might be something I can do for Ace."

Getting cleaned up took more time than Cara expected. Venting her anger was fun while it lasted, but now she had to pay the price. The wavy mirror over the dresser in her bedroom revealed bits of eggshell and stringy yellow yolk in her hair. While she heated water for a bath, she washed her hair with tepid water from the rain barrel. Taking a towel and her comb, she went out the back door, sat on the stoop in a patch of sunlight, and worked the tangles out. Her dress front was soaking wet, but nobody could see her out here, and the sun felt so good.

She felt her muscles relax. How long had it been since she'd had a moment not laden with worry? Her fingers worked her damp hair into a braid that hung halfway down her back. The teakettle whistled on the stove, calling her. She twisted the braid into a knot and secured it with pins, then hurried inside to finish her toilet.

Cara felt refreshed as she walked with Big Boy up the lane to the Sheltons'. Pancake followed, stopping now and then for a morsel of grass.

"So, what's the latest?" Big Boy asked.

"You won't believe this," she replied. "The sheriff has charged Dance."

"Charged her! With what?"

"Lord help us. He thinks Dance tried to kill Ace." Turning to face Big Boy, Cara walked a few steps backward. "He figures Dance followed Ace all the way up that mountain and whacked him in the head with the hatchet Ace kept for killing chickens."

"That's a stretch," Big Boy said.

"Isn't it just?" Cara said, her voice rising in anger. "Then she's supposed to have walked home and cool as a cucumber laid the hatchet back on the chopping block."

"I never figured her for such a woman as that," Big Boy said.

Cara stopped dead in her tracks. "You mean you believe it!" His words made her mad enough to melt.

"Now, missus, I never said that."

Cara plucked a leaf from an overhanging tree limb, shredded it, and let it fall. "I'm sorry. I'm just so angry I don't know what to do with myself."

"Did the sheriff lock her up?"

"Oh, on the morning he came for her . . . Big Boy, it was awful. I reckon the sheriff was fixing to drag Dance away from the sickbed with all the young'uns looking on. But, praise the Lord, Elder Foster intervened."

They started up the path again, walking slowly as they talked. Pancake passed them by. He knew the way by heart.

"Poor Jean, she's practically living at Dance's now. Elder Foster gave his word to the sheriff that Dance wouldn't *escape* if the sheriff would leave her home until the law could prove something one way or the other. Escape," Cara spit the word out. "Where's she supposed to go? What's she supposed to do with her children?"

Cara could feel anger and sorrow settling on her shoulders like stone. If she stood still, the weight of it would drive her right into the ground. She'd be just another bump in the road. "And Fairy Mae's taken a turn." She paused and shook her head. "I'm afraid all this will do Dance in. Oh, if only Ace would wake."

Big Boy picked up a pebble and let it fly. They could hear it smack against a tree in the distance. "Has anybody been back up there where Ace was killed? Anybody besides the law, I mean."

"I don't rightly know," Cara said, "but I don't think so. Why?"

"What say you and me do a little scouting early in the morning?"

"I don't know as I can go back to that spring. What could we do anyway?"

Big Boy whipped another rock through the trees. "Maybe beat the law at its own game. We'll take Jay along and that other little fellow too, if you want."

"You mean Wilton? I don't know about that, but it might be good for Jay. He has a lot of questions."

"All right then," Big Boy said. "I want to see everything you saw that day."

CHAPTER 29

CARA WAS PLEASED when she entered the cabin after her walk over with Big Boy and Pancake. Dance was sitting at the kitchen table with Jean, breaking green beans into a cooking pot. Her dress was clean and her hair was caught up prettily with tortoiseshell combs. A couple Cara didn't know was sitting beside Ace's bed.

"You must be Cara," the woman said, standing. "I'm Ace's mother and this is his father."

The man tried to smile and acknowledge her but instead a sob broke out. He pulled a kerchief from his pocket and blew his nose, then made a beeline for the door.

"I'm sorry. This is terribly hard on all of us." Leaning over the bed, Mrs. Shelton pushed a strand of hair off Ace's pasty forehead. "Maybe we'll go over to Mrs. Whitt's. We haven't seen the other children yet. And of course we need to call on Fairy Mae anyway." She stopped by Dance's chair on her way out and patted her shoulder. "Should we take Wilton and Jay with us?"

"That'd be fine," Dance said. "If they want to go. I can't hardly get Jay to stray farther than the porch."

"We'll have dinner ready when you get back," Jean said.

Cara pulled out a chair. "When did Ace's folks get here?"

Dance took a handful of beans from a basket. "Not long after you left this morning. They came whilst the doctor was here."

Cara could hardly believe all this had happened in the short time she was gone. "Was it the same doctor as before? What did he say?"

"Ma," Wilton yelled through the screen door, "me and Jay's going with Pap and Granny."

Dance made a shooing motion with her hand. They could hear Wilton's feet pounding across the porch. Dance's hand shook so hard the beans fell to the floor. She bent down to pick them up. "Yeah, he's the one that saw Ace right after, and now he's saying Ace might never . . ." Her voice wobbled like the green beans she held.

Cara couldn't take her eyes off those beans. She wanted to reach out and steady them—steady Dance for the news she held. While Cara waited, Jean did just that. Her work-worn hand cupped Dance's and came away with the wavering string beans.

Dance took a deep breath. "The doctor said Ace might never be more than he is now—just a shadow of his self."

"Oh no. Oh, Dance, don't give up hope," Cara said.

"I've made my peace. I'll take care of him." Dance began to clip the end caps off more beans, pulling green strings down each side. "Besides, doctors ain't always right. Sheriffs ain't neither."

Cara thought they had successfully kept the sheriff's suspicion from Dance. "How long are Ace's parents staying? Do you want them to sleep over to my place?"

"I don't rightly know how long they aim to linger here. I ain't thinking past the moment." Dance lifted her chin. "I'm glad, though—glad they come." She looked tired but resolute. Cara figured she was drawing on whatever strength she had left.

"Cara," Dance said, "there's a slab of bacon in the smokehouse. Would you mind to cut a piece for these beans?"

Jean worked beside Dance, peeling potatoes. A peel hung from her knife like a long brown ribbon. "We've had news from Fairy Mae's," Jean said.

Cara blanched. News was bad these days. Fairy Mae was worse, she reckoned.

"My husband went to check on Fairy Mae and brought back a piece of mail," Jean continued.

Dance pulled a postal card from her apron pocket. "Darcy Mae is having herself a fling in the midst of my tragedy," she said with a spark of her old self, flipping the card across the table.

Cara studied the front, a pretty scene of trees and flowers. *Humboldt Park* was printed across the bottom.

Snapped beans jumped across the tabletop. "Makes me mad as blue blazes," Dance said.

Jean collected the errant beans. Cara looked to her for guidance, not wanting to say the wrong thing. Dance could go either way quick as a cat's sneeze. Jean's face was as calm as her manner.

"This sure is pretty," Cara ventured.

"Humph." Dance slammed beans into the pot. "All Darcy's ever had to do was be pretty. Read the tuther side."

"'Dearest Mammaw and family,'" Cara read aloud. "'This is a nice park I saw one day while touring. I am well and trust you are too. You will be glad to learn Henry and I are wed. I will be home shortly after. Devotedly, Darcy.'"

"Touring," Dance snorted. "Devotedly," she mocked. Pouring water over the beans, she began to wash them one at a time. "Are you going to get me a hunk of bacon or not?"

Cara raised her eyebrows and looked at Jean, who lifted her shoulders the merest bit. "Sure thing, Dance."

Pauline's mewling cry called Dance to the cradle. "Didn't I just feed you?" she asked.

"I'll be right back, Dance," Jean said, following Cara out the door and across the porch.

Cara kept her voice low. "Dance seems to be some better. What do you think?"

"The doctor was pretty frank with her," Jean said. "He laid it all on the table—talked right to Dance, not around her as everyone else seems to be doing. Of course he doesn't know her history."

"Dance may have odd ways, but she really loves Ace. There're times I've seen them tease each other—kindly like dancing except with words. It would make me laugh. I guess you'd have to spend time with them to understand." Cara shook her head. "I can't believe Ace won't get better. Is that what the doctor said exactly?"

"The word I latched onto was *might*." Jean picked up a boy's knit sweater discarded during play. "*Might* could go either way, don't you think?" She gave the sweater a shake, then folded it over her arm. "I could swear Ace smiled when his mother kissed him. We have to keep on praying. Praying hard."

"I reckon I've been as worried about Dance as I have about Ace. I've never seen her praying," Cara said.

"Nothing prepares you for what has happened to Dance—her husband sorely injured, herself accused, her grandmother near death." Jean smiled thinly. "I wanted to tell her to lean upon the Lord, but I was afraid she'd throw me out of the house."

"Shouldn't she though? Shouldn't she lean upon the Lord?"

Their skirt tails stirred up puffs of dust as they walked toward the smokehouse. Jean lifted her skirts just the barest bit. Cara followed suit. Jean was such a lady.

"I'm not sure where Dance stands on things," Jean said. "In times like this, I've found it's best to show God's love rather than preaching it. If Dance feels cared for, if she feels safe, she'll search Him out."

"I wish I were more like you, Jean."

Jean stopped beside the smokehouse. A row of tall, white holly-hocks brightened the gray, weather-beaten wall. Cara remembered the spring day when Ace had planted the seed. He was always a man to brighten things up.

Lifting the latch, Cara stepped inside the dark structure. She inhaled deeply. The briny, smoky scent of cured meat rewarded her senses. Hams dressed in heavy brown paper and tied in flour sacks hung from wires attached to the rafters. Jars of sliced meat preserved with salt, pepper, and pulverized saltpeter sat on a shelf between wall studs. A slab of bacon lay on a wooden table, waiting for a knife.

Cara sawed at the heavy rind and freed a good-size piece, then cut some thick slices for tomorrow's breakfast, two jobs done in the time of one.

Leaning out the door, Cara asked, "Should I bring in some of these jars of meat?"

Jean stepped in and looked them over, selecting two. "I didn't know all this was in here. Ace is a good provider."

"I reckon he and Dance did well together," Cara said, filling her hands with bacon. "This is all so strange. I scarce can take it in."

"I know." Jean set the jars down long enough to close and latch the door behind them. "It's like you don't know what awful thing is going to happen next."

"I sure wish Darcy were here to help out some."

"I expect you and Dance are a little put out with her," Jean said. "But you know she never could have perceived of this happening to her sister."

"I know," Cara said, thinking of the egg incident this morning. "I think I'm working out my mad toward her."

Jean rewarded her with a smile. "You know, Cara, I've watched you just blossom lately. When Dimmert went away, you were timid as a young girl. But look at you now. Why, you're a strong woman standing on your own two feet. I'm so proud of you."

Cara felt herself bloom at Jean's simple words. She stood tall. She was every bit the sturdy hollyhock; her back might be against the wall, but nothing kept her from moving forward.

"Goodness me, what's that ruckus coming from the barn?" Jean asked.

"Oh, I forgot all about Big Boy. He was looking for something to tend to. Do you know Big Boy Randall?"

"No, but I believe I've heard that name bantered about."

"He's good as gold. Big Boy's the one who went to visit Dimm in prison."

"That's good enough for me," Jean replied.

"Jean," Cara said, "do you think Darcy's truly wed?"

"Well, yes. I suppose so. I don't think she'd say she was if not. Why?"

"It's just so quick. The whole thing's caught me off guard. And I reckon I'm like Dance, just a little jealous that Darcy's off having fun while—"

Jean stopped in the yard to eye a small, errant sock. "Boys," she said, expertly flipping the sock into the air with the toe of her boot. It landed atop a meat-filled jar. "Was Wilton even dressed when he left?" She shifted her load, then laid the sock over the woolen sweater. "We don't know she's having fun, but I surely hope so, because no matter what, she still has to come home to all this."

"I hadn't thought about it that way," Cara responded.

"Your heart's too good to hold on to envy. We must pray for Darcy too. Pray that she is truly happy and pray for a safe journey home."

Cara nudged the kitchen door open with her elbow and held it for Jean. Dance was nursing the baby. Ace lay on his other side; obviously Dance had turned him. Darcy's postal card lay bright as a bouquet of flowers in the middle of the table. Cara looked it over again. Only time would tell if Darcy was happy or not.

It was with considerable dread that Cara followed Big Boy to the spring early the next morning. Jay led the way, and they let him. It seemed to be something he needed to do. Big Boy showed up early at the Sheltons', before the rest of the household stirred, as they had agreed to. Big Boy said he didn't want to take a chance on meeting anyone else there. Meaning the law, Cara surmised. The rooster crowed half a crow as they started across the yard, as if it was too early for the real thing.

The weedy path was tramped down now and easy to find. A heavy mist swirled like smoke and dampened Cara's skirts and her shoes. She carried a linen sack, containing bacon biscuits and a green Mason jar of cold coffee, slung across her chest. Her steps were not as sprightly as they might have been. She was having trouble keeping up.

Every so often Big Boy would stop to let her catch them. "Wait, Jay," she'd hear him call.

As the day commenced, rays of morning's first light filtered through the canopy of trees, burning off the heavy dew. Birds chirped and squirrels chattered from their nests high overhead. A striped ground squirrel shot across the path in front of her. The world was waking, starting its day.

Too soon, they reached the edge of the meadow where Ace had built his sweetwater run. The meadow was small, less than an acre, and was ringed by giant trees that cast a shadow like a pall over the area. Even there, still at the edge of the forest, she could hear the dancing burble of the spring. Jay waited. He didn't ask a thing.

Cara took the lead. "Let's have a little breakfast. I'm near weak with hunger." Finding the now-familiar fallen tree limb, she spread a feed sack towel across the trunk and passed around the coffee.

Jay took a sip. His face scrunched up. "Whew, I ain't ever had coffee bare before."

"Goodness, Jay, I should have thought to bring some cream. Want me to water some down for you?" Before Cara gave it half a thought, she was searching for the tin cup Ace kept by the spring. Finding it easy enough, she caught a stream of water and took it back to Jay.

As soon as she sat on the limb and picked up her bacon biscuit, it came to her what she had done. *It's simple as that,* she thought. You could do most anything when you focused on someone else's need instead of your own. Munching on her biscuit, she tucked that thought away, sure she'd need to think on it again.

As soon as Jay finished his breakfast and his watery coffee, he stood. "I want to see where Daddy got hurt."

"All right." Cara reached for his hand and led him to the spring. "He was just there, like he was resting in the water." She kept her voice clear and resolute. She would not foist her fear upon this child.

Jay nodded. "I'm going to build something for Daddy." Pulling loose from her touch, he rolled up his britches and waded into the stream that issued from the spring. "When Daddy gets better, we'll come here again."

"I'm sure he would like that," she remarked.

Jay began to lay smooth stones in a circle. "I'll have to use heavy ones, else the water will carry them off."

"You're smart. Your daddy would be proud."

Jay tapped the side of his head. "Daddy said always use your noggin."

Cara walked back to the fallen limb, where Big Boy was waiting. "Tell me everything," he said.

So she told the story again. Sometimes it seemed like the only one she knew. From her seat, she watched Big Boy scout the scene. It seemed he thought every blade of grass and each tree scattered across the meadow was a clue. He stopped the longest time by the hickory where she had found the hat, then motioned for her to come.

"This is where Ace was laid into," he said, kneeling and parting a thick clump of rye grass. "See here? Old blood and bits of tissue. Human blood and tissue, I warrant. The tree has protected it somewhat."

Cara felt sick. She looked to make sure Jay was still busy at the spring. "I don't want Jay to see."

Like she had, Big Boy looked toward the spring. He dropped his voice. "If the sheriff's theory was indeed fact, Dance would have had to drag Ace from here to the spring. Now, she's tall but she's slight, and a body is deadweight."

Cara stepped back, covering her mouth with one hand, swallowing hard.

"Sorry, missus, I shouldn't be so blunt," Big Boy said, standing.

"No. No. It's all right. I'm just queasy." She took in a fresh lungful of mountain air. Her mood lightened. Big Boy could save Dance. "We have to get the sheriff back here."

"I'll go into town this afternoon and fetch him. Surely he'll see the light."

"I hope so. But he seems set on finding fault with Dance."

"Some men have a hard time admitting when they're wrong, and that sheriff's hard-nosed." Big Boy dropped to his haunches and ran his hand through the grass. "If we could just find something else."

The sun rose ever higher in the sky. A hearty breeze rustled through the trees, showering them in autumn leaves of red and gold.

Cara shivered. "Who could have done such a dreadful thing? Why Ace of all people?"

"All's I know for sure is Ace didn't fall off no cliff, and his wife didn't do him in. I figure Ace caught somebody busting up his stuff. There was an argument, and things got out of hand. But who did it? I don't have a clue. Everybody liked Ace."

"Come and look, Aunt Cara," Jay called.

The boy had built a small tower of gray and brown rocks. He'd chinked the stones together with clay mud. From the very top, a long brown feather waved in the breeze. He stood in the springwater with a look of satisfaction.

"It's beautiful," Cara said.

"You got an eagle feather there, boy," Big Boy said. "They're not easy to find in these parts."

Jay ran his fingers lightly over the feather. "Huh. I thought this here was from a hawk."

Big Boy stepped over beside Jay. "See how long it is? And see how thick the quill?"

"That means it's old, right?" Jay asked.

Cara gathered her things and stuck them in the linen sack while Big Boy talked with Jay. This time had been good for the boy, she reckoned. But she felt a growing unease. A riddle tickled her mind. There was something here she was overlooking. With the sack slung across her chest, she leaned against the fallen log just pondering.

"Aunt Cara," Jay yelled, "let's go. I want to show Daddy the feather. That's sure to wake him up."

"Don't run," Cara cautioned as Jay took off down the mountain. "You're liable to take a spill."

"That boy's nimble as a goat," Big Boy said, "and smart. I've never seen a smarter young'un. Like he said, that feather he found is way too old to have laid in the weather for long. I think it was brought up here recently. Could be a clue."

Cara's blood quickened; she could feel her own heartbeat. Clear as day, she saw herself leaning over a shadow-box table, admiring a collection of Indian artifacts in Henry Thomas's office. She turned to Big Boy. "I know who hurt Ace."

CHAPTER 30

AFTER THEY CAME DOWN from the mountain, Cara was so
excited she ran the two miles to her cabin, praying all the way that
the thin length of leather was where she thought it was. She found it
in the cupboard innocently curled in the bowl of a cup. She tucked
the thong in her pocket and set the cup aside. She would never drink
from it again.

A stitch in her side kept her from racing back. She prayed all the
way to the Sheltons'. *Please, Lord, let the sheriff believe me. I know I'm
right. I know it.*

A group of folks milled about in the Sheltons' yard. Jay was in the
middle showing off his eagle's feather. Everyone looked Cara's way,
and she held out the piece of leather triumphantly. If her side didn't
hurt so badly she might have done a little dance.

"Yee haw!" Big Boy shouted. "Let's go see the sheriff."

"Hold up, folks," Elder Foster said. "We need to make a clear-
headed plan and not just rush off willy-nilly."

Everyone quieted and looked at Elder Foster for guidance.

"First let's get our evidence together." He put the feather and the
leather strip on the very chopping block that had turned the sheriff's
eyes toward Dance.

269

Dance placed Darcy's postcard beside the other items. "This is proof of where he's at."

Cara's exultant mood plummeted. The items looked so insignificant laid out that way. What had made her think an old feather and a worn string bore witness to a crime? Henry Thomas's items probably still lay under glass in his office. Besides, it made no sense that Henry would take Darcy off to Chicago if he had just tried to kill Ace, and Darcy would surely discern that something was wrong. The sheriff would laugh in their faces.

"It's worth a try," Big Boy said. "If we go several strong, the law will have to listen."

Elder Foster wrapped their paltry evidence in a clean white handkerchief. The card he handed back to Dance, who offered it to Cara.

"Do you want to go along?" Cara asked, sticking the card in her pocket.

"I ain't leaving Ace," Dance said. "I'll be all right here with the young'uns."

"We'll stay with her," Ace's father said.

"I'm going." Jay jumped into a buggy. "Ain't nobody stopping me."

It was late afternoon before Cara, Jay, Big Boy Randall, and Elder and Jean Foster gathered on the sidewalk in front of Henry Thomas's office door.

The sheriff jimmied a heavy lock. "Have to do every little thing myself since my deputy broke his leg," he muttered. The door was stuck. The sheriff applied his shoulder. "You folks wait out here. Henry could be in there dead for all we know."

Not likely, Cara thought but kept her mouth shut. At least the sheriff had responded to her story about the string of leather she'd found the day Ace died and then stuck on a shelf, forgotten until the feather jogged her memory.

"That's kind of fanciful thinking," he'd said. "Why would Henry Thomas try to kill Ace Shelton?"

Cara wondered that herself, but the sheriff had come here to look. She had to give him credit for that.

They all rushed the door when they heard a long, low whistle.

The lid to the shadow-box table stood open, and the sheriff leaned over it, fiddling with something. "Well, lookee here."

Cara ventured closer.

"See that?" The sheriff pointed at the tomahawk. "And right alongside the hatchet is a faint stain. Leather will bleed sometimes, you know." He positioned the leather thong just so along the marking. "Looks like a match."

The sheriff carefully placed the eagle's feather on the handle of the hatchet. With his hands on his bent knees, the sheriff looked up at Cara. "Mighty suspicious. You just might have found the weapon used in the crime."

Pushing off from his knees, he straightened and opened the door to the back room. They could see a big black safe standing with the door hanging open, empty. "I expect it will be a sight harder to find Henry Thomas."

"He's in Cincinnati, Ohio," a man said. "I heard him say it not three weeks ago."

"Say, that's right," another said.

Cara looked around. The office was full of folks who had slipped in quiet as mice through the open door, all ogling Henry's empty safe.

"Hey," the sheriff said, "you all get on out of here. Anybody talked to Henry meet me at the office."

The folks were slow to move.

"Go on, get." When the door was closed, the sheriff said, "Cincinnati's a right big place. I'll contact the law there."

"He's not in Cincinnati," Cara replied with alarm. "He's in Chicago, and he has Darcy with him."

The sheriff looked at her like she'd sprouted two heads. "You're a fount of information."

"We've had mail," she said, handing the postcard to the sheriff.

The sheriff flipped the card from front to back. He rubbed his chin with one hand. "This gal could be in considerable danger. I'd advise you folks to keep everything you've seen in this room under your hats for the time being." Pointedly, he made eye contact with each one.

Cara pulled Jay close, and he tightened his grip on her hand.

"For pete's sake, Sheriff," Big Boy said, "half the town was gawking when you laid out that strip of leather."

The sheriff fingered his badge. "I don't much like a smart aleck, Mr. Randall. There's a bunk in the jail that still remembers your hide."

"I didn't mean no disrespect," Big Boy said. "I just want to help out is all."

"What we need is a reason—a motive, so to speak," the sheriff said, stepping behind Henry's wide desk. "What would drive somebody like Henry to do such a thing? The answer could be right in here." He tugged at the desk drawers. Each was locked.

"Want me to bust them open?" Big Boy asked.

With crossed arms, the sheriff stood back. "Go to it."

Big Boy took a hunting knife from a sheath on his belt. Sliding the blade behind the lock on the middle drawer, he made a swift motion. Soon—*pop, pop, pop, pop*—all the desk drawers stood open.

The sheriff extracted papers from a manila folder and spread them across the surface of Henry's desk. He whistled. "Can I trust you folks?"

They all nodded as he turned the papers toward them.

"My word," Elder Foster said. "Henry was planning to take over all the Whitts' property. Here would be your motive, Sheriff."

"Exactly," the sheriff responded. "Let's keep this to ourselves. I expect there will be a trial, and this will be strong evidence against one Henry Thomas."

"But what about Darcy?" Cara asked.

"You're right to be worried," the sheriff said, finally sounding like he cared. "I'll have to get ahold of somebody to deputize. Somebody smart enough to find Chicago."

Big Boy stepped forward. "I'll go."

The sheriff stacked Henry's papers and placed them back in the manila folder. He gave Big Boy a long, appraising look. "Come by the jail and get a badge. I'll find someone else to go along. There might be trouble."

"My son Dylan will go with Big Boy," Elder Foster said. "He's always wanted to be a lawman."

Slapping the folder against his leg, the sheriff replied, "That's settled then."

Cara thought she was beyond surprise, but when she got to the Sheltons' after the visit in the sheriff's office, she found that was not so. A somber group was sitting over coffee around Dance's kitchen table. The doctor was holding forth; everyone else was listening intently. She caught the screen door behind her and eased it shut. Ace's father rose and indicated for her to take his seat. He leaned against the wall as she sat down.

The gist of what the doctor said was that Ace was stable and that he could be moved. In reply to Mrs. Shelton's pleading inquiry, he said there was no way of telling how much function Ace would get back. But—and this was an important *but*—he was pleased at how Ace was doing so far. Just that morning he had turned himself in bed and asked—feebly but he asked—for water.

When the doctor finished, he took his black bag and left. Cara wondered how long Ace would have lived if Dylan had not found that man and brought him over the mountain to care for Ace. The doctor had made the long trip several times since that dreadful day.

As soon as the door closed, Mrs. Shelton turned to Dance and asked, "Would you be willing to let us take him home for a while? We have more than enough room for all of you, and there is a hospital nearby."

Cara was as sure that Dance would say no as she was that her eyes were gray. No way would anyone get Dance off this place. Cara wanted to tell her that they could take care of Ace right here. Instead she kept her place. Who was she to interfere? And Dance was free to go now that the sheriff knew the true culprit. Take her kids and flee this troublesome place.

Later she walked with Dance out by the clothesline as they folded the sheets and pillowcases and towels Mrs. Shelton had washed this morning. "What is in your heart to do, Dance?"

Her friend's face was etched with worry lines. Cara bet she'd lost ten pounds since this all started. "I'm bone weary. My young'uns deserve better. Ace deserves better. And his parents are so kind." Dance stood for the longest time, looking off into the distance, holding a folded dish towel against her chest. "I'm going. I reckon it's time to put Ace first." She reached out and grabbed Cara's arm with one thin hand. "We won't be gone long. Ace will be up to his old rascally self soon. I just know it."

"What can I do to help?" Cara asked. "Do you want me to keep the children so you can focus on getting him well?"

"Maybe for a couple of weeks. Just the big ones, I couldn't leave Pauline or Cleve. We'll see. Jay might not want to go and Wilton won't go if Jay don't."

"I'll do whatever you need me to," Cara said, sliding the clothespin bag along the line. "I can move over here and stay with the kids until you get back or take them to my house. Whatever you think best."

"I'll think on it." Dance picked up the full clothes basket and carried it to the house.

Cara stayed under the line for a while. Everything seemed hopeless, beyond her ability to comprehend, until she looked toward the riot of color on the mountain. The fall day was quite beautiful if you stopped to notice. *Please, Lord,* she prayed, *give me strength and show me what I must do to help.*

A warm west wind stirred the trees, and a whisper of leaves danced through the air. Laughing, she pulled an errant leaf from her hair. Suddenly she realized what she had sought since Dimmert had been taken from her. She was not alone. She was never alone. God's comfort and peace were hers for the asking.

"'Even them will I bring to my holy mountain, and make them joyful in my house of prayer,'" she said aloud, Scripture she had memorized just the night before. Memorized but not fully understood until this moment. She spread her arms toward the sky and danced in the shower of God's blessing. Everything would be all right.

CHAPTER 31

THE GIRLS in Darcy's lodging house were all atwitter. They flocked around the windows that looked out onto the wide porch as someone knocked at the door. There was some shoving and lots of giggling as they jockeyed for position.

"It's a man come calling," one said as the sound of the door knocker continued.

"And he's got flowers," another said. "Hope they're for me."

"Not likely," the first said.

Mrs. Oldham crossed the room. "It's simple enough to open the door and find out, girls."

"Oh, my," Darcy said when she finally got a peek. "It's Henry." She smoothed her hair and pressed her lips together. There was no need to pinch her cheeks; she could feel them blooming as pink as the rose bouquet Henry held.

Darcy nearly burst; she was that glad to see Henry on the other side of the door.

"I've come to see Miss Whitt," he said, all formal.

"Please come in," Mrs. Oldham replied.

"If it's all the same, we'll visit out here."

"Of course." She said in an aside to Darcy, "You know my policy."

"Yes, ma'am." As if any of the girls could forget. The rules were printed and hung on each bedroom door: No visitors not approved by the house. No kissing. No touching. No lingering. No callers after dark. . . . Among many others. Mrs. Oldham read them aloud to each girl who boarded in her house.

Darcy felt light as air; she might just float away. Henry indicated a seat on the porch swing. She could feel his longing charge the air between them. *It's a wonder we don't set the porch afire,* she thought.

"I've sure missed you, Henry."

"Darcy," he said, his voice cracking with emotion, "I should never have brought you here."

That was not what she expected to hear after her weeks of waiting. It most assuredly was not. "What do you mean?"

"Look," he said, "is there someplace we can go? We need to talk privately."

"I'll just take these in," she said of the roses, "and get my hat."

Mrs. Oldham took the flowers. "You should take someone along," she said in answer to Darcy's request.

Bridgett followed out the door and down the walk. As soon as they were out of sight, she dropped several feet back, allowing privacy.

"There's a park close by. We can talk there, Henry."

He took Darcy's hand and rubbed his thumb across her knuckles. Her skin responded to his tender touch as if it had lain dormant until that moment. She never felt so alive.

"I do love you, Darcy Mae. Just remember that."

"You're scaring me a little," she said.

The slatted-wood park bench where they chose to sit was painted dark green. A boy ran past chasing a hoop, and a man called out for his dog. Bridgett sat a few benches over. Her back was turned.

Henry leaned forward. His elbows rested on his knees. He cleared his throat, took off his hat, and put it beside him. She watched his hair, dark as a crow's wing, fall across his fine forehead. She longed to brush it back.

"I've done a terrible thing."

"Don't tell me yet," she said. "Give me a minute."

A minute—that was all it took to change the world.

"You said you love me, Henry."

"I do, but that doesn't amend what has happened."

Darcy watched his face and saw it was true. Something was woefully wrong. One tear slipped down his cheek. She reached to wipe it off.

He caught her hand and brought it to his lips. "If I had only listened to my heart," he said with a groan. "You were all I needed all along."

"Whatever has happened can surely be fixed," she said. "I'll stand by you."

Henry swallowed hard. She could see the jut of his Adam's apple working. "Listen before you make promises you can't keep," he said and then started the whole terrible story.

When the tomahawk met with Ace's skull, she jumped up and ran to the fountain that sat in the middle of a brick-floored square bounded by the benches. Water splashed merrily over the rims of the three-tiered fountain and drowned out the sound of her sobs. He didn't follow. She knew he wouldn't try to stop her if she walked right out of the park. Her family was waiting at home probably worried to death about her. Henry sat disconsolate on the bench. The choice was hers. She sat back down but kept her distance. "Tell me the rest," she said.

When Henry was finished, they were both crying.

"I have to go back," he said. "They'll send me to prison, and I deserve it."

"How could you?" she said around a clot of tears. "How could you do such a thing?"

"I got so mad," Henry said. "Please believe I went there with no intent to hurt Ace. It just happened—I don't understand it myself."

Despite herself she cupped his face and kissed him like a woman would kiss a man she's sending to a place where she could not follow, with love and heartbreak and yearning all mixed up together.

"Don't you hate me?" he asked.

Darcy felt she'd aged ten years between the time of leaving the lodging house and now. Sorrow washed over her. Poor Dance. Poor Ace—he had been good to her. How could she still feel love for the man who sat weeping beside her on the park bench? He had hurt her sister's husband. Still, all she wanted to do was offer him the comfort of her arms. "I don't hate you. I love you."

"How could you after what I've done?"

"I don't rightly know. But I can't just turn my love off like I was turning down the wick on a kerosene lantern." She dabbed at her nose with a delicately embroidered hankie. "We'll go home and face the music together."

"Oh no," Henry said. "I'll not take you down with me."

"You don't have a choice in that."

"What do you mean?"

"I'm your wife, and if my suspicions stand correct, I'm carrying your child."

He gasped and placed his hand on hers. "Oh, Darcy."

She moved her hand away. "I'm not ready for your touch yet. I might touch you, but you aren't to touch me."

"A baby," he said. "How could this have happened?"

"Surely you can figure that out," she snapped.

"I'm sorry," he said, twirling his hat in his hands. "I'd take it all back if I could."

"Stop that. There'll be no sorrow over this baby." She spread her hand over her belly. "Think about it this way—at least I'll have this much."

"I'm sorry," he said again.

"Henry Thomas, if you say that again, I'm going to pinch your head off. Sorry doesn't count right now."

"Your family will stand by you. I might be gone a long time."

"I suppose they would," Darcy said. "I'll stay home until the baby is born, but after that, wherever you are, that's where we'll be. I'm not sitting around on Troublesome Creek being gossip fodder for the rest of my life. I have a trade and I can support myself. Prisons have visiting days, I expect."

"There's no need to worry about how you'll live. There will be enough money to last you."

Darcy sighed. "Don't you get it? Money and greed are what got us in this mess. Your money. Your greed."

As if her words were poison-tipped arrows, he jerked, then slumped back against the bench.

Darcy's eyes smarted. Her blood simmered with anger like a pot of beans on a back burner. Right now she didn't understand herself or him. She should get off the bench and walk away, not even look back. Instead, she took a moment to compose herself. She thought of her grandmother and the troubles she'd faced in her lifetime. Mammaw had stayed stalwart and strong through it all. Darcy would claim that endurance as her heritage from Mammaw just like her button nose and her short stature.

"I could have given you the world," Henry said in a choked voice.

"I never wanted the world. I only wanted you." Darcy turned toward him. She wanted to see his eyes. It felt like her life rested on his answer. "Just tell me one thing. Why didn't you run while you had the chance?"

"I couldn't leave Ace's wife to stand accused. I thought I could." He tossed a bit of stale pretzel he found on the bench over the heads of the pigeons to a hopeful squirrel. "When I heard those men say the law was after Dance, I figured I was the luckiest man alive. I came back here to collect my stuff, figuring to head out west. But there was the Bible on my nightstand and old man Follett's admonition—I'll tell you about him another time. Anyway, I spent two days and nights on my knees with that Bible. The Lord wouldn't give me any rest."

She bit her lip. That was a good answer, but it wasn't the answer she longed for. "I'm glad you found the Lord. You know He forgives you. Maybe everyone else will in time."

"I know you don't want me to touch you, but I can't help myself." Henry rubbed her lower lip with his thumb, then kissed her ever so gently. "I couldn't leave you, either, little Darcy. I thought to, believe you me. I've cursed myself for bringing you into this. But I couldn't resist you. You're the best and brightest thing that ever happened to me. I never loved anyone until you."

"Do one thing for me," she said, handing him her gold band. "Put my ring back on."

Henry was not surprised to find a welcoming committee outside Mrs. Oldham's boardinghouse when he and Darcy Mae returned. He heard her gasp, and the hand she rested in the crook of his arm tightened.

"Something has happened to Mammaw," she said while they were still out of earshot. "Dylan's come to tell me."

But Henry had seen the wink of sunlight off a badge on Dylan Foster's chest. Big Boy Randall was a puzzle, though. The sheriff must be getting desperate. The street was busy this time of day, and they hadn't been spotted. There was still time to make a run for it. Henry's muscles coiled tight as a spring. Every ounce of his being begged self-preservation, but he kept his forward trek. It was put up or shut up now.

"Darcy Mae, be brave. They've come for me." Oh, how he wished he could protect her from what was to come. "Open your purse."

She didn't question as he slid three bankbooks into her purse but received his gift and pulled the drawstrings tight. Right then he knew she stood with him, whatever befell. It was a powerful moment.

"That's something for your eyes only, Darcy. I worked hard for each penny recorded in those books. There's more than enough to take care of all your needs and Dance Shelton's too. Spend it as you like."

Just then he saw Foster elbow Randall, who was jawing with some ladies. Big Boy fumbled with the holster on his hip. Henry almost laughed. *Some fine lawmen,* he thought as he raised his arms in surrender.

CHAPTER 32

THE WHITT FAMILY CEMETERY was crowded with folk on the bleak November day Reverend Jasper laid Fairy Mae to rest. Women drew shawls tightly against the cold wind, and men held on to their hats. Trees skirting the graveyard lifted bare black branches as if in supplication to the cloud-whipped sky. Leaves piled ankle-deep squelched under booted feet. Leaf mold mixed with the scents of dry bark and mushroom spores. Cara stifled a sneeze and tucked Merky underneath her mantle.

This funeral was especially hard. Mammaw was well loved. To keep her mind off the gaping hole in the red, raw earth, Cara studied the folks gathered round. Dance was holding up surprisingly well considering how close she'd been to her grandmother. Ace's mother was right at her elbow—just in case, Cara figured. Jay stood in front of his mother with one hand on Wilton's shoulder. He was such a little man. Cara was glad Dance made it home in time to tell Fairy Mae good-bye. And glad Ace was well enough for her to leave him in the care of his father for a short time. They'd all be coming home next spring if Ace continued to improve.

Darcy. It pained Cara somewhat just to look at her across the yawning grave. She grieved for the loss of the sweet friend Darcy had once been to her. She was different since she came back. There was a far-off feel about her nowadays.

People change, Cara reckoned. She herself was not the same as she was before Dimmert went to prison. She was strong now like a seam mended with double thread. And truly, if anybody should understand Darcy's pain, it was she. Henry Thomas's trial had been swift but merciful. He got five years of hard labor. Most folks thought he should have hung. Cara was glad he didn't—for the sake of Darcy and her baby, if for no other reason.

Even the sheriff had come to the service. Cara smiled to see Big Boy standing respectfully behind him. Big Boy's badge shone on his chest. Talk about a change. These days Big Boy was tracking criminals instead of being just short of becoming one. Wilton tore around the grave to where Big Boy stood. Big Boy lifted the tad over his head and settled him on his broad shoulders. Jay stayed with his mother.

And there was Dylan. Bless his heart. It was no secret he once carried a torch for Darcy. He'd be all right though. He was young and about to leave for the big city, where he'd gotten a good-paying job in Lexington's police department.

A commotion caught her eye. Henry's dog Daisy pushed through the crowd to stand by her new owner. That hound was never far from Remy, and now her long tail beat a happy dance across the back of Remy's knees. If she wasn't careful, Remy might topple over. Cara shuddered. What if she fell into the grave? Who would fetch her out?

It had been a sight to see Big Boy and Dylan carrying Remy up the mountain to the boneyard in a sling made by their crossed arms. Remy had sat there upright as a queen on the throne, holding her crutch like a scepter.

Cara bet that dog slept in the house—not very cleanly by her standards, but then she'd once slept with a mule's head in her window. Oh, that Pancake. Cara felt a smile twitching at the corner of her lips and clamped them shut. She should concentrate on the service, show some respect. Brother Jasper was talking about streets lined with gold. . . .

Merky dropped her dolly, and Cara set her down so she could

retrieve it. She'd dragged it everywhere with her since she'd come to stay with Cara. On the morning the family had loaded up to head off to Maryland, Merky was the only one who cried to stay. The doll seemed a comfort to the little girl. Maybe Darcy would make it a new dress. Wouldn't it be dear if she made one for Merky also? Matching dresses, a good idea.

Miz Copper looked good. Cara was glad to have her friend home from Philadelphia, glad everything had turned out okay for her and the babies. My, my. Twins. It was no wonder that the doc wouldn't let her travel until they were born. There was to be a dinner for the mourners at the Pelfreys' following the funeral. Maybe she'd get to hold the babies. Miz Copper bent down and whispered something in Lilly Gray's ear. The girl nodded solemnly and leaned back against her mother.

The wind picked up. Dead leaves swirled in a cone, hopping and skipping across the ground like a tiny tornado. Cara's arms ached from the weight of Merky. She nuzzled the girl's head with her chin. Merky was more like hers than Dance's now, although Cara knew that wouldn't last long. She couldn't take the place of a mother.

When the Sheltons came back, she supposed they would move into Fairy Mae's place. Jean told Cara that Darcy aimed to build onto the house so Dance would have plenty of room. Cara wouldn't know. Darcy didn't let her in on her plans anymore. Maybe Darcy blamed her for the sheriff finding Henry in Chicago before they had a chance to return on their own. If so, Cara couldn't be sorry for it.

Six pallbearers stepped up to the coffin. She caught Darcy's eye. Darcy lifted her chin. *Be that way,* Cara thought and then felt shame. It was Darcy's beloved grandmother the men were lowering by ropes into the grave. Nobody could fault Darcy on her care for Fairy Mae, least of all Cara, who'd done little enough. What was that Bible verse about ignoring a beam in your own eye whilst you were exclaiming a mote in your brother's? She'd have to ask Big Boy about that. And soon she needed to have a heart-to-heart with Darcy. There was fault enough on both sides.

Somebody started singing. Soon most of the folks joined in. Cara couldn't, for she was choking on sobs. Funeral music always did her in.

"'There's a land that is fairer than day,'" rang out pure and simple across the mountain top. "'And by faith we can see it afar; for the Father waits over the way . . .'"

When the first shovelful of clay dirt hit the coffin with a dull thud, Cara looked off into the distance in a bid to keep from breaking down. She chanced to see a flock of migrating wild canaries spread across the topmost branches of the bare trees. A ray of sun broke through the gray and gloomy cloud cover and lit the yellow birds from behind like handblown ornaments on a candlelit Christmas tree. Cara gasped and pointed before she remembered where she was. Everyone turned to look. Cara listened to the song's sweet promise: "'In the sweet by and by, we shall meet on that beautiful shore . . .'"

The bright birds soared high and swooped low over and over in perfect cadence to the melody.

Thank You, Jesus, Cara praised. *Fairy Mae would love this.*

⌁⌁⌁⌁

After the service, the Pelfreys' house was packed with folks sharing Fairy Mae stories. Cara loved listening to the older women talking, the ones who had known Mammaw since she was a girl. The women were in Miz Copper's spacious kitchen, slicing ham and bread and adding a pinch of salt or a sprinkle of pepper to the dishes. Soon they were tittering at a story Fairy Mae had told on herself, how when she was a girl she broke half a dozen eggs into a hot skillet and then couldn't turn them for love nor money. Nobody'd taught her about greasing the pan first. Fairy Mae was like that, everyone agreed, always laughing at her own self. Always humble.

"She'll be sorely missed," Jean said, blotting her cheeks with the corner of her apron.

One of the ladies asked Cara about Dimmert. "I heard he was coming home," the lady said. "I heard he got a pardon."

Cara wished she hadn't asked. She'd never liked to be the center of attention, and now all the women strained her way, waiting for the answer. "It's up to the governor," she replied. "I heard from the warden at the prison that he had sent the paperwork. It's waiting for governor's signature. Of course he might say no."

"Pshaw," the lady said. "Dimmert should never have been sent away. It's not like he killed somebody."

There was a murmur of agreement among the other women.

From the corner of her eye, Cara saw Darcy take the water bucket and head outside. Cara followed. This might be the only chance she had to come to terms with her friend. The empty bucket Darcy carried bumped against her leg all the way to the well house.

Miz Copper's well had a newfangled pump so you didn't have to lower the bucket on a rope. Cara stood in the doorway and watched Darcy hang the bucket on the pump, then jerk the handle up and down until water gushed out the mouth.

"That's amazing," Cara said. "How'd you know to do that?"

"The place where I stayed in Chicago had one in the kitchen. You didn't even have to go outdoors to fetch water."

"I studied about that once," Cara replied. "In ancient times a king watered his garden from the river with a series of pulleys and gears and whatnot. Kindly puts me in mind of Ace's sweetwater run."

Darcy's face turned beet red. She pumped so hard, water overflowed the bucket and spread wastefully across the stone floor. "Did you come out here to remind me of what Henry did?"

Cara could have bit her tongue right off. How thoughtless could she be? "I'm sorry. I never meant to hurt your feelings. Here, let me help you tote that bucket." Cara took hold of the handle, but Darcy jerked it away. Water cold as ice splashed out, soaking Cara to the skin. She stood in shock for a moment before she wrested the half-empty bucket away and dumped it over Darcy's head.

Darcy sputtered and stammered, then dissolved in laughter. Holding her sides, she collapsed on the bench just inside the well house door. When she caught her breath, she grabbed Cara's hand and pulled her down beside her.

"Gracious, Cara," she finally got out, "I forgot how much I've missed you."

Cara fanned her soaked skirts. "Good way to show it," she said before she got the giggles her own self.

They sniggered like girls until they were rocking on the wooden bench. "I've laughed so hard I reckon we'd best visit the other little house," Cara said. "I've heard it's a two-seater with linoleum on the floor."

"And lace curtains at the window." Darcy howled and clutched her belly. "Oh, you've set the baby to kicking."

Like spies scouting for Indians, they peeped out the door. Since no one was about, they scampered across the barren garden and down the long path to the outhouse, swinging their hands together.

Less than two weeks later, you would have thought spring was just around the corner instead of winter. Why, the day was almost balmy.

"Let's do a wash," Cara said to Merky. "Let's wash all the bed-clothes and hang them to dry in the sun."

"My get Dolly's blankie," Merky said, jerking the cover from the doll bed. Her doll tumbled headfirst to the floor. She held the doll up to Cara. "Her's got a boo-boo."

Smiling, Cara kissed the wooden head. "Be gentle with your baby, Merky."

"Her's all better now," Merky replied as she dragged the doll by one arm.

While water heated under the iron wash kettle, Cara hung two woolen blankets on the line and beat them soundly with a rug beater. She'd let them soak up the warmth of the sun until the wash was done. Rarely did she wash a wool blanket. It was a tedious chore and not one she relished, washing by hand in cold water and then stretching them on a curtain frame to keep shrinkage to a minimum.

By noon the clothesline sagged under bleached white sheets and colorful quilts. Cara surveyed the morning's work. Nothing made a body feel better than a wash line full of laundry on a pretty day. Merky stood right beside her with her tiny fists seated at her waist, miming Cara.

Cara swung her up and kissed her rosy cheeks. "Are you hungry, little chickadee?"

Merky's eyes drooped. "Sleepy."

Back in the kitchen, Cara crumbled corn bread into a mug and then poured sweet milk over it. She spoon-fed Merky before wiping her face and tucking her in for a nap. She knew she was spoiling the girl, but she couldn't help it. And Merky was so easy—such a sunny child. Cara watched as Merky drifted off. Each day with her was a blessing.

Leaving the child to sleep, Cara took her egg basket and headed to the henhouse. It would break her heart when Merky went home, but at the same time she couldn't wait until the entire Shelton family was back within visiting distance, back where they belonged. Eggs were plentiful today. Good, Merky liked scrambled eggs for supper.

A shadow crossed the doorway. The day was turning cloudy. She'd best see if the quilts were dry.

Then she heard a dear, familiar voice. "Cara. Cara-mine, I'm home."

Her heart stood still as she turned toward the door. There Dimmert stood, big as life. She dropped the basket, eggs and all, on the ground. In two long strides he was across the packed-dirt floor and folding her into his strong arms. She leaned back and looked at his face, ran her fingers through his ginger-colored hair, straightened his collar.

"Is it really you?" she asked, resting her head on his broad chest.

He kissed her hard in answer to her question. She was weeping with joy, and he dashed tears of his own.

"Where's old Pancake?" he asked.

Cara smiled and shook her head. No doubt about it—her Dimmert was home.

ABOUT THE AUTHOR

A retired registered nurse of twenty-five years, Jan Watson specialized in the care of newborns and their mothers. She attends Tates Creek Christian Church and lives in Lexington, Kentucky. Jan has three grown sons and a daughter-in-law.

Sweetwater Run follows Jan's Troublesome Creek series, which includes *Troublesome Creek, Willow Springs,* and *Torrent Falls.* Her awards include the 2004 Christian Writers Guild First Novel contest and second place in the 2006 Inspirational Readers Choice Contest sponsored by the Faith, Hope, and Love Chapter of the RWA. *Troublesome Creek* was also a nominee for the Kentucky Literary Awards in 2006. *Willow Springs* was selected for *Library Journal's* Best Genre Fiction category in 2007.

Jan's hobbies are reading, antiquing, and taking long walks with her Jack Russell terrier, Maggie.

Jan invites you to visit her Web site at www.janwatson.net. You can contact her through e-mail at author@janwatson.net.

DISCUSSION QUESTIONS

1. The opening scene in *Sweetwater Run* is the arrest of Dimmert Whitt. Do you think he was treated unjustly? Would this be as likely to happen in today's judicial system?
2. How did the arrest of her husband affect Cara Whitt?
3. Cara turns to Bible study and prayer to help her deal with her stress-induced hypochondria. Does this work for Cara? Have you ever dealt with an internal struggle in this way?
4. If you have read *Torrent Falls*, were you surprised that Darcy Whitt became a self-supporting woman? Would that have been unusual for that time and place?
5. Dance Shelton has obvious mental health issues. What might her diagnosis be if her story played out today?
6. Is Ace Shelton an admirable figure in this book? What did you think of the relationship between Ace and Dance?
7. Henry Thomas is portrayed as a selfish, greedy man. Why do you think Henry became that way? Did you see any redeeming qualities in him prior to his conversion?
8. Have you ever had a brief spiritual encounter with another person that affected you as deeply as Henry's with old man Follett?
9. Did you believe the assault on Ace Shelton by Henry Thomas was an accident? What did Ace do that triggered Henry's violent response? Or was Ace an innocent victim?

10. Why is Cara's friendship with Big Boy Randall important to the book?
11. Was Darcy wrong to follow her heart and her man to Chicago? Was her love for Henry a true love? Was Henry Thomas a better man because of Darcy?
12. What impact did the life of Fairy Mae Whitt have on the other women in *Sweetwater Run*?

Do you love to read?
Do you want to go deeper?
Are you in a book group?
ChristianBookGuides.com
Visit today and receive free discussion guides for this book and many other popular titles!
BONUS!
Sign up for the online newsletter and receive the latest news on exciting new books.
CP0071